Wer

She had the most erot[...] sweetly curved, naked of p[...]

"You're beautiful," she [...], tracing her long, slender fingers over the curve of his chest. "Are you real?"

"As real as you, my dream," he said.

Then her witchy gaze captured him, silver with magic. She bent to kiss him, her mouth wet and burning. As she moaned against his lips, he set himself to pleasure her, swirling his tongue between her teeth. Her corner teeth felt oddly sharp, but he didn't care.

He caught the back of her head in one hand. Her hair felt as soft as a cat's fur. Discovering the sensitive whorls of one delicate ear, he stopped to explore. Unlike his own, it wasn't pointed. "You're human," he murmured.

"Not really," she whispered . . .

MASTER
of the
MOON

ANGELA KNIGHT

B

BERKLEY SENSATION, NEW YORK

THE BERKLEY PUBLISHING GROUP
Published by the Penguin Group
Penguin Group (USA) Inc.
375 Hudson Street, New York, New York 10014, USA
Penguin Group (Canada), 10 Alcorn Avenue, Toronto, Ontario M4V 3B2, Canada
(a division of Pearson Penguin Canada Inc.)
Penguin Books Ltd., 80 Strand, London WC2R 0RL, England
Penguin Group Ireland, 25 St. Stephen's Green, Dublin 2, Ireland (a division of Penguin Books Ltd.)
Penguin Group (Australia), 250 Camberwell Road, Camberwell, Victoria 3124, Australia
(a division of Pearson Australia Group Pty. Ltd.)
Penguin Books India Pvt. Ltd., 11 Community Centre, Panchsheel Park, New Delhi—110 017, India
Penguin Group (NZ), Cnr. Airborne and Rosedale Roads, Albany, Auckland 1310, New Zealand
(a division of Pearson New Zealand Ltd.)
Penguin Books (South Africa) (Pty.) Ltd., 24 Sturdee Avenue, Rosebank, Johannesburg 2196,
South Africa

Penguin Books Ltd., Registered Offices: 80 Strand, London WC2R 0RL, England

This is a work of fiction. Names, characters, places, and incidents either are the product of the author's imagination or are used fictitiously, and any resemblance to actual persons, living or dead, business establishments, events, or locales is entirely coincidental.

MASTER OF THE MOON

A Berkley Sensation Book / published by arrangement with the author

PRINTING HISTORY
Berkley Sensation edition / May 2005

ISBN: 0-425-20357-3

BERKLEY® SENSATION
Berkley Sensation Books are published by The Berkley Publishing Group,
a division of Penguin Group (USA) Inc.,
375 Hudson Street, New York, New York 10014.
BERKLEY SENSATION and the "B" design are trademarks belonging to Penguin Group (USA) Inc.

PRINTED IN THE UNITED STATES OF AMERICA

10 9 8 7 6 5 4 3 2 1

ACKNOWLEDGMENTS

Several good friends helped me get this one into your hands. As always, there was my wonderful critique partner, Diane Whiteside, who helps me spot the howlers as I go along. Then Morgan Hawke and Sheri Ross Fogarty gave it a fresh read and helped me find still more stuff to fix.

And as always, my thanks go to my editor, Cindy Hwang, who gave me the chance I'd always dreamed of.

Thanks, ladies!

PROLOGUE

The Palace of the Cachamwri Sidhe
401 A.D., Christian Calendar
2033rd year of Dearg Galatyn's Reign

Llyr Galatyn paced the chamber, fear and hope warring in his chest. If anyone could save his father from the wound he'd suffered, it was Merlin. The alien wizard's powers were greater than any Sidhe's.

But the Dark One who had struck down Dearg Galatyn was also a creature with vast powers, and the magic that had tipped its poisoned blade was slowly eating the Sidhe king from the inside out. None of the Sidhe healers had been able to reverse the spell.

Dearg was perilously close to death.

"Do stop that pacing," Ansgar Galatyn growled. "You wear on my patience."

As if he'd ever had any. Still, Llyr obeyed, moving instead to the window to look out at his father's garden. The sound of falling water pattered from the nearest of the three fountains, and a deceptive peace lay over the flowers bobbing gently in the night breeze.

Dearg had always loved his roses.

Grief rising, Llyr breathed in their rich perfume. Just that morning, the stench of the battlefield had gagged him as he and his father fought the Dark Ones who had ambushed them. The war to save their human cousins from the demonic invaders had been costly indeed. "If Merlin can't reverse the spell, Father won't last the night," he said. "I don't know what I will do without him." The thought of the old man's death lay on his heart like a stone.

"Well, I, for one, plan to make a great many changes." There was a note of menace in Ansgar's voice.

Llyr looked over his shoulder. His brother lounged in his favorite chair, dressed to catch a woman's eye in a blue tunic, thick hose, and boots, all richly worked with gems and gold thread. He'd braided sapphires into two locks of his hip-length black hair. There was no grief at all in his slight smile.

With his father dying, Llyr had donned a plain black jerkin and leggings; he hadn't had the patience to fuss with full court garb. "Aren't you getting ahead of yourself?"

The smile turned into a sneer. "You can't imagine he'll name you his heir? You're a child."

He was one hundred and two. Though young by immortal standards, he was no child. Ansgar, on the other hand, was two centuries older.

Llyr's first memory was of his brother's kick.

He'd always known why Ansgar hated him, and he was

just angry enough at his brother's callousness to use that knowledge now. Flexing an arm, Llyr drew attention to the outline of a dragon curled around his biceps, shimmering with ancient magic. "You may be firstborn, brother, but you're not the Heir to Heroes."

Rage leaped in Ansgar's eyes. Despite himself, Llyr had to control his flinch. When he'd been a child, his brother often beat him when he wore that look. Afterward, Ansgar would use his magic to heal Llyr's injuries so he could deny the crime if the boy was foolish enough to go to their father. Then he'd beat him again for tattling.

Llyr hated his brother with a pure, incandescent passion. He also knew if Ansgar became king, it wouldn't take him long to see that Llyr met with a fatal accident.

But before Ansgar could spew more of his venom, the door of their father's chamber opened. Llyr turned, hope leaping.

It was dashed at the look on Merlin's ageless face. "There's nothing we can do," the alien wizard said, as his mate Nimue slipped out after him. "I have attempted a dozen spells, but the poison overcomes them all." His gaze met Llyr's in warm sympathy. "He wishes to see the two of you."

"Finally." Ansgar rolled out of his chair and strode eagerly toward the chamber door.

Llyr frowned at Ansgar's back, wondering whether his brother's hands were entirely clean in the ambush that had left their father dying. Surely even Ansgar was not capable of such treachery. If Llyr ever discovered he had been . . . His fingers tightened on the hilt of his sword as he followed his brother into the chamber.

He saw with bitter cynicism that Ansgar had fallen to his knees beside the old man's bed, holding Dearg's hand, shoulders shaking in a fine imitation of grief. "Father," he said, voice breaking. "Oh, Father . . ."

Dragon's Breath, Llyr ached to call his brother out, but the side of Dearg's deathbed was not the place to do it. The old man loved Ansgar with a father's doting blindness.

Controlling his anger, Llyr moved to the other side of the bed and took his father's icy hand. Tears welled in his eyes as he looked down into Dearg's face, and he blinked them back fiercely.

The king had been youthful and handsome just that morning, but barely five hours after the ambush, his face was as drawn as a skull. The body that had been so powerful when they'd sat down to breakfast now appeared little more than a bundle of dry twigs, and his opalescent eyes were dull and filmy.

"Father," Llyr managed, a dozen desperate words flooding his tongue. He didn't think he could say any of them without losing control of his grief. The king's fingers tightened on his in response.

"Listen, my sons," Dearg husked. Each faint syllable seemed a work of vast effort. Llyr and Ansgar had to lean close to hear him. "My time is short. I will not speak of my love for you. You know of it."

"Oh, whatever will I do without—" Ansgar burst out.

"Shh . . . listen. I cannot leave one of you the kingdom and give the other . . . nothing. There'd be . . . trouble. Our people have had enough"—he had to stop and pant before he could finish—"enough of war."

Llyr ached to deny he'd lead a rebellion if Ansgar became king, but he held his tongue. For one thing, he wasn't sure it was true. Ansgar would be a nightmare as king. Even war would be preferable. But Dearg had never seen his eldest son's faults.

His father gave them a tight, painful smile. "So it's fortunate I have . . . two kingdoms for . . . for my two sons."

Ansgar stiffened. "What?"

"You, Ansgar, will be king of the Morven Sidhe . . . while you   you, Llyr, will hold the Cachamwri throne."

"No!" Ansgar spat, throwing aside the old man's hand as he exploded to his feet. "You can't give the Cachamwri to this puppy! I was to rule both kingdoms—I am firstborn! The Morven are a conquered people, while we have ruled the Cachamwri ten thousand years." He shot a deadly glare at Llyr. "I will not take his leavings."

Dying or no, Dearg's icy will showed in his eyes. "You lack the mark, Ansgar. The king of the Cachamwri Sidhe . . . must wear Cachamwri's Mark. As the Heir to Heroes . . . Llyr can call the Dragon . . . in the hour of our greatest need. As he must answer when Cachamwri calls. This is our pact with Cachamwri, the Dragon God."

"This for your pact." Deliberately, Ansgar spat on the floor beside the bed. Furious at the insult, Llyr dropped a hand to his sword. "Cachamwri is a fool, if he'd choose this whelp to wear the Mark over me."

"No!" Dearg rapped out with surprising strength. "You will not kill one another. Heed me now!"

The brothers turned, startled, as the king lifted one frail hand. Magic flared around it, sparking and glowing.

Whoooom!

Before either could react, the magical blast slammed into them both with a cold, burning ferocity. Each cried out in shock. "What have you done, old man?" Ansgar gasped, falling to one knee as Llyr struggled to hold his feet.

Dearg's hand fell weakly to the bed. His voice dropped to a faint, dying whisper. "If one of you attempts to slay the other with magic, my curse will turn that magic on you threefold. I will not have you . . . fighting . . . No more . . . war . . ." His eyes went fixed as his spirit fled.

"He used his own life force to power that spell," Llyr whispered, stunned. "Why would he . . . ?"

"Because he knew I'd kill you the first chance I got," Ansgar snarled, climbing to his feet, his eyes blazing with fury in his white face. "So I'll just have to look for another way." He whirled and stalked out the door.

Llyr didn't turn as the door slammed behind Ansgar. Slowly, he sank to one knee at his father's bedside and took the cold, still hand in his. Dropping his forehead against Dearg's icy fingers, he wept.

One Year Later

Llyr sat on the throne that had once been his father's, looking over intelligence reports from his spies in the Morven Kingdom that Ansgar now ruled. His brother had been all too busy of late, ordering the execution of those who complained about the freedoms he'd stripped from the Sidhe accustomed to his father's kind hand.

So far, though, he'd made no move against Llyr. With any luck, Dearg's protections would be enough to make sure that dubious peace continued.

As if the curse was insufficient, Dearg's will ordered that if either king tried to kill the other by physical means, the nobles of both courts were to rise against him and strip him of his crown. Llyr wasn't sure it would be that easy, but hopefully the provision would never be put to the test.

Hearing the throne room's double doors open, he glanced up. "The wizards Merlin and Nimue," his guard captain announced in ringing tones.

Llyr straightened as the two aliens strode across the throne room toward him, both smiling. The lovers looked like mortal youths—barely old enough to *be* lovers—but an air of power hung around them that proclaimed they were far more than they seemed. He put his reports aside and gave them a welcoming smile. "Well met, my friends."

The two didn't kneel, and Llyr didn't ask it of them. Their eyes held such age and wisdom that he found them slightly intimidating. "You look better," Nimue said in her delicate, chiming voice. Blond, lithe as a nymph, she wore a delicate froth of ivory silk that belled around her tiny feet. "I am pleased to see your grief weighs less heavily on you, Your Majesty."

"I only wish we could have done more for your father," Merlin added with a sigh.

"I was grateful you made the effort," Llyr told him. "None of our Sidhe healers were able to help him either."

Merlin shrugged. "It was the least we could do, after all Dearg did to help us drive off the Dark Ones."

His father had been skeptical of Merlin and Nimue when the alien couple had first arrived on Sidhe Earth two years before. After all, the last group of starfarers the Sidhe had encountered had been the invading Dark Ones thousands of years before.

It had not been an auspicious introduction. The Dark Ones preyed on the life force of others through murder and torture, and they had decimated the Sidhe people. It had taken centuries and the help of Cachamwri himself to banish them.

Even then, the Dark Ones had only fled to the next dimension over, Mortal Earth. That world was a copy of the Sidhe version except that magic barely functioned there. As a result, the humans who occupied it had no magical abilities, and the Dark Ones had been able to prey on them with impunity.

At least until the starfarers Merlin and Nimue arrived and convinced Dearg to help them drive the Dark Ones from Mortal Earth. Dearg had finally agreed, fearing the Dark Ones might otherwise decide to attack the Sidhe again.

In the end, the Sidhe and their allies had defeated the

demons and imprisoned their leader, Geirolf. Unfortunately, that victory had cost the lives of Dearg and two thousand Sidhe warriors.

With an effort, Llyr lifted his head and shook off his grief. "Have you selected your champions yet?"   •

Merlin had told him the two aliens intended to create a race of guardians who would guide and nurture the human race into adulthood. To that end, they had created a magical grail that would genetically alter those who drank from it, making the women magic-using Majae, and the males, powerful vampire shape-shifters.

The wizard nodded. "Actually, that's why I'm here. My Magekind—"

"Magekind?"

"That's what we're calling our creations," Nimue explained in her soft voice.

"They need a base of operations on this dimension's Earth," Merlin explained. "Because they have so little magic on their own, they'll need to live here to replenish their powers."

Llyr sat back on his throne with a frown. "Merlin, this world belongs to the Sidhe. I don't want an alien colony here."

"You need not worry, Your Majesty. Avalon will be located on the other side of the planet from the Sidhe kingdoms."

And the Sidhe bred so slowly, it would be millennia before there need be much contact between the two realms. Particularly given their recent casualties. "Still . . ."

Those wise, dark eyes gazed into his. "I believe you'll come to find them useful allies, Llyr."

Which, coming from Merlin, sounded like a prophecy he didn't dare ignore. He sighed. "Very well, then."

"Good. They're a decent lot, especially King Arthur and

his knights." Merlin hesitated, his young face troubled. "But if there is ever trouble with them, we have created a safeguard race."

"Another one?" He wasn't sure he liked the sound of that. "Are they going to want to live on this Earth, too? Merlin—"

"Oh, no," Nimue said quickly. "They'll live among the humans on Mortal Earth. We call them Direkind. They're a race of wolf-shifters."

"If my guardians trouble you or try to enslave the mortals for whatever reason, you'll find allies in the Direkind." Merlin spread his hands in a graceful gesture. "They will help you deal with Magekind, should it ever come to that."

"Let's hope it doesn't," Llyr said coolly.

"I'm sure it won't," Nimue said. "So. We must say our farewells then."

"Oh?"

"Yes," Merlin said. "Our work on mortal Earth is complete. We have another race to attend to now."

"Ah. Safe journey to you, then."

"And good fortune to you, King Llyr Galatyn," Merlin said. He lifted a slender hand, and a dimensional gate swirled into being before them. With an offhand wave, he and Nimue stepped into it. Even as they did so, Llyr thought he saw the aliens become something . . . else. Then the gate was gone.

He sat a long time, wondering exactly what it was he'd seen.

ONE

Llyr opened his eyes to see a woman standing over him in slim and glorious nudity, her body gleaming in the moonlight. As is the way in dreams, he didn't question who she was or what she was doing in his chamber. He only gazed at her and felt his need rise.

She was all lithe muscle, like a young cat, with small, sweet breasts and rose nipples rising flushed and swollen. But it was her scent that teased him to full, aching hardness—the scent of woman and deep forests and wild, ancient magic.

And passion, feral and urgent.

Yet though desire surged in response to her body, her eyes drew his soul. Almost too big for her sensual face, they shone wolf-pale under the darkness of her short-cropped black hair.

"I'm in need," she said in a low voice that seemed to cup his sex in heat. She had the most erotic mouth he'd ever seen—full, sweetly curved, naked of paint. "Will you make love to me?"

"Yes. Oh, yes." Llyr watched hungrily as she slid onto his bed with the weightless grace of someone far stronger than she should be. "We're going to be together," he told her, knowing this was more vision than dream. "Soon, we'll meet each other."

"Not soon enough," she said, her eyes going even paler until they glowed like molten silver. "I burn tonight."

"Come to my arms then," he said, reaching for her. "And I'll make you burn even brighter."

She slid the length of his body, her skin so hot and smooth, he gasped in pleasure. "You're beautiful," she murmured, tracing long, slender fingers over the curve of his chest. "Are you real?"

"As real as you, my dream," he said, and cupped one sleek breast. She sighed and let her head fall back. He sat up and drew her astride him, groaning at the sensual delight of her silken backside settling over his thighs. A cool breeze blew into his face from the open window, blending the scent of Sidhe roses and the potent musk of her arousal. A fountain tinkled from the courtyard, a backdrop for her sigh.

Her witchy gaze captured him again, silver with magic. She bent to kiss him, her mouth wet and burning. Llyr set himself to pleasure her, swirling his tongue between her teeth. Her corner teeth were oddly sharp, but he didn't care.

He caught the back of her head in one hand. Her hair was as soft as a cat's fur against his fingers, and he stroked it, loving the sensation. Discovering the sensitive whorls of one delicate ear, Llyr stopped to explore. Unlike his own, it wasn't pointed. "You're human," he murmured.

"Not really," she whispered, and pulled back to look at him with those burning silver eyes.

It was then that he knew. "Oh," he said, "that's going to be a problem."

King Llyr Aleyn Galatyn jolted awake to find himself naked and alone, his cock hard as a broadsword. He looked around wildly, but all he saw was the pale gleaming marble and gem-inlaid wood of his chamber. His magical lover had vanished, as if she'd never been there at all.

Which of course, she hadn't been.

He fell back against his silken pillows with a huff of frustration, eying his rampant prick. It seemed to eye him back. "Yes, I know, I woke too soon," he told it, smiling in reluctant amusement.

Then, with a sigh, he took his shaft in one royal hand and attended to the problem himself.

Diana London sat straight up in her bed, panting and sweat-damp.

The beautiful blond man was gone.

She rolled out of bed to stand in the moonlight, gasping with frustrated need. Every nerve burned with erotic hunger. She shut her eyes, remembering the way he'd looked sprawled across those dark sheets of his, his hair a fan of gold beneath his broad, muscular shoulders. He was built like a runner, lean and long and sculpted, with eyes that gleamed up at her like opals, filled with magical sparks of color. When they'd kissed, his wide, firm mouth moved against hers with such delicious skill, she ached even more just thinking of it.

And his cock . . .

Better not think about his cock. Not when she was alone with the Burning Moon blazing in her blood.

She'd never had a dream so intense, so real. So erotic. The need for release burned in her blood until her skin felt small and tight.

Diana glanced at the nightstand where she kept the vibrator that had become a necessity since her Burning Moon began. She grimaced. The dream had ignited a hunger cold plastic couldn't soothe.

She needed to run.

Diana strode naked to the window and jerked up the sash so hard, the glass reverberated with a booming rattle. A cool breeze blew in, chilling the sweat on her body as she stared out into the night. The moon rode full over the shadowed trees behind her house. A whippoorwill called, its voice high and mournful in the darkness, sounding as lonely as she felt. Traffic sighed from the interstate. Somewhere a train whistle blew a long, wailing note.

The wooden privacy fences on either side of the yard were higher than a man's head. No one could see her.

Stepping back, Diana closed her eyes and concentrated. Magic raced over her body in a wave of burning sparks. She caught her breath in a gasp as muscle knotted and bones and reshaped themselves. Sinking to the floor, she felt the telltale itch of fur rippling its way across her skin.

When Diana opened her eyes again, she was a wolf.

Bounding through the window, she began to run on four swift paws, trying to escape her clawing need for the dream man's touch.

* * *

"It's bald-faced police harassment, is what it is!" Clara Davies leaned onto the podium and glared. Her thin, wrinkled face was so flushed, Diana was half afraid she'd keel over where she stood. Even her carefully teased blue-tinted perm vibrated with her rage.

At the front of the room, the seven members of the Verdaville City Council wore expressions of polite skepticism. Diana gave silent thanks that the council was pleased with her work as city administrator, or Davies's accusations might have met with a different reception.

Which wasn't going to stop the old bat from trying to take Diana down anyway.

Clara pointed a gnarled finger in her direction. *"That woman* has ordered the police to torment my Roger. He can't set foot out the door without one of this city's hick cops pullin' him over or charging him with beating up on some tramp."

"Diana," Mayor Don Thompson said, making a show of giving her an evenhanded stare. He was a tall man who'd probably been handsome in his youth, with spadelike hands and a long nose. In her more whimsical moments, Diana suspected he used that Romanesque snout to sniff the political winds. "Is there any truth to this?"

She fought to keep her angry frustration off her face. Dealing with idiots didn't normally bother her, but it was her Burning Moon, and her patience wasn't what it should be. "No one is harassing Mrs. Davies's son, Mayor Thompson. Roger has a hot temper, and he's a bit too willing to take it out on his girlfriends, the police, and anybody with the bad fortune to encounter him when he's drunk. Which is most of the time, judging from his three DUIs in the past six months."

"You see?" Clara shrilled, her wrinkled face going mottled. "Lies! Nothing but lies! My Roger does not drink. I raised him to be a good Christian boy. I did my duty!"

"I'm sure you did," Diana retorted coolly. "But he's a man now, and you can't control his behavior anymore." *If you ever did.* "Which makes it our job."

"Your job," Clara sneered. "You're not a real cop. You just like to put on that blue uniform and prance around giving people a hard time." She turned a fulminating glare on Thompson. "I told you three years ago you shouldn't hire her. Women have no business in positions of authority. She certainly doesn't."

"Now, Clara—" Thompson began.

"You listen to me, Don Thompson," the old woman snapped, pointing a gnarled finger at him. "You tell her to quit passing herself off as a police officer and leave Roger alone, or I'm going to sue her and this city. And you, too!"

Gathering up her purse with a jerk, Clara wheeled around and stomped from the council chamber, her mint polyester slacks whispering with every step.

Well, that was over. Diana relaxed as the mayor announced the next item on the agenda, and the council segued into an argument over window treatments for City Hall.

After the confrontation with Clara, her head was pounding and her nails had grown beyond the limits of her champagne polish. She carefully fisted one hand around her Cross pen to hide them.

Most of the time, being Direkind was no big deal. The whole bit about turning into a ravening monster every full moon was a load of crap. She kept her human intellect even in wolf form, and she'd never killed anybody in her life.

In fact, eleven months out of the year, Diana actually enjoyed being a werewolf. It certainly came in handy in her job as volunteer police officer. Her nose for drugs and fleeing suspects had raised the Verdaville Police Department's conviction rate 30 percent.

But one month a year, she went into the werewolf equivalent of heat as her hormones ran wild with the drive to mate. It was like PMS squared, with a side order of nymphomania.

All with no suitable male in sight.

That was when being Direkind seriously sucked. Her body demanded sex with such savagery, there were times she could barely resist the need to molest the first hapless male she met.

But somehow she'd always managed. She knew all too well that if she lost control, she could end up infecting somebody with Merlin's Curse. And if he couldn't handle it, her brother would have a duty to kill the poor bastard to keep him from exposing them all.

It was a tightrope Diana had been walking every year since she'd turned fourteen, including all five years as city manager of Verdaville and an even smaller town before that. You'd think it would start getting easier.

Instead it only got harder.

And listening to the council snipe about the merits of blinds over drapes wasn't exactly helping. Diana jotted down notes, fighting to concentrate.

But despite her best efforts, her thoughts began to wander. *The man's powerful torso gleamed gently in the moonlight, muscles flexing in long ripples as he swept his silken blond hair back from an arrogantly handsome face. Opalescent eyes gleamed as he watched her come to him. "We're going to be together," he told her. "Soon, we'll meet each other."*

Just the memory of his deep male purr drew Diana's nipples into peaks under her blouse, making her glad for her linen jacket. When she crossed her legs in the matching charcoal slacks, she could smell her own heat.

God, if only there really was some safe, luscious sex god around to take the pressure off. The Burning Moon seemed worse this year than it ever had been before.

Glancing around the room, she saw a man in the audience staring at her, his eyes hot and glazed. Diana swore silently. Men weren't consciously aware of her scent, but they still reacted to the pheromones her body produced during the Burning Moon. Which didn't make the lust any easier to deal with.

"What do you think, Diana?" the Mayor asked.

Her eyes flicked back to the council table to see all seven members staring at her.

"That decision is up to the council. I'll do whatever you direct." After a delicate hesitation, she suggested, "Maybe this is a good time to bring the question to a vote."

With the meeting over at last, Diana retreated to her office to pack up for the night. She was just collecting her purse when Thompson spoke from the door.

"Just wanted to let you know, we're all real pleased with this month's financial report," the mayor said. "City's in good, solid shape. Think we'll be able to avoid a tax increase this year?"

She slung her purse strap over her shoulder and eyed him. This time of year, she never liked being alone with a man, even one a good thirty years older than she was. Not that she couldn't handle him if he got obnoxious. Tall and wiry though Thompson was, her Direkind strength gave her the edge even in human form. Still, having to fend off a pass would certainly complicate her life.

"I haven't finished compiling the budget, but I see no reason we'd need an increase," she told him cautiously. "Revenues seem to be hitting the two million mark, which is enough to run the city." Diana grimaced. "As long as the fire department doesn't wreck another aerial truck, anyway."

"Good. That's real good." Thompson's bony face twisted into the good ol' boy grin he often used to set opponents up for the kill. "Thing is, there's more to running Verdaville than understanding budgets."

Yeah? That's not what you said three years ago, when you hired me to save your ass after you ran this town into the ground. "Oh?"

The grin faded. "You need to watch Clara Davies, Diana. Her son's a bastard, but she's got influence. She could stir up a whole lot of people if she takes it into her head. And we don't need that kind of grief."

Diana didn't quite manage to bite the words back in time. "So, what? You want me to let Roger skate the next time he beats the snot out of his girlfriend?"

Thompson made a placating gesture with his big, spade-like hands. "Now, I didn't say that, Diana. You're a smart girl. You'll do the right thing when the time comes."

Steaming, she watched him flash that grin and saunter out of her office. *I am a professional city administrator,* Diana mentally chanted. *Professional city administrators do not turn into wolves and bite the mayor on the ass.*

Even when he really, really deserved it.

By the time Diana left the building, it was after ten P.M. and the city hall parking lot was deserted. As she locked the front doors, she looked up to scan the redbrick front of the building, automatically making sure none of the floodlights had burned out. Doric columns flanked either side of the two-story double doors, and the windows reflected her face, pale against the darkness.

Once upon a time, the structure had been the main office for a textile plant. Diana suspected its resemblance to a Southern plantation had been intended as a subliminal message from company management. *Y'all don't get uppity, now.* That message went double for the city's employees, at least as far as the council was concerned.

"Hey, Diana!"

She turned to see a Verdaville police car pulling up to the curb behind her. The blue Ford Crown Victoria bore the city's coat of arms on its front doors, picked out in gold paint. "Hey, Jer! What can I do for you?"

The officer hooked one arm out his open window. "Chief needs you at a crime scene. Want to follow me?" Jerry Morgan was a short, stocky ex-Marine whose usual expression was a sly grin. Tonight he looked pale and tense.

Diana frowned. Jerry was a Desert Storm vet; he liked to say his tour of the Highway of Death had left him with a cast-iron stomach. Anything bad enough to make him blanch had to be pretty damn bad. "I'll get my car," she told him, and strode to the spot where she'd parked her ten-year-old Honda.

The trip did not take long. No drive within the Verdaville city limits did. Two minutes after leaving City Hall, they pulled into one of the mill villages that formed the core of the town.

The little clusters of homes had been built by the town's textile plants as employee housing. Most of the four-room houses dated from the 1920s, when employees rented from the mills, picked up their mail in the mill office, and shopped in the company store. That lifestyle had slowly disappeared as Verdaville had grown. Even so, the town had been left with a gaping economic wound when the plants closed, one that still hadn't healed two years after the last one shut its doors.

Plant closures or not, though, the villages were tight-knit little communities where everybody knew everybody else. Diana wasn't surprised to see a crowd gathered outside the yellow police tape strung around one particular bungalow. Anywhere else, this kind of group would have worn avid expressions of morbid curiosity. Here, they visibly grieved for somebody they'd probably known all their lives.

She knew there would be relatives in the crowd, too, notified by neighbors the minute the cops pulled up—all of them ready to pounce on the first authority figure to show his or her face.

Sighing in resignation, Diana reached into her glove compartment for her badge and gun. After she and Chief Gist had reached their understanding, she'd obtained a commission as a reserve officer, training for six weeks in everything from how to shoot a gun to issuing traffic tickets. Such volunteer cops were invaluable to small-town departments that couldn't afford much manpower, and Verdaville's ten-man police force was no exception.

Sometimes, though, her badge was a mixed blessing. This was one of them.

Knowing what was coming, Diana felt her stomach tie itself into a knot as she got out of the car. She'd barely managed to clip her badge onto her belt and slip on her shoulder holster before somebody in the crowd called her name.

Oh well. She really hadn't thought she could get through this mob without being recognized anyway. She made the front page of the local weekly too often.

As one, the entire bunch surged in her direction, voices lifted in anger, fear, or distress. "Miss London, do they know—"

"Have they caught—"

"*. . . need to see my brother!*" That last was a howl from a sobbing young woman whose face was swollen with tears. She tore herself from the restraining hands of a young man and lunged to grab Diana's wrist. "You've gotta tell me what happened! Is he dead? They said he's dead. Please, please tell me what's going on!"

Diana froze, battling half a dozen conflicting instincts. She'd never liked being grabbed, but this was a particularly bad time of year for a stranger to lay hands on her. Especially a woman.

It took her a moment to squelch her more lethal impulses enough to speak. "I probably know less than you do right now. If you'll let me by, I'll send the chief out to talk to you." Her voice emerged at a rumbling register that didn't sound quite human. *Oh, hell.*

The woman jerked away from her as if scalded. Fear blazed up on a score of faces as those near enough to hear shrank back. "You . . . you do that," she managed finally, obviously trying to convince herself she'd imagined whatever she'd seen in the city manager's face.

"I'll send the chief out in a minute." Diana nodded shortly, put her head down to hide her burning eyes, and strode toward the front door of the house. The crowd melted from her path. Humankind might be at the top of the food chain now, but they still knew a predator when they saw one.

Whether they could admit it or not.

Dammit, Diana thought. *I've got to watch that.* In old movies, pulling crap like that was what got the torch-carrying mob after the monster.

"Sorry I wasn't here sooner," Jerry panted from behind her. "Had to park up the street. By the time I got back, they were all over you." She looked around to see him wearing an apologetic smile. He'd evidently missed her near transformation. "Maybe you should start keeping your uniform at City Hall so you can change. Public's not as obnoxious when you're in blues."

She grinned, remembering some of her own recent adventures. "Unless they're drunk. Then they're worse."

He grinned back. "There is that."

Jerry led the way up the irregular cement steps and pushed open the screen door. As Diana crossed the narrow front porch behind him, she automatically sized up her surroundings. The white vinyl siding was relatively new, though she'd bet the house itself was pushing ninety. The shutters and wooden door were the same shade as the steps, though in the dark it was hard to tell the color. Even so, she could make out the wooden swing hanging at one end of the porch. A couple of lawn chairs stood across from it, looking out over a postage-stamp yard that had been recently cut. There was no trash or beer bottles in the yard. The owner might not have much money, but he'd cared about appearances.

Poor bastard.

Jerry paused in the act of reaching for the door to meet her eyes. At five-eleven, she was actually an inch taller than he was, a fact that had never stopped him from trying to protect her like the Southern gentleman he was. Diana wouldn't dream of telling him just how little she needed his protection. "It's pretty bad," he warned her.

"I figured that out. Please tell me it's not a kid."

His white smile flashed in the dim light. "Grown man."

"Good." She grimaced. "I hate it when it's kids."

"Everybody hates it when it's kids. But what the killer did to that guy—well, it's sickening."

He opened the door. Death spilled out with the ripe stench of blood and human waste. Even in this form, Diana's sense of smell was so acute, she had to swallow hard. "What'd they do, gut him?"

"Pretty close." Jerry lifted a brow at her as he led the way inside. "You could tell that from the smell?"

"I've got a good nose."

"That ain't exactly a blessing in here." He jerked a thumb at a closed door to the right. "Chief's in the bedroom. Unless you need me, I'll be in the kitchen."

"No, that's fine."

Jerry gave her an absent wave and headed across the little den for the even smaller kitchen, where male voices rumbled in conversation. The Sheriff's Office must have sent men to help out, since the Verdaville PD couldn't muster enough people for a crowd on its own.

Somebody laughed, but the sound held the strained note of a man trying very hard not to think about whatever he'd just seen.

Oh, yeah. This was going to be bad.

TWO

The Grand Palace of the Cachamwri Sidhe, Mageverse Earth

Llyr's soft boots scuffed over dew-soaked grass as he walked into the courtyard garden carrying his sheathed great sword in one hand. Three of his personal bodyguards trailed behind him, silent as wolves, but he was scarcely aware of them.

The milky glory of the Mageverse spread overhead, and around him, the palace rose in curving elegant shapes of creamy marble. The extravagant beauty of the courtyard was normally a balm to his spirit, but not tonight. Tonight he craved the sweat and effort of a good fight, and he knew the captain of his guard would give it to him.

Llyr had dressed for their weekly practice session in

leather leggings and boots, but he wore neither shirt nor armor. His magic would protect him against any blows gone awry.

Though in truth, he would welcome a few bruises. It was no more than he deserved.

Strange how guilt seemed to have a taste to it. Last night, Llyr had been so far under the dream woman's spell, he'd not thought of Janieda even once, not even when he brought himself to climax. Yet by the time he had awakened this morning, guilt had filled his heart until he could taste it on his tongue, sour and cold.

Today he'd been able to think of nothing else. Janieda, his fairy sprite, who'd loved him enough to give up the essence of herself to save him from a demon.

They'd been lovers since his last wife fell to his brother's assassins a century ago, and Llyr had loved Janieda as much as a king can afford to love anyone. She wanted to be his queen, but he thought she'd lacked the steadiness he needed in a wife. The lives of ten million people hung on his every decision, and he couldn't afford to make a poor choice.

Llyr had already lost four wives to his brother's assassins, which was why he'd been so determined to secure one of Arthur's magic-using witches for a bride. Besides being more fertile than a Sidhe woman, a Maja would have had the power to handle Ansgar's hired killers. Janieda, on the other hand, would have been easy prey.

Unfortunately, being his mistress proved equally hazardous.

Sixteen hundred years after Merlin imprisoned him, the Dark Ones' demonic general, Geirolf, escaped from his Mageverse cage. The demon kidnaped Janieda to force Llyr to turn over a Magekind couple he was sheltering. Geirolf planned to sacrifice the two in a spell that would have wiped out Merlin's race of guardians, giving the demon free rein on mortal Earth.

Llyr had been willing to do anything to get his lover back. He'd even linked his magic and his soul with Erin Grayson, the Maja Geirolf had demanded in trade.

Pretending to betray his allies, Llyr handed over Erin and her lover Reece Champion to the demon, who promised to release Janieda. To nobody's surprise, Geirolf failed to follow through on his end of the deal.

At first, everything went as planned. When the demon tried to sacrifice Erin and her lover, the Maja blasted all her borrowed power into his face. The spell had ripped away Geirolf's magic so Reece could finish him off.

But then the demon's vampire followers turned on Reece and Erin. Janieda had known if Erin died, the link between them would kill Llyr, too, so she'd fought to defend the drained and powerless witch. When Janieda fell to one of the vampires, her last act was to pour her magic into Erin so the Maja could defend herself.

Yet barely a week after her heroic death, Llyr had dreamed about another woman. He winced in guilt.

"My liege?"

Llyr looked up to see the captain of his guard waiting for him. Kerwyn Arberth was a big man, as dark as Llyr was blond, and a full head taller. Despite his hulking build, Kerwyn had an open, laughing face and a wicked wit as sharp as his considerable skills with a sword. He'd been Llyr's closest friend for six centuries.

"Well met, Kerwyn." Llyr swept his friend a salute with the sheathed sword. "I'm in desperate need of a good fight. I trust you'll oblige me."

The captain looked him over with a frown. "Are you sure, my liege? You look tired."

Llyr shrugged. "Guilt and lack of sleep."

Kerwyn's mouth tightened. "Janieda."

Llyr wasn't surprised his captain could read him so well. "That, and the vision I had last night." He drew his blade with the scrape of steel on leather, absently aware his guards had fanned out to watch for his brother's assassins. "I dreamed of an exquisitely beautiful woman with dark hair and silver eyes. I believe we're destined to meet. But she's a Direkind shape-shifter, and I fear it will not end well."

Kerwyn stiffened, but his tone was carefully controlled as he drew his own sword. "Janieda gave up her life for you but a week past."

Llyr nodded. "How could I even think of anyone else?"

The captain shrugged and fell into guard, the thick ropy muscles of his chest rippling. "Well, it was not as if you truly loved her, my liege."

Stung, Llyr lifted his head. "Of course I loved her. I wouldn't have stayed with her a century if I hadn't." Detecting a fractional drop in Kerwyn's guard, he lunged, but the bigger man brought his blade up in a ringing parry. Their blades met with a satisfying jolt the instant before Kerwyn launched his own attack. Llyr knocked it aside and retreated with the oiled smoothness his centuries had taught him.

"You know as well as I that you'd grown tired of her," Kerwyn said as they circled. "Her taste for drama had begun to grate, and she was insanely jealous. If you even spoke to another woman, she'd rage at you for days."

"She did have a passionate nature." He brought his sword up and around in a swinging overhead attack, knowing Kerwyn's magic would block the blow even if he missed the parry. Llyr usually had to be more careful with his practice partners, since he could attack faster than most could either parry or cast a shield spell. Kerwyn, however, was just as fast as he was. "She never held back. She always gave everything she had."

As expected, the captain parried his blow. For a moment, they surged against one another, testing each other's strength, nose to nose. Llyr had to work at it: Kerwyn's greater size gave him the advantage.

Then his friend lost his easy expression in a snarl. "She was a fool."

Pain pricked Llyr's ribs. Startled, he disengaged and jumped back. Glancing down, he saw a narrow trail of blood snaking down his side. Confused, he looked up to see a dagger in Kerwyn's left hand. "I didn't think we were practicing with two blades tonight." Automatically, he reached with his magic to conjure a second weapon for himself.

Nothing happened. His left hand remained stubbornly empty.

"You're not." Kerwyn's mouth curved in an ugly grin.

Llyr reached out again, but the usual snap and crackle of Mageverse energies were beyond his reach.

And he knew.

The king stared at his oldest friend as the three bodyguards stepped from the garden to surround them. He had no delusions about whose side they were on. "How much is my brother paying you, Kerwyn?"

"A great deal, but this isn't about money." The big man began to stalk him. "I loved Janieda for decades, but she had eyes for no one except you. Yet all you cared about was putting a queen's crown on one of your precious Majae and securing an alliance with Arthur."

Llyr saw the flicker of motion from the corner of one eye. Acting on sheer instinct, he twisted and dropped to one knee, avoiding the sword swing that would have decapitated him. He thrust upward, his blade slicing into the underside of the guard's jaw. The man fell, dead before he had time to deflect the blow with magic or sword.

Steel flashed. Llyr rolled, avoiding another traitor's lunge. Surging to his feet, he rammed his blade into the gap between his opponent's chest plate and armored hip. His victim screamed and toppled to the dewy grass to twitch out his life.

"A king is not so easy to kill, traitor," Llyr sneered at the third guard, whose eyes flickered in alarm. He'd gone pale as milk in the moonlight.

"Watch yourself, fool," Kerwyn barked. "The spell may have blocked Llyr's magic, but he's faster with steel than most are with magic." He launched a blinding set of attacks, forcing his prey to retreat.

"Why didn't you just poison that dagger instead of enchanting it, Kerwyn?" Llyr demanded over the clash of swords.

"I wanted the pleasure of killing you with my own hands." The captain's eyes glittered with hate as he sought an opening. "I would have made Janieda happy, but she refused me over and again. All she cared about was you. Now she's cold in her grave and you're already hot for another woman, you faithless whoreson."

"So you'll hand my people to Ansgar because a woman refused you?" And Llyr had considered this fool a brother! "He'll make the Cachamwri Sidhe slaves, torture and rape them at his pleasure, drain away their magic. They'll curse your name!"

Kerwyn's face contorted until he was barely recognizable. "At least he won't be you!" He lunged, swinging his sword in a viscous overhand blow.

As Llyr parried, the third traitor saw his opening and sprang. Llyr drove an elbow into his face, but not before the guard's sword sliced into his side. Steel grated on bone as it punched out his back just over his hip.

Roaring in pain, Llyr spun, swinging his great sword. The traitor's magical shield glittered up an instant too late.

As the guard's head spun away, Llyr grabbed the blade buried in his side. The pain drove him to one knee with its chill savagery, but he forced himself to grip the bloody hilt. The weapon was lodged in the muscle of his waist, barely an inch into his side. If he could tear it free . . .

He looked up to see Kerwyn looming over him, sword lifted in both hands. "Heir to Heroes, eh?" the traitor sneered. "See if you can call the Dragon God now, you bastard. Beg him to save your worthless life!" He brought the blade slicing down like an executioner's axe.

Llyr threw up his own sword, parrying one-handed as he levered the turncoat's weapon from his flesh with the other. White-hot pain ripped a bellow from him. Blood flew.

He swung out with the guard's sword, chopping into the side of Kerwyn's chest. The sickening jolt told him it was a death blow. "It seems I don't need the Dragon after all."

For a moment, Kerwyn's wide, shocked eyes met his. He could sense his former friend reaching desperately for the energy of the Mageverse, trying to heal the wound.

Nothing happened.

Llyr smiled bitterly. "I gather you bespelled the guards' blades, too."

He heaved himself to his feet as Kerwyn fell to his knees, fighting desperately to breathe around the blade sunk in his chest.

"I'm glad Janieda refused your suit, you bastard," Llyr panted. The pain in his side burned like a white-hot poker. "She may have deserved more from me than she got, but she definitely deserved better than you."

A single stroke of his sword cleaved Kerwyn's head from his shoulders.

For a long moment, the king of the Cachamwri Sidhe

stood under the Mageverse moon, blood pouring hot down his side as the bodies of those he'd trusted cooled around him. Then, slowly, teeth gritted against the tearing agony, Llyr hobbled across the stone courtyard toward the nearest palace entrance.

He'd go directly to his grandmother's quarters; at the moment, the Dowager Queen was the only healer he was willing to trust. She'd be able to take off the spell blocking his powers.

Then he'd see if his brother had suborned other traitors among those he loved.

Diana spotted the Grayson County Sheriff's Office evidence tech down on one knee in front of a coffee table. He was carefully brushing fingerprint dust on a couple of wineglasses. One had a quarter inch of something pale pink in the bottom.

She moved to stand beside him. "White zin?" Bending, she sniffed the glass.

"Yep." The tech pulled a strip of tape from his box of gear and carefully applied it over a print he'd found.

"He served white zinfandel to his killer?"

The tech shrugged. "Must have had a lady friend here, too. From the size, these are a woman's prints."

Diana lifted a brow. "Killer could have been his wife or girlfriend."

The tech glanced up at her. "No woman could have done that kind of damage."

"You might be surprised."

He shrugged and pulled off the tape, lifting the print. "Hey, don't get me wrong. I've known of women to do some serious overkill. But unless she brought a rottweiler, this one ain't a woman's work."

The bedroom door opened, releasing a stench that made Diana choke. Even the tech gagged.

"There you are," Chief William Gist said to her. "I want you to check this out."

"What the hell for?" she heard the tech mutter, so softly Diana doubted the chief heard. The man plainly thought she couldn't. "She's a fucking reservist."

Ignoring him, Diana slipped past Gist into the bedroom, carefully holding her breath.

The victim lay spread-eagled on the double bed under a cheerful yellow canopy. The matching bedspread beneath his naked body was covered in tiny blue flowers and splatters of drying blood. His empty eyes stared at the canopy, his face slack and waxen.

Looking at the ruin the killer had made of him, Diana wondered if he'd begged God to let him die.

Once he'd been a handsome, well-built young man whose blond hair and blue eyes had probably attracted more than his share of feminine admiration. Now his groin was a mutilated ruin. Above that, deep furrows scored his muscular belly, revealing pink coils of intestines. *Well, that explains the smell.* He was probably headed for a closed-casket funeral; Diana doubted even a skilled mortician would be able to hide the butchery.

"Sweet Jesus." Diana stepped closer to examine what was left of him. She winced. "What have we got, Chief?"

Gist flipped open his notebook. "Ronnie Jones, twenty-four, worked first shift over in Carson at the roller bearing plant. Lived with his brother, who works for UPS. Tim Jones had the extreme bad fortune to come home from work and find him."

Diana glanced up at Gist. "He alibied?"

Gist frowned, his long face lengthening even more. "We've got the brother under wraps, but I doubt we'll charge him unless you find something. Given his job, Tim could easily have come home and killed the guy, but somehow, my gut says no. He's too busted up over it."

She nodded. "And whoever did this was seriously pissed."

"Right. If Tim had been the killer, he couldn't have faked that kind of grief."

"Makes sense." Frowning, she bent closer to the corpse. "Looks like the killer used a knife. But where's the blood? Are those injuries postmortem?" There was a great deal of splatter on the bedspread, but Diana knew if Jones had bled to death, the mattress should have been soaked right down to the box springs.

On the other hand, if the killer had hacked him up after his heart had stopped beating, there wouldn't have been as much blood. She frowned and twisted her head, examining the angle and length of the splatters.

"Coroner said he thinks the guy probably bled out."

Diana glanced up at him. "I'd feel more confidence in that assessment if George Miller had an M.D. to go with his ego." Under South Carolina state law, a county coroner had to have a high school diploma, but that was about it. The theory was that anybody could tell when somebody was dead. Which was how Miller had managed to get himself elected based on his standing in the community rather than any knowledge of medicine. That wouldn't have been so bad, if the man hadn't been a media hound who loved to make pronouncements about cause of death.

"Yeah, but if Miller's right, where did the blood go?" Gist raked a hand through his salt-and-pepper crewcut, his bony face tired. His wife always ironed his blue uniform until the creases were sharp enough to cut paper, but it was visibly wilting now. "I thought maybe he'd been killed somewhere else and moved here, but there's just enough blood in the mattress to indicate otherwise. Besides, look at his arms and legs."

Thick bands of red, scraped flesh circled wrists and ankles. "He was bound," Diana said. "Looks like some kind of manacles."

"Chained to the bed. You can see the bedposts are scored, too. He must have fought like hell to get loose."

Diana looked up at Gist. "So where are the restraints?"

The chief shook his head. "We haven't been able to find them. Or the murder weapon, whatever it was."

"Maybe I'll have better luck." She looked at the closed door. "That lock?"

"Took care of it while you were checking out the body."

Diana nodded shortly and closed her eyes to visualize the form she wanted. A tingling sensation gathered under her scalp and spread down her body, intensifying into a hot burn as muscle and bones contorted. The bottom dropped out of her stomach, as though she was riding an elevator that had gone into free fall.

When Diana opened her eyes again, a wall of yellow fabric stood in front of her. She'd always been grateful that she wasn't color-blind in the German shepherd form she assumed when playing K-9.

She resisted the urge to give her body a doglike shake, having no desire to contaminate the crime scene with black fur.

"I'll never get used to that," Gist said, rocking back on his heels as he looked down at her. He suddenly seemed much taller. "I always hope that I'll see the moment when you change, but I never do. It's just too quick. And where the hell do your clothes go?"

Automatically, she tried to answer—*It's magic, Chief*—but the first word emerged as a soft woof, reminding her to shut up before somebody heard her. This was not a form with human vocal cords, though at least her brain didn't seem to change. Which was probably why Diana became such a damn big dog; she needed a skull with enough room to house it. She'd never been able to turn into anything smaller.

As it was, this form actually weighed more than her human body. She had no idea where the extra mass came from, any more than she knew where her clothes went. It was, as she'd tried to tell the chief, magic.

Unfortunately, she had an ugly suspicion she wasn't the only one in Verdaville capable of working a spell.

Rising onto her hind legs, Diana braced her forepaws on the mattress, then extended her long nose for a sniff at the body. If anything, the smell of death was even more overwhelming in this form, but somehow she didn't find it as horrific.

But there was something beneath the ripe smell of blood and waste, an overlay of . . .

Alien.

Her canine lips curled into a snarl as a deep growl rumbled in her throat. Instinctively, she dropped down and backed away from the bed, repulsed.

"What is it?" The chief looked down at her, a frown on his face. "What'd you smell? Dammit, would you turn back? I feel like I'm trapped in an episode of *Lassie.*"

Diana ignored him, forcing herself to approach the corpse again. She'd never smelled that particular scent before, and she had to make sure she wasn't mistaken. This time, though, she lowered her head to the carpet, hoping to sample whatever it was without the distracting overlay of death.

As she'd expected, the scent trails around the bed were even stronger. There was the victim's—a healthy young man in his prime with a taste for Stetson cologne and Dial soap.

And there was his killer's.

A woman. Or something that looked like a woman, anyway. She'd been human once, but she certainly wasn't anymore. The alien magic in her scent made Diana's hackles rise.

She dared. She dared come into Diana's town and kill Diana's people. She was going to pay for that.

And what the hell was she, anyway? Maja? Diana cursed silently. She'd never met one of Merlin's witches and had no idea what they smelled like, so she couldn't say whether the alien taint in the killer's scent was Maja or not.

Still, though Merlin had created the Direkind in case of just such an eventuality, Diana had a hard time believing a Maja could do something so horrific. She'd grown up listening to her grandfather's tales of heroic Arthur, his vampire Knights, and the witches of Avalon.

No hero did this.

The chief huffed. "Would you please turn back into something that can talk instead of pacing around the room snarling to yourself?"

Rumbling in frustration, Diana closed her eyes and visualized her human form. Magic raced over her skin, tingling and burning by turn. When she opened her eyes again, she was dressed once more in the conservative charcoal slacks and jacket she'd put on that morning, badge and holster in place. "The killer's not human," she told Gist, scrubbing both hands through her short-cropped black hair in frustration.

"Not . . ." Blinking, he looked wide-eyed at the body. "What do you mean, he's not human?"

"It's a she. And I mean she's"—Diana huffed out a breath—"like me. Some kind of magical whatever."

"A werewolf?" The chief's eyes flickered. She could almost see him imagining the consequences of a magical killer lose in Verdaville.

She waved off the suggestion. "No, not a werewolf; the smell's wrong. Something else. I won't know for sure until I find her. Look, I need to track this monster, if that's even possible in the muddle of scents with all those people outside. Can you . . . ?"

He nodded. "I brought Luna's stuff, just in case."

"Good. Oh, that reminds me," Diana added, as the thought of going outside into the crowd made her remember the victim's sister, "you're going to need to talk to the sister. She's outside."

"Coroner said he was going to take care of that. He's probably with the family now."

"Good." She took a deep breath. "Okay. Then it's time to play K-9 Corps before the trail goes cold."

Llyr staggered through the hidden passage into the Dowager Queen's quarters. Woozy from loss of blood, he tripped on the threshold and threw out a hand to brace himself against the wall. "Grandmother!" He grimaced as he noticed he'd left a bloody handprint on one of her floor-to-ceiling tapestries. "Oh, I'm in for it now."

Tiny wings whirred. He turned his head. "Janieda?" No, that couldn't be right. Janieda was dead. Fresh grief stabbed him.

He'd failed another of his women.

A tiny face stared into his, startled. "Your Majesty!" Instantly, the Demisidhe grew to his full height—Becan, Oriana's chamberlain. Normally as dignified as he was tall and wiry, the man looked panicky now as he wrapped a surprisingly strong arm around Llyr's shoulders. As he helped him hobble toward the nearest chair, Becan lifted his voice in a shout. "Oriana! Come quickly!" In his anxiety, the chamberlain neglected to use the Dowager's royal honorific. He corrected himself the next breath. "Your Highness, it's the king! He's been hurt!"

"What?" Light feet pattered in from the next room. Llyr looked up blindly and found himself instantly surrounded by the familiar warmth and scent of his grandmother's arms. With a sigh of relief, he let his head rest against her delicate shoulder.

His grandmother had raised him after his mother fell to a Morven rebel when he was barely an infant. Even after all these centuries of manhood, the scent of her was enough to remind him of his boyhood.

"What have they done to you?" Her voice was fierce with rage that anyone had dared touch him.

"Stab wound," he managed. "Through the side. Poisoned me with something that blocked my magic."

She caught her breath, no doubt remembering the injury that had killed her son. Gently, Oriana laid a long, slender hand against his ribs. Magic rushed from her palm in a wave of warm power, knitting the wound closed in an instant. He moaned in gratitude as the pain drained away.

At least this wound had yielded to a healer's magic.

The Dowager Queen scanned his body anxiously. "Is that your only injury? Where are your guards, boy?"

Llyr lifted his eyes to hers. She was a lovely woman still, with the exotic features and almond eyes of her Morven Sidhe heritage. A mortal would have mistaken her for no more than fifty, though in fact she was in her fifth millennium. He gave her a tight grimace. "Who do you think did this? Four of them turned on me."

"No!" Her long, dark hair seemed to crackle with sparks of magical ire. "Which ones?"

He slumped, defeat rolling through him even as his body strengthened. "Kerwyn and three others. I had to kill them all."

"Oh, no." Oriana sat back on her heels, the white silk of her nightgown settling in heavy folds around her slim body. "It was over Janieda, wasn't it?"

Llyr glanced up, startled. "You knew he loved her?"

"Yes, but I would never have expected him to turn on you. I thought that boy loved you."

"I thought so, too. Evidently we were both wrong." He stood, sighing in relief at his returned strength. Magic stirred and crackled at the edge of his consciousness. His grandmother's healing spell had lifted the block, too.

Becan walked in, carrying a tray with a pitcher and two goblets. Llyr took one with murmured thanks, then added to his grandmother, "Another point to Ansgar. What need has he to brave my father's curse, when he can hire my own men to kill me?"

"I should have drowned that one like a puppy," Oriana hissed. "When he was born without the Dragon's Mark, we all should have known right then what he'd turn out to be."

Llyr turned a brooding look at the full-length mirror hanging on Oriana's wall. Bending his right arm, he watched the intricate outline of the Dragon curl around his flexing biceps in brilliant shades of red and blue. It looked like a tattoo, but in fact, it was a magical birthmark signifying his status as the Heir to Heroes. "Kerwyn taunted me about that. He told me to call on Cachamwri if I could."

Oriana watched him with sympathy in her eyes. "Did you try?"

He shrugged. "No. But then, Cachamwri has never answered me before, not even to save my wives or children. Why should he heed me now?"

"Apparently, you didn't need him. You did defeat Kerwyn."

Llyr shrugged, turning away from the mirror. "There'll be others."

There always were.

THREE

The county coroner had evidently done his job: Gist and Diana made it through the gauntlet of friends and family without having to stop more than twice to say, "We don't know who did it yet. We're following up on all leads. Have you talked to one of our detectives about what you know?"

Finally they escaped the crowd and started toward the chief's SUV. "You're awfully damn jumpy," Gist said finally as they strode up the darkened sidewalk. He'd evidently parked some distance away. "It's that time of year again, isn't it?"

"Is it that obvious?"

"I could tell by the way you reacted whenever anybody in the crowd got too close." He sighed, sounding thoroughly put out. "Among other things. I don't normally get a boner at a crime scene, especially when somebody's guts are spread all over the place. Those pheromones of yours are damn inconvenient."

Gist was happily married, but that didn't stop his body from reacting when he and Diana were in close quarters too long during the Burning Moon. Luckily he seemed to find the reaction more embarrassing than titillating. That, or he was completely turned off by the fact that she ran around on four legs half the time.

Either way, Diana was grateful. God knew she didn't need the complication of an amorous police chief right now.

Coming out of the kennel to Gist several years before had been one of the biggest risks Diana had ever taken, but she'd had no choice. They'd been in the midst of a string of violent Main Street armed holdups that had terrorized the city's merchants and customers. Everyone had known the bandit would eventually murder one of his victims.

As luck would have it, Diana had been getting her hair done when the robber burst into the beauty shop waving a pistol and demanding the customers' purses. Even through the mask he wore, it was obvious he was high—not only on drugs, but on the terror of his victims.

Diana had known if she made a move toward him, he'd open fire on everyone in the shop. Gritting her teeth, she'd handed over her handbag like the rest of the customers and watched him run out the door.

The minute he was gone, she told the stylist to call the police and followed him. Trailing the bandit into the concealment of a stand of trees behind the shop, she transformed into wolf form and took off in pursuit.

Diana chased him into a house barely five blocks from the businesses he'd been terrorizing. From the scent trails that surrounded it, she knew she'd found the bandit's home.

However, since she didn't want to simply kill him out of

hand, Diana had been forced to go to the police with what she'd discovered. If she hadn't, somebody would have eventually ended up dead. And that she simply couldn't allow.

She tried to talk her way around revealing how she'd managed to track the robber, but Gist, unfortunately, had a cop's nose for a lie.

Diana finally gave up and transformed for him. He'd been terrified and disbelieving at first, but he'd also worked with enough police dogs to grasp the possibilities as soon as he calmed down.

Since then, Diana had helped the chief solve a number of cases. Since she could hardly testify in court that she'd identified the defendant by turning into a wolf, she'd tell Gist what she'd learned and let him collect the necessary evidence by more mundane means.

This murder, however, was an entirely different can of worms. Diana had no idea what she was going to do when and if she caught the killer. You didn't just lock up somebody with that kind of power.

The chief had parked his blue SUV in a patch of shadow between two street lights. Besides the usual Verdaville coat of arms, the big vehicle was emblazoned with the words K-9 UNIT: STAY BACK. Heavily tinted windows ensured no one could look in to see there was no dog inside.

The chief was reaching for the hatch to open the truck when Diana heard a faint sound. She whirled just as a flash went off in her face.

"Hi, Diana!" a cheerful voice said from downwind. Recognizing it, she suppressed her instinct to lunge at its owner.

"Thanks a lot, Bobby, you jerk," Gist said, sounding good-natured even as he clamped a restraining hand on her shoulder. He knew how short-tempered she was during the Burning Moon. "I'm totally blind now."

"Sorry," Bobby Greene said, not sounding sorry at all. Letting the camera hang by its strap from around his neck, he pulled his notebook out of his back pocket. "So what can you tell me about this murder, Chief?"

"This isn't the time, Bobby," Diana growled. She forced herself to straighten and clear her throat.

"We're trying to catch this guy," Gist said quickly. "Come by the office tomorrow, and I'll give you the scoop."

"It'll have to be early," Bobby said. "*The Verdaville Voice* goes to press at noon."

"First thing in the morning," Gist promised.

"Okay." The reporter turned to eye the crowd standing around the house. "I think I'll go see who I can find to interview." He wandered off.

"Damn, Diana," the chief said as soon as he was out of earshot. "I thought you were gonna eat him."

"Nah, I wouldn't do that. I don't like the taste of vulture. Besides, there's somebody I want to bite a lot more." Diana took a quick look around. Nobody was watching, but she jumped up into the back of the van for a little extra concealment anyway. "Okay, let's do this."

He nodded. She let the power go. Magic raced over her body, changing her once again into the shepherd form she used when posing as a K-9. Diana actually preferred being a wolf—her senses were more acute, her body better suited for the chase—but it drew too much attention. So shepherd it was.

Settling back on her furry haunches in the bed of the truck, she watched as Gist got her collar and leash out of the toolbox he kept it in.

Diana lifted her chin and he buckled the canvas collar around her neck, then clipped on the leash. "Okay, Luna," he said finally, calling her by the name he used for the shepherd, "let's go find the bad guy."

With a soft *woof*, she hopped out of the truck and the two of them started off down the sidewalk.

Diana trotted along with her nose down, sifting through the confusing jumble of scents from the crowd. Concentrating ferociously, she was scarcely conscious of the musical jingle of her chain and the scrape of Gist's shoes on the sidewalk as he followed her.

"Look, Mommy! The policeman has a dog!"

"Shh!"

"Wonder how much that mutt costs the city," somebody else said. "It must eat ten pounds of dog food every day. What is it, part Clydesdale? Biggest damn shepherd I've ever seen."

"Coming through, please," the chief said patiently. "Give Luna here room to work."

Alien. Blood. Death.

Diana stopped dead, almost gagging. She'd hit the killer's trail.

Despite the instinct to back away, Diana forced herself to breathe in the scent of carnage, committing it to memory as her hackles rose. She started off again, following the trail carefully, not even feeling the tug of the leash anymore in her excitement. The crowd melted back as she followed it down the sidewalk away from the house.

The wind shifted, carrying the overwhelming stench right into her face. Lifting her head, she stared out into the darkness.

The bitch who'd butchered one of Diana's people was out there. In the woods. Watching.

And she was going to pay.

Diana didn't even think twice. She shot off in pursuit,

barely even noticing Gist's shout as she tore the leash from his hand.

She was running flat out by the time she hit the concealment of the woods, plunging around trees and bounding over brush with the killer's scent goading her every time her paws hit the leaves.

As she ran, Diana realized this fight called for something more substantial than a dog. She transformed into the wolf form she used for combat without even breaking stride, magic rolling down her body like a hot wind.

When she burst into a small clearing, Diana found the killer waiting.

Her first impression was of deceptive fragility—a pale, oval face, big green eyes, and a shimmering tumble of red hair. The killer wore a tight black skirt and a cutoff T-shirt that exposed a neat silver belly button ring. She was splattered from head to toe with drying blood, and the scent of the man's death hung around her like a particularly nauseating perfume. She grinned at Diana as if the wolf was somebody's goofy pet. "Why, hello there, White Fang. What's got your—"

Diana didn't even break step as she leaped right for the killer's throat. The woman dodged with a startled, "Whoa!"

Diana sailed by and hit the ground, instantly wheeling in a flurry of leaves to lunge at her enemy again. This time her fangs scored the woman's wrist. She growled in pleasure as the taste of blood flooded her mouth, but before she could get a good grip, something slammed hard into the side of her head. The blow tumbled her a dozen feet across the slick leaves before she managed to get her paws under her again.

For an instant she and the killer eyed one another in

simmering rage. "You're fast, furball, I'll give you that," her opponent spat. "What the fuck are you?"

She just concentrated and let the magic spill. The woman's eyes widened as Diana grew, falling back on her haunches, stretching upward and upward until she towered on two long legs.

Diana rarely became the Dire Wolf. In fact, she'd never before used the guise in combat. The seven-foot biped monster was the tactical nuke of her arsenal; too deadly, too blatantly magical to use except in the worst emergencies.

Which this was.

With a sense of pleasure, she watched the killer back up a pace.

Unlike her other canine forms, the Dire Wolf was capable of human speech. "Verdaville is my fief," Diana said, pacing toward the woman with hackles raised and a deep growl vibrating in her throat. "Its residents are under my protection. You don't come into my territory and kill my people." She displayed every tooth in her long wolf muzzle. "Not and live."

The killer bared fangs almost as long and sharp as Diana's. Whatever she was, it definitely wasn't human. "Wrong." As she lifted her hands, a glowing nimbus appeared around them, crackling with tiny lightning bolts. "I go where I want. I kill who I want. And that includes you."

The magical blast detonated in Diana's face with a roar, its heat and light blasting her back on her haunches. It stung, but Diana's people were designed for magical combat. She shook it off like a wolf shedding water. "Nice shot." Her muscles bunched under her as she prepared to fling herself at her foe. "But can you take as much as you dish out?"

An expression of fear flashed over the witch's face as

she realized Diana was magic resistant. Then her eyes narrowed with calculation. "Oh, yeah. But you know, just now I'm not in the mood. Later."

Sensing the build of magical energies, Diana leaped.

Too late. Even as she opened her jaws to rip out the witch's throat, the killer disappeared in a swirl of energy.

Unable to stop, Diana crashed into the tree just beyond. Pain exploded through her head in a shower of stars, and she hit the ground hard.

Luckily she could take a lot of punishment in Dire Wolf form. Growling savagely, Diana rolled to her feet and glowered at the spot where her foe had stood. "Now *that* is a bitch."

"Luna!" The chief called the name of his mythical K-9 as he crashed through the woods toward her. It was a good thing the witch was already gone, or he'd have handed her a hostage.

Diana cursed and muttered. "Yeah, yeah, I'm coming, dammit." Transforming herself back into the shepherd, she trotted toward Gist, dragging the leash that had reappeared with her shift.

"You okay?" he murmured as she reached him, dropping to one knee to examine her anxiously.

Diana woofed softly even as she turned to look back at the clearing. She wished she could tell the chief this was over, but she knew better.

In fact, she had the ugly feeling her new enemy was only getting warmed up.

Llyr walked into the Great Hall of Avalon flanked by his six most trusted bodyguards, including the twins Egan and Bevyn Cynyr, and Iden Naois, an intense young man he'd elevated to guard captain.

Llyr and Oriana had placed truth spells on all two hundred of the remaining palace guards and questioned them ruthlessly. They'd all passed the test, but the Cynyr brothers and Naois were the most fanatically loyal, as well as the most skilled. He decided to make the three his primary security team.

Even so, the guards were even more grimly paranoid than usual. Their beloved captain and three comrades had attempted regicide, and they hadn't seen it coming. Now they all eyed one another and kept one hand on their swords.

Not exactly the spirit of trust and teamwork Llyr wanted in his men.

To make matters worse, the news had spread through the palace. He'd expected as much; there was simply no way to keep something like that quiet. Unfortunately, the end result was a mood of fear among the Cachamwri Sidhe, in part because Llyr was well-liked, but also because none of them wanted to be ruled by his brother. It was known the Morven Sidhe suffered under Ansgar's heavy hand, and the Cachamwri hated him.

Llyr had decided the best way to reassure his people was to go about business as he usually did, while cementing his alliance with the Magekind. He'd need it if things heated up even more with Ansgar. That meant helping the Liege of the Magi with his current problem. Tricky, but still a better solution than the arranged marriage Llyr had sought. Arthur would have supported Llyr if he'd made a Maja his queen, but this deal was much more certain.

Unfortunately, it also meant hunting vampires.

Before Reece and Erin managed to slay Geirolf, the demon had gathered around himself thousands of mortal followers who had provided him with human sacrifices. Deciding he might need a more physically formidable force, Geirolf had used a magical rite to transform them into vampires. Unlike the heroic Magi, however, Geirolf's vampires were tainted with his evil—killers with a taste for sadism and murder.

When Geirolf died, Steven Parker, one of his priests, had used the energy of the demon's death to scatter his vampire army all over Mortal Earth. Now the Magekind had to find them all before they did any more damage.

Arthur looked up when Llyr entered with his men at his back, a smile of welcome on his deceptively boyish face. He wore trousers in some coarse, dark blue fabric and a short cotton tunic with the legend GRATEFUL DEAD. Llyr puzzled over it as he crossed the room, wondering what the dead would have to be grateful about.

Otherwise, Arthur looked little different than he had when he'd been High King of Britain all those centuries ago: stocky and muscular, with warm brown eyes and a thick brown beard. He hadn't been king in hundreds of years, but his people had elected him Liege of the Magi's Council, so he still had an active role in leading them.

Llyr was skeptical of democracy. It seemed to him a form of government designed by those with a short attention span. Still, he had to admit there was a certain attraction in the idea of actually being chosen to lead by one's followers.

Not that he'd dare propose such a concept to the Sidhe. His people disliked change on general principles, believing if something was working, there was no reason whatsoever to tinker with it. It was a philosophy Llyr had certainly benefitted from. His family had ruled since the first Galatyn helped the Dragon God slay Uchdryd the Dark One.

"Welcome, Your Highness," Arthur said, striding toward Llyr. Llyr's bodyguards simultaneously dropped their hands to their swords. He stopped, a dark brow lifted.

"A recent assassination attempt," Llyr explained, adding

to his men, "At ease." They obeyed, though Naois aimed a dark, warning look at the surrounding Magekind.

Arthur nodded in understanding. "Ansgar?"

"To my knowledge, no one else wants me dead."

"That may change, if you insist on helping us with our vampire problem," Reece Champion said from where he sat with his new wife. He was a big man, as dark and intense as Erin was beautiful and blond. If he held a grudge over Llyr's attempt to woo her before their marriage, it didn't show.

Llyr gave him a tight smile. "It's worth the risk, if you help me deal with Ansgar afterward."

"That is the arrangement," Arthur said.

"It's also a lot easier said than done." Morgana Le Fey straightened from the thick tome sitting on the table. She was lovely enough to be a Sidhe herself, with waist-length dark hair and a face as cool and elegant as a goddess's. Unlike her half-brother, she wore a white linen suit, its short skirt showcasing a pair of legs Llyr thoroughly appreciated. "Apparently, Geirolf's little henchman, Parker, did far more than just scatter his brood of vampires all over the planet. He also managed to shield them from magical detection. I have no idea how we're going to find them."

"Look for the bodies," Champion said. "That bunch will leave a trail."

Erin Champion nodded. "Which means you should be able to Google 'em."

Llyr frowned. Human slang changed so quickly it was impossible to keep track of it. "Google?"

"She means you can use the Internet to search online newspapers for unusual murders," Champion explained.

Llyr glanced at Arthur. "Did you understand any of that?"

"They're talking about computers." The immortal

grinned and slapped him on the shoulder. "You've really got to start keeping up with the times, Llyr. Try watching MTV once in a while."

Ignoring the dig, Llyr lifted a brow at him. "So do you have one of these 'computers'?"

"They don't need one," said the massive book at Reece's elbow, flipping itself open. "They have me. And I can access newspapers that are not even online."

Interested, Llyr walked over to the table as the others crowded closer. The enchanted tome known as Merlin's Grimoire was the alien's ultimate bequest to his followers. Sentient as it was, there weren't many questions the great book couldn't answer.

Llyr watched over Erin's shoulder as she began to flip the pages, each of which seemed to have turned into a newspaper front page. Their mastheads read the *New York Times,* the *Atlanta Constitution,* the *San Francisco Chronicle.* And others, too, towns he'd never heard of.

Each had similar headlines: TWO MEN VICTIMS OF BIZARRE MURDER, BODY FOUND DRAINED IN FIELD, POLICE: WOMAN SACRIFICED IN BLACK MAGIC RITE.

"Are all these our escaped vampires?" Arthur asked, leaning closer to read over Erin's shoulder.

"I can't say for certain," the Grimoire said. "But all of them share characteristics that suggest vampire killings or occult elements."

"Makes sense," Champion said. "Geirolf's cultists were committing bizarre murders to power his magic even before he turned them into vampires. Now that they've got powers of their own, it's not surprising that they'd still be killing people."

"Plus, Geirolf starved his troops," Erin added. "One reason they were so eager to fight is because they were hungry."

"Add all that up, and you've got an excellent motive for some spectacularly nasty murders," Arthur said. "This is going to get ugly."

"It was already ugly," Llyr told him grimly, watching as Erin flipped another page over. His eyes widened as he recognized a familiar face staring out at him. "Wait. That one. I know that woman."

The grainy color photograph, obviously taken at night, showed a man in a police uniform standing beside a woman in front of a big vehicle. Her eyes shown in the light of the flash with an eerie luminescence that didn't look quite human.

It was the woman from his dream.

"The *Verdaville Voice*," Llyr read. "What's that?"

"A weekly newspaper in Verdaville, a small town in the state of South Carolina," the Grimoire announced.

"The caption says she's Diana London, city administrator," Erin said, then looked up at Llyr. "How did you meet a city administrator from some podunk South Carolina town?"

"I haven't. Yet. I had a dream about her," Llyr said.

Erin groaned. "God, not another dream." Both Janieda and various Majae had experienced prophetic dreams about the confrontation with Geirolf.

"Don't underestimate the power of dreams, Erin," Llyr said, staring intently at the photograph.

"In this job?" She snorted. "Not a chance."

"Do you want to check this one out, then?" Arthur asked.

"Check it out?"

"Investigate it. Find out if it's one of Geirolf's vampires doing this killing, or just a random human lunatic."

Llyr looked down at the paper. "Oh, yes. I definitely want to see more."

The next day

Diana's nervous system seemed to be buzzing like a cicada as she fought to concentrate on the report the head of the sewer department was giving her. Last night her mind had insisted on conjuring all kinds of dark, bloody dreams. Which was probably no surprise given the circumstances.

What was a surprise was the number of times the blond sex god also put in an appearance, delicious and flexing. And there'd been a dragon, too. She had no idea where the hell that had come from.

"We're going to have to get the sludge pumped out of the treatment pond, or DHEC's going to eat our lunch," Randy Johnson warned her, breaking into her preoccupation.

Diana grimaced. The state's Department of Health and Environmental Control was notoriously hard-nosed when it came to small-town water treatment plants. DHEC was fully capable of fining Verdaville thousands of dollars if it decided the town had violated water quality standards. Money they didn't have, which would mean raising taxes. Which, in turn, would bring outraged voters down on the city's hapless head. "How much is it going to cost to pump out the sludge?"

As Johnson quoted a figure at her, the office door opened and Gist slipped in. Most department heads knew better than to arrive late for the weekly staff meeting, but Diana cut Gist some slack because he was usually out answering calls.

"Sounds like we're going to have to dip into the emergency fund for that one," she told the sewer department head, eyeing Gist as he dropped into a chair. "I'll call a special meeting of the council, get 'em to okay it."

Diana paused, frowning. The chief's smile was downright dreamy. Something about it made the hair rise on the back of her neck. "Judging from the happy face, you must have had a break in last night's murder. What's going on, Chief?"

"It's off our plate," Gist said. "FBI's taking over."

She sat up in her chair. "What? Since when does the FBI get involved in a run-of-the-mill homicide?" Actually, this case was far from run-of-the-mill, but the Feds had no way of knowing that.

Gist shrugged. "All I know is, a special agent showed up this morning and took right over."

Diana shot a look at the other department heads, who were following the conversation with interest. "I think I've taken up enough of your time, gentlemen. Why don't you go tend the city's business?"

She waited until they'd filed out of the room before she spoke. Something about this just didn't feel right. "Did you ask the FBI to step in, Chief?"

Gist blinked at her. "Who, me? Hell, no. You know how I feel about the Feebees."

Yes, she did, which was why she was wondering about his loopy smile. "Somebody had to. Murder's a state offense. The Feds have no jurisdiction. Do they think this is a serial killer?"

The chief shrugged.

Diana frowned at him. "So you're all right with having a bunch of suits come in and pull this case right out from under you?"

"Well, they are better equipped to handle this kind of thing."

She stared. "You're under some kind of spell."

He blinked at her. "What? What are you talking about?"

Diana got up and walked around her desk to crouch in front of him. His eyes looked faintly out of focus. Her temper began to steam. "Where's this FBI agent now, Chief?"

"He's down in my office."

She rose and started for the door.

"Where are you going?"

Diana looked back over her shoulder at her normally razor-sharp friend. He looked confused. "Don't worry about it, Bill. I'm just going to go kick some ass."

He nodded vaguely. "Okay."

She turned and stalked through the door, resisting the urge to slam it. "And I'm going to kick really, really hard."

Diana strode down the short carpeted hallway, nodding absently to the city clerks who waved at her as she passed. She was too busy worrying about what waited for her down in Gist's office.

It couldn't be the killer. Surely the bitch wouldn't be bold enough to just waltz in and put the Verdaville Police Chief under a spell with Diana right there in the building.

Unless she didn't realize the seven-foot werewolf she'd fought the night before was actually a five-foot-eleven city manager. Which, now that Diana thought about it, sounded a lot more likely than she'd first assumed.

Her stomach coiling into knots, she hit the stairs, heading for the police department, which took up City Hall's basement.

Shoving the door open, she stormed down the hallway, her heels clicking angrily on worn vinyl tiles that had peeled away in spots, revealing the cement floor underneath. She barely noticed the crackle of the police scanner or the murmur of the clerk's voice as she talked to an officer over the radio. Diana's narrowed gaze was focused on the chief's door at the end of the hall, opposite the locker room.

She didn't bother to knock.

Three business-suited men she didn't know whirled as she barged in. Each, oddly enough, reached for his hip rather than the shoulder holsters visible under their jackets. The closest one aborted the gesture and grabbed for her instead. Diana jerked away, her lips pulling back from her teeth. "Back off!"

But before the man could touch her—or she could lunge for his throat—a deep male voice said, "Stand down!"

The barked command drew Diana's gaze to the man sitting behind the chief's desk, crime scene photos spread out in front of him across a litter of reports.

For a moment, she felt heat flood her cheeks at the thought that these men really were FBI. Then she realized every one of them had hair halfway to his butt, in colors not found in humans. And she'd be willing to bet those exotic shades didn't come from a bottle.

"Hello, Diana," the blond said, in a voice as deep and smoky as Kentucky bourbon.

Diana frowned. "Do I know . . . ?" She broke off, realizing she did indeed recognize her unwelcome visitor.

Except the last time she'd seen him, he'd been naked and prowling through her dreams like an erotic ghost. She hadn't noticed the pointed ears last night. Or the smell of magic that clung to everybody in the room like a very expensive cologne.

This couldn't be good.

"What in God's name are you?" Diana demanded, instinctively tensing for combat.

The blond man leaned back in Gist's chair, a very male smile curling his handsome mouth. "Actually, I'm the King of the Fairies."

FOUR

The King of the Fairies.

Diana would have been less shocked if he'd punched her. She'd grown up hearing her grandfather's stories of Merlin, Arthur, and the Sidhe. "You're King Dearg's son." Remembering one tale in particular, she took a wary step back. "Llyr or Ansgar?"

One of the other three men—he had hair the color of spring grass—squared his impressive shoulders and announced, "You are in the presence of King Llyr Aleyn Galatyn."

Oh, the *good* one.

She'd almost banged Llyr Galatyn. At least in her dreams. Granddad would be tickled—if she ever told him, which she wouldn't.

"These men are my personal bodyguards," Llyr told her,

rising from his chair. Something about the way he moved made Diana's libido purr. He dropped a hand on the shoulder of the green-haired man. "Bevyn Cynyr." An elegant gesture pointed out a second breathtakingly handsome man, this one with shimmering blue hair. "His brother, Egan," Another sweep of a royal hand indicated the one who'd almost jumped her when she walked in. "And Iden Naois." Naois was big and broad, his dark, hip-length hair shimmering with iridescent highlights that might have looked effeminate, had his face not been so thoroughly masculine. He watched her with a feral intensity that made her hackles rise.

Staring right back at him, Diana readied herself to transform, though she knew she was seriously screwed if they attacked her. Powerful as she was, she wasn't up to taking on four Sidhe warriors. Not if Granddad's stories had any truth to them at all.

"I'm Diana London." She edged away from the dark one. He didn't move. His eyes were so black, they seemed to have no pupils at all. Diana gave him a hard, warning glare before turning to the Sidhe king. "I'm the Verdaville city administrator. Which brings me back to my original point—where the hell do you get off, putting a spell on my police chief?"

Llyr lifted his chin, surprise flickering in his gaze. After a pause, he tapped one of the photos arrayed on the desk in front of him. "I thought it best. Your police may not be equipped to handle this murder. There's a good chance the killer is not human."

Diana snorted. "Yeah, I picked up on that last night when she almost fried me with an energy blast."

Every Sidhe in the room came to alert. "You fought her?" The king's eyes searched her face. They glittered with tiny flecks of light, like opals.

"She was waiting for me in the woods, about a quarter of a mile from the crime scene," Diana told him, trying to ignore her body's response to his. "What is she, anyway? She casts spells, but she's way too strong to be a Maja. She one of yours?"

"A Sidhe? Dragon's Breath, no. She a vampire."

Diana frowned. "There are no female vampires. Magi are always male."

"Merlin's Gift had nothing to do with this one. She's the product of a death spell. A demon named Geirolf . . ."

"Geirolf? Isn't he the one who killed your father?" She braced her fists on her hips and studied the Sidhe king. Damn, but he was beautiful.

"The same. Merlin locked him in a cell in the Mageverse sixteen hundred years ago, after the Great War." Diana listened with interest as Llyr described Geirolf's escape and the battle to defeat him. "Unfortunately, Stephen Parker, Geirolf's lackey, used the demon's death to power a spell that scattered his vampire army all over Mortal Earth."

"Wait—vampire army? That doesn't sound good."

"It's not. When Geirolf escaped his cell, he founded a network of death cults . . ."

"The cults are connected to that creep? Figures." When Llyr lifted a brow at her, she shrugged. "I watch CNN like everybody else."

For months now, the news had been dominated by the crimes of a network of death cults that were allegedly responsible for murders all across the country. Part of the media's fascination was born of the fact that the cults seemed to have nothing in common. Some were ecoterrorists, others were blatantly Satanic, and still others were violently racist. Their weapons ran the gamut from strychnine in cold medications to human sacrifice. They'd driven the public into a panic, and the media was having a field day speculating on why so many lunatic groups had cropped up at one time. In retrospect, it made sense they'd all be related.

If one of those cultists had come to Verdaville, the situation was even worse than she'd thought.

And it was, she realized, as Llyr described the way Geirolf had fed off the deaths of the cult's victims. "Then he decided to eliminate both the Magekind and the Sidhe," the king continued. "He designed a death spell he meant to power by sacrificing Grayson and Champion. If it had worked, it would have instantly killed every witch and vampire on either Earth."

She lifted her brows. "Must have been a hell of a spell."

"It was, but it wouldn't have worked on my people. For that, he needed a magical army. So he transformed his cultists into vampires, planning to turn them loose on the Sidhe."

"But then his Magekind sacrifices sprung their booby trap and killed him," Diana guessed, piecing it all together. "And Parker used the energy of the demon's death to scatter all those vampires all over the planet."

"Where they've been murdering people ever since. The Magekind are attempting to track down and destroy them. I volunteered to help." He spread his hands and sat down again. "So my men and I will track down your killer, eliminate her, and be on our way."

Diana looked at him as he sprawled in masculine elegance in Gist's chair. She was tempted to dump the whole thing in his lap and let him handle it. After all, Llyr could work magic. She might be a shape-shifter, but the kind of power blasts Vampire Bitch had thrown around last night were beyond her.

Besides, this was the Burning Moon. Diana didn't trust herself to keep a choke chain on her libido with the King of the Sidhe flexing under her nose. All she needed was to lose control, rip the enchanted Armani off his luscious body, and bang his fairy brains out in front of God and the

Verdaville City Council. And every time she inhaled the scent of magical masculinity, she was seriously tempted.

A smart city manager would leave the whole mess to Llyr and go off to fight with DHEC over the sewage treatment pond. Only . . .

Diana sighed. "Like I told Fang Face last night, this is my fief. Its people are my people. She killed one of my people, she's mine." She met Llyr's glowing opalescent gaze. "But I wouldn't turn down help."

Something in Diana's direct stare made blood pool in Llyr's groin, much to his irritation. He'd like to help her, all right. He'd like to help her with the sexual hunger that rolled off her in hot waves.

Llyr felt a stab of shame. Janieda had given her life for him. He owed her more than to go up in flames for a stranger when she was barely cold in her grave.

Yet Diana fascinated him. Every breath he took in her presence carried the scent of wild passion, and there was a lithe strength in the way she moved that he found darkly arousing. Even the bold challenge in her gaze called to him. He wanted to test himself against her, wanted to bend her over, strip down those mannish slacks, and investigate her sweet cream heat.

Oh, yes, he wanted to ride her, badly. Despite his dream-inspired conviction that they were destined for each other, that was all he wanted.

Dream or not, it was all too obvious Diana wasn't the queen he'd been seeking. She was too feral, too sensual. The animal lay too close to the surface in her; his people would never accept her.

What was worse, she was mortal. He'd buried too many queens as it was.

So despite his dreams, there could be nothing between them but sex. Any woman he wed would be queen of the Cachamwri Sidhe, and had better be worthy of the honor. Though Diana's obvious dedication to the people of Verdaville was a point in her favor, it wasn't enough.

And yet every breath he took of her scent made his need rise.

As he stared hungrily into her face, Diana lifted a brow. Belatedly he remembered she'd implied a question: would he work with her to catch the killer? He cleared his throat. "You know your fiefdom better than I. We'd do well to work together, rather than at cross purposes."

"I couldn't agree more." She extended a long, slender hand. Lust hit him like a fist, and he drew in a breath, staring down at those slim fingers. "Partners, then?" she asked, her voice a honey rasp that seemed to stroke over his skin.

"Partners," he agreed hoarsely, and somehow managed a handshake instead of dragging her into his arms. Her skin felt like velvet against his palm, sending another bolt of lust through him. "Please, be seated."

Nodding briskly, she dropped her hand and moved to a chair. When she sat down and crossed her long legs, every man in the room caught his breath.

Llyr glanced around at his bodyguards and realized he wasn't the only one who ached to touch her. He wasn't at all sure she wouldn't let them, either.

And he'd just agreed to work with her.

"May I suggest that if you're going to continue posing as FBI agents . . ." Diana's silky brows drew into a frown. "Does everybody see the hair?"

He blinked. "I beg your pardon?"

"You boys have more hair than an eighties rock band. It doesn't exactly fit your cover."

Mortal slang could be so irritatingly obscure. "I'm afraid I'm not familiar with your terminology."

"FBI agents wear their hair cut short, Your Majesty."

"We're surrounded by a glamor. Your people will see what they expect to see."

"Handy talent to have." She drummed her nails on the arm of her chair, frowning. "If you're going to pose as FBI, I would advise you to check into the motel in town. It would attract less attention than popping in and out."

Llyr gathered she was talking about an inn of some kind. He considered the idea before nodding slowly. He didn't want the vampire to know he was in pursuit. "You have a point."

"Good. I'll take you over. I assume you don't have a car?" She lifted a brow.

"If we need one, I'll create one."

"Wish I could do that." Diana glanced at her watch. "Look, I've got some duties to attend to before I start squiring y'all around. I'll meet you back here in an hour, if that's acceptable?"

He nodded. "Whatever is convenient."

"That would be." She rose from her chair. "See you then."

Llyr watched the feminine sway of her hips as she walked out the door, closing it carefully behind her. He listened to the click of her heels down the hall, the easy murmur of her voice as she spoke to one of her employees. In the distance, another door closed.

"Mmm," Naois said. "I'd love to put a leash on that."

As Llyr stiffened slightly, the brothers laughed. "Aye, she's a hot one," Bevyn agreed, tossing back his green hair with a shake.

Egan smirked. "A true bitch in heat. And I, for one, wouldn't object to giving her exactly what she needs."

"She's also our host," Llyr growled. "And I expect her to be treated with respect."

His guards looked at him with dismayed surprise. He glared back. They'd been with him so many years, they sometimes forgot themselves. "We intended no disrespect, Your Majesty," Naois said. "Our apologies."

The brothers chorused an agreement. "It will not happen again," Egan added.

"I am relieved to hear it," Llyr said coolly. "I would be most displeased. Please take your posts."

Chastised, the three stiffened and hurried into position, one stepping outside the door, another just inside, the third at his back. Simultaneously, they drew themselves to attention with an audible click of the heels, backs rod straight, chins up, stomachs in. Normally, he'd tell them to assume a more comfortable pose, but this time Llyr left them like that as he turned his attention to the file on the murder.

Inwardly, he was a bit surprised at his own incandescent reaction. His men had not said anything he hadn't been thinking himself. But that was irrelevant, he told himself. Diana was their hostess. Treating her with such blatant disrespect was rude.

And that was his only concern.

Adsulata Cynyr snapped her head up over the scrying bowl she used for visions. Its surface danced, the water showing the image of her husband, Egan, as he fell into attention outside the office where the king sat.

"Bastard," she growled, rising from the bed to pace the room in long, angry strides. She wasn't at all surprised to find Egan sniffing after the werewolf. He screwed every other female he came in contact with—why not an animal woman? It was just the kind of thing he'd do.

Goddess, but she hated him.

Adsulata had been spying on Egan since she'd discovered his whoring a year before. It had been a simple matter to enchant the Bond Bracelet he wore as a mark of their marriage so she could use it to spy on him through her scrying bowl. It was the only method that would have worked, since Llyr traveled with powerful magical shields as a protection against his brother's assassins.

But he'd not reckoned with the deep, subtle magic that bound a husband and wife.

Neither had Egan.

Of course, if either the king or Egan had discovered her trick, she would have been imprisoned for it. But Adsulata didn't care. She'd been betrayed by her faithless husband. She deserved her revenge. And she knew just how to get it.

Her violet eyes narrowed as she lifted her hands in an intricate gesture. In the air before her, a tiny point began to glow with Mageverse energies. She poured power into the point, and it swelled, opening a hole in the air. Beyond it, trees shimmered under the moon of the Mageverse.

With a thought, Adsulata clothed herself in a glittering gown that bared more of her lush body than it hid. A single stroke of her hand drew her violet hair into soft, sleek waves.

Then, content with her beauty, she stepped through the gate to meet the one she loved. Her nipples tingled and hardened, her arousal heightened by the knowledge that she'd found the one lover who would enrage her husband most.

As the gate vanished, King Ansgar Galatyn smiled slowly, and her heart beat faster at the hint of cruelty in the curve of his lips. "Well met, my darling."

When Diana returned to the chief's office an hour later, she found the blue-haired guard standing at attention outside the door. He stepped forward with a snap and opened it for her.

Lifting a brow, she walked in and he shut it behind her. Naois stood inside just to the left of the door, chest out, back straight, heels together. Which didn't prevent him from watching her like a hawk.

"Hello again, Your Majesty," she said to Llyr, pausing to look up into the dark guard's inhumanly beautiful face. "Before we leave, I think there's a couple of things I'll need to make clear."

The king glanced up from the thick tome he was reading. With a gesture, he made it disappear as he leaned back in his chair. "Go on."

Diana inhaled, drinking in the scent of magic and masculinity as she looked up at Naois. Rising onto her toes, she leaned toward the guard and angled her head, not quite touching him as she gave him a slow, seductive smile. His black eyes widened. Testing, she rested a hand on his chest, feeling the warmth and muscle beneath the linen of his suit. He tensed, then relaxed slightly as she did nothing more. She paused another moment, letting him breathe her magical scent. His heart began to pound under her hand. She licked her lips. Heat blazed up in his eyes. Around the room, the other men shifted restlessly.

"First," Diana said softly, "I think you should know that any man who tried to put a leash on me would regret it." Her nails extended, growing into curving, two-inch claws. "Deeply." She dropped her hand. "And second, the Dire-kind have better hearing than the Sidhe."

Point made, she turned away from the astonished guard to meet Llyr's chagrined gaze. "Now that we've got that settled, I'll take you to your motel."

The king hesitated a moment, obviously taken aback. "I apologize if my men's comments offended you."

Diana gave him a smile that felt more than a little stiff. She'd been steaming for the past hour. *Leash, my ass.* "Think nothing of it. Shall we go?"

When she turned to lead them from the room, she was satisfied to note wary respect in Naois's dark eyes.

Diana led her handsome Sidhe parade out of the building and into the parking lot to Gist's big, black SUV. "We wouldn't fit in my car, so I borrowed the chief's," she explained, keying the lock open with her fob and reaching for the driver's door.

The four men watched as she opened it. Egan awkwardly copied the motion with the back door and stood back as Bevyn and Llyr slid inside.

"How long has it been since any of you rode in a car?" Diana asked as she and Naois got in.

"Never." When she looked in the rearview mirror at him, he shrugged. "I haven't been to Earth in a century or so." He examined the upholstery. "Though this is much more comfortable than the last coach I was in."

"Glad you approve." Deciding she didn't even want to attempt to explain seatbelts—the Sidhe were immortal anyway—she started the truck and pulled out. The motel was located out on the interstate, so they had a ten-minute drive ahead of them.

"Tell me about your encounter with the vampire," Llyr said as they started off.

Diana complied, trying not to inhale as she spoke. There was far too much delicious masculinity sitting much too close, but she was determined to ignore her rumbling sexual hunger. After the bitch in heat crack, she had no intention of handing her arrogant Sidhe visitors any more ammunition.

It was really too bad. If they weren't such jerks, the

Sidhe would be the answer to Diana's Burning Moon prayers. She wouldn't have to worry about infecting one of them if she got carried away during sex and bit her partner.

That much of the myth was true: Merlin's Curse spread through Direkind saliva, something like rabies. The Fey wizard had designed it that way, at least according to Granddad. The idea was that if the Magekind ever went evil, the Direkind could create an army in the space of a few days just by biting their new recruits. And since the Direkind was practically immune to magic, they could take anything their rivals could dish out.

The problem was, Merlin's Curse was even more contagious during the Burning Moon. A werewolf female had to be damn careful who she slept with at that time of year. One-night stands were out of the question, since it was too easy to infect a casual lover. Werewolf males, at least, only got really contagious when they had a strong emotional attachment with their partner, so one-night stands were all they did.

Luckily the Sidhe were magical creatures, immune to the bite. She couldn't infect one of them if she tried.

Diana flicked her gaze to the mirror to catch a glimpse of Llyr's face. Something in her tightened and purred. Seducing him would shut her libido up for a while, making it easier to concentrate on the problem of the vampire.

Trouble was, it would also confirm the Sidhe's "bitch in heat" theory. She really didn't want to give them the satisfaction.

Diana frowned, drumming her nails on the steering wheel as she stopped at a light. Glancing toward the passenger side, she noticed Naois was staring at her hand. She looked down and realized her nails had grown into claws again. She stopped drumming and curled her fist around the wheel.

This was ridiculous.

By the time they pulled into the motel parking lot, her

body was buzzing like a cricket. But as she reached for the truck door to get out, a thought pierced the fog of lust. "Wait a minute—how are you going to pay for the motel?"

Llyr shrugged, watching Egan try to figure out the door latch. "With gold, of course."

"That's what I was afraid of. Your Majesty, you can't do that."

"It's perfectly good gold," he said, offended.

Diana grappled for patience. "Gold is not legal tender in the United States. The motel clerk would have no way to convert it. Besides, he's going to expect an FBI agent to use a credit card."

"What is this?"

She grabbed her bag from the passenger side floorboard, her libido growling like a Doberman when she reached past Naois's legs to do it. Digging out a credit card, she handed it back to the king.

Llyr glanced down at it. Light flared between his fingers, and there were two cards in his hand. "Now we have a credit card."

"Neat trick. May I see that?"

The king handed it to her. The brush of his fingers touching hers sent a bolt of heat through her she tried to ignore as she looked down at the card. "This is my card, Your Majesty. It's got my name and bank number on it."

Even his frown was gorgeous. "And this signifies?"

"That the rooms would be charged to me. And I'd have to pay for them. The card means I have an account and a line of credit with this bank, which I pay on every month. It's a loan."

Llyr gestured. Light flashed between her fingers. She looked down, and wasn't remotely surprised to see the name now read Llyr A. Galatyn. Diana sighed. "Did you magic an account with this bank?"

He shrugged. "No, because I do not know how the system works."

"Give the mortal a bag of gold," Naois growled, impatient. "And bespell him into accepting it."

"Yeah, and then when he tries to deposit it, real FBI agents are going to show up asking real questions I really can't afford to answer." Patience was definitely not her long suit at this time of year. "Which would also apply if you tried to create cash. You'd get the serial numbers wrong, and then I'd end up charged as an accessory to counterfeiting."

"This is wasting time," Llyr said. "We will simply gate from the palace when we need to."

"Look," Diana snapped, "I don't want you beaming in and out in front of people like Captain Kirk. It'll cause talk."

"If I don't want them to talk," Llyr said coolly, "they won't talk."

She threw up her hands. "I'll pay for the damned hotel room, okay?" Swinging the door open, she got out and slammed it with more force than was strictly necessary.

"As you wish." Her lupine hearing picked up Llyr's reply as his men figured out how to open the door latches. "I'll give the gold to you."

"Fine," Diana muttered. "It'll make a great paperweight."

Twenty minutes later, she was trying to show the Sidhe how to use a key card to open one of the rooms.

The second time Bevyn flubbed the sequence of *insert card-wait for green light-turn handle,* Llyr gestured. Magic flared. The door swung open, and his men trooped in to check for assassins. "You make everything more complicated than it needs to be," the king told her.

Diana showed her teeth. "Bite me."

She thought he muttered, "I am tempted."

FIVE

The little werewolf was abrupt and arrogant, verging on rude. Llyr had never been treated with so little deference in his very long life. She obviously had no understanding of his power and authority, and not the faintest concept of how to deal with royalty.

He had no idea why he found her so appealing.

Leaning against the bathroom door, he watched her try to demonstrate the workings of the plumbing to his guard. He didn't bother telling her how inadequate these quarters were for a king and his retinue.

"Would you object," Llyr asked finally, "if we gated from inside this room? There's no reason for us to actually stay here."

"No, of course not." She smiled slightly, looking around at the two beds with their ugly blue coverings and the furniture that was made of pressed sawdust rather than solid board. "This isn't exactly a palace, is it?"

"Would you like to see a palace, Diana?" The offer was pure impulse, but he found himself hoping she would accept. "You are welcome to take the noon meal with us. We could discuss strategy."

She turned to look at him. A shaft of sunlight through the window sparked a flash of silver in the depths of her lovely eyes. "I'd like that."

It was her turn to hesitate when he opened the Mageverse gate. Llyr listened to her gasp at the magic that rushed over her skin as she followed him through the glowing opening. When he turned to look at her as she saw the palace towering around them for the first time, her expression of awe made his chest warm.

He couldn't resist taking her on a tour.

It was odd. Llyr had lived in the palace for all seventeen hundred years of his life, but it was as if he'd never seen it until he saw Diana's eyes light up.

White marble gleamed underfoot, checkered with jeweled tiles. He looked up with pride at the soaring columns that supported the marble ceiling with gold buttresses. Intricate tapestries shimmered on the wall, woven with the protective wards that guarded the palace. Vases of enchanted flowers filled inset niches, and the furniture was as intricate and glimmered with Sidhe workmanship.

Llyr found himself folding Diana's long, soft hand into the curve of his arm as he led her around the palace. Her eyes rounded as Sidhe in silk, velvet, and jewels paused to bow to him in greeting. As he spoke to them, he breathed in her scent—human, yet not, tinged with something feral and sweet. It was fortunate he wasn't wearing his usual doublet and hose, for lust hardened his sex behind the fly of his mortal-style breeches. He remembered his dream the night before, recalled the way she'd stroked over him like a cat. Shuddering, he hardened still more.

Even as need clawed at him, he knew he should ignore it. He had a killer to catch, not to mention a whole list of responsibilities to his people and his line. Poor Janieda was scarcely in her grave. And she was only the latest in the list of women who'd died in his war with Ansgar.

Despite his dream, Diana was not his destined queen. She couldn't be.

He glanced down. She'd turned her face away from his, apparently studying one of the tapestries they passed. Hot red painted the elegant curve of her cheek.

She was blushing.

Llyr took an involuntary breath, and her scent told him why. She'd gone wet. It was as though just the touch of his arm, the brush of his body had aroused her with the intensity another woman might feel after an hour of serious foreplay.

He remembered her voice in the dream: *"I burn . . ."*

And now so did he.

Diana tried to concentrate on the lovely face of the Dowager Queen as Llyr introduced them. Oriana Galatyn did not look like any grandmother she'd ever seen, and those iridescent eyes were sharp as they flicked from her face to Llyr's.

Diana didn't think she was imagining the disapproval in the Dowager's gaze. *Another Sidhe in the bitch-in-heat camp,* she thought, and was relieved when Llyr led her off on the rest of the tour.

The trouble was, she was beginning to feel that condemnation wasn't all that far off the mark.

At any other time, Diana would have been fascinated by the intricate frescoes and paintings, the parade of exquisitely beautiful people who stopped and nodded and spoke, worshipping Llyr with their eyes.

But with the Burning Moon breathing fire across her skin, all she could feel was heat. She kept remembering the way he'd looked in the dream, his golden hair spilling across his pillows, his opalescent eyes sultry with need.

With her hand tucked into the curve of his arm like this, it was too easy to feel the apple-firm muscle of his biceps shifting beneath his fine linen jacket. The warmth of his body radiated right up through the fabric. Every time he took a step, his hip brushed hers.

Diana ached to peel that jacket off him and claw away the shirt until she could touch bare flesh. Her head was so full of his scent, she could almost taste him on her tongue.

I'm not an animal, dammit. Despite the times she felt like one.

Diana was so busy struggling with her hungers she didn't even notice when he led her into one of the rooms until the *click* of the closing door brought her out of her stupor.

Glancing around, she saw they stood in a bedroom filled with furniture so elegant and delicate, it would have made Versailles look vulgar. An enormous bed hung with red silk took up one side of the room, while a beautiful bathing pool occupied the other. A tapestry depicting a magnificent blue dragon swirled across one wall, shimmering with magic that illuminated the entire room.

Diana's heart gave an annoying bounce at the thought of being alone with Llyr in such a room, so she looked around for his men. They were nowhere to be seen.

"Where are your guards?"

"Guarding." Llyr's smile was tight. "From outside the

door." From the heat in his eyes, the Sidhe king was as tired of denying his body's needs as she was.

Diana took a deep breath. "This is not a good idea."

He didn't even acknowledge her point. "Do you remember the dream?" His voice sounded low, rough, far from its usual urbane purr.

She looked away and cleared her throat. "What dream?"

"You know perfectly well what dream. The one where I almost took you."

"Or I took you."

The triumph in his grin made her curse her unruly tongue. "As you will."

Diana stepped away from him. Her heart was pounding. "Like I said, this really isn't a good idea, Your Majesty."

"It may, however, be the only way either of us will stay sane."

"Or it may make a bad situation worse."

"You're wet." He said it like a challenge as he started toward her, stalking. "I can smell it."

Diana wished he hadn't mentioned that, because now that she thought about it, she could smell his need, too. Spotting a window, she strode over to swing it open. Even the shutters were edged in gilt.

A cooling breeze flowed into her face, smelling of alien flowers. "It's the Burning Moon," she managed. "I can't help it. My hormones always go nuts this time of year. It tends to . . . affect men."

"It's certainly affected me." Llyr stopped just behind her. She could feel the heat of him all up and down her body. He took another step, and she felt the brush of his coat against her back. "In the dream, you said you burned, Diana." His breath caressed the side of her face in a warm puff. "I offered to make you burn brighter." The king's voice dropped to a register she could feel in secret, female places. "The offer is still open."

Yessss, the Need whispered.

Diana closed her eyes, trying to fight it. But God, it was hard. Year after year she'd battled the Burning Moon, and every year it had grown worse, as though her lack of a mate offended it.

And there were easily two more weeks of this to go. She couldn't survive it, not if she was supposed to work with him. Not if he was going to push her.

A growl rumbled deep in her throat. Diana was scarcely aware of it. She whirled on him. Opalescent eyes stared down into hers. And then she was kissing him with all the hunger in her starving soul.

Llyr's arms came around her, warm and hard and strong. Suddenly desperate, she grabbed the lapels of his jacket, dragged at it, trying to unwrap his luscious body so she could feast her hands and her mouth and her eyes. Something tore. He laughed, the sound at once ragged with hunger and rich with male satisfaction.

The king hooked strong fingers in the lapels of her blouse, jerked. Buttons bounced, clicking on the marble floor, but she was too busy trying to get him out of his jacket to care. Cupping her breasts, he studied the lace cups that covered them. "What is this?"

"Bra," she gasped.

He caught the fabric in both hands and pulled down. Her nipples popped free, swollen violently pink. "I like it." Then his hot mouth covered the nearest peak, and she cried out.

Her hand tightened into a fist in the back of his jacket. Jerked. Half the coat came away under her Direkind strength. "Sorry," she managed. "Didn't mean to do that."

He was too busy swirling his wet, clever tongue over her nipple to answer.

She dropped his coat and reached for the back of his shirt, hungry to feel bare skin. Her nails rasped over the linen.

He lifted his head. "Claws."

"Sorry." Diana tried to retract them, but she couldn't seem to manage the concentration.

Before she could figure out the trick, the world swung around her, and she realized he'd scooped her into his arms. She clung to him, dizzy and panting. "Where are we going?"

"My bed." He dropped her onto something soft and yielding, then pounced, warm and bare. Somehow they'd both become naked.

"Where'd our clothes go?"

"They were in the way," Llyr growled back. "Too many buttons."

Then his mouth returned to her nipple again. Teeth raked gently, sending fiery curlicue spirals up her spine. She writhed against the silk beneath her, feeling her mind spinning away, drowning in heat.

He suckled her in long, deep pulls that wrapped up in her consciousness and dragged everything to a tight and quivering point. Mind reeling, Diana grabbed for his head as the only stable thing in her universe. Her fingers slid into the long, sweet-smelling strands of his hair and bunched into fists, holding him tight. The cool slide of blond silk in her hands made her moan.

Touching him was so seductive she just had to go exploring, stroking her palms over the warm contours of muscle and bone, over satin flesh dusted in short blond hair. Breathing in deeply, Diana groaned. "You smell so good. Like magic and sex."

Llyr chuckled and lifted his head. His opalescent gaze

met hers, bright with dancing flecks of color. "You smell of mortal soap and wild things." His mouth curled into a smile. "I like it. All buttoned-up and prim on the outside, hot and feral underneath." One big hand brushed down her thigh. She gasped as he slipped a finger between her labia. "Very hot. Dragon's Breath, you're wet."

Diana smiled and reached down the length of his body, found something jutting and thick. "God, you're hard."

"I've got to taste you." He slid down her body, and she groaned at the feeling of his strength. His cock brushed her thigh as he moved, maddening her with its erotic tease.

She lifted her head, gasping at the feel of his long hair slipping across her skin. "If you're going to do that, I want a bite, too."

He looked up her torso as he settled between her thighs. "I think not. I suspect you have fangs to go with those claws." Then, angling his head, he contemplated her sex and lowered his head to lick.

The first pass of his tongue had her arching off the bed with a shout. Before she could writhe free, he wrapped his arms around her thighs and pinned her. His tongue flicked over her clit. "Ah!" She threw back her head at the fiery pleasure.

"You taste just as good as you smell," he said, with another delicate lick between her lips.

"You're going to drive me insane!" She pumped her hips pleadingly, dying for another pass of that magnificent tongue.

He caught one of her lips between his teeth and gave it a gentle, teasing tug. "Mmmm. I do believe I might like that." Then his tongue thrust deep into her sex, wet and hot. He lapped slowly, as if enjoying an ice cream cone.

Diana sucked in a breath and groaned. "If you don't quit teasing me, I'm going to bite you!"

Llyr lifted his head to smirk. "Sweet, people who threaten kings get clapped in irons." His wicked grin widened. "Come to think of it, that isn't a bad idea."

"Don't you dare!"

"But you'd look so good in bondage." He contemplated her wet, spread sex. "And just think what I could do to you, once I had you at my mercy."

"Oh, God," she whimpered, as his tongue began its hot dance over her clit. "I'm already at your mercy."

"Now that," he rumbled, "is what a man likes to hear." Then his mouth locked over her clit and sucked. She exploded like a bottle rocket with a scream of delight.

Diana's nervous system was still sparking and fizzing when Llyr fell on his side beside her and propped his head on his fist to grin down at her, smug and very male. "Did you like that?"

"I'll tell you—"she had to stop and pant—"once I can string a sentence together again."

"Ahhh." Llyr rolled over onto his back, and her mouth went dry at the sight of his perfect strength. "In the meantime, I have another question."

Deciding she'd better get another taste of him before he got high-handed again, Diana sat up and contemplated his powerful body. "And that is?"

"Are you ready to play again?" He flung his arms out in invitation across the silken disorder of his hair. His shoulders looked wider than the pile of pillows he was propped against, and his torso was sculpted in ridges and tempting hollows, thick pectorals capped by small brown nipples.

She reached out and ran one forefinger down the washboard ripples of his belly. His chest hair curled in thick, bright gold strands. "Definitely."

"Good." He smiled lazily at her, and the light in his eyes made her sex clench, "I want to watch you ride me. Now."

It didn't occur to Diana to deny him. She rose, slung one thigh over his waist as he caught his cock and angled it upward. Aimed. And, with a groan, sank onto the thick, delicious shaft, knowing even as it slid deeper and ever deeper that she was making a very big mistake.

She just didn't give a damn.

She looked like his dream.

Diana's sweet, warm little backside rested across Llyr's hips as her sex gripped his cock, hot as melted butter and strong as a fist. She'd thrown her head back at the sensation of being impaled on him, and her soft, pink mouth gasped as her lashes lay like long feathers on her cheeks.

Hungrily, he let his gaze slide down the length of Diana's body. She was lithe as a pixie, her breasts small, exquisitely sensitive, her legs long and muscular as they gripped his flanks. And the way she felt . . .

Llyr threw back his head and gasped as she moved, sliding upward slowly, her small, soft hands braced on his belly. He felt something pricking his skin and realized her claws were still out, long and curving, a silent warning she wasn't quite in control.

Dragon's Breath, that was arousing.

She flexed her fingers again, unconsciously kneading his belly like a cat. Claws pricked, but didn't quite dig in. Llyr rolled his hips upward, driving his cock deeper into that slick satin body.

"Ah!" Diana flung her head back at the sensation. Her face was framed by dark, wispy strands of short hair, like an elegant silk cap. White teeth nibbled her upper lip. She leaned back, grabbing her slender ankles and bowing her torso up into an erotic arch, the better to grind down on his cock.

Her next thrust very nearly clawed an orgasm out of him. He held on by bare will and gritted teeth. She braced her knees farther apart, rose, and forced herself down again, impaling her slick, sweet sex on him.

Pleasure blazed its way up Llyr's torso and seared right into the base of his brain, agonizing and gorgeous. He'd long since lost count of the women he'd had, yet he'd never had one like her. He hadn't known strength could be erotic in a woman, but the power of her slim body gripping him, riding him, was hotter than anything he'd ever known.

Hungry to touch her again, he reached up and cupped her small breasts. Tight nipples pressed into his palms as he squeezed the dove-soft flesh. Diana groaned and rolled her hips, doing exquisite things to his cock.

His fragile grip on control snapped. Llyr caught her by her waist and rolled her under him, mad to ride her. Wide silver eyes blinked up into his, and she gasped as he came down over her. He speared deep in one long thrust. She felt even slicker and tighter like this. Llyr drew back and powered into her again. "God!" She writhed. "God, you feel so good!"

"Yes," he gritted. "You're . . . ah! You're snug." He lunged again, unable to resist the temptation of her slick, gripping heat.

She lifted her long legs and wrapped them across his working ass as she slid her arms around him. Claws pricked at his back like little spurs.

And Llyr went mad.

Bracing his weight on stiffened forearms, he ground deep, drew back, slammed inside again, ground—each thrust pounding pleasure through him like a spike.

"Llyr!" She convulsed under him, her eyes widening

with shocked delight. He watched her climax take her, arching her body up and back, her pretty mouth opening in a long, strangled scream. She flung her arms out, gripped the mattress. Something ripped violently. He didn't care. Her inner muscles milked his cock in long rippling swallows, and he could feel his own orgasm boiling up out of his balls.

He went over with a roar.

Maddened, submerged in a blazing climax, Diana watched the Sidhe king come, tendons standing out in tight cords on the sides of his neck as he threw his head back. She'd never seen anything more beautiful, masculine, or wild.

All that elegant royal culture is a mask, she realized. *He's as feral as I am.*

It was her last thought as her climax drowned her brain in pleasure under Llyr's pounding cock.

When he finally collapsed back onto the bed, it was to wrap his arms around her and pull her half onto his chest. Diana was perfectly content to be there, listening to his galloping heartbeat and breathing in his erotic Sidhe scent.

Absently listening to his rough breathing quiet, she ran her fingertips over the muscled ridges of his belly. "Thank you."

He laughed, a little breathless. "Ah, sweet, believe me—the pleasure was most definitely all mine."

Diana smiled. "Well, not *all* yours."

"That's good to hear."

They fell silent again, concentrating on breathing.

Unfortunately, that gave Diana too much time for certain unpleasant realizations. She'd just had a nooner with the King of the Fairies. That couldn't be good. There'd be those "bitch in heat" comparisons again, not that he'd ever be so vulgar as to say such a thing aloud.

Okay, stop that, she told herself sternly. Yes, she'd banged Llyr only a few hours after she'd met him, but that made her Direkind, not a slut. She might look human, but she wasn't. The rules were different.

But stupid, said a voice in the back of her head, *is still stupid.*

Silently, Diana groaned. Why couldn't anything ever be easy?

Sighing, she sat up and raked her hands through her short hair. It was probably standing up all over her head. "Ummmmm."

He opened one eye. His expression was easy, relaxed. "If you're about to spoil the mood, don't."

"I do have to get back to the office," she told him reluctantly. "I told my clerks I was only stepping out for lunch."

Llyr grinned. "And a lovely meal it was, too."

She grinned back, unable to resist his wicked smile. "I'm glad you approved, Your Majesty. Unfortunately, however . . ."

". . . Duty calls," he finished for her.

"Loudly." She started climbing reluctantly out of bed. "And then there's the whole killer-vampire-on-the-loose thing. I've really got to stick a stake in that bitch."

"I do intend to help you with that," he pointed out, lifting a brow. He frowned, his mind visibly shifting gears to their common problem. "By the way, did the killer leave anything behind—hair, blood, anything of that nature?"

"You mean physical evidence?" Diana looked around absently, searching for her clothes. "I don't know. I could check with the chief. If he found anything, he's probably planning to send it to the state lab for DNA tests." She grimaced. "Unfortunately, given the backlog at SLED, it'll take months to hear back."

"SLED?"

"The State Law Enforcement Division. South Carolina's answer to the FBI, only even more underpaid and overworked. Did you see what happened to my clothes?"

Llyr waved a regal hand. Diana's eyes widened at the tingling rush of power over her skin. When she looked down, she was dressed again in her charcoal gray pantsuit and red blouse. "Now there's a time-saver."

"My pleasure. About the killer . . . I could work a locator spell with a few strands of hair, if you can get them for me."

"I'll see what I can do. How am I going to contact you if I manage it?"

He nodded and extended a hand toward her. Automatically she reached out to take it. Light flashed, and he held a hand mirror. She accepted it awkwardly. It was so heavy, it must be solid gold. Diana examined it wonderingly. "What's this?"

He smiled slightly. "Magic. Say my name to it, and it will call me."

There were actual honest-to-Tiffany jewels set in the back. And she'd bet they were real, too. Diana looked up with a nod. "That'll work. In the meantime, could you create one of those gate things and send me back to the hotel?"

"Of course." She watched with admiration as he rolled out of bed. Another absent wave, and he wore a dark blue velvet doublet, snug blue hose, and a jeweled codpiece she knew from personal experience he did not stuff.

It was all she could do not to drool. "Wow."

"Wow?" He cocked his head. Bright golden hair shifted across the dark velvet. "I'm not familiar with this term."

She dragged her gaze away from his codpiece with difficulty. "It means if you don't make that gate for me in the next five minutes, I'm going to have to dock my own pay for taking a three-hour lunch."

He smiled slowly, seductively. "But Diana, darling, it's only been two."

"Exactly. Gate, please."

It shimmered into being. She stepped through with Llyr's rich chuckle echoing in her ears.

Llyr watched her go with a mental purr of satisfaction. He'd had more than his share of women over the centuries, including four wives and ten mistresses, but none had ever matched Diana London in sheer lush enthusiasm.

She might not make a good queen, but as a lover, she was everything he'd ever dreamed of.

Smiling in sated delight, he strolled into the formal chamber. He still had tasks to take care of if he meant to go on a vampire hunt.

But as he started to seat himself at the desk with its pile of waiting work, guilt pricked his conscience.

Janieda.

Much as it pained him to admit it, perhaps Kerwyn had been right after all. He hadn't loved her.

She'd fascinated him, yes, and he'd thoroughly enjoyed her passion in bed. But more than that, he realized with a prick of regret, she'd been safe. She'd kept the other Sidhe ladies at a distance with her jealousy, so Llyr hadn't had to worry about becoming involved with any of them.

Meanwhile he'd kept Janieda herself from expecting more by his search for a queen among the Majae. Though she'd resented it bitterly, the gambit had worked. None of the assassins who had tried for him over the next century set their sights on Janieda.

Unlike his wives and the other women he'd courted, she'd been safe. At least until Geirolf kidnapped her.

Diana would be even safer, if what Merlin had told him about the Direkind was true. The Fey had designed Diana's werewolf people to fight the Magekind if need be, so they were highly resistant to magic. She'd be more than a match for any assassin.

So he'd woo her. It shouldn't take long, since she needed him right now as badly as he needed her; the arrangement would suit her as well.

He'd just have to make damn sure neither of them got his or her heart broken.

SIX

Suddenly the outer door banged open. Llyr conjured his sword into his hand and lunged to his feet.

He relaxed as his grandmother pushed her way past the guards in the hallway. "For the record, Llyr Aleyn Galatyn, I do *not* want puppies for grandchildren!"

Laughing, he put the sword aside. "I have no intention of marrying her, Grandmother."

Oriana glowered at him. "Does she know that?"

He settled back into his chair. "She's not a fool."

"Well, that's obvious," the Dowager said, impatient. "And she seems a nice enough child, Direkind or not. Not enough to be Queen of the Cachamwri Sidhe, mind you, but personable and bright."

"I'd agree with you there. Your point?"

"You are very hard on your women, grandson. Or at

least, that wretched brother of yours is. Keep in mind who'll pay the price for your pleasure."

Llyr stiffened, stung. "The pleasure is not mine alone, Grandmother. And the little werewolf is more than capable of taking care of herself. Why do you think I'm even considering making her my mistress?"

Suddenly his frustration boiled over, and he rose to pace. "Dragon's Breath, I tire of this. If it weren't for Father's curse, I'd have settled it when Ansgar's pet murderer killed Isolde and our son. Perhaps it's time I begin hiring assassins of my own. See how my dear brother likes it."

"Don't go down that road, grandson." Oriana's voice was low with warning. "You won't like its end. And neither will your people, when your nobles rise up against you as your father instructed."

He wheeled on her. "And what of Ansgar's nobles? Why do they sit silent when he flouts Father's will over and over?"

She shrugged. "They have no evidence of his crimes, and he has them too cowed to look for any. But you, my boy, are justly unwilling to brutalize your people enough to cow them. You must abide."

"Or die." Llyr curled his lip. "Sometimes it would almost be worth it to have an end to this."

Oriana's eyes widened. "That is not a welcome jest, boy."

"I'm not joking." Pacing to the window, he braced a hand against the wall and gazed out over the gardens. "Sometimes I wonder if it's cowardice, this abiding by Father's will. One magical strike against Ansgar . . ."

"Would kill you, too, when Dearg's Curse sent the same magic against you." Urgently, she crossed the room and caught him by the shoulder. "It's not worth it, boy."

"But the Sidhe would be free—not only the Cachamwri,

but the Morven kingdom, too." He turned to look his grandmother in the eye, a bitter smile twisting his lips. "Isn't that what a hero would do?"

"Llyr—"

"Fear not, Grandmother. I am no hero." He laughed shortly and turned away. "Perhaps that's why Cachamwri doesn't answer when I call."

The basketball hit the pavement with a ringing *thud* and bounced back into Gerald Bryce's hand. A spring breeze kissed his shirtless chest as he feinted with the ball and broke right, circling a knot of his jostling, laughing friends.

Gerald dribbled down the asphalt court in a hail of cheerful insults in the bright glare of the lights. In the darkness beyond the park's outdoor basketball court, lightning bugs flashed in the honeysuckle-scented air. He didn't even notice. He was too intent on proving a point to the boys from home.

Spotting an opening to the chain net, he surged for it, dribbling skillfully. A long brown arm snaked around his body in an attempt to bat the ball from his hand, but he threw an elbow back at its owner. Tyrone yelped and faltered, and Gerald kept going. Leaping up, he grabbed the metal rim of the hoop and stuffed the ball inside. It bounced on the pavement below, and Gerald hung from the rim, grinning at his frustrated friends. "Who's a pussy now, huh?"

Tyrone grinned at him. He'd never been one to hold a grudge. "You got lucky, college boy. Let's see if you can do it twice."

But as Gerald dropped to his feet, the sound of hands slowly clapping drew his attention. He turned, saw who was applauding, and stared.

She was, hands down, the whitest woman he'd ever

seen. Her long red hair was teased into a mane that tumbled halfway down her back, like a really early Janet Jackson style. She wore this black bustier deal, showing off a pair of really nice boobs that jiggled as she strutted across the concrete in thigh-high black leather boots. Her leather skirt was so short, he'd bet she showed cheek when she bent over. Two pairs of handcuffs hung from her wide, studded belt, jangling over fishnet stockings. Pretty legs, but somebody really needed to tell the chick it wasn't 1985.

"Who the hell is that?" Bill whispered as she came toward them. "She looks like a hooker."

"Ain't no real hooker dresses like that," Tyrone said, his voice low.

And he was right. Verdaville prostitutes wore T-shirts and jeans and not much in the way of makeup. If any of them had ever dared go out dressed like this girl, every good Christian mama within ten miles would be calling the police to come get her off the street.

The girl came to a hip-shot stop, handcuffs jingling a cheerfully kinky note. "Very nice," she cooed, giving Gerald a blatant once-over. "I'm impressed."

"Can we help you?" He asked with the automatic courtesy his mama had drummed into his head. Then he had to drive an elbow back into Bill's ribs when the boy snickered at him.

"Why yes, I do believe you can," she said in that seductive rasp, and took a step closer until Gerald felt the chill of the handcuffs brush his belly. It took a lot of effort, but he managed to resist the urge to look down and see what her boobs were doing in that low-cut top. Then, to his absolute shock, the lady put out a hand and laid it right in the middle of his sweaty chest. "What nice muscles. You must work out hours every day."

"Uh . . ." Gerald had no idea what to say. Behind him, his ex-friends broke up, falling all over themselves laughing at him. He shot them a glare, then returned his attention to the girl. Her eyes were big and green and pretty. "Are you lost?" It was the first thing that came into his head.

She started tracing a design on his chest with her long red nails. "Well, now that you mention it, I am new in town. And I'm really thirsty."

Damn, she was giving him a hard-on. He swallowed. "Yeah?"

"Yeah. I had a nice glass of white zin last night, but tonight . . ." She smiled. A dimple flashed in that pale cheek. "Tonight I think I'm in the mood for coffee. Something black and strong and full of cream. You know where I can get a really good cup of coffee, Gerald?"

Wait a minute—how did she know his name? He frowned, but as he started to ask her, she looked up, and he forgot the question. Instead he heard himself say hoarsely, "Yeah, I know a place."

"That's good." She hooked an arm in his. "Why don't you show it to me?"

"Oooooh, Gerald!" Tyrone hooted. "Dawg!"

His friends yelled catcalls as she drew him gently away, but he didn't hear them. He was too busy looking down into her lovely face.

For just an instant, he thought he saw something flash in those big, pretty eyes, something . . . horrible. But then it was gone.

He must have imagined it.

Diana pulled into the carport of her little brick ranch and parked. Collecting her purse, a bag of groceries, and the takeout she'd bought from Verdaville's sole Chinese restaurant, she slid out of her Honda and headed for the door.

Damn, she desperately craved a quiet evening in front of the boob tube. After the day she'd had, she wasn't up for another run-in with vampires, fairies, or anything else that went bump in the night.

Though Llyr bumped really well.

There had been one nice thing about that nooner, Diana decided as she unlocked the door one-handed and pushed it open with her hip. At least it'd had the effect of turning the Burning Moon down to a simmer. Her body was still purring, even after an afternoon spent arguing with a DHEC inspector about the treatment pond.

Murder or no murder, the city's business went on.

Diana flicked on the overhead, sending light washing over her sunny yellow kitchen. She dropped her purse and packages on the marigold center island and noticed her answering machine was blinking. She hit the PLAY button and went to put away the soft drinks she'd bought.

"Hellloo, Diana!" her mother's recorded voice caroled from the answering machine. "Your father sends his love. Call me, sweetie. I was talking to your third cousin, Sandra Waltz—you remember Sandra from the big family reunion . . ." Actually, Diana didn't. The annual Direkind Reunions were madhouses with thousands of attendees. God knew which one Sandra had been. "Anyway, she knows this very nice young . . . lawyer." Werewolf. "And she'd love to introduce you. Call me, sweetheart. You're not getting any younger, you know! Love you! Bye!" The machine beeped, signaling the end of its messages.

Diana tilted her head back and groaned up at the ceiling. "Oh, God, just what I need. A blind date with a horny shifter during my Burning Moon. I'd be pregnant before breakfast. No, Ma, uh-uh." With a disgusted snort, she pulled a can of soda from the six-pack, collected her bag of takeout, and made for the living room. She'd call her mother later. Hopefully after Marly London had forgotten all about her candidate for fuzzy fiancé.

Plopping down on her blocky, overstuffed couch, she scooped up the remote, turned on CNN, and started rummaging in the paper bag for her carton of shrimp chow mein.

At least she didn't have to worry about Llyr getting her knocked up, she thought, delving a plastic fork into the carton in search of shrimp. Direkind could only get pregnant with other Direkind; werewolf DNA was just different enough to make it impossible to crossbreed with either a regular human or humanity's Magekind cousins, the Sidhe.

On the other hand, if you bit a human and infected him with Merlin's Curse, his DNA would change and all bets were off. Either way, Diana had no intention of getting involved with anybody. In a few years, she hoped to be hired as city manager somewhere much bigger than Verdaville. Once that happened, she could think about finding a mate.

Diana had worked her way through half the carton and most of a news cycle when the phone rang. She scooped it off its kitschy Porky Pig base. "Diana London."

"What happened to 'hello'? You are not at work, sis." Her brother's deep voice was amused.

Diana grimaced and tucked the phone between her shoulder and cheek. "Sorry. Habit. How's it going?"

"Decent," Jim said. "Getting ready for the gallery show next month. You're coming, right?"

"Wouldn't miss it." Her brother's paintings of the rural South, with their sense of lurking magic and darkness, had started attracting attention in the American art world when he was barely twenty-five. The upcoming New York show would be his third major opening in five years. Diana loved attending the shows, if only to see people's reaction to Jim He didn't exactly fit the stereotype of a pale, sensitive artist, not with those quarterback shoulders and feral black eyes. She loved to tease him that he'd gotten so popular because critics, female and otherwise, tended to fall violently in lust with him. There was absolutely no grounds to the accusation—he really was that good—but it never failed to put his tail in a twist.

"Have you spoken to Mom yet?" he asked.

"Oh, God, are you going start on me about that damn . . . lawyer?"

There was such a long pause she groaned, knowing he was about to do just that. Finally he sighed. "You're not a male, Diana. You can't afford to play games with the moon. You keep this up, you're going to turn somebody who isn't suitable. And then I am gonna have to kill him."

It wasn't a figure of speech. Jim was the family's warrior male, now that Dad was in his fifties and too old to fight. If she turned somebody not worthy of the Curse, it would be Jim's duty to take care of her mistake.

"Give me credit for a little sense," Diana said hotly. "I'm not going to have sex with the first redneck I pick up in a bar." Now, the King of the Fairies . . .

"Diana, you're thirty years old. Every year that goes by, the Burning Moon gets worse. How long do you think you can stay celibate before you snap? You need to—"

"I'm not celibate." The minute she blurted out the words, she winced. She was normally a better politician than that, but she'd never been able to play games with Jim.

His silence went on so long, it grew ominous. "I really don't like killing people, Diana."

"You're not going to have to kill this guy, Jim. He's Sidhe."

"Sidhe?" She heard a thump she suspected was his big feet hitting the floor. "How the hell did you meet a Sidhe?"

"He came to town investigating a vampire murder and—"

"Wait, wait—one of the Magekind went off the rails in Verdaville? Dammit, Diana, why haven't you reported it? This is the very thing we were created to prevent!"

"The killer is not Magekind. She was made by some kind of demon alien or something. It's complicated."

There was a long, ominous silence, during which Diana winced. Finally her brother said quietly, "Then maybe you'd better explain it to me."

For a moment Diana gave serious thought to cussing him out and hanging up on him. She decided against it. He'd just show up in town tomorrow, looking to kick vampire ass. Jim took his duty as family warrior seriously, never mind that Verdaville was her responsibility. And she did not need to juggle him and the Sidhe *and* a psychotic vampire.

After she finished the story, there was another long pause, this one simmering with amusement. "You *slept* with Llyr Galatyn?"

"Uh, yeah."

Jim's laughter boomed in her ear. "Man, Granddad would chase his tail for joy. You go, girl."

She grinned. "Glad you approve."

"My little sister, Queen of the Fairies."

"Don't you start!"

"I can see it now. He'll fall in luuuuv, and the next thing you know . . ."

"If you dare mention this to Mother, I will drive to Atlanta and bite you. I'd never hear the end of it."

"Oh, come on! You seriously don't expect me to keep this to myself?"

"I wouldn't have told you if I'd known you'd repeat it!"

"But King of the Sidhe! That's just too good."

"It was a one-night stand, Jim. Look, Llyr Galatyn is not gonna fall for a werewolf. Heck, his men were talking about putting a *leash* on me."

"They what?"

Oh, God, he was back in protective alpha male mode. "Don't sweat it. Llyr put a stop to that line of conversation in a hurry."

"Good. Cause, you know, I can come to Verdaville and knock some teeth down fairy throats."

"Yeah, and after that you can run around peeing on trees. The city's shrubbery isn't up to it, Jim. Go paint something. I'm hanging up now."

"No, wait. Seriously, do you need help? Because I can break away for a couple of days and come up."

She sighed. "I appreciate the offer, babe, but Verdaville is my responsibility. And if I need help, I'm sure Llyr would be happy to provide an army to back me up."

Diana could hear the grin in his voice. "Well, God knows I'd hate to horn in on a budding romance—"

"Oh, shut up." She dropped the phone back in its cradle, cutting off his rolling laugh.

Diana was in the middle of a deeply erotic dream involving Llyr's blond head between her thighs when an insistent ringing woke her. Blearily, she reached for the phone and fumbled it off its cradle. "London." Glancing at the clock, she stiffened as adrenaline instantly started pumping through her blood. Three A.M. calls are never good news to a city administrator.

She was right.

"We've got another one, Diana," the chief said. "I need Luna again."

"Damn. Okay, let me call . . . the FBI agents, and I'll be right there."

"Two thirty-five Fairview Drive. Wear your uniform," he said, and hung up.

Stopping only long enough to drag a T-shirt out of a drawer—she really didn't want to call Llyr naked—Diana padded into the kitchen in search of her purse. She pulled out the heavy gold mirror from the side pouch she'd tucked it into, frowned at its reflection of her disordered hair, and dug for a comb. Once it was relatively neat again, she briefly considered reapplying her makeup. Then she decided she was being ridiculous. "Llyr?" Clearing her throat, she tried again. "King Llyr Galatyn?"

Nothing. Was she doing it right? "Your Majesty?"

The mirror suddenly blazed with light so bright she was forced to glance away. When she looked back, Llyr stared out at her, his expression grim. Evidently three A.M. calls weren't good news for Sidhe kings either. "Yes, Diana?"

His throat and shoulders were bare. She tried not to wonder if he was naked. "There's been another murder, Your Majesty. I thought you'd want to know."

"Are you there now?"

"No. Gist just called me."

"As soon as you arrive, use the mirror. I'll come to you."

She nodded. It was the middle of the night—if she called from somewhere private, nobody would see him gate in. "I'll do that."

He murmured some Sidhe farewell, and the mirror reflected her own face again. She tucked it back in her purse and went to get dressed.

Diana parked the next street over from Fairview Drive, beside a section of sidewalk where the streetlight had burned out. She made a mental note to have the street department replace it and got out of her car. After making sure there was no one around, she pulled out the mirror. "King Llyr?"

A point of brilliant light appeared in the air in front of her. Diana took a hurried step back as the point swelled into a gate. Bevyn and Naois stepped out, dressed in suits. A moment afterward, Llyr himself appeared, Egan and a Sidhe she didn't recognize behind him.

"Well met, Diana." The king rocked back on his heels to study her. "What sort of costume is that?"

"It's not a costume, it's a police uniform." Diana rested a self-conscious hand on her weapon's belt. Her PR-24 rapped against her hip, leather belt creaking. Her sidearm was holstered next to the baton, while other pouches held ammunition clips, handcuffs, and a canister of pepper spray. "I'm a reserve cop. A volunteer."

A wicked smile teased Llyr's mouth as he contemplated her. "I approve." His guards showed no expression at all, but she could almost smell their amusement.

"Yeah, well, unfortunately we're not here for fun and games. We've got another murdered man and a vampire to worry about." Turning on her heel, she stalked toward the corner.

"You're right, of course," Llyr said, following her. "I'll have my men quarter the area to ensure the killer isn't nearby."

"Don't bother. I'll do it." Diana shot him a glittering look. "If you hear any howls and screams, come running."

Then, reaching for her magic, she changed.

To Llyr's Sidhe eyes, the transformation looked like an explosion of magical light. When it faded, a huge black wolf stood where his slim lover had been. Before he even had time to speak, she was running, a dark, furred blur swallowed almost instantly by the darkness.

Llyr cursed softly and ran after her, his hard mortal-style shoes ringing on the sidewalk, his men at his heels.

"Your Majesty, what are you doing?" Egan called. "You could be pursuing this creature into you know not what danger!"

Oh, he was well aware of the risk. That was why he had no intention of letting her go alone.

Unfortunately, he had not reckoned with the werewolf's supernatural speed. Though he was faster than any mortal, Diana was even faster than that on her four legs, and she soon outpaced him.

Luckily, she also left a hint of magic in the air that made it possible to track her. Surefooted in the light of the moon, the Sidhe followed her across yards, jumping hedges and colorful objects that appeared to be children's toys. Llyr found himself splashing through a wading pool made of some kind of fabric, grimacing as he soaked his breeches to the knee. He didn't break step, though he allowed himself a moment's smile at the splashing and growled curses as his men hit the same obstacle behind him.

But none of them stopped.

"You see?" Adsulata gestured at the scrying mirror she'd conjured. Its silvered surface showed Llyr's back as he ran through the night, pursuing the Direkind woman. "It's as I said. That werewolf has Egan and the king chasing vampires on Mortal Earth."

Ansgar Galatyn sat back against the headboard of his bed, watching the mirror with narrow-eyed interest. His little spy was right. Llyr was trying to cement his alliance with Arthur by aiding the Magekind on this latest idiotic quest of theirs.

He was just going to have to do something about that.

Silently, Ansgar counted his brother's bodyguards. Four. Nowhere near enough, but then, Llyr had always been convinced he could handle any assassin Ansgar sent.

Unfortunately, he'd been right. Ansgar's men had succeeded in killing Llyr's wives and children, but never the bastard himself. It was as if Cachamwri himself protected him.

Tits of the Goddess, it was frustrating. Ansgar would have much preferred to simply challenge the lackwit and kill him, but he didn't dare. Dearg had seen to that, interfering old bastard. Ansgar wished he'd known that before he'd betrayed his father into that demon ambush. He'd have eliminated Llyr first and saved himself the trouble. As it was, he had to make sure Llyr died in a way that was not immediately traceable to him.

Ansgar stroked his spy's bare breast and considered the image she'd created for him. This quest of Llyr's had real potential as something he could use.

Particularly this murderous vampire. How convenient it would be if she killed Llyr. Nobody would be able to trace the assassination back to Ansgar.

All he had to do was find the vampire first.

Llyr caught up to Diana when she stopped between two houses, her wolf ears pricked as she stared at whatever lay beyond them. Odd patterns of blue light struck the building and disappeared. He threw up a fist as he stopped, and his men skidded to a halt behind him, going silent and alert.

Cautiously, Llyr moved up beside Diana. A cluster of mortal vehicles lined the street, some of them parked at haphazard angles that seemed odd compared to what he'd noticed earlier in the day. The vehicles were topped with long electric lights that produced the blue flashes he'd noticed. Some of the cars were marked with VERDAVILLE PO-

LICE, others with GRAYSON COUNTY SHERIFF. All terms for their officers of the law. The home must be the location of the murder.

Magic shimmered, and suddenly Diana was standing next to him in human form, once more in her blue uniform. "Oh, hell."

"What?" He glanced over at her. Her expression was so grim, he tensed.

"We've got media. This isn't good. And what the hell are they doing out here at four in the morning, anyway?" She glanced at him. "Hey, that glamor thing of yours—does it fool television cameras?"

"That depends. What is a television camera?"

"Mechanical device. Collects digital images, which that live truck"—she nodded at a large, boxy vehicle parked down the street—"beams back to a television station, which broadcasts it to a hundred thousand people or so. At least in this market."

"What market?" Llyr frowned; he hadn't seen any sort of bazaar. Then he dismissed the question as yet another overcomplicated mortal reference. "The answer is no, in any case. A glamor is a spell that only affects people in my immediate vicinity."

She rolled her eyes. "Which means the entire television audience will wonder how my police chief mistook members of a rock band for the FBI."

"You do realize I understood perhaps two words in that entire sentence?"

Diana indicated the men behind him. "Let me break it down for you—the butt-length pastel hair is a problem. I don't suppose y'all could cut it?"

Llyr winced. "No."

"Tie it up and stuff it under a hat?"

"What kind of hat?"

"A fedora, maybe."

"A what?"

"Haven't you ever seen a Bogart movie? Oh, forget it. We don't have time. Maybe we can take you in the back way, avoid the cameras."

"Or perhaps I will tell the mortals not to use their devices on us." He started across the grass toward the truck.

He'd never understand why mortals had to make simple things so complicated.

SEVEN

The young man sat slumped in the wooden chair, his throat and groin ripped to bloody shreds. His intestines had been torn from his abdominal cavity and draped over his body like tinsel around a Christmas tree.

Chief William Gist crouched in front of the corpse, smoking a cigarette and contemplating his own guilt. It was brutally obvious this case was related to the one two nights before. He couldn't understand why he'd dropped it the minute that FBI asshole told him to.

Regardless of what they thought, the Feebees were not God's gift to law enforcement. Besides, the people of Verdaville were his responsibility. It was his duty to protect them from this kind of shit, and he hadn't.

With a sigh, he rose to his feet and glanced at his watch. Where the hell was Diana? He needed her nose for this.

They had to find this prick and put him away. Preferably tonight.

Light flashed behind him. Must be the crime scene photog. Gist turned. "'Bout time you got here. I want a—" He broke off and stared.

The guy was built like a running back for the Carolina Panthers, but he had black hair down past his ass. He wore some kind of poofy shirt with a velvet vest, tights, knee boots, and a cape that draped over one shoulder and under the opposite arm. Gist barked out a laugh. "What the fuck are you supposed to be? And how did you get in here, anyway? Hey, Jones! Get in here. I need you to—"

"Silence," the fruit growled.

And suddenly Gist couldn't say a word. Looking into the man's cruel black eyes, the chief suddenly felt a raw, cold terror greater than anything he'd ever known before.

Mentally cursing, Diana hurried in Llyr's wake. He might have the world's most luscious ass, but he was a loose cannon. She could already tell she was going to have her hands full keeping him from making a bad situation worse.

She'd been tempted to tell him she didn't need his help, but she suspected he wouldn't listen. Besides, the galling fact was, she did need him.

Diana's quick and dirty circuit of the area had revealed not so much as a whiff of vampire. She was going to have to spend quality time with her nose on the pavement to trail the little psychopath. Assuming, of course, the vampire hadn't created one of those magical gates and zapped herself wherever.

All of which meant Llyr's magic hands might prove useful in more than just the carnal sense. Diana was just going to have to grit her teeth and keep an eye on him.

As they approached the live truck, a spill of bright light made her lengthen her stride. Sure enough, she saw as she neared that the light was coming from a camera. They were interviewing somebody.

"So you were the one who found your son, Mrs. Bryce?" The reporter was a slim redhead with a sympathetic smile and sharp blue eyes, dressed to the teeth even at this ungodly hour. Diana knew and liked Sandra Kent from previous encounters. She was ambitious enough to go out on a story at four in the morning, good enough to find out entirely too much, and bright enough to get it right.

In short, she was the last reporter they needed.

"Yes, I found him." The lady Kent was interviewing lifted her chin. Her eyes were swollen from crying, and her dark face looked much older than she probably was, lined and gray in that particular way Diana had learned to associate with sudden, traumatic loss. Her blue jeans and knit shirt were scrupulously clean. "I got home from work at the Kwick Mart just after midnight. I knew something was wrong when I opened the door. It smelled like something had . . ." She broke off, and her round chin quivered. "I went into my Gerald's bedroom and I found him. He'd been . . ." The woman began to sob, shoulders shaking with the violence of terrible grief.

Diana winced, remembering what she'd seen two days before. Llyr, standing just beyond the circle of light, turned to look at her. He gestured at the photographer, a muscular young man who held a video camera balanced on one shoulder. "Is that one of those camera devices you were talking about?" he asked in a low voice.

She nodded and gestured at him to be quiet. She wanted to hear what the woman had to say.

"Could you tell us what had happened to him, Mrs. Bryce?" Kent asked gently.

"He'd been . . ." She stopped with a gasp, then tried again. "I can't talk about it. What I came out here to say was one of the police told me the same thing happened to a boy just night before last." Now anger lit her gaze, lending animation to her grief-blasted face. "If this is some kind of serial killer, they got to tell people. People got to know so another boy don't die like this."

"Are you saying you think there's a cover-up?" Kent asked.

"That's exactly what I'm saying! The city's hidin' this just because it don't look good, and that ain't right. My boy wouldn't have died like that if we'd known! He wouldn't have gone off with whoever did this. The police as good as killed him!"

"That's enough!" Llyr growled, laying a big hand over the top of the camera. Its halogen light flared and went out as he stepped past its operator.

"Shit!" the photographer spat. "Sandra, I'm off! Camera's gone dead."

"Well, get it back," Kent ordered, assessing Llyr. "Check the battery. Sir, I'm Sandra Kent, WDRT News. And you are . . . ?"

"In charge. Leave."

The reporter's eyes went blank. Without another word, she and her cameraman went to work packing up their equipment.

Diana swore silently and tried to decide how to handle the new disaster the Sidhe king had unleashed on her head.

Mrs. Bryce watched, confused. "Wait, the interview's over? I wasn't finished! People need to know about this! Somebody could . . ."

Llyr turned to her. "Madame, I regret your loss. Rest assured, your son's killer will pay in very short order. But accusing Diana's men of involvement in these crimes accomplishes nothing, and you will not do so again."

The woman's eyes went as blank as the news crew's. "All right."

"Llyr!" Diana gasped. "What the hell do you think you're doing?" But the king and his entourage were already headed across the sidewalk toward the house.

Growling, she touched the lady's shoulder. Dark, vague eyes lifted to hers. "Do you have family in town, ma'am? Or maybe a friend? Somebody you can call who can come help you?"

"I've got a brother. I've already called him. He's coming."

"Okay, good. Why don't you come with me, and I'll have somebody wait with you until your brother can take you home with him."

As she led the woman across the yard, the news truck's doors slammed, and Kent and her photographer drove off. Diana didn't envy them their coming conversation with their news director, who would surely want to know why they didn't have anything on the murder they'd been sent to cover.

She didn't doubt that Llyr had completely fried both the camera and the digital tape they'd shot. The whole thing was going to drive Kent nuts as soon as the spell wore off.

Well, there was nothing she could do about it now. She collared the first Verdaville cop she saw and told him to take care of Mrs. Bryce, then went to find Llyr.

The Bryce home was a two-story rental, which smelled as if it had been recently painted. Padding through the kitchen over scarred vinyl flooring, she automatically checked the sink. Unfortunately, there were no handy glasses or dishes standing around that looked as though they might host the killer's fingerprints.

Diana continued through the living room past a forty-two-inch television that had probably cost twice as much as the sagging couch. The unmistakable scent of violent death led upstairs, where she found Gist, the Sidhe, and what was left of the poor young man who'd been Mrs. Bryce's son.

She stopped dead in the doorway, staring at him in nauseated horror. "Oh, Jesus. Poor bastard. And his poor mother."

Llyr turned and looked at her, his expression grim. "Well, the vampire witch has outsmarted herself. She's left enough traces here to make it possible to track her. All I have to do is follow her trail, and we'll have her."

Diana sighed in relief. "That's the best news I've had all day." She closed the door behind her and eyed the boy's ruined body grimly. "Let's get started. I owe this . . . person, and I'm looking forward to collecting."

Llyr nodded and turned toward the body. As Diana watched, a spark of light appeared, then another, then another. The tiny points of energy began to swirl over the corpse, slowly at first, then faster. They rose in the air, dancing like a storm of fireflies, streaming toward the ceiling. But just before they reached it, the stream went out.

Llyr frowned. "Huh."

"What?" She moved closer. Around her, Llyr's Sidhe guards shifted in surprise and unease. "What happened?"

"Something's blocking the spell."

"The vampire?"

"I'm not sure." He stared at the ceiling, his expression grim. "It could be, but if so, she is surprisingly powerful. But how did she know she needed to spend that kind of energy on a shield?"

"Dammit." Diana sighed, then straightened her shoulders. "Okay, so we'll just have to do this the old-fashioned way." She looked at Gist as she turned toward the door. "Chief, let's go get Luna's leash and take a look."

But Gist remained where he stood, staring at the boy's body, a cigarette smoldering forgotten in his hand.

"Chief?"

He didn't respond.

"Bill?" Diana touched his shoulder, but he didn't move. "Oh, shit." Teeth bared, she swung toward Llyr and gritted, "Goddamn it, Llyr, I told you to leave my police chief alone! I'm tired of you putting spells on my people every time I turn around!"

His opalescent gaze examined her with chill displeasure. "What are you talking about? I haven't done anything to your man."

"Well, somebody has. Look at him!" She shot a suspicious look the guards.

"We would certainly cast no such spell without His Majesty's permission," Naois told her coolly. "You are mistaken."

"No," Llyr said slowly. He'd stepped nose to nose with Gist, who gazed back at him with blank eyes. "He's definitely been bespelled."

Diana cursed. "The vampire. She must have still been in the house when the police arrived. Can you break it?"

Naois spoke up. "Your Majesty, we should search the house. The killer may still be here. With her powers, the mortals might not even be aware of her."

Llyr nodded shortly. "Naois, you, Egan, and Kelar search. Bevyn, you remain here."

The guards nodded and trooped out.

Diana stepped closer, examining the chief's blank face in concern. What if he didn't come back to himself? What if he was stuck like this? "Llyr, help him. Please."

"If I can." The king reached out and cupped the side of Gist's head in his palm. Sparks of energy spilled around his hand.

Instantly, Gist's eyes widened and focused. He jerked back in surprise. "Whoa. Where did you come from?" Backing up another wary pace, he tensed, obviously ready to punch Llyr in the teeth. "Who the hell are you?"

Diana caught him by the shoulder. "Bill, it's okay. He's a friend."

Gist frowned, staring into Llyr's face. "You're that FBI agent, aren't you? What's going on?"

"We're not sure," Diana explained. "You seemed to be in some kind of trance."

Bewildered, the chief glanced around, spotted the body, and winced. "Damn. I don't understand this. I've never had blackouts in my life." He smiled dryly. "Not without a whole lot of beer being involved, anyway. And I definitely haven't been drinking."

"What was the last thing you remember?" Diana asked.

"I . . . think I was kneeling in the floor smoking a cigarette. Then . . . I don't know. You were here. It was like you just appeared."

"You don't remember us walking in at all?"

"No."

Diana turned toward Llyr. "How did he seem when you walked in?"

The king shrugged sheepishly. "I didn't notice. I was concentrating on the body."

"I don't like this." She bit her lip and eyed Gist. "I don't like it at all."

"Neither do I, but there doesn't seem to be much we can do about it," Llyr said.

Gist spoke up. "Diana, do you want to walk out to the truck with me? I need to get . . . Luna."

"Bill, Llyr knows what I am."

"You *told* him?"

"Yeah. Let's see what kind of scents I pick up in here."

Diana gathered herself and concentrated. Again, she felt the tingling rush of energy that reshaped muscle and bone. Then she was once more on all fours.

Pausing, she breathed deep, focusing her canine senses. All she could smell was the nauseating scent of the boy's death. With a low *woof* of frustration, she dropped her head to the floor and sniffed her way over to the corpse.

Nothing.

She circled it. The killer's scent should be all over the body—it certainly had been with the first victim—yet she smelled nothing but the boy. Stubbornly, she went on working the room, but there was no trail at all.

Finally Diana transformed again and propped her fists on her hips. Her baton rapped her thigh with the motion. "Hell."

"What?" Gist demanded. "What'd you smell?"

"Nothing. Our killer somehow erased her scent trail."

"That's not possible," Gist protested.

Diana met Llyr's grim gaze. "I'm afraid it is."

"If she could block my power, anything is possible," Llyr agreed.

They decided to return to the Mageverse to discuss strategy.

Stepping through the gate with Llyr and his guards, Diana found herself in yet another lushly appointed room in the Sidhe palace. Chairs lined the walls, and the floor was covered with a huge hand-worked rug that practically glittered with magic. Every time she stepped, the image the fibers depicted changed—a hunting party pursuing a dragon; armored men doing battle with demonic creatures; inhumanly beautiful Sidhe men and women dancing. It made Diana dizzy.

MASTER OF THE MOON   113

She looked around for Llyr and found he'd flung himself onto a massive wooden throne, one leg hooked over the arm as he drummed his fingers on the jeweled armrest.

"It's time to try something different," he told her, frowning in concentration. "This vampire is a great deal more powerful than I anticipated. I'm going to have to move my base to mortal Earth for the duration of this hunt."

"But Your Majesty, that will increase the risk to you," Naois protested. "We cannot protect you as effectively there."

Llyr looked up at him. "But we can't detect this murderer here, and the entire point of this is to find the killer and stop her. There's so little background magic on Mortal Earth that if she works any significant spell at all, she'll light up the entire area like a bonfire. I'll sense it, and then we'll have her."

"But what of Ansgar?" Egan protested. "If he should attack in force . . ."

Llyr snorted. "The minute he opened a gate big enough to bring that many men through, we'd all know it. Besides, he doesn't dare violate the will that blatantly. Not only would he not gain my kingdom, he'd lose his own."

"Where will we make our base, Your Majesty?" Naois asked.

"The inn Diana bespoke for us. I will increase the number of guards to ten." He gave his guardsman a sardonic smile. "Will that make you feel any better, Naois?"

The dark-haired Sidhe smiled tightly. "Somewhat, Majesty."

"Good. I'd advise you all to get a few hours' sleep. I doubt you'll find those mortal beds as comfortable. Arrange for your relief shift for the remainder of the night."

"As Your Majesty bids." Naois bowed shortly, then he and the others marched from the room.

As Diana watched, Llyr rose from his throne and sauntered across the room to a table where a pitcher and goblets
waited. "These additional men of yours," she said, her
Burning Moon temper at a simmer. "Am I paying for their
rooms, too?"

Llyr looked up at her. "I will repay you, Diana."

"Yeah—in fairy gold. I wonder how I'm supposed to
explain that one to the IRS?" She rested a hand on her gun-
belt and glowered at him as he approached her in that slow,
tempting walk of his.

Llyr handed her a goblet. "You're snapping, my she-
wolf."

"She-wolf? You're pushing it, fairy." She took the drink
from him and put it aside on the arm of the nearest chair.
"And you're damn right I'm snapping. I'm sick of the way
your people treat my people—putting spells on them and
screwing with their brains every time they get the itch."

Llyr sipped from his own goblet, watching her over its
golden rim. "I'm not responsible for what the vampire
does, Diana and she is not one of mine, in any case."

"Yeah, well, you are responsible for the way you messed
with Linda Bryce's head. Not to mention Sandra and her
photographer. They could lose their jobs because of your little stunt!"

He shrugged, a graceful lift of broad shoulders. "If so,
'tis no more than they deserve. They spoke against those
who lead them."

"Llyr, this is America. Speaking out against your leaders
when they screw up is practically a civic responsibility."

An elegant blond brow lifted. "And undermining your
authority is supposed to make the situation better?"

It wasn't fair that anybody so pigheaded should smell
that good. Diana spun away from him and began to pace.
"But she was right! Mrs. Bryce had a real point. If I'd

warned the public, that boy might not have gone off with his killer. What happened to him is my responsibility."

A strong hand hooked her upper arm and dragged her to a halt. She faced him. He frowned down into her face. "Do you seriously believe this creature needs her victim's consent? It didn't matter whether he went off willingly or not. She'd have taken him anyway."

"But we don't have to make it easy! I owe it to people to warn them."

"Warn them about what? That a vampire is murdering young men, but they should not fear because their leader is a werewolf with the King of the Fairies for an ally?"

Diana glowered at him. "Don't be obnoxious. I'm going to issue a press release warning the public to use caution because there may be a serial killer on the loose." And Mayor Thompson would be in her office an hour later, popping a vein. He hated anything that could even remotely make the town look bad. And it didn't get much worse than a sadistic murderer who eviscerated young men.

"And what will this accomplish?" Llyr's gaze searched hers. "Realistically?"

She sighed. "Realistically we'll get swarmed by local media. And if we're really unlucky, we'll get the national boys, too."

He frowned. "I do not care for the sound of that. What if one of these reporters uses their devices when I am not aware of it, and broadcasts something I don't care to have seen? I cannot allow that, Diana."

She raked a hand through her hair. "So we *are* going to cover this up. Perfect. Just perfect."

Llyr rocked back on his heels and tilted his head to one side. "I do not understand why you wish this to be known. It will only make an already ugly situation more complicated while accomplishing nothing."

"It's like I said, Llyr: This is a democracy. When something affects public safety, the public has a right to know about it."

"Given that there is absolutely nothing they can do to safeguard themselves, I must ask—why?"

Frustrated, but knowing perfectly well he was right, she spun and shoved her nose inches from his. "Because I'm not a glorified dictator, unlike some people I could name!"

His eyes narrowed and sparked with temper. Belatedly, she remembered that she'd just insulted a king. He took a step forward, right into her. "No one in this entire kingdom dares speak to me in that tone. I'll not tolerate it."

Diana opened her mouth to apologize—just as he grabbed the back of her head with one big hand and kissed her, his mouth plundering hers like something out of a pirate romance. She managed a shocked "Mmph!" before his other hand caught her butt and he pulled her full against him. Somebody growled, a deep rumble of pleasure.

To her shock, Diana realized it was her.

God, he tasted good. Like some exotic wine, all spices and heat. She breathed in deeply but he didn't smell nearly as good as he tasted.

"The scent of death still clings to you," he whispered against her lips, as if reading her mind.

"Too much time trying to get a scent off that poor kid," she murmured back. "I need a bath."

Llyr drew back from her, his eyes crinkling with amusement. "I can help you with that." He looked off to one side.

She followed his gaze and gasped. The intricate rug became a pool set into the marble floor. Bubbles floated on its surface, and steam rose into the air, smelling deliciously of jasmine. "Damn. Nice trick, Llyr."

He leaned down to whisper in her ear, "People do not

only hesitate to offend me because I'm king, Diana." His grin was wolfish. "I have more than one kind of power."

She shot him a grin. "No wonder you're spoiled."

"Spoiled!" Eyes widening in mock offense, he rocked back on his heels.

Diana smirked and reached for the buttons of her uniform shirt. "Spoiled."

"Wench, I'm a warrior king. I am most certainly not spoiled." A wicked light lit his eyes, and he gestured.

Glancing down, Diana discovered her clothing had disappeared—all but her weapons belt, which rode her naked hips. "Not just spoiled—*kinky* and spoiled." Giving him a dry look, she reached for the buckle of her belt and opened it.

"Kinky?" He tilted his head. "I gather this has more than the usual meaning."

"It means sexually perverse." Dropping the belt, she stepped down into the pool and sighed at the warm, silken water settling around her skin.

"Yet another insult. Why do I find you so appealing?"

Diana smirked at him, slipping deeper into the water. "Because you're kinky."

"Well," he purred, "if it's sexual perversity you want, I can accommodate you."

Suddenly she found herself frozen in place. Startled, Diana realized her arms were stretched behind her, wrists locked together in steel manacles. As if that wasn't kinky enough, her legs were spread wide, ankles shackled. "Llyr!"

"Oh, love, what did you expect?" he rumbled. She heard water splash as he entered the pool. "People who anger a king find themselves in chains."

She jerked, but the shackles barely clinked. "I'm going to bite you."

Big, warm hands brushed over the taut flesh of her ass.

As she twisted around to aim a mock glower at him, he grinned. "Not before I bite you. This is a very nice bottom."

Diana felt a wicked little thrill. He could do whatever he wanted to her. Determined not to make it that easy for him, she gave her bonds another hard tug, but she couldn't move at all. Yet the chains seemed attached to empty air. "What have you chained me to, you royal pervert?"

"Nothing. That's why they call it magic, darling." He bent to scoop up a handful of water, then splashed it over her back. Long, wet fingers stroked over her skin, tracing over her arms, the tensed muscles of her shoulders, along the curve of her spine.

Despite her irritation, Diana sighed as pleasure shivered in the wake of his hands. "That's nice."

"I'm delighted you approve." He moved around in front of her and went to his knees, reaching beneath her body to stroke and cuddle her hanging breasts, his fingers tugging gently at her nipples. The sensitive tips hardened at the lazy delight he gave her with every gentle stroke.

Moaning, she closed her eyes and surrendered to the sweet, glowing pleasure. She'd fought the Burning Moon so long, it was wonderful to simply give in and let herself feel her own need.

A breath against her lips warned her Llyr was about to kiss her. Then his mouth was there, moving over hers as slowly and seductively as his hands.

Diana opened for him with a sigh, and he stroked his tongue in deep. She suckled gently. He rewarded her with a passionate groan and deepened the kiss, one hand softly busy on her breasts as he cupped the back of her head in the other.

When they finally had to stop to breathe, he gave her lower lip a gentle nibble. "You are insolent," he murmured against her mouth. "And you have no manners whatsoever. Why do I find you so charming?"

"I have excellent manners," she protested. "I'll have you know, I was raised a good Southern werewolf."

He laughed, a deep chuckle that made something warm inside her. "Oh, I'm sure you're a very polite werewolf. But a courtier, you are not."

Diana gave him an impish grin. "Courtier. Isn't that another word for brownnoser?"

Tiny lines fanned around his magical eyes as he smiled. "I have an ugly suspicion about what that phrase means. Please tell me I'm wrong."

"You're not."

His smile became a grin. "You do realize you're going to pay for that."

She smirked back. Despite everything, a bubble of almost ridiculous happiness rose in her chest. "I can't wait."

EIGHT

Diana really was astonishingly delicious. The long, elegant contours of her body made Llyr's blood run hot, particularly bent over as she was now. And when he looked into those pale, wild-wolf eyes, he felt the bottom drop out of his chest with something more than lust.

But the hot throb between his thighs made it impossible to think about what that sweeter ache might mean. Instead, he straightened to his full height, gave her his best marauder's smile, and waded around her bent, helpless body. The pose displayed that magnificent bottom of hers to best advantage, sending hot blood flooding into his cock to raise an aching erection. He contemplated her backside lustfully, feeling his pulse beat. "Well, now," he purred, "this is a lovely view."

"You do say the sweetest things." She twisted her head

to look back at him, one brow lifted sardonically. "You could turn a girl's head."

"Oh, I intend to do more than turn it." Testing, Llyr reached between her long legs. The lips of her sex were soft, furred in dark, curling hair. And as he probed between them, he found her very wet. "Much more."

She caught her breath. "Just . . . how much more?"

He added a second finger, probing deeply, slowly. "I'm going to make it spin, she-wolf."

Diana tilted her head back and groaned. "Oh, you're doing that already."

"Good." Lust sizzling along his nerves, he stroked a finger back and forth across the tiny button of her clit. She squirmed. He inhaled, breathing in the delightfully erotic scent of Diana in heat. It reminded him of just how delicious she tasted.

Dropping to one knee, he parted her delicate lips for his tongue. She jerked and gasped as he gave her a long, slow lap. "God, Llyr! Damn, you're good at that."

He grinned. "Thank you, milady. I do try." Angling his head, he stabbed his tongue across her clit, enjoying her shudder of arousal. She tasted just as sweet and wild as he remembered. With a rumble of hunger, he closed his lips around her button and suckled until she ground her hips back at his face. He rewarded her by sliding two fingers deep again and scissoring them open and closed.

Then, plying tongue and fingers with cheerful ruthlessness, he proceeded to work her to a shuddering orgasm that tore a scream of raw ecstasy from her lips.

By the time he drew back again, she hung in her bonds, gasping for breath. "Oh, man."

He grinned. "Did you like that?"

"God, what do you think?" She groaned. "Damn. That's

the second time you used your mouth on me. Don't I owe you one or something?"

He licked his lips as his cock leaped at the thought of thrusting into Diana's sweet mouth. "Well, if you insist . . ."

She laughed. "Be my guest."

To his amusement, Llyr found his legs weren't quite steady as he walked around to present his cock to his willing captive's mouth. Standing over her, relishing the wicked sensation of dominance, he aimed the aching shaft for her lips. She opened for him with an eager little groan and sucked him right in.

The delicate sensation of Diana's hot mouth pleasuring his cock was so intense, it was all Llyr could do not to come right on the spot. He managed to hold on by sheer will as she danced her tongue over the sensitive head of his cock, then shaped her lips around him for a deep, drawing suckle.

"Dragon's Breath!" he gasped as her teeth nibbled delicately.

She drew back. "Glad you approve, Your Majesty."

"Wench." He drew in a hard breath as she engulfed him again, sucking so hard he saw stars. He'd never be able to last if she kept that up. With a desperate groan, he pulled free of her lips.

"Hey!" she protested as he moved around behind her. "Where do you think you're going?"

"Where do you think?" He caught her by one slim hip.

"Oh."

Llyr laughed. "Oh." Stepping in close, he took his cock in his hand. When he stroked the blunt head between her lips, the wet heat made him shudder. Drawing in a breath of anticipation, he slowly began working his way inside.

"Ahhhh, that's nice." Her groan of pleasure echoed his own as her fine muscles clamped around him. He kept going, hungry for more. By the time his belly rested against her silken backside, he was gasping.

"Oh, man," she whimpered.

"Yes. Dragon's Breath, yes." He drew out slowly. She squirmed, doing magnificent things to his aching shaft.

"More," Diana breathed.

He wrapped his fingers around her slim waist. "As my lady wishes." And he drove to his balls in one hard thrust that almost made his knees buckle with its ferocious pleasure. Her shout of passion goaded him. Maddened, he clenched his teeth and began to stroke, in and out, faster and faster yet, tormenting both of them with the wet silk slide of skin on skin.

Diana's delicious channel gripped him hard. She braced herself and surged back at him, slapping his hips with her backside.

Llyr threw his head back and shut his eyes as his climax roared down on him like a comet. Another hard, ramming thrust, and it struck, showering him with hot sparks of molten pleasure. He roared, distantly aware of Diana's cry as she came, milking him in sweet ripples.

He wouldn't have thought it possible: It was even better than the first time.

Diana hung in her chains, barely capable of coherent thought, wrung out from the pleasure Llyr had so wickedly inflicted.

Suddenly her shackles vanished. Before she quite knew what was going on, he scooped her into his arms and started wading through the pool.

"What?" she murmured. "Where are we going?"

"To bed, sweet," he said, his chest rumbling against her

cheek with his speech. "I feel a sudden need to sleep beside you."

Diana yawned so hard her jaws popped. "Sounds good."

He lifted her like a child, put her down on something exquisitely soft, and crawled in next to her. Somewhere along the trip to bed, they'd both become dry and warm. She sighed in contentment as he pulled her back against his muscular chest.

Just before she fell asleep, it occurred to Diana that she could get seriously addicted to Llyr Galatyn's spectacular lovemaking.

Llyr listened to Diana breathe as she curled against him, silken and warm. So sleek, so lovely.

"So soon," a familiar musical voice whispered in the darkness, sounding mournful. "You've forgotten me so soon."

His eyes flared open. Janieda stood over him, her iridescent wings spread in the moonlight, her eyes inexpressibly sad.

"He's forgotten us all," the women whispered, drifting from the shadows. All his wives—dark, lovely Isolde; blond Shayla; laughing Carili; even cool Teriva, with her summer-grass hair piled high on her head.

"Even me," Isolde said, her voice sweetly familiar even after more than a millennium. "And you told me you loved me."

Llyr tried desperately to move, but his body was frozen in place as his lovely ghosts surrounded him. His very lips felt cold with terror.

"Does the wolf girl know she's next?" the boy asked. His hair shimmered the same golden shade as Llyr's as he stepped into the moonlight. He'd been a man grown when he died, but he looked no more than ten now. His opalescent eyes met Llyr's. "Does she know you'll let him kill her, too?"

Llyr jerked upright with a strangled shout. Wildly, he looked around the room.

They were gone.

A dream. It had been a dream, thank Cachamwri.

He lay back with a relieved huff. His sweat-damp shoulder touched Diana's, and he glanced at her in the moonlight. For such a formidable creature, she looked delicate and defenseless in sleep.

Does she know you'll let him kill her, too?

Dragon's Breath.

What did he think he was doing, involving her in the bloody chaos that so frequently engulfed his life? Yes, she was a werewolf, but that did not make her invulnerable. Just the reverse. For all her magic, she was still mortal. At least his wives and children had been immortals. Even when they fell to assassins, they'd still had far longer lives than Diana would ever know.

It was criminal to put at risk what little life she did have.

Of course, they still had to work together if they were going to capture the vampire. But that didn't mean he had to make her his lover—and a more tempting target for Ansgar's assassins.

He had to keep his distance. There could be no more sleeping with her. No more seductions. No more joking. He had to limit contact to what was strictly necessary to catch the killer.

Next to him, Diana sighed and rolled against him, slipping one slender arm around his chest as she laid her head against his shoulder. Her hair tumbled over his skin like fine silk. One soft little nipple beaded as it came in contact with his forearm.

Llyr closed his eyes and gritted his teeth. *Distance,* he chanted to himself. *Keep your distance.*

Susan Anderson lay dozing in the darkness, stuffed with the blood and life force of the boy she'd killed. Behind her closed lids, she could still see him, struggling and screaming.

And helpless.

She smiled to herself as she remembered the way he'd come to her with such dazzled trust. There had been a time when a man like him would have had nothing to do with her. Would have seen her as the skinny, bookish, ugly little freak she'd been in high school.

But that was before she'd become beautiful and immortal. Before she'd become one of the demon god's worshippers, and tasted the power Geirolf rained down on those who loved him.

Susan had joined Death's Sabbat last year, looking for something to give her empty life meaning. She'd found it in the cult, with its dark secrecy and promise of forbidden knowledge.

But when the cult's leaders started talking about human sacrifices, Susan had been frightened. What if they were caught? Still, she'd been intrigued, too. What would it be like to break society's ultimate taboo?

What would it be like to commit murder?

Besides, she didn't want her new friends to turn on her. She knew that if they began to doubt her, she might end up being the sacrifice herself.

So Susan went along for the ride when they abducted an old homeless man who lived under the Highway Eleven bridge. They all knew nobody would care. He lived in a re-frigerator packing crate, for God's sake. He wasn't exactly a loss, was he?

Susan quickly found that though he was dressed in rags and smelled bad, the fear in his eyes was intoxicating. When the cult leader plunged in his knife, the power of that moment made the hair rise on the back of her neck.

Then it happened. With a crack of thunder and the stench of brimstone, Geirolf appeared to drink the dying man's life force.

The demon towered over the altar, his great horned head thrown back, roaring in pleasure as their victim gasped out his life. Susan realized she was in the presence of a god.

The idea of serving a being like that entranced her. This wasn't the invisible, kindly, gray-bearded wimp god she'd learned about in Sunday school. Geirolf loved blood and death and power, and he was real.

Suddenly there was no good and evil. There was only pleasure and power and the dark god. Susan threw herself into the cult with everything she had, plotting with the others to obtain sacrifices for him. Women or men, rich or poor, all were prey to the knife.

And Geirolf rewarded her.

She was summoned with the others to appear before him at his hidden temple. She drank from his perverted version of the Holy Grail and welcomed the pain of trans-formation. She became a vampire. Part of his army.

Suddenly Susan had more power than she had ever dreamed of, not to mention the face and body of a super-model. She was no longer even human. She'd remember the joy of that moment for the rest of her life.

But just when everything was within her grasp, those Magekind bastards killed Geirolf.

Susan had been standing in the sanctuary watching the

sacrifice of the Magekind couple when it happened. The god had lifted a knife in either hand, preparing to plunge it into the chests of the witch and the vampire. Instead, the Maja had blasted him with some kind of death spell, and the vampire had beheaded him.

Susan had screamed in rage and disbelief, hearing the congregation howl around her. How could her god die?

As if that wasn't bad enough, suddenly the sanctuary was full of Sidhe and Magekind enemies, ready to kill them all. Furious, Susan attacked, wanting only revenge, determined that they would pay for what they had done.

Some fairy was the first to fall to her sword. Then she'd found herself face to face with King Arthur himself. She'd attacked him, confident in her power.

He'd disarmed her as if she was nothing more than a child.

Shocked, terrified, she'd watched him lift his blade. She'd known she was about to die.

But then Parker's final spell had swept over them all, mixed with the death energy of the god himself. Even as Excalibur descended, Parker's magic swept her away.

She'd found herself here, in Verdaville, alone. But powerful.

And hungry.

Now the entire town had become her personal feast. The police would never catch her. Even the werewolf could do nothing. And she was safe underground where they would never find her.

How could they? Her lair did not even have doors. She'd used her magic to dig it out of the solid rock of a hillside, and furnished it with beautiful things she'd seen in magazines. The floor was covered in a thick, royal-blue carpet that felt like velvet under her feet. Her bed, like the bureau and vanity, was massive, carved of solid oak.

Bloodred silk sheets covered it, and the mattress felt like a pillow of air.

When she needed to see anything, she illuminated it with her magic. Anything else she needed—anything at all—she could create with a thought.

The men she had killed had given her a great deal of power, and she could use it any way she liked.

Smiling in pure happiness, Susan hugged her pillow close.

Then, from the darkness, a man's voice spoke. "You've been a very wicked girl, haven't you?"

Susan yelped, rolling off her bed as her heart catapulted into her throat. "Lights!" she gasped, and her spell illuminated the chamber.

The man was a good eight inches taller than she, his hair a crow-black tumble around broad shoulders. He wore black armor, intricately engraved and blatantly magical, trimmed in gold that glittered against all that darkness. In one huge hand, he held a massive sword, its hilt embedded with alien gems.

"Who the hell are you?" With a jerk of one hand, Susan summoned her own armor. The shimmering magical plate instantly appeared around her body, gleaming bloodred. "Answer me!" She lifted her sword.

He shrugged those powerful shoulders. "My name is Ansgar."

"Well, Ansgar, get the fuck out of my house!" She took a threatening step toward him. "I don't like uninvited visitors!"

"I wouldn't either, if I'd done to a man what you did to that boy." His mouth curled into a cruel smile as he settled lazily into guard, his black eyes watchful. "Draping him in his own intestines. Tsk. I do believe you deserve to be soundly punished."

"Dream on, asshole." Heedless frenzy whipping through her, Susan leapt for the invader, bringing her sword down in a vicious, two-handed chop.

He parried it with an ease that made her shoulders shriek in protest at the impact. Jesus, he was strong!

Snarling, she swung again, aiming for his head, only to be deflected by another ringing parry. To her fury, he looked almost bored.

His return attack staggered her with its power. She backpedaled frantically as he hammered at her, their swords ringing with every blow. Something hit the back of her knees, and she fell backward to sprawl across the bed. Frantically, she brought up her sword, barely blocking his downward chop. Jackknifing her body up and over, she rolled off the mattress and backed away from him.

"You're going to have to do better than that," Ansgar said, rounding the bed as he came after her.

Susan snarled at him. His big body seemed to take up all the available space as he slowly stalked her. She had to get more room to fight or she was finished.

Sweating, she launched another attack, banging her blade against his, not so much to land a strike as to keep him busy. At the same time she flung out her will in a spell, generating a gate in the woods above her lair.

The moment it was open, she whirled and dove through it, hitting the ground in a hard roll on the other side. Crickets went still as she surged to her feet. She threw a quick glance around, trying to get her bearings. Thick pine trees circled the clearing she stood in. There was just enough light to warn that dawn wasn't far away. She'd better wrap this up fast, or the sun would catch her. And unlike a Magekind vampire, the light could kill her.

Ansgar shot through the gate before she had time to close it and instantly went on the attack. She scrambled away, parrying his relentless attacks as her shoulders screamed with effort.

This wasn't working. He was too good with that blade. It was time to change the rules.

Susan reached for her magic, pulled a fireball out of the air, and sent it screaming toward Ansgar's head. He ducked. It hit a tree behind him, instantly igniting a blaze.

"Much better," Ansgar said, extinguishing the fire with an offhand gesture. "I was beginning to get bored."

"Can't have that," Susan growled. She swung her sword at his ribs, then as he parried, followed it with another energy ball. The spell splashed off his armor like napalm, and he shouted in pain.

"Got you."

He shot her a black-eyed look glittering with such malice even Susan felt fear. One mailed hand lifted in an intricate gesture, and she caught her breath as his spell snapped toward her.

She threw up a shield and fell back, but the magic ate like acid at the mystical barrier. Susan tried to reinforce it, but the spell kept coming. An instant later, the white-hot splash of power touched her skin and burned. She cursed as her stomach clenched in fear.

The power she'd stolen from the boy was running out.

She had to defeat Ansgar quickly. A lethal gamble: It meant giving him everything she had. If it wasn't enough, she was finished.

Gathering herself, Susan shrieked like a banshee and lunged at him. Even as she rained sword blow after sword blow on him, she followed up with bolts of magic. Ansgar had no choice except to retreat, his sword flashing to meet hers, his eyes burning as he blocked her magical attacks.

Yes! Now she had him! "Bored now?" She grinned savagely into his face.

"You're doing better." He shot a fireball at her head. She ducked aside and swung her sword with all her strength. As he went for the parry, she blew all her remaining power right into his face.

Ansgar fell back with a roar of rage. His hair was burning. With a shriek of triumph, she brought her sword scything around, intent on taking his head.

Instead she struck an invisible shield so hard she felt the reverberation in her shoulders.

She was still staggering from that when his fist struck the side of her head. The world spun around her as she flew across the clearing. Her back slammed hard into something, then the ground came up and punched her in the face.

For a moment Susan lay stunned. Her head ached savagely. So did every muscle, bone and tendon.

And Ansgar wasn't through yet.

Desperately Susan reached for the power. This time, it didn't come. She'd given him everything she had. There was nothing left.

She was dead.

Susan heard the scuff of booted feet in the leaves as he moved to stand over her. Dizzy and sick, she lifted her head and looked up at him. Her heart sank.

The side of his face was blackened from her spell, and the rage in his eyes was terrible. He reached for her. She lifted a leaden hand to swat him away, but he ignored it, wrapping a fist in her hair as he dragged her mercilessly to her feet. She cursed him hopelessly.

Ansgar tightened his grip, shaking her slowly back and forth. "Watch your tongue. You speak to a king."

"Fuck you!"

His slap made her taste blood. He tightened his grip on her hair still more and dragged her onto her toes. "Do you have anything left?"

She spat in his face.

He grinned, spittle running down his cheek, his eyes glittering with rage. "I didn't think so. I could kill you now, vampire. Your life is mine."

Susan sneered. "Then cut the cornball speech and do it."

"Are you in such a hurry to die?"

She glared at him. Her entire body rang with pain. She could feel blood running down her face, taste it in her mouth. She could smell her own sweat, acrid with terror. He should have already killed her. "What do you want, you bastard?"

Ansgar tightened his grip on her hair, cranking her another inch onto her toes. "Your services."

"I'm not a whore."

"You flatter yourself." He shoved her away. She tripped and fell, landing hard in the leaves. Pain jarred through her body.

She didn't dare take her eyes off him. He seemed to grow, drawing in power out of the very air. Susan knew she was an instant from annihilation. "All right!" She threw up a hand in

"What I want," he growled, "is the services of a killer."

"Seems to me you do just fine on your own." Rolling onto her hands and knees, Susan pushed her way slowly to her feet.

Ansgar let her rise. "Unfortunately it isn't that easy. I can't be connected to this death."

Rubbing her bruised shoulder, she studied him with calculation. "So you want an assassin. Why the hell didn't you just ask?"

"This isn't an easy target. I had to know if you were capable."

Susan wiped the blood from her cut lower lip. "Am I?"

His smile spread across his sooty face. "You will be— with a little more power."

Power. Now that she understood. "Who do you want dead?"

Ansgar stepped through the gate and into his chambers. He was limping, and his entire body throbbed like a toothache. Normally he would have cast a simple spell to heal his injuries, but he'd lent Susan too much power. He didn't have it to spare.

He hoped she'd use her new magic with a little more wit. It had been a simple matter to track her from the scene of her last murder. If he hadn't erased her mystical trail with a spell, Llyr would have found her as easily.

"Your Majesty!"

He whipped around in alarm, then relaxed when he saw it was only Adsulata.

She would not betray him. He'd see to it.

The Sidhe hurried toward him, her eyes wide and anxious as she scanned his battered body. "My love, what happened? Was it Llyr?"

He snorted. "As if I'd be such a fool to battle him openly. No, I was testing a new . . . employee."

"And he did that to you?" Bracing her slender hands on her lush hips, Adsulata frowned. "I trust you punished him."

"To the contrary, I found her performance entirely satisfactory." Coolly, he studied his spy. She wore a whisper-thin gown obviously designed for seduction, its fine lace a delicate veil over hard rose nipples. When he inhaled, he scented sex. She was already wet for him. In a breath, the triumph of finding the new assassin turned to lust. He gave her his best purr, knowing it would make her heat. "Tell me, my dear, where is your husband?"

She lowered her lids as she moved toward him in a slow, hip-swaying strut. "Back at the palace. He sleeps."

Ansgar stiffened, arousal dashed. "And you dare come here right under his nose? What if he wakes?"

She took a step back. "No! I put a spell on him to make sure his sleep is deep. Egan will not so much as open an eye for hours yet."

He relaxed slightly. "Still, you took a chance."

Adsulata gave him a pleading look, as though he could be swayed by those kitten eyes of hers. "I had to see you."

Fool. He forced himself to smile. "It's well you did. You may tend my injuries."

"It would be my pleasure!" Slender fingers traced a design in the air.

Healing energy slid over his skin like a warm spring rain. Bruises faded, cuts closed. Strength poured through his body, and he sighed. "Very nice."

The spy smiled, slow and seductive. "Ah, sire—believe me, it's an honor to serve you." Dipping her head, she looked at him from under her lashes. "Is there anything else I may do?"

She really was quite beautiful, with those high, pert breasts and long legs. "I'm sure I can find a use for you."

NINE

Ansgar thrust heavily into Adsulata, groaning at the slick, satin pleasure of her grip. She writhed beneath him, gasping, her long calves riding his ass. He could feel her fighting for that last bit of sensation she needed to spill over into orgasm.

He didn't wait for her. Throwing his head back, he roared his pleasure at the ceiling as he spilled.

After the last spasms poured his seed, he rolled onto his back with a groan. Adsulata lay still. He could practically feel the waves of her frustration. He ignored them.

She'd become a problem.

He contemplated his magical reserves. Her healing spell had done its work; he thought he had enough for what he needed.

"Effective spies, my sweet, don't drop in unannounced at will."

She reared up onto her elbows, her eyes going round and wide. He basked in the fear in them. "I'm . . . I'm sorry. I didn't think. I just needed you so."

Ansgar smiled easily and rolled out of bed. "I understand. But I'm afraid our time is up. I have much to do."

Adsulata scrambled hastily off the mattress, watching him like a mouse cornered by a tiger. "I'll go, then. And I'll . . . wait for your summons."

It would be a long wait. "Do. But before you go, a kiss."

Her expression lightened with relief as she stepped into his arms. "Of course."

Ansgar caught her slim body against his, savoring how small and delicate she felt. It was an erotic sensation. Then he took her lips.

And began to take still more.

The spy stiffened as she felt the spell slice into her, but she couldn't break his hold. His mouth muffled her scream as he drank in her life force. It was hot, delicious, filling the void left when he'd given Susan so much of his power.

Drinking, he ignored her desperate fists as she pounded at him, feet drumming at his shins. Drank until her struggles weakened. Drank until she was all gone.

Ansgar opened his arms, and she fell to the floor. Her huge eyes stared up at him in shocked bewilderment.

Crouching beside her, he told her corpse, "You betrayed your husband, your king, and your people, my sweet. I didn't care to be the next one you betrayed."

Then he rose and walked away, leaving her empty eyes fixed on the spot where he'd stood.

There was a great deal to do.

* * *

Llyr's deep voice spoke in her ear. "It's time, Diana. We must rise." Strong hands caught her shoulders and gently lifted her from the broad, warm chest she lay across.

Diana moaned in protest. "God, already? I did *not* get enough sleep." She pried open her eyes and was rewarded by the sight of Llyr's mouthwatering backside as he walked away from the bed. Her Burning Moon hunger stirred. "Mmm. I'm feeling better already. Wanna play, Your Majesty?"

"Much as it pains me to remind you, we do have a killer to catch." He gestured, and was instantly attired in a magnificent black velvet doublet trimmed in gold and set with sapphires. At least his black tights and codpiece made the most of his magnificent legs.

She eyed his gleaming boots. "Oh, come on, just a quickie. Have I mentioned I've got a thing for leather?"

His handsome face chilled. "I do not take my duty lightly, Diana."

She frowned at the dig, but her belly chose that moment for a ferocious growl. "Oh, God, I'm starving. Turning into a wolf is murder on the blood sugar. Is there any way I could get my paws on something to eat? Eggs, sausage— hell, point me at the royal deer and I'll get my own."

She'd hoped her joke would warm his cool expression, but he only gave her a regal nod. Llyr flicked his wrist. A table appeared by the bed, groaning with food. Rolling naked off the mattress, Diana looked it over. Not only was there a plate of eggs and a big round loaf of dark bread, but he'd included an entire ham, neatly sliced, along with a jug of something that smelled alcoholic. "Cool! Let's eat." Grinning happily, she snatched a piece of ham and looked up. His expression was so distantly polite, the smile froze on her face.

"I'm afraid I can't join you," Llyr said, turning toward the door. "I have too much to do. Enjoy your meal."

"What—? Wait!" But he had already opened the door and stepped outside. "Where are my clothes!" Magic rushed over her skin, and she looked down to see her uniform had reappeared.

Llyr glanced over his shoulder. "When you're ready to leave, let me know. I'll be in the next room meeting with my advisors." The door clicked closed behind him.

"What the hell was that?" She sank down on the edge of the bed, staring at the closed door. "Not even an 'I'll call you sometime.' Damn."

Hurt bloomed in her chest. She turned her gaze to the table and mechanically picked up another piece of ham. Her appetite had disappeared, but she knew perfectly well her werewolf metabolism would be clamoring again in another ten minutes. She bit into the meat and chewed.

It was delicious. Didn't it figure?

Just beyond the closed door, Llyr put his head down and cursed himself at the memory of her wounded eyes. But it was better to break this off now than wait until they had begun to fall in love.

Brooding, he walked to his throne and dropped into it, hooking a knee over the armrest. The dream hadn't exaggerated. Every relationship he'd ever had with a woman had ended in pain and violence, starting with his mother—killed by a Morven rebel fighting his father—and continuing through all four of his wives. Even his children had been slain, one by one, leaving gaping wounds in his spirit that never ceased to ache. Janieda had only been the latest victim of what he'd begun to think of as his personal curse.

And with every loss, the weight of his guilt and grief had grown heavier, his isolation deeper.

True, Diana was tougher than any of them, but she was also mortal. Even if she could handle any of the assassins his brother would send after her, she could not defeat time. In a couple of decades at most, she'd begin to slow down, and then she'd be easy prey.

He didn't want to see that happen to her.

Suddenly he huffed out a breath, impatient with his own self-deception. *Be honest, Llyr. You don't want to risk falling in love.*

He didn't think his heart could survive breaking again.

The door opened and one of his advisors stuck his head in. "Your Majesty, I have an issue I'd like to discuss."

Llyr thrust aside his personal concerns and nodded. "Come in. I need to brief you all anyway. It seems I will be away from the palace for the next several days."

Llyr was listening for Diana when she walked into his audience chamber half an hour later. Even in her police uniform, she looked as cool and distant in her disapproval as any queen he'd ever had. "I'm ready to leave now."

He fought to keep the regret off his face. "Where do you want to go?"

"Back to my car." She hesitated. "If you can make sure nobody sees the gate."

Llyr nodded. "I can arrange that. Visualize your vehicle for me." With the ease of long practice, he picked the image out of her thoughts and opened the gate.

Diana walked over and studied the dimensional gateway cautiously, satisfying herself that none of her townspeople waited on the other side. Over her shoulder, she said, "If you need me to arrange additional accommodations for your men, let me know."

"I will. Until we meet . . ."

She stepped through the gate before he could get the rest of the sentence out of his mouth. He hid a wince.

"It was for the best, Majesty."

Llyr glanced around and met Naois's sympathetic gaze. He wasn't surprised his guard captain knew what he was thinking. The man had been with him for centuries, much of it as Kerwyn's second-in-command.

Llyr gave him a long, assessing look, wondering if that was a flicker of satisfaction he saw in the guard's eyes. After all, Diana had threatened Naois with her claws in retaliation for his joke about leashing her. For a man as proud as the captain, that would grate. "Indeed?"

Another man would have retreated in the face of his frosty disapproval, but Naois was made of steadier stuff. He shrugged. "It will go easier for us all now that she knows her place."

"And what place is that?"

The captain's eyes flickered at Llyr's tone, but he didn't back down. "She's mortal, Majesty, she knows nothing of the court, and she has the manners of a barbarian. As intriguing a bedmate as I'm sure she is, that's all she can ever be." He bowed slightly. "As you are wise enough to see."

It was exactly what Llyr had been thinking. Why, then, did it sound so distasteful aloud? Uncomfortable, he glanced away from the captain, his gaze falling on Egan. The bodyguard stood frowning, his thoughts obviously elsewhere. "Is there a problem, Lieutenant?"

Egan started and lifted his head, blue hair swinging. "It's my wife, Majesty. She wasn't home when I awoke this morning. She does not usually get up so early. I tried to touch her thoughts, but I could not make contact."

He frowned. "Do you believe something has happened to her, then? Do you wish to search for her?"

Egan hesitated. "No," he said at last. "I'm sure she simply did not want to speak to me." Reading the question in Llyr's gaze, he shrugged. "Our union has hit rough waters of late."

Bevyn sneered. Llyr knew he'd never liked his brother's wife, largely because the two fought incessantly. "Most like she's off with a lover."

Egan forced a smile. "Mayhap you're right. Perhaps she'll be more tolerant of my lapses, then."

"I doubt it," Bevyn grumbled.

Llyr lifted a hand, cutting off the conversation. "In the interim, we have another mystery to solve. I would like to find this killer and eliminate her before she does any more damage to Diana's people." He'd already made arrangements for his council to assume the reins of the kingdom until his return.

Llyr aimed a thought at his doublet and hose, and it obligingly became one of the suits the mortals were so fond of. As his men made similar transformations, he opened a gate into their hotel room and led the way through.

Diana contemplated the row of budget figures and rubbed the throbbing spot between her eyebrows. South Carolina law required local governments to pass budgets by June thirtieth of each year. She needed to have a proposal put together by next month's council meeting, but between the murders and amorous fairies, she hadn't looked at the package all week.

At the moment, something was bugging her about the

fire chief's budget request, but she was damned if she could put her finger on it.

Probably because her thoughts kept wandering to Llyr—the way those drugging kisses had made her head spin, the heat of his thick cock forcing its way into her sex.

And the chill in his eyes when he'd cut her off at the knees this morning.

With a growl of disgust, Diana tossed her pencil down on her legal pad of scribbled figures. If she wasn't careful, she was going to make some embarrassing mathematical error that would end up in the paper in forty-point type: *City Manager's Figures Don't Add Up.* Implication being that the city manager couldn't add. Just what she needed on her résumé.

Restlessly, she rose from her desk and walked to the window. Looking out across the parking lot, she could see the city park basketball court where Gerald Bryce had met his murderer.

This morning Diana had yielded to the inevitable and drafted a press release about the killings. The mayor hadn't been happy about it, but Thompson had known as well as she did that trying to cover up serial killings was the equivalent of holding an orgy in city hall. People were bound to find out, and when they did, they'd be pissed.

Even now, the fax machine was working its way through its programmed list of newspapers and television and radio stations. Any minute, her phone would start ringing like a bookie's during the Super Bowl.

What the hell was Llyr's problem?

The thought that had been chugging along in her mental background for hours now suddenly burst to the surface. He'd been so warm and passionate last night, but this morning, he'd practically given her frostbite. Diana would have wondered if he was married if she hadn't known for a fact he wasn't.

Okay, she told herself firmly. *So he's a jerk with really good protective coloration. You don't see him coming until he's already gone. Who cares? It's the Burning Moon, you're horny, you banged him, it's over. It's not like you were expecting to live happily ever after with the King of the Fairies. You're a werewolf, for God's sake, not Snow friggin' White.*

She rested her forehead against the glass and blinked her stinging eyes. *I just expected better of him. Damn him.*

Behind her, her desk phone rang. She sighed, lifted her head, and went to deal with the media.

When Llyr moved himself and his ten guards into the hotel, he took no chances. He stationed seven of them in and around the hotel's lobby and entrances, all in mortal garb.

Meanwhile, he and his core team pushed what passed for the motel room's furniture out of the way so he could create a magical map of Verdaville in the center of the room. They were discussing the best way to lay a warding spell over it when someone started pounding on the door.

Llyr looked up, frowning as his men instantly went on alert.

"Egan!" a female voice called. "Egan, I must talk to you! Now!"

Bevyn frowned at his brother. "Is that Adsulata? What in the Dragon's name is she doing here?"

Impatient, Llyr scowled at the lieutenant. "Deal with her, Egan. This is a complicated bit of spell casting. I don't need hysterical wives distracting me in the middle of it. I'd hate to accidentally turn Diana's fief into a crater."

Visibly irritated, the guardsman started for the door. "Adsulata knows better than to interrupt me when I'm on your business, Majesty. I'll send her back to the palace."

Llyr, returning his attention to the spell, barely noticed when he walked out.

"All right, what is it?" Egan demanded as he stepped out into the narrow hallway. "And it had best be important."

Instead of answering, his wife whirled and strode off down the corridor, silken skirts twitching. "Not here. I do not want them to hear what I have to say to you."

"Cachamwri give me patience," Egan muttered under his breath. Adsulata's taste for drama could be tiring. He hurried after her. "My wife, I am on duty! We can discuss whatever is bothering you when I return to the palace."

"Not this time," she snapped, throwing open a door and clattering down the cement stairs beyond it.

He gritted his teeth and followed. "Where were you this morning, anyway? When I woke, you were gone." Egan hit the landing just as she stopped and turned toward him. For the first time, he caught her scent.

And realized the woman before him was not his wife.

Her hand shot toward his ribs. He automatically tried to knock it aside, but even with his guardsman's reflexes, he was an instant too late for her blurring speed. Something thumped into his ribs.

His eyes widened as he looked down. A jeweled hilt protruded from his chest. Even as he realized he'd been stabbed, the pain hit, a dagger of ice in his heart. Grabbing her wrist, Egan tried to jerk out the stiletto and throw up a healing spell.

Too late. A wave of death magic rolled up the blade, freezing the bellow of warning in his throat even as it ripped his magic from him. Frantically, he tried to send a mental shout to the king, but his power was gone.

As blackness crashed in, the last thing he saw was his

killer's smile. "Your wife died this morning," she purred, "betraying you."

Susan watched in satisfaction as Llyr's guardsman fell dead at her feet, spilling the energy of his life into her mind. It had been much easier than she'd expected.

Ansgar's power had her consciousness humming like a high-voltage electric line. He'd appeared to her the minute she woke up this evening to suggest the plan and feed her the image of the guardsman's wife. She'd been skeptical at first, but the gambit had worked just as he'd promised. Using Adsulata's guise, she'd been able to approach each of the Sidhe bodyguard patrolling the grounds and lobby. One by one, she'd killed all seven.

There'd been one bad moment when she'd looked around to see the hotel clerk reaching for the phone, no doubt to call 911. A quick fireball had incinerated him before the handset left the cradle.

Now speed was key. She had to kill the Sidhe king before a horde of local law enforcement showed up. Not that they could stop her, but they could certainly complicate her life.

Llyr, however, was a much more serious problem. He was said to be as powerful as his brother. And he did have those remaining guards.

She would need to improve the odds a bit more before she could afford to strike.

Llyr did not look around when the door opened behind him. The architecture for the spell was not cooperating.

"Bevyn? I need your help," Egan said from the door.

"For Cachamwri's sake, Egan, just send the bitch home! We do not have time to deal with her histrionics!"

"She won't leave until she talks to you."

"Since when does she want anything to do with me?"

"Bevyn, please!"

"Bevyn!" Llyr growled. He'd have the spell if they'd leave him alone for five more minutes. "Tell her whatever she wants, just get rid of her!"

"Aye, Majesty!" The guardsman stalked out to meet his brother. The door snapped shut behind him.

At Llyr's elbow, Naois said suddenly, "Why didn't she just gate into the room?"

He glanced up to meet his guard captain's suspicious gaze. Chill horror slid over him. "Dragon's Breath!"

But even as the two Sidhe whirled toward the door, they heard a choked scream.

Bevyn.

"Bloody fuck!" Naois cursed as he drew his blade and threw a barrier spell over the door. Even as his magic took hold, something slammed hard into the barrier. He grunted and threw out a hand, sending another spell to reinforce the first. "She's trying to get through—and she's strong enough to do it. Gate back to the palace, Majesty!"

The thought of retreat was galling, but Llyr knew he didn't have the luxury of allowing some vampire to kill him. Not if it meant leaving his people to Ansgar's brutal mercies. He reached for the Mageverse . . . and slammed head-on into a magical shield.

Naois cursed. "She's thrown up a spell barrier."

"So I'll crack it," Llyr growled. "I'll not be trapped by some vampire bitch." There was no doubt in his mind that was who they faced.

Whoom!

The door blew inward, sending both men staggering back, barely raising shield spells in time to block the chunks of wooden shrapnel pelting the room.

"Why, hello there." A woman stood in the blasted hole,

red hair tumbling to her shoulders. Fangs gleamed in her smile. She was dressed in magical armor, the scarlet plate mail ornately worked with runes. "I've never killed a king before." A fireball bloomed around her hands and shot toward him.

"And you haven't killed one now." Llyr flung up a shield. The flames splashed off, hitting the carpet, which ignited at his feet with a *whoosh* of heat and flame. He threw a suffocation spell over the floor, and the fire winked out.

"We must leave, Majesty!" Naois cried, whirling to blow a chunk out of the back wall. The room shook.

He was right. They needed space to fight. Llyr started toward the hole, but before they could escape, the vampire stepped into the room, a magical sword appearing in her hands. "Don't leave yet—I want to play."

Naois turned back toward her, his own armor shimmering into place around him. "Go, Majesty!" He lunged at the witch, howling the kingdom's battle cry: "Cachamwri!"

Llyr hesitated, knowing he had a duty to leap for safety. But he couldn't just leave the captain to die. Cursing himself, he wheeled to go to his bodyguard's aid, creating armor around him as he went. He'd be spitted if he'd lose another man to that vicious bitch.

Naois hacked at the vampire's head, but she parried his sword easily. The blades rang and scraped, sparks flying. Llyr snarled, knowing she was drawing on the death energy she'd stolen from the men she'd killed. He badly wanted to feed her a blast of power she'd find a lot less pleasant.

Unfortunately, the captain was in the way, his broad back blocking the shot. Growling, Llyr circled, looking for an opening as Naois hacked at the vampire in a frenzy of rage.

She parried, then parried again. The blades rang like a blacksmith's hammer on an anvil.

His mouth curled into an snarl, Naois lifted his sword again for another two-handed swing Suddenly the vampire jabbed for his ribs with her empty hand.

The dagger appeared the instant before it hit, sliding right through the armor like an axe through burnt bread.

"No!" Llyr roared, leaping forward.

Naois gasped, the sound soft and shocked. For just an instant, his eyes met his king's over the vampire's shoulder. Llyr saw the death spell take hold, stealing Naois's life in a rush.

"Cachamwri!" Llyr roared, and swung his blade with all his strength right for the vampire's chest.

But she was already spinning, blocking the blow with a spell shield as she swung her own sword at his throat. Llyr jerked aside and the big blade struck him in the shoulder, slicing through his armor. Cold steel cut through flesh and muscle.

The spell came roaring up the blade. Desperately, Llyr drove his own power to block it with the full force of his will. Magic met magic in an explosion of energy.

Boom!

The detonation blasted Llyr right off the sword blade and through the hole Naois had blown in the wall. Wind whipped past his face as he shot across the night like a cannonball. Stars spun around him. He glimpsed a flash of moon. Instinctively, he tried to throw up a protective shield, but it barely shimmered. Too weak . . .

Something slammed into his head. Light exploded behind Llyr's eyes with a burst of white-hot pain. He didn't feel himself hit the ground at the base of the tree.

Sirens shrilled. Male voices shouted.

"God, lady, are you all right?"

Susan opened her eyes and blinked away the blood. A face loomed over her, and she tried to spell her sword into her hand. It didn't come.

What had happened to her power?

"Lady, are you alive?" The man's round face was white as a ghost's, and his eyes were so wide they literally bulged. "It sounded like World War Three out there! And then you came flying through the wall. I figured you were dead, but you opened your eyes. How the hell did you survive all that?"

Thank Geirolf—just an innocent bystander. Who had been thoroughly traumatized, judging by the way he was babbling.

And he wasn't the only one. She felt like she'd been beaten with a hammer. The fairy king hadn't liked that last spell at all. He'd blown her through a couple of walls into a neighboring room.

Struggling onto her hands and knees, Susan realized she was naked. Damn, all her power must be gone, if even her magical clothing had disappeared.

The anxious fat man was still babbling. "What happened to your clothes? Maybe you better just lie still. I called 911 when all hell started breaking loose, and the lady said she was sending an ambulance."

Which meant the cops would be here any minute. And her with no magic. No way could she create a gate without it. "Great," Susan growled. "Just great. Now what the hell am I going to do?"

Her eyes fixed on the man's beefy face as he crouched by her side. Come to think of it, he might come in handy. She didn't have time to feed, not with the cops so close, but there was one good way to restore her power.

She gave him a grin.

He paled and rocked back on his heels, staring down at her in horror. "Your teeth . . ."

"Yeah, my teeth. You really should have minded your own business, lard ass."

Diana contemplated the bottom of the ice cream carton. It was a good thing she burned calories so fast, or she'd have put on five pounds tonight just from going through all this fudge ripple. There were advantages to being a werewolf.

Too bad they weren't sufficient to let you hang around with the King of the Fairies.

The phone rang.

Diana winced. "Oh, Jesus, tell me there hasn't been another murder." She sighed, rose to her feet, and scooped her cordless phone off the coffee table. "London."

"We've got trouble, Diana," Gist's voice said brusquely. "I need you over at the hotel. Looks like somebody set off a bomb. And we've got bodies. At least twelve."

It felt as if her heart had stopped. "Llyr?"

"The FBI guy? Can't tell. But the manager said one of the dead guys is in one of the rooms the agents had."

"On my way." She hung up the phone, flung it aside, grabbed her purse, and ran for the door.

TEN

When Diana roared into the motel parking lot five minutes later, two fire trucks, three ambulances, and five police cars were already there. She jumped out of the car and ran for the hotel entrance. Several corpses lay scattered around in poses of violent death, but she could see at a glance none of them was Llyr. Most of them were disturbingly naked, and she wondered how the killer had stripped them all. A cop looked up from throwing a sheet over one, and she snapped, "Stairs?"

Recognizing her, the officer pointed. She ducked down the hallway he indicated, spotted a metal door, and clattered up them toward the second floor.

Diana found the next body on the landing, already covered in a sheet. Heart in her mouth, she stopped to lift a corner. She winced at Egan's wide, empty eyes. He, too, was naked. The spell that had clothed him must have collapsed with his death. The reek of blood clung to him and she spotted the wound in his chest. "Jesus, I'm sorry. I should have been here!"

Sick at heart, Diana dropped the sheet back over his face and took the rest of the stairs two at a time.

Bevyn sprawled in the hallway, his bright green hair matted with blood, his eyes empty above a slit throat. A crime-scene photographer stood over him, snapping pictures. "I thought these guys were supposed to be FBI," the man said, snapping another shot.

"They were," she said dully, looking over at the door to Llyr's room and dreading what she'd find.

"Then what's with the hair and the Spock ears?" He nodded at the elfin points showing through Bevyn's tangled hair. "And why did the killer strip them all?"

"I have no idea," Diana lied. Grimly, she rose and strode for the hotel room, stopping only briefly to examine the hole that had been blasted into the hallway wall from inside the room. Across the hall, something had blown another human-sized hole through the Sheetrock. Glancing inside, she saw still another body draped in a sheet. This one wore socks, though, so he was probably just an innocent bystander.

Catching her breath in dread, she stepped into the room she'd obtained for the Sidhe. Naois lay sprawled, his brawny body covered in blood. She knew he'd fallen protecting his king.

Gist crouched beside him, making notes in a pocket notebook.

"Llyr. Where's the blond FBI agent?" Diana demanded.

The chief looked up. "We haven't found him yet." He nodded at another hole, this one punching right through the hotel's brick exterior to overlook the woods in back of the hotel. "He might be out there."

Diana stepped up to the opening and looked out.

More than a hundred feet away in a straight line lay a stand of trees. She thought she saw something crumpled lying at the base of one of them, but even with her Direkind vision, she couldn't be sure. *Sweet God, I hope it's not Llyr.*

She didn't hesitate. Magic flared across her skin as she transformed herself into a wolf and flung herself out of the opening.

"Diana!" Gist yelled, startled. "What the hell are you doing?"

She hit the ground running.

Diana found Llyr lying in a bloodied heap, just as naked as the others. Judging from the litter of broken branches around him, he must have hit the tree like a rocket.

She whined, wolflike, at the thought of what the impact must have done to his body. But as she sniffed at his face, she was relieved to detect the faint sigh of his breath, bruised and bloodied though he was. She reached for her magic and became human again. "Llyr? Your Majesty?" Gently, she ran her hands over him, looking for broken bones and the wound that had produced all that blood.

There was a vicious gash in his left shoulder, which looked like a sword wound, and the entire side of his body was sticky with drying blood. Gritting her teeth, she carefully rolled him onto his back. He moaned, but his eyes didn't open.

"Llyr, wake up. Come on, you pigheaded fairy, talk to me. We have to contact your people!" It was painfully obvious he'd need magic to heal the injury; he'd lost a lot of blood. "Llyr!"

He murmured something incomprehensible in what was

probably the native Sidhe tongue, then finally opened his eyes. He frowned, looking up at her. *"A'cki ve?"*

"It's Diana London, Your Majesty. Come on, babe, focus! We need to move you before the cops get here."

His gaze cleared. "Diana?"

She sighed in relief. "Yeah, it's me. You need to open a gate and get back to your palace. The shit has hit the fan, and you're not safe."

"What?" He lifted his head from the leaves and looked around. "My guards. Where are my guards?"

Diana drew in a breath. "I'm afraid they're all dead, Llyr. Something nasty got hold of you."

He dropped his head back on the leaves. "The vampire. But where in the Dragon's name did she get the power to do all this?"

"I have no idea, but I didn't see her body back at the hotel, which means she's still loose. You need to go home and heal."

Llyr drew in a breath, gasped at the pain. "Yes. Yes, you're right. But, Goddess, my men. Naois, Egan, Avar and Bevyn, Gayln and Camyr. All the rest. All dead. She killed them all."

"Which is why you'd better create that gate *now*."

He nodded, his gaze sharpening. Diana looked around for the expanding point of light that was an opening dimensional gate.

Nothing happened.

She frowned. "Llyr, where's that gate?"

"I . . . It's not responding." His eyes met hers, very wide. "My powers are gone!"

"What?"

"When she ran me through with her sword, I sensed a death spell roll up the blade. I tried to block it. The two spells . . . exploded. They blew me through the wall."

"You've got no powers at all? Are you sure?"

Llyr licked his lips and concentrated again, obviously straining. Finally he let his head drop back to stare blindly up at the tree overhead. "Nothing. Everything's completely gone."

"Well, when will they come back? They *will* come back, right?"

"Let's hope so." His handsome face was grim. "Either I've burned myself out blocking that spell, or the spell itself was designed to steal my powers. Either way, healing the loss will take time."

"But how are you going to get home? Can you call somebody?"

Llyr glanced up at her, his expression wry. "There isn't exactly telephone service to the Mageverse, Diana."

"What about my magic mirror? The one you gave me. It's in my purse . . ." She started to stand.

"Not anymore. When the spell stripped me of my power, the mirror would have vanished." He grimaced and stopped to pant in pain. "Just like my clothes and weapons."

She sat back on her heels and stared at him in dismay. "Oh, hell."

"That is about the size of it."

"We can't leave you here, Llyr. They're going to find you. And your glamor has collapsed. Somehow I don't think you want you and your pointed ears under a microscope."

His mouth twitched. "I doubt I'd fit."

"You know what I mean. Besides, you're naked." Gnawing her lip, Diana thought fast. "Okay, look, I'm going to go get my car. I'll take you back to my house until we can make contact with your people and get you back home."

He let his eyes close. "Whatever you think best."

She studied him anxiously. "You're being too damned agreeable."

Llyr grunted. "I'm not exactly in a position to play autocrat."

"Guess not. Look, just wait here. I'll be back in five minutes." She stood, then stopped and looked around. "You don't think the vampire's anywhere around?"

"I have no idea."

"Great. Just fucking great." She hurried off.

Fortunately, Diana had parked the car beside a fire truck, out of the immediate view of the hotel. She slid in, started the engine, and drove off across the parking lot without turning on the lights.

Reaching the edge of the lawn, she drove across the expanse of yard to the spot she'd left Llyr. With any luck, nobody was watching. Unfortunately, Gist was probably at work organizing a search around the hotel for any injured, so she'd better act fast. Parking the car as close to Llyr as she could get, she got out and started toward him. If he couldn't walk, she'd have to transform into the Dire Wolf and carry him.

"You want to tell me what the fuck you're doing?" Gist demanded.

Startled, she spun to see him standing just downwind, all but invisible in his dark uniform, his hands on his hips. "What are you doing here?"

"After the way you dove out that damn hole, I was afraid you might be in trouble. Instead, I find you sneaking around in the dark."

She took a deep breath. "I found the FBI agent. He's been hurt."

"So we'll get the ambulance over here."

"We can't. He's not human."

The chief stiffened. "Shit. First the killer, now him— what is this, a spook convention?"

"That's about the size of it. We can't take him to the hospital. I'm going to let him recover at my house."

Gist searched her face in the dim moonlight, then nod- ded. "Think he'll be okay?"

"I hope so."

"Need a hand?"

"Probably." She led him over to where Llyr lay. The Sidhe king didn't move. "Llyr?"

Gist dropped to one knee beside him as Diana knelt at his shoulders. "Jesus, don't these people own clothes? He looks like somebody chewed him up and spit him out. And that wound in his arm is ugly. You sure you don't want to take him to the doctor?"

"Yes." She bent to listen to his broad chest. To her relief, he was still breathing, his heartbeat steady if a little fast. "Llyr? Come on, Your Majesty, we've got to get you into the car."

"Your Majesty?"

She ignored the chief's incredulous stare and shook the Sidhe by one broad shoulder. Opalescent eyes opened. "There you are. Think you can get up? We've got to get you into the car."

He groaned something that sounded like a Sidhe curse and rolled over onto his hands and knees, his wounded arm tucked against his body. Even bruised and bloody, his broad back was magnificent. As he started to push himself to his feet, Diana crouched to help. The chief took the other side, then hastily shifted his grip to the king's waist as Llyr hissed in pain.

He eyed Gist woozily. "You are her policeman. What are you doing here?"

"It's okay, Llyr, the chief can keep his mouth shut," Diana said.

Gist snorted. "Wouldn't keep this job long if I couldn't."

Between the two of them, they managed to get the Sidhe into Diana's car. Judging from the tight, pale line of his mouth, it hurt. A lot. Diana buckled him in—he tolerated the process in stony silence—and hurried around to the driver's side.

As she opened the door, Gist stepped up and caught it to stop her. "I don't like this, Diana," he said in a low voice. "I think you're in over your head. I know for damn sure I'm in over mine. What the hell are we fighting here?"

She looked at him, weighing what to tell him. "It's a vampire, Bill."

His eyes widened. "Shit."

"Yeah." Diana got in and started the car, then drove across the yard. The car bumped over the curb and back onto the street. She hit the gas and headed for home.

Llyr, sitting pale and silent, suddenly spoke. "It is not a good idea for mortals to know so much about us, Diana."

"I told you, the chief can keep his mouth shut."

"Not if someone casts the right spell on him."

"Okay, that's a point," Diana admitted. "But when I first told him about me, I never expected to encounter any other magical beings. Direkind rarely have any contact with the Mageverse."

He nodded reluctantly. "I suppose not."

She stole a glance at him. To her hyperacute senses, he didn't smell healthy. "How are you?"

"Half blind. My head feels as though someone has driven an iron spike into each eye, and my shoulder feels like raw meat." His voice dropped. "But I am still far better off than the men who died for me."

Diana winced. "I'm sorry about your guards."

"I should have protected them. I . . ."

"Llyr, who was whose bodyguard?"

He threw her an impatient look. "They were my guards, but I was their king. It's my responsibility to protect my people against magical threats."

"Isn't that a little unrealistic? The President of the United States doesn't expect to protect the Secret Service."

"Your president does not have my power." He turned a brooding gaze out the window. "Yet I allowed my men to be separated and butchered because I was so intent on creating that spell, I didn't realize what was happening."

"What spell?"

He shrugged. "Something that would have allowed me to sense when the vampire appeared so we could stop her."

"Damn, I wish you'd been able to complete that. It would have come in handy."

"Yes." He sucked in a breath as they bounced over a pothole. He must be in serious pain. She only wished she could do something for him.

"How fast do you guys heal on your own?"

The car rounded a curve and he hissed as the shoulder belt put pressure on his arm. "I do not know from personal experience, but I'm told it's fairly quickly. With any luck"—Llyr blew out a breath—"the shoulder should be fine by tomorrow."

"It had better, or I'm taking your ass to the hospital," she told him grimly. "A one-armed king wouldn't be much good to the Cachamwri."

"Let's hope it does not come to that," Llyr said. "Going to your hospital would make matters entirely too complicated. Once my powers return, it's possible I could bespell the mortals into forgetting about me, but I would prefer to avoid the problem altogether."

Diana drummed her fingers on the wheel. "When do you think your people will realize something's wrong and come looking for you?"

He started to shrug, then froze with a wince. "That depends on whether someone has a vision that I'm in need of help. If that were to happen, they could locate me almost immediately. Unfortunately, my advisors knew I intended to remain in Verdaville for several days while we searched for the vampire, so it could be some time before they start looking."

"And in the meantime, I've got to keep the vampire from killing you."

He sent her an icy look. "I am more than capable of protecting myself."

"Thus the ten-man bodyguard team." She snapped her teeth closed. *Great going, Diana. Stomp the man's ego.*

"I am alive, am I not?" Llyr growled. He immediately looked stricken. She knew he was thinking about the men he'd lost.

Diana pulled the car into her driveway and pulled as close to the door as she could get before she went to help Llyr.

By the time she reached the passenger side, however, he'd already opened the door and was levering his way grimly to his feet. His expression was set and white, and from the stiff, too-careful way he moved, she knew he was in a great deal of pain. She reached for his waist, but he warned her off with an icy glare. "I can walk."

"You can also fall on your face."

"If I do, it's my affair."

She scowled at him in frustration. "You're being impossible. You know that, right?"

"Yes, but I don't particularly care." He started toward the door, his steps much shorter than his usual confident stride.

Diana huffed, bit back the half dozen comments on male pigheadedness that leaped to mind, and went to open the door for him. He hobbled past her.

"It's a good thing it's four o'clock in the morning," she said, trying for a mild joke. "Otherwise it would be all over town tomorrow that the city administrator brought a naked man home."

He grunted.

Okaaay, Diana thought. *We're definitely not in the mood for humor.*

She directed him through the living room and down the hall to her bedroom. Flipping the covers back, she watched him gingerly lower himself onto the mattress. Bruises had begun to bloom across his body like huge purple flowers. The gash in his shoulder had stopped bleeding, but drying blood covered his left side.

She frowned, looking down at him. "I have got to get you cleaned up. You can't sleep that way."

"I'll . . ." He lifted one hand as though about to cast a spell, then lowered it with an expression of disgust. "Still nothing."

"So we'll do it the old-fashioned way." She went off to gather what she needed.

Diana returned a few minutes later with a basin of water, a cloth, and some kind of metal box she held tucked under one arm. Llyr suppressed a sigh of resignation, knowing this was probably going to be a painful process, given the state of his battered body. Though frankly, his head was pounding so viciously, a little extra pain would hardly make a difference one way or another.

"Fortunately, the mayor gave me a first aid kit for Christmas one year," she said, putting the basin down on a small table beside the bed. "I don't generally keep medical supplies in the house, since I can heal damn near any wound just by transforming." With ruthless efficiency, she started tearing clear wrappings off the box.

Llyr sighed. "The last time I was powerless, my grandmother put me back to rights with one spell." He shifted on the pillow as Diana flipped open the box and rummaged inside. He had to bite down on his lip to keep the grunt of pain behind his teeth. "I'd dearly like to have her here now."

"Well, you're just going to have to make do with me tonight. Or this morning. Or whatever—ah! Ibuprofen! Just the thing for that headache." She pulled out a small bottle, uncapped it, and poured some pills into her hand, then handed them over. "Hang tight, handsome. I'll go get you some water to take those with."

Llyr watched her pretty rump roll as she got up and headed for the bathroom. Her cheeks in those tight blue pants were deliciously rounded, seeming to beg for his hands. Despite his pounding headache and the tearing pain in his arm, his cock twitched. He smiled without humor. *I must be in better health than I thought, if I can get a cockstand just watching her cross the room.*

Then again, Diana could probably give a corpse a cockstand. Particularly this time of year, with her body producing all those potent pheromones.

Listening to the sound of running water from the bathroom, Llyr bounced the pills in his palm and contemplated the idea of a seduction. Unfortunately, he had a feeling he'd disappoint them both. He felt wretched.

If she'd even let him get close after the way he'd slapped her down this morning. Llyr grimaced in regret, knowing he should apologize.

By the time she came out a moment later, his cock had surrendered to both reality and guilt. But when she bent to hand him a goblet of water, the curve of her breasts was enough to make it twitch in interest. She lifted a brow at his sigh. "Just bemoaning my injuries," Llyr said, his gaze lingering on her breasts.

"Take the pills."

"Human medicine." He snorted. "Any Sidhe child could do better."

"Yeah, well, unfortunately we don't have any Sidhe kids here, so you're going to have to settle for the pills. You might be surprised. When I've got a headache and it's inconvenient to transform, they work wonders."

As he obediently downed them, she dipped the cloth in water and rubbed up a lather with a bar of soap.

He was forced to pull in a breath when she went to work cleaning away the dirt and blood. Yet despite the sting of the cloth rasping over his injured skin, her touch was so light and deft, he found himself swallowing his protests. True, he was perfectly capable of washing his own hurts—but it was so much more enjoyable when she did it.

Which reminded him. He cleared his throat. "I'm sorry."

She looked up at him, a dark brow lifted. "For what?"

"For the way I treated you this morning."

She stiffened slightly. "Oh. That."

"Yes, that." Llyr hesitated, trying to think of a way to explain. "What happened to my guards today isn't really all that unusual for me. I've lost four wives and ten children to assassins."

Her eyes widened. "My God."

"Being someone I care about isn't a particularly healthy role."

She gave him a long, cool stare. "So you're saying this morning's brush-off was your way of keeping me safe."

He owed her honesty. "And myself, as well. I have grown weary of losing people."

Diana fell silent, stroking the cloth over his skin. They fell into a dark silence while he remembered the wives he'd lost. And the children, all his handsome, bright children . . .

"My father says there's nothing a parent fears more than burying a child," she offered finally.

Llyr nodded sadly. "Particularly for my kind, for the Sidhe are much less fertile than humans. And to lose so many is particularly painful. Mind you, all my children were adults when they fell to Ansgar's assassins—the oldest was four hundred years old. But the point is, they were immortal. They should not have died at all."

He let his head fall back against the pillow as the memories poured in on him. "Ansgar has a great deal to answer for," Llyr said softly, as his shoulder and head throbbed in renewed pain, an aching backdrop for his grief. "And one day, I'll make him pay full measure."

It really wasn't fair, Diana thought. Llyr was obscenely beautiful even when he looked as if he'd gone fifteen rounds with a tyrannosaurus Rex. What was more, the sadness on his handsome face only added to his appeal.

He lay back against the mound of pillows, his brilliant hair tumbled around his brawny shoulders. She made a mental note to brush it for him; there were leaves and sticks tangled up in it from his flight through the trees.

Diana had never considered herself much of a nurturer, yet she found it oddly satisfying to tend his injuries. When the water went cool and rust-colored, she returned to the bathroom, emptied the plastic basin, and refilled it with warm, soapy water again.

Stepping back into the room, she found herself stopping just to look at him. He seemed to be dozing, as though finally worn out by pain and sadness, his athletic body lax against the sheets.

Frowning, she wondered if she should wake him. She seemed to recall that people with head injuries shouldn't sleep. And considering the way he'd slammed into that tree, he was virtually guaranteed to have given himself a good concussion.

She went to sit beside him and cleared her throat. "How's your head?"

"Aches." He didn't open his eyes. "But your mortal pills do seem to have helped."

"What year is it?"

"Sixteen hundred and four."

Oh, hell. " 'Fraid not, Majesty. Try 2005."

He cracked one eyelid. "Sidhe years, not your calendar. It's the sixteen hundred and fourth year of my reign."

Diana stared at him. "The Sidhe calendar is based on how long you've been on the throne?"

"The Cachamwri Sidhe's is. Though the calendar of the Morven Sidhe is the same, since my brother took his throne at the same time."

Damn. He'd been king sixteen hundred years. "It's a wonder you're not even more arrogant than you are."

His tone went dry. "Thank you."

"You're welcome." Tilting her head, she appraised him. "You seem to be tracking pretty well, assuming you're right about the date." Scooting closer, Diana gently probed his head. His eyes drifted shut. She got the distinct impression he enjoyed her careful touch. "No lumps," she said finally, after a thorough exploration. "That's a miracle in itself."

"I managed to put up a cushion the instant before I hit. Must have been the last of my magic."

"I hate to think the shape you'd have been in if you hadn't. No way in hell would I be capable of treating a head injury like that." Relieved, she dipped her cloth in the water and went back to washing him off.

"I don't know. You're doing quite well."

Meeting his brilliant eyes, Diana felt heat pour into her cheeks. *Oh, great, I'm blushing*. She ducked her head. "Thanks."

Finished cleaning him off, she bandaged the sword wound in his shoulder with a sterile pad and tape, then went on to treat the rest of his cuts and scrapes with a tube of antibiotic gel. He relaxed with a sigh.

She'd just finished bandaging one of the nastier scratches on one arm when she realized he had an erection. The long, heavy shaft lay over his belly in a rigid curve, thick and flushed dark.

Diana's Burning Moon sex drive instantly awoke with a low mental rumble. Damn, that was all she needed.

This really isn't the time, she told it. It didn't seem to care.

ELEVEN

"You can't possibly be turned on," Diana protested faintly.

"And yet, the evidence suggests otherwise." There was dry amusement in Llyr's tone.

"It certainly does." God, she wanted to wrap her hand around his thick, hard shaft, cup those heavy balls in her palm . . . Diana dragged her eyes away.

His gaze dropped to her chest. "What do you call that tunic you're wearing?"

She glanced down. "It's a T-shirt."

"I like the way it hugs your breasts." His voice rasped. "Though I don't particularly care for the wording."

Diana grinned. Printed in big white letters across her bust was 25% SWEETHEART—75% BITCH. "It was a gag gift from my brother. He said it's only fair to warn people. Not that I wear it out in public, since the mayor wouldn't exactly approve."

"Neither do I. You're not a bitch, Diana."

"Oh, I can be. Believe me."

"I'm not talking about your wolf form."

"That's not the only one I do, Llyr." She thought about showing him the Dire Wolf, then decided against it. There was nothing like watching his sex partner turn into a seven-foot monster to give a man a sudden case of impotence.

A big, warm hand descended on her thigh. "I would like to make love to you," he said softly. "But I fear not being able to finish what I start."

Her libido gave a disappointed growl, but she shushed it and rose to her feet. "I'm pretty wiped out myself. Good thing it's Friday." Bending to pick up the basin, she paused. "Actually, Saturday morning." She shrugged and dropped the washcloth into the water.

He watched her carry the basin into the bathroom. "What difference does that make?"

"Means I don't have to work tomorrow. Most mortals work Monday through Friday. Which means we both get time to recuperate." Diana emptied the basin down the sink. "Here's hoping Vampire Bitch takes the weekend off."

"Unfortunately, I doubt we'll be that lucky."

"I do, too." She washed out the basin and rinsed the rag before tossing it into the dirty clothes hamper, promising herself she'd do the laundry later. "Then again, maybe you hurt her and she'll stay holed up a while."

"It's possible. That explosion when our spells collided probably hit her as hard as it did me."

Diana, on her way back into the room, stopped in her tracks. "Well, that would explain the holes in the wall. Looked like she was blown right out of your room, across the hall, and into another one next door. Where she evidently killed the occupant."

He raked a brawny hand through his hair. "We have got to do something about her. She can't be allowed to continue this."

"We'll get her."

"If she doesn't get me first."

Diana woke to the scent of aroused male. The Burning Moon sizzled through her blood in response, and she opened her eyes.

Llyr lay next to her, still gloriously naked and deeply asleep, despite an impressive erection.

An erection that had figured prominently in the hormone-addled dreams she'd enjoyed curled up against his delicious body.

She rolled onto one elbow and contemplated him. One or the other of them had kicked the covers off during the night, and the flowered top sheet lay wadded at their feet. Diana could look her fill.

Sunlight poured across the pale contours of the king's body, gleaming in his golden hair. His cock reared over his belly in a long, smooth curve. Her first impulse was to pounce on it, but mindful of his injuries, she squashed the urge.

But as she scanned him, Diana was delighted to note the constellation of bruises and scrapes had already disappeared. Carefully, she peeked under the bandage on his shoulder. To her relief, it, too, had faded into a faint pink scar.

"You really do heal fast," Diana muttered. "Good thing, too. I've got a feeling we'll be seeing more of Vampire Bitch."

Looking up, she checked out the alarm clock standing

on her bedside table. It was just after noon; they'd slept the morning away.

The question is, her libido purred, *is Llyr up to a brisk game of erotic Twister with a very horny werewolf?*

"Well, his cock certainly thinks so," she muttered. "And who am I to argue?"

She rolled onto her belly beside his hip and contemplated his straining erection. Shooting a wicked glance up his torso at his sleeping face, Diana purred, "Wakey, wakey, Tinkerstud. I want to play with your magic wand."

He stirred, but his eyes didn't open.

She decided she wasn't going to wait. Catching his cock in one hand, she swooped her mouth down over its tight, flushed head in one eager gulp.

Llyr was in the middle of another confused dream—his body's reaction to his bedmate's pheromones warring with his guilt over his bodyguards' deaths—when hot, wet pleasure jolted him awake.

He opened his eyes to the sight of Diana's mouth engulfing his shaft inch by delicious, teasing inch.

For a moment, all he could do was lay there, his brain reeling at the sizzling eroticism of the moment. Then she paused midway down his shaft and sucked so hard her cheeks hollowed, and he thought the top of his head was going to blow off.

Llyr groaned, the sound heartfelt and tormented. Diana lifted her head, releasing his cock with a wet *pop*, and gave him an impish grin. "Good morning."

He had to swallow before he could answer. "It certainly has been so far."

"Glad you approve." She bent her head and sucked him back in again, one slim, possessive hand cupping his balls.

Llyr found himself digging his fingers into the mattress as he fought not to come. "You know," he gasped, "if you have plans of me being any good at all to you, it might be wise to stop." A particularly hard pull forced him to add, "Now."

Diana lifted her head. "Why, Majesty. Am I getting to you?"

"Yes."

"Good." She bent again. Before she could swoop his cock back down her seductive throat, he grabbed her by the shoulder, flipped her over, and pounced. As sternly as he could considering his aching erection, he growled, "Enough!"

Diana considered the question. "No. No, I don't think so."

"Wanton." He took her mouth in an act of sheer self-defense.

She rumbled in silken approval, arching her lithe body against him. Her lips tasted so sweet he couldn't resist lingering.

Llyr kissed her slowly with famished heat. She moaned into his mouth and slid her arms around his waist, simultaneously opening her legs to him. He settled into the warm cradle of her hips with a happy sigh and kept right on kissing her.

Diana's rose-petal lips were just as skilled as they were soft. She kissed him in gentle nibbles, suckling softly at his lower lip, swirling her tongue around his. Llyr had kissed countless women over his long life, but he'd never realized how delicately erotic the act was.

He loved the way she felt, undulating against him like a cat demanding a petting. He adored the wet, soft heat of her mouth, the smell of her skin, the slim strength of her body under his. Experienced seducer though he was, it all seemed as entrancing as if he was a virgin, lost in the sheer, sweet pleasure of passion for the first time.

Llyr was so absorbed in the simple pleasure of her mouth, long minutes went by before he decided to seek the rest of her body.

Diana had gone to bed wearing that T-shirt and a tiny pair of silk panties, but even that felt like too great a barrier to his starving body. He reared off her just enough to give himself room to push the hem of her shirt up, baring her small, delectable breasts. Her nipples were a tight and eager pink.

Llyr stopped and just looked at them for a long moment, admiring the way they rode the gentle mounds. "You're so lovely," he said in a low voice.

"You're not bad yourself, Tinkerstud."

" 'Tinkerstud?' Should I ask you what that means?"

Diana laughed, the sound a bit ragged with hunger. "You don't want to know."

"I think I should teach you to have a little more respect." He looked down at those tempting nipples. "Later." Bending, he sucked one into his mouth. It stabbed his tongue, as deliciously firm as a grape. Ravenous, he drew on it in deep, slow pulls, circling his tongue over and around the tiny peak.

Cupping the other breast in his hand, he closed his eyes in pleasure at the satin sensation of her flesh, so warm and soft in his. She made an approving little rumbling sound, and he caught her nipple between thumb and forefinger. Carefully, he tugged, enjoying the way she caught her breath. When he rolled the tip back and forth between his fingers, she pumped her hips against him pleadingly.

He lifted his mouth from the nipple he was pleasuring. She met his gaze, her eyes wide, pale and unfocused with the force of her need. "More?" he asked softly, teasingly.

"God, yes." Diana wrapped her legs around his waist. As she moved, the feral perfume of her lust teased his senses. It was his turn to pant as his hunger spiraled.

Reaching a hand down, he wrapped his fingers in the waistband of her panties and twisted. Silk tore.

She laughed even as she pushed her head back into the pillow in extravagant pleasure. "You're murder on my underwear, you know that?"

"I'll magic you more as soon as my powers come back." Hungry to learn if she was as wet as she smelled, Llyr eased his hips up enough to give himself room to probe her sex with his fingers.

He found her just as richly slick as he was hard. Her snug little channel gripped his index finger, obviously yearning for something thicker. His cock throbbed, eager to oblige.

Pulling off her, Llyr sat back on his heels, knowing he needed a moment to cool off. He was far too close to spending.

Dragon's Breath, she was beautiful. She smiled up at him, her pale wolf eyes bright with cheerful passion, her lips curled into a smile. Her short hair was completely disordered from rubbing against a pillow all night. It stood straight up in a crown of dark, waving curls that curled his lips into a besotted smile.

But the demanding throb in his balls wanted even more. With a growl, Llyr scooped her delicious behind off the sheets, draped her knees over the crook of his elbows, and positioned her over his aching cock. For a moment he hesitated, just looking down at her bounty, so pink and wet and nakedly erotic. "Dragon's Breath, you drive me insane."

"You have the same effect on me." Her smile was hot and wicked. "Why don't you start getting all that cock in me? Now's good."

"Your wish is my command." Taking his erection in hand, Llyr slowly, deliciously, began to work his way inside. Her tight little sex welcomed him with snug, slick walls.

The first inch was almost enough to make him come, but somehow he held on. He slid deeper, listening to her heart-felt moans of pleasure as he went.

The challenge only got greater when Llyr was finally in to the balls. As his groin settled against her velvety backside, he hoped he could last long enough to give her what she needed. Teeth clenched, he began the slow, delicious withdrawal.

"God, Llyr," she gasped. "You feel so good!"

"May I—*ah!*—say the same, my lady."

She bucked once, violently. "You're making me crazy. Please—more!"

The sensation of her burning, wet-satin heat clamping around him as she ground her hips snapped his control like a lute string. With a growl, he began to ride her, lunging hard in her delicious grip. He could feel his orgasm getting ready to break, but he clenched his teeth and fought it. He was damn well going to hold on long enough to share it with her.

Diana did not wait passively. She tightened her muscled legs, dragging him close and deeper as she hunched against him. Slim fingers tangled in his hair. "Harder!" she gritted.

"As my lady commands!" He braced his fists on the mattress and pounded, his pelvis slapping against hers.

"Yes! Oh, yes, that's it!" Her eyes stared up into his, dazed with passion, her mouth swollen with his kisses. Llyr knew he'd never seen a woman more beautiful, not even the ones he'd married.

Fire roared over him. He tumbled willingly, stiffening as he came, emptying his balls into her in burning pulses. She writhed against him, her legs gripping his backside hard, holding him deep. "Llyr!"

"Yes! Diana!"

He came until his trembling arms would no longer hold him braced. Until he collapsed into her arms to hold on to her as the electric jolts of pleasure faded.

"Well," Diana said hoarsely when she was capable of speech, "that's one way to kick off a weekend."

"Does that mean you approve?"

"Oh, yeah."

He rolled off her with a groan and collapsed onto his back, only to immediately reach over and haul her into his arms, draping her across his chest like a scarf. With a collective sigh, they settled into comfortable bliss.

His heartbeat thundered in her ears. Their skin felt damp and sweaty with delicious effort. Time spun away.

Long moments passed before Diana had the strength to lift her head again. There were still leaves in his hair from the night before. "Don't take this the wrong way, but you need a shower. And somebody needs to currycomb that mane of yours."

"Currycomb?"

She flashed a grin at him. "Seems appropriate for a stallion." Rolling off the bed and onto her feet, she looked down at him. He sprawled in brawny, exhausted masculinity and didn't even stir. "Come on, Llyr. Hi ho, Silver."

He cracked an opalescent eye. "That sounds like another obscure mortal reference."

She snickered. "I need to park you in front of the television and make you watch TV Land for a couple hundred hours. We have got to do something about that appalling cultural ignorance."

"I'm not sure I'd call whatever you mortals have 'culture.'" Llyr raked his hair out of his face and grimaced when his hand caught in a tangle. He flicked his fingers in an attempted spell and scowled when it failed. "My powers are still gone. And my hair is a dragon's nest."

"That's why we ignorant, uncultured mortals invented the comb. Come on, I'll wash it for you. It'll be easier to work with wet."

It didn't take Llyr long to grasp the erotic potential of a shower, particularly when combined with mounds of shampoo lather. Diana soon found herself pressed against the tiled wall with her legs wrapped around his waist while he pounded them both to another dizzying climax. By the time they staggered out again, the water was cold and her thigh muscles were quivering.

"Mortal plumbing leaves much to be desired," Llyr told her with a groan as she handed him a towel.

When he stared at it, clueless, she took it from his hand and started briskly toweling him off. "I'm deeply sorry I didn't foresee the need for a hot water heater big enough to let you work your way through the Kama Sutra. Do you ever do *anything* without using magic? Where did you get these muscles?"

"Sword practice and hunting."

"What, you don't just fry the poor little beasties with a fireball?"

"Magic leaves an unpleasant aftertaste in the meat."

She stared. "You're kidding me."

Llyr smirked. "Mortals are so gullible."

"Remind me to take you hunting for a rare, endangered Earth creature. It's called a snipe."

"Does it breathe fire?"

Diana shot him a disgusted look as she grabbed a fresh towel and started drying herself off. "Sucker. Kids take other kids out in the woods and use the lure of a snipe hunt to get them to run around after rustling bushes in the dark. But I've gotta ask—do most of the things you hunt breathe fire?"

"No."

"Well, that's good."

"A few of them breathe acid."

Diana stopped and stared. "You're pulling my leg."

"I haven't touched your leg. But I am deeply interested in your breasts." He reached for a nipple.

She stepped nimbly away. "It's a figure of speech, pervert. It means you're playing a joke on me."

"Ah. No, I am quite serious." He watched her breasts bob as she finished toweling herself. "After all, if I never did anything but lie about and work magic, how would I defend my people against genuine threats? I might freeze the first time I was in danger."

"That makes sense." Though it was harder to imagine Llyr frozen with terror than it was to picture an acid-breathing magical monster. She lowered the commode lid and turned to get a brush and comb from a drawer. "Have a seat. We need to get started on that mane of yours before it dries."

After persuading him to sit sideways on the toilet lid, she stepped up against his broad back, picked up a silken hank of his hair, and went to work. "Seems to me fighting mystical fire-breathing critters is the kind of activity that would drive your bodyguard nuts."

"Actually, it's not as dangerous as you might think. So many Sidhe turn out to watch, if I did get seriously hurt, someone would heal me."

He fell silent. Diana discovered a complicated snarl and concentrated on combing it out. There was something deeply sensual about coaxing the wet, gleaming mass to straighten out and lie flat down his broad back. "You know," she said, stroking the brush through his hair, "something's been bugging me. What's Ansgar's problem with you, anyway? Why does he keep trying to kill you? And why kill your wives and children?"

Llyr shrugged. "He wants both kingdoms. Besides, he's hated me since the day I was born."

"Sibling rivalry?"

"And because of this." He extended his uninjured shoulder, drawing her attention to an intricate dragon curled around his biceps.

Diana bent closer to admire it. The detail was so exquisitely fine, each iridescent scale shimmered as if alive. She took a sniff and whistled soundlessly. "You know, whatever took your powers obviously didn't affect this tattoo. I can still smell the magic."

He shook his head. "It's not a tattoo. I was born with it—it's the Dragon's Mark. And yes, it's definitely magic. For thousands of years, one son of each generation of my line has been born with this. It's called the Mark of Heroes, and it means that, at least in theory, I can call on Cachamwri in my hour of greatest peril."

She blinked, impressed. "The God of Dragons? Cool."

"You've heard of him?"

"Oh, yeah. My grandfather loved to tell all kinds of stories about the Mageverse, the Sidhe, and the Magekind. He especially loved the ones about Dragonkind and Cachamwri."

"Did he tell you how Galatyn the First helped save Cachamwri from Uchdryd the Dark One?"

"No, but I'm always up for a story." She picked a waterlogged twig out of his hair.

Llyr settled back against her with the air of a man getting ready to tell an old and favored tale. "When the Dark Ones first came to this world, they invaded Mageverse Earth first. In those days, the Sidhe were as mortal as humans . . ."

"Yeah? How did you become immortal?"

"I will get to that. As I said, the Sidhe were much like our human cousins then, mortal and prolific, though unlike them, we had evolved welding magic. Still, we did not have the strength to fend off the Dark Ones. But the dragons of our world did, and they had no interest in sharing Sidhe Earth with such as the Dark Ones."

"Judging from what I've heard about that bunch, I don't blame them."

"Indeed. The Dark Ones were just as unpleasant to Dragonkind as they were to humans, killing and torturing as they chose. So Cachamwri, King of the Dragons—he was not yet a god then—decided to lead his people against the Dark Ones."

"Good for him."

"Yes, but unfortunately, the attack was repelled and Cachamwri was captured."

"Ouch. Bet that got ugly."

"It did. He was imprisoned deep inside the fortress of the Dark Ones' high general, Uchdryd, where he was tortured and starved. It was there that my ancestor found him—Galatyn the First, who had slipped into the fortress with a party of his raiders to take revenge for the death of his woman."

"Oooh. Romantic. What happened to her?"

"That's a story for another time. As I was saying, Galatyn found Cachamwri in the dungeon. Now, the dragons and the Sidhe had always been enemies, but Galatyn put aside his hate in favor of forming an alliance. He worked a spell with the dragon, giving him the power to break free. Then he and Cachamwri went through the fortress and killed every Dark One they could find, with the Dragon absorbing the life force the aliens had stolen from his people."

"Poetic justice."

"Indeed. By the time they slew Uchdryd himself, Cachamwri had absorbed so much magic, he'd become a god. The remaining Dark Ones fled to Mortal Earth, and he chose not to pursue them. Instead, he rewarded the Sidhe by making them immortal. In gratitude, our tribe adopted Cachamwri's name and made Galatyn their king. But that wasn't the end of his honors, for Cachamwri put a mark on him so that the Dragon God would always recognize the heroes of his line. From then on, my people have been allies with the dragons, and certain chosen Galatyn males have been born the Heir to Heroes. The Dragon's Mark obliges them to serve Cachamwri at his call, but he also vows to lend us his power in our hour of greatest peril."

Suddenly a great deal was very clear. "Ansgar didn't get the mark. And you did."

"Exactly. He was two hundred years old when I was born with Cachamwri's brand, and he hated me from then on."

"Considering his personality, it's amazing he didn't arrange for you to meet with some unpleasant accident in childhood."

Llyr shrugged. "I probably would have, but Ansgar believed our father favored him, mark or no. It was only as Dearg lay dying that the terms of our inheritance were revealed."

"So why haven't you just taken him out? Under the circumstances, it sounds as if you'd be justified."

"Perhaps, but my father had no intention of allowing it. He laid a deathbed curse on us. If either of us tried to kill the other with magic, the curse would kill him instantly."

Diana gave him an incredulous look. "But the curse doesn't kick in if Ansgar uses assassins?"

"No, but my father ordered the elders of both kingdoms to repudiate whichever of us kills the other."

"Dearg didn't realize Ansgar would attempt it anyway and just try to cover it up?"

"Apparently not."

"Fantastic." She mulled the implications for several minutes before she noticed his air of dark brooding. "What's wrong?"

"I was thinking about my men." His gaze was bleak. "And Janieda. I dreamed of her again last night."

Diana froze, the comb midway through a hank of blond silk. Deliberately, she started combing again. "Janieda? I don't believe you've mentioned a Janieda."

"No." He was definitely brooding.

She let the silence slide past until she couldn't stand it anymore. "If that's your wife, I'm going to pull that shower rod out of the wall and beat you over the head with it."

Llyr twisted to look at her, surprised. "If I had a wife, I would not have made love to you. Sidhe kings do not break their vows. My people are fairly tolerant of infidelity, but not in a ruler."

"Yeah?" Diana grinned, more relieved than she cared to show. "I'd tell a Clinton joke, but you wouldn't get it."

"I get very few of your jokes."

"I noticed that."

"You wouldn't get mine either, which is why I'm too polite to tell them."

"Two orcs walk into a bar? Heard it." She smirked and scooped up another handful of blond hair.

"And everybody else runs out the back."

Diana frowned down at the top of his head, where a truly impressive tangle had taken up residence. "What in the heck are you talking about?"

"The joke. Two orcs walk into a tavern, and everyone else runs out the back."

"Wait a minute. That's a real joke?" She bent over to

look him in the eye, incredulous. "And that's the punch line?"

He gave her an innocent blink. "Why, yes. I thought you'd said you'd heard it."

"That's the stupidest joke I've ever been subjected to in my entire life."

"Not really. If two orcs walked into a tavern, everybody *would* run out the back."

This time she caught the sly glint in his gaze. "You lyin' Sidhe devil! You ought to be ashamed, taking advantage of me like that."

He grinned. "But I love taking advantage of you, Diana. Each and every way I can."

Diana planted her comb in the knot and gave it a hard yank. When he yelped in outrage, she said sweetly, "Did that hurt? I'm so sorry."

"When was the last time you were spanked?"

"I don't remember. I ate the last guy who tried it."

Satisfied with the results of their sparring, the two fell into a companionable silence while she worked on his hair. Finally she asked, "So what's with this Janieda?"

Any humor vanished from his voice. "She's dead. She died ten days ago protecting me. She was my mistress."

TWELVE

Llyr's last mistress was dead. Had Ansgar got to her, too?

Diana stilled. "Oh."

"We were lovers for a century," he said, his voice soft. "I thought I loved her. And yet, I have barely thought of her since I've been here."

"What happened?"

"I had bound myself with a Maja into a death spell in order to kill Geirolf."

"That was the demon god, right?"

"Indeed. The spell worked, but the Maja was left powerless. She was attacked by one of Geirolf's vampires, but Janieda used her own magical essence to protect her rather than escaping to safety. Otherwise, the spell was so powerful, it would have dragged me into death with the Maja."

He slumped. "Janieda died in that battle. Too often, that seems to be the way it ends."

Diana put the comb aside and stoked her fingers through the smooth, bright silk of his hair. "It's not your fault, Llyr. You're not responsible for the crimes other people commit."

"Perhaps not, but I do seem to provide the inspiration." He twisted around to face her. "You said you would protect me if the vampire came after me again, but I don't want you paying that price. You aren't one of my people. You don't have that duty to the Cachamwri." He rose and strode naked from the bathroom.

Automatically admiring his muscular ass, she murmured, "We have got to find you something to wear." Then she strode after him. "Look, Llyr, I'm Direkind. Merlin designed us specifically to contain the Magekind if they lost their collective minds and started preying on mortals. We're highly resistant to magical attacks in a way other humans—even Sidhe—aren't." She caught him by the elbow, dragging him to a stop. "That means if Fangface throws a ball of fire at me, it'll probably just splash off."

He sighed. "I'm aware of that, of course."

"Yeah?"

"Merlin approached me before he created your people. After the way the Sidhe helped the Fae defeat Geirolf and the Dark Ones, he trusted us. Or, at any rate, me. He wasn't as impressed by Ansgar. But he asked me to aid the Direkind if it ever became necessary, and I took a vow to do so. Which is why I never told Arthur about you."

"So you know I'm not helpless."

"That isn't the point . . ."

Diana was opening her mouth to answer when the phone rang. "Dammit." She started toward the nightstand beside her bed. "With my luck, that's another killing."

"Unlikely, since it's the middle of the day. She wouldn't be out this early."

"Damn, I hope you're right." She reached for the phone. "London."

"Is that Llyr guy still naked?" Gist demanded.

Sighing in relief—at least it wasn't another murder—Diana shot the Sidhe a look. He stood glowering at her, his fists on his bare hips, his head lifted at a regal angle. "Yep, I'm afraid the emperor still has no clothes."

"Figured. I got to thinking about that this morning. He's a big guy; I'll bet you don't have anything to fit him."

"You bet right. You got something you could lend us?"

"Yeah, I have a pair of sweatpants and a T-shirt that would fit. And flip-flops he could probably get on those big feet. Does this guy have money, or is he gonna have to sponge off you?"

"Don't worry about it, Bill. He's good for it. And yeah, if we can borrow the clothes until we can hit Wally World, that'd be great."

"You want to come get them, or shall I drop 'em off?"

Her gaze flicked to Llyr's. "I . . . don't want to leave him. Some people are very unfond of him."

"Yeah, I picked that up when I saw the bodies spread all over the Sleep Saver. You want me to come over and help guard him?"

"And get caught in the crossfire with the rest of us? Uh-uh." Besides, considering his vulnerability to magic, the vampire could easily turn Gist into a weapon against them.

"You sure about that?"

"You know me, Bill. Anybody who messes with me, I'll eat."

"Jesus, don't even joke about that. Okay, I'll be over in a few."

"Great. See you, buddy."

"She may not come after me again," Llyr pointed out after Diana hung up.

"I don't know that we can say that, since we don't know why she came after you to begin with."

"She must have discovered I'm hunting her."

"So am I, but she hasn't shown up to blow the hell out of *my* house." Diana frowned, another question occurring to her. "And why *did* she jump you, anyway? If I was going to make a list of people to hit, I damn well wouldn't have taken on the King of the Fairies and all those badass Sidhe bodyguards. That was a big risk to take, when she was doing such a great job of ducking all of us. Why not just go on playing hide-and-seek while she butchered people and laughed at us? Why carry the fight to you like that?"

His eyes narrowed in realization. "Ansgar. She's working for Ansgar."

As promised, Bill Gist showed up half an hour later bearing a paper bag full of clothes. Leaving Llyr upstairs trying to master the concept of the plastic safety razor, Diana went to deal with the chief. Like the nice Southern werewolf she was, she asked him in for a glass of sweet tea.

He followed her into the kitchen, looking troubled. "I met with the coroner this morning. 'Fraid he's going to be a problem."

Diana, reaching into the refrigerator for the tea, looked at him over the door. "Oh, God, what now?"

Gist leaned a hip against a kitchen counter and folded his arms, watching while she poured them a couple of glasses from the pitcher. "You know there were ten of your buddy's dead friends, right? Miller had autopsies done on all of 'em. Now he thinks he's discovered aliens in our midst. Evidently Dr. Garrison told him there were serious 'anomalies' in their blood, though the organ arrangement looks roughly the same."

That made sense; the Sidhe were basically human, though they'd evolved on a magical version of earth. "That's all I need." She handed him a glass. "When's the press conference?" Coroner George Miller was a notorious publicity hog, in part because he was an elected official with no real medical qualifications. The pathologist at the local hospital did autopsies.

"I think Garrison's refusing to cooperate," Gist said, and took a sip from his glass. "He's afraid this is some kind of hoax, and he doesn't want to look like a fool. So he wants to have some more tests done—like DNA—but they'd have to come out of the coroner's budget, and George doesn't want to pay for them."

"He knows County Council would have a mass stroke." Diana downed a deep swallow from her own drink before adding, "And if Garrison doesn't find anything, Miller will have spent a chunk of change his opponent will hang him with in November."

"So you've got some time, but not much. Miller has heard those guys were supposed to be FBI agents, which they're obviously not. He wants to call the real FBI."

"Shit!" And once the Feebees started investigating, they'd connect the dots straight to Diana—and Llyr.

"Don't panic—I told him it was an unfounded rumor, and then I told my guys to keep their fucking mouths shut if they want to keep their jobs."

Diana stared at him. "Oh, Bill. You shouldn't have done that. The girls in my office know they're supposed to be FBI, too. Which means that by now, everybody in town knows. We're not going to be able to keep a lid on this."

The chief shrugged his shoulders. "Yeah, I know, but what the hell was I supposed to do?"

Llyr spoke from the doorway. "It will be taken care of."

"Jesus." Gist scooped the bag he'd brought off the counter and tossed it to Llyr, who caught it automatically. "Go put some clothes on, will you? There's a lady present."

He lifted a golden brow. To Diana, he said, "Once my powers return, I believe I can work a spell that will cover the people who know of this. They'll forget we were here."

"What if it gets on the news?"

"That . . . becomes problematic. That kind of memory change on even a small number of minds requires a great deal of power. Once enough people know it, I won't be able to do anything."

"And you can't do anything now until your powers come back." She rubbed a hand over her stomach. "I think I'm getting an ulcer."

"Powers?" Gist asked. "What is he, a witch?"

"Actually, I'm King of the Fairies."

Gist looked at him. "That would have been my next guess."

"Let's try to keep this quiet for a couple of days," Diana said. "If we can keep it out of the media until Llyr gets his powers back, we'll both be able to keep our jobs." She sighed. "I can't believe I'm involved in a frigging cover-up."

"You do realize if this goes bad, keeping our jobs won't be the problem," Gist said. "If the FBI gets wind that we helped those guys pass as agents and then covered it up, we could go to jail. Obstruction of justice. I'm violating the hell out of my oath."

She sighed. "I know. If it gets out and the FBI shows up, cooperate. Tell the Feebees I ordered you to lie."

He gave her a horrified look. "Like hell."

"I don't want you going to prison for me, Bill."

"Nobody will go to prison," Llyr growled, a stormy expression on his face. "I will not permit it."

"Whatever, Your Majesty," Gist said. "Would you please go put some clothes on? I'm tired of looking at the royal dick."

With a growl, Llyr, wheeled and stalked out of the kitchen.

The chief looked at Diana. "You're doing him, aren't you? You're too laid-back for this time of year otherwise."

"Laid-back?" She stared at him. "This is laid-back?"

"For you, when you're on the Wolfie Rag? Yeah, it is. I expected to have to talk you out of eating the coroner."

"I don't really eat people, Bill."

"This time of year, I'm never sure." His grin faded. "You really like that guy, don't you?"

"Who?"

"Fabio in there."

"I'm going to bite you."

"See what I mean? Bitchy." When she quit laughing, he asked, "You sure you know what you're doing with him?"

Uncomfortable, she looked away. "Hey, it's that time of year, Bill. And he's the first guy I've ever met who's safe."

Gist gave her a long look. "If you think *that* guy is safe, you're not paying attention."

"Susan, you disappoint me."

The vampire jolted out of sleep to find Ansgar standing over her, hot, black rage in his eyes. With a muffled yelp, she rolled out of bed and landed on her feet. He started toward her, and she backed away, her heart pounding. "I fought him!" Susan blurted. "I killed his guards!"

"But you didn't kill Llyr. And you could have." He

clenched his big fists. "The spell worked. It rendered him powerless. You had a perfect opportunity—*and you let it slip through your fingers!*"

His roar made her cringe. "But it rendered me powerless, too. I couldn't . . ."

"You could have found a knife and finished it!" His hand flashed out and wrapped around her throat. He dragged her close. "Fortunately for you, he hasn't regained his powers. You still have a chance."

She swallowed, licking her lips. "I still haven't recovered my full power. Perhaps you could . . ."

"Lend you more of mine?" He laughed shortly. "Not likely. You don't need it. If you must have more, do what you do so well. Kill somebody and feed. Then take care of Llyr."

"Why?" Susan almost quailed at his expression, but forced herself to lift her chin. She didn't dare let him think he could bully her. With Ansgar, it would be a short step from lackey to slave. "Why should I risk myself again? He almost killed me. I see no reason to go against him and the wolf bitch for nothing."

His lids shuttered those glowing black eyes. "Is your life nothing, then? Because if you refuse to do as I order, you're no good to me. And those who are no good to me . . ."

Damn him to bloody hell. "Fine! Fine, I'll kill the little bastard." All she had to do was get rid of him, and then she'd disappear.

Ansgar's fingers tightened around Susan's neck until she gagged. "Don't presume to think you can trick me, vampire. I am a king of the Sidhe, and I have more power than you can imagine. If you disobey me, I will find you. And I will give you such a death as to make your Christian hell a welcome relief."

Shit. "I understand."

"Good." Those black eyes scanned down her body. She was uncomfortably aware of her T-shirt, which was all she wore. With her magic so low, she'd been reduced to wearing her mortal wardrobe again.

A slow smile curved Ansgar's lips, and the shirt vanished.

"Hey!" Instinctively, Susan tried to struggle. "What are . . . ?"

"Stop it." He shot her a single black glance.

Just like that, she was unable to move, bound in magic. She realized what he intended. "No!"

"Oh, yes. I believe you need a lesson in the wages of displeasing me." With a casual flip of his wrist, he tossed her onto the bed.

Susan hit the mattress and bounced. Bound and immobilized, she was unable to keep her face from smacking hard into the stone wall. She fell back onto the bed, stunned.

Dazed, she watched Ansgar stride toward her. His clothing had disappeared, and he had an erection that swayed with each step.

The grin on his face made her blood chill.

"There's a technique to this," Diana told Llyr. "First you swirl it in the ketchup. Then you eat it." Leaning across the picnic table, she popped the fry into his mouth.

He munched thoughtfully. "That's amazing. It's almost edible."

"Okay, so it's not hummingbird ass dipped in ambrosia sauce, or whatever the hell you fairies eat. What do you expect for five bucks?"

"Something a little less greasy." But despite the complaint, he dipped another fry in the blob of ketchup and ate it.

"Snob." She scooped up one of the cheeseburgers they'd picked up at the late-night drive-through. Her radio crackled from its speaker on her shoulder, carrying the news that Jerry Morgan, the other Verdaville cop on duty, had just arrived at the local bar to take care of an unwanted customer.

After their shopping expedition that afternoon—she'd brought Llyr two pairs of jeans and three polo shirts—Diana had decided it would be a good idea to work the third shift in her capacity as a reserve police officer. There was a good chance the vampire would try to claim another victim, and she wanted to be there as soon as the call came in.

Too, Gist had told her that between overtime and illness, manpower was getting dangerously low on that shift. She didn't want Jerry working it alone.

Since Diana had no intention of leaving Llyr alone either, he was playing civilian ride-along. Dressed in his new jeans, a pair of white running shoes, and a blue polo shirt, which brought out the blue flecks in his eyes, he looked much more handsome than he had any business being. She'd carefully tied his hair back so it covered his pointed ears, but the style only emphasized the rough male beauty of his face.

Diana was having to exert real effort in order not to simply stare at him in besotted fascination.

Suddenly Jerry Morgan's voice blasted from the radio on her shoulder. "Code Zero-zero! London, I need some help over here!" To someone else, he snapped, "Get back, sir!"

Zero-zero was the city police code for officer needs emergency assistance. Her heart in her throat, Diana clicked the button on her mike. "Morgan, what's the problem?" She released the button and waited, tense.

He didn't respond.

"Morgan, copy."

Nothing.

"Shit." She jumped up, grabbed her half-eaten sandwich and fries, and shot them toward the nearest trash can as she sprinted for her patrol car. "Come on. We've got trouble."

Llyr scrambled into the front seat and slammed the door as she started the engine and threw the ancient patrol car into gear. She reached down to flip on the lights and sirens, and the car filled with the cycling wail as they screeched out of the city park parking lot.

"What's happening?" Llyr demanded.

Diana didn't answer, too busy keying her shoulder mike. "Verdaville Charlie One-Nine en route to Danny's Bar and Grill to assist Charlie Two-Four. Requesting S.O. assistance."

"Will do, Charlie One-Nine," the county dispatcher replied.

"Diana, what is going on?" Llyr asked again.

She didn't even glance at him, too intent on keeping the patrol car on the road. The 1990 Crown Vic had 120,000 miles on it, and its steering tended to get mushy at high speeds. "Sounds like somebody jumped the other Verdaville cop at our local bar. Could get really nasty, which is why I asked the Sheriff's Office to back us up." The car swerved as she rounded a corner. Diana corrected, swearing. "Dammit. I told the cheap-ass city council we needed to replace this relic, but noooo. We'd have to raise taxes. Well, they don't have to drive this thing at ninety miles an hour through town. Stay on the road, you piece of shit."

"Diana, my love," Llyr said, his voice arch with understatement. "Please remember I don't have my powers. I'm not sure, but I suspect running into a tree at this speed would not be pleasant."

"Neither is a drunk beating Jerry Morgan to death. Dammit, it would help if Mike Williams hadn't called in with the flu. And Jimmy Patterson worked fifteen hours of overtime on the murders and took the night off. We've got to do something about manpower . . ."

They rounded a curve and the bar appeared ahead of them. Diana started slowing the car in preparation for pulling in and got a good look at the parking lot. "Oh, fantastic. Every redneck in twenty square miles must be out on the town."

A crowd of people milled around in the bar's parking lot. A flurry of motion close to the door of the business had all the taletell signs of a brawl.

Diana's heart began to pound as her stomach knotted. This could get ugly, even with her powers. She drove the car right into the crowd, the members of which immediately began to scatter like cockroaches.

But the knot of brawlers kept right on going, pounding at one another in a flurry of punches. She grabbed her shoulder mike and reached for the door with the other hand. "Verdaville One-Nine, 10–23 at Danny's Bar. Where's our backup?"

"Ten-four, Verdaville. Nearest S.O. units are tied up. They say it'll be fifteen to twenty minutes before they can respond."

And then they'd have to drive all the way to Verdaville. "Fan-damn-tastic. You stay in the car," Diana said to Llyr as she threw open the car door.

"I think not." He swung out after her. "I don't care for the odds."

Diana didn't have time to argue with him. "Fine. Stick with me, then. And for God's sake, try not to kill anybody." She grabbed her PR-24 baton and started pushing her way through the crowd, making blatant use of her Direkind strength, Llyr striding at her heels.

They found Jerry Morgan rolling on the ground with

three other men who were all enthusiastically whaling away on him. Two more knots of combatants brawled nearby, but Diana didn't even break stride as she ran to help her fellow cop.

Something slammed hard into the side of her head. Glass exploded as beer showered her face. Stunned, she went down on one knee.

Llyr roared in fury. She sensed rather than saw him shoot by.

Diana reeled to her feet and swiped at her wet face. Her hand came away smeared in blood. She snarled, looking for the person who had coldcocked her.

Llyr had a man down on the ground, pounding his opponent without mercy. She grinned, knowing it was probably her attacker.

Since the Sidhe obviously had matters well in hand, she went for the knot of brawlers currently beating on Morgan. Reaching in, she grabbed the back of a shirt at random, hauled the owner out with Direkind strength, and shot her fist into his face.

Blood went flying. A wild-eyed face screamed into hers as the man grabbed for her, drawing his own fist back.

A big hand landed on his shoulder and smashed him onto the pavement. Then Llyr hit him twice. That was all it took before the drunk's eyes rolled back.

Diana turned and aimed her PR-24 in a powerhouse swing toward a fat-padded shoulder. Its owner howled and rolled off Jerry. She pounced on the fat bruiser, planted a knee in the small of his pudgy back, and grabbed his wrist, dragging it back for the handcuffs she pulled out of her shoulder pouch. He cursed and bucked under her, but she bore down and got him cuffed anyway.

Suddenly somebody slammed into her, rolling her off the

thug. She had an impression of red eyes and a five o'clock shadow before a huge fist plowed into her face. Her head snapped back into the pavement so hard she saw stars.

Then the weight of the man was gone, and she heard Llyr cursing steadily in Sidhe between grunts of effort punctuated by thuds.

Diana staggered to her feet just as a bloody face loomed at her elbow. She'd drawn back a fist before she recognized the badge on the man's chest. "Damn, Jer, you look like hell."

"You don't look so good yourself." Morgan's uniform was covered in blood and dirt, and his left eye was swollen shut. He jerked a thumb over his shoulder. "Who the hell is *that*?"

Llyr surged to his feet, having finished off the last of the fighters. The collar of his new shirt was ripped, and his hair had come half out of the tail she'd tied it into, falling around his blood-smeared face. As he whirled, teeth bared, she strongly suspected most of the blood was not his own. His too-pale eyes did not look entirely sane.

"Chit' ca virat keva!" he roared at the mob around them, throwing out a brawny arm to point at her. "The next man who touches her dies!"

The crowd fell absolutely silent, staring at him as he stared back, blood running down his face. They might be drunk enough to tangle with a couple of city cops, but they weren't sure what the hell Llyr was. Other than very big and very pissed-off.

Finally he bellowed, *"Go home!"*

To Diana's surprise, the lot of them turned away and started moving off toward their cars.

"I repeat," Jerry muttered in her ear, "who the hell is *that*?"

"My boyfriend." The words were out of her mouth before she could call them back.

"Think we can recruit him?"

Diana stuck her tongue in her cheek. "I think he's already got a job."

She spent the next several hours bouncing between the county hospital and the county jail, checking on her fellow cop and booking the brawlers. Jerry ended up needing a head X-ray. Luckily, his concussion turned out to be mild, but she took the report for him anyway, since he wasn't quite up to the task.

It seemed the three original drunks were friends of Ronnie Jones, the first victim of the vampire. When Jerry had shown up to deal with an unruly bar patron, the three had questioned what he was doing rousting drunks when he should be off catching a serial killer.

They hadn't liked his explanation, and he hadn't liked their attitude. Neither did Diana, who charged all three with aggravated assault and battery on a police officer, not to mention resisting arrest and public drunkenness. She fully intended to add more charges as soon as she could think of them. Local prosecutors tended to drop a few charges; the more counts the idiots faced, the more likely one or two were to stick.

Clara Davies's son, Roger, was the one who'd cold-cocked her with the bottle, only to suffer Llyr's impressive Sidhe revenge. Remembering the mayor's instructions to let Roger walk the next time he fell afoul of the law, Diana bared her teeth and charged him anyway.

Clara and the mayor could kiss her ass.

The other two guys were the ones who'd jumped her when she'd tried to help. Warrants on them had to wait until they were released from the hospital; both had needed patching-up after Llyr got through with them. The Sidhe himself was in the clear, since he'd been defending Diana at the time.

Finally she'd worked her way through all the paperwork, and she and Llyr were free to head back to town for the rest of the shift. She planned a stop off at the house first, since she still smelled like a brewery from the bottle Roger had broken over her head. It was a good thing she healed fast, or she'd be cooling her heels in the ER with Jerry.

However, Diana also knew if she were to encounter any Verdaville citizens in the course of what remained of the night, they'd immediately leap to the conclusion she'd been drinking, just from the smell. Which made the shower a political necessity.

Llyr had been surprisingly quiet since their little battle at the bar. Now, between his silence and the drive back to town, she had plenty of time to think about the night—particularly the feral expression on his face when he'd threatened to kill the next man who touched her.

Diana felt a bloom of warmth within her chest. There was nothing like a man willing to break heads on her behalf to make a girl feel wanted. She felt she should mention it—Llyr deserved her thanks at the very least—but the whole topic made her feel strangely shy.

It wasn't as if it meant anything, after all. Maybe if he'd been another man, things would have been different, but he was King of the Cachamwri Sidhe, and Diana was a werewolf.

And that was really all there was to it.

THIRTEEN

"Why do you do it?" Llyr asked suddenly from his side of the car.

"What?"

"This . . . police business." He looked at her, a muscle flexing in his square jaw. "I heard them say at the jail that you are some sort of volunteer. You are not even being paid."

"Well, no, but I have a responsibility. You of all people should understand that. I'm stronger than most humans, damn near impossible to kill, and the department is chronically shorthanded. If I can back the cops up, I should."

"But they said reserve officers normally drive around with a paid officer who supervises them. You take a great risk."

"Somebody said a lot." She made a mental note to find

out who it was and have a long talk with him. "Anyway,
I'm not just your average wannabe playing cops and rob-
bers. I'm city manager. Gist knows I can be trusted."

"You could have been hurt tonight." His eyes flashed at
her. "I don't like it."

"I know what I'm doing, Llyr. And what I'm doing is
my duty."

Party to forestall further conversation, she reached over
and adjusted the volume on the police radio. "At least we
haven't heard from Vampire Bitch tonight. Normally she's
killed somebody by now."

"Aye." He drummed his fingers on his bent knee. "I
wonder what she is doing?"

Susan lay still in the utter darkness of her lair. Moving
hurt. She ached deep inside, where that bastard Ansgar had
pounded her without mercy. Even after he'd finished, he'd
used his fist on her a few times, just to underscore his
point.

Damn, she'd love nothing better than to leave this rotten
town and its fairies behind her, but she didn't dare. The
bastard would find her.

So she had no choice. Ansgar's brother had to die. But
not tonight. Tonight she wanted only to lay still and heal.

Tomorrow would be soon enough.

Llyr tossed the shimmering ball of magic at the Sidhe
child. Kevir threw up a magical shield, but he was a trifle
late. The enchantment reached him, carrying the sensation
of tickling fingers digging into his little ribs. He fell into
the grass, his merry laughter ringing like birdsong as he
kicked and wiggled.

Llyr pounced on him and swooped him up into his arms for a smacking kiss. "You've got to learn to be quicker, boy."

The child collapsed bonelessly in his arms, his cheeks bright, long lashes veiling his opal eyes in gold. His hair was even paler than Llyr's, almost white.

But though his coloring was his father's, the shape of his face was all Isolde. Sometimes looking into the child's face brought a stab of pain to Llyr's heart as he remembered his lost wife. Luckily, the boy didn't seem to remember the day his mother had tried to shield him from the assassin when their bodyguards fell.

Thank Cachamwri Llyr had arrived in time to rescue him. He only wished he could have been fast enough to save Isolde herself. Conscious of the risks the boy ran, Llyr put the child back on his feet. "Come, Kevir. Try the shield again."

The boy pouted, his lips a pink curve. "But I don't want to. I'm tired of doing magic. Anyway, I don't need to know how to shield. You'll protect me."

Llyr tousled his son's bright hair. "But I cannot be there every minute, child. I have a kingdom to run. Come now, once more."

"No!" Stormy anger blazed up in the child's eyes. Whirling, he ran.

"Kevir!" Frustrated, Llyr raced after the child, but his son moved with amazing speed. Still calling, Llyr ran on in pursuit. Fear stabbed his chest. He didn't dare let the boy out of his sight.

But his legs felt like lead, and every running step he took drained the strength from him.

As he pounded along, all the light faded from the woods around him until he was racing through darkness. The air

MASTER OF THE MOON   203

was so bitterly cold, he could see his own breath. "Kevir! Dragon curse you, boy, where did you go?"

There. Bright gold in the moonlight. The boy's hair. "Kevir!" He charged on, forcing his leaden limbs to carry him.

His son lay in the leaves, a heap of pale limbs and court velvet. He'd grown into a man in the last few minutes—a man with a trace of Isolde in the shape of his mouth, yet with Llyr's strong build.

A crossbow bolt protruded obscenely from the center of his chest.

"Kevir!" Llyr fell to the boy's side and scooped him into his arms. His laughing jester of a son felt cold, leaden. "No! Oh, Dragon's Breath, no!"

Suddenly opalescent eyes opened. "You were supposed to save me. Why didn't you call the Dragon to save me?"

"I tried!" Llyr cried out, stroking his cold face as tears spilled free. "I tried, but Cachamwri would not heed me!"

Suddenly the pain in his chest became tearing agony. He fell back with a hoarse bellow. Writhing, he looked down in horror as the front of his tunic distorted as if something was forcing its way out.

Cachamwri's head exploded from his chest. "Why would I answer you?" the Dragon God sneered. "You're *nothing*."

Llyr's eyes flew open as he jerked upright in bed, sweating and cold. His heart was thundering so hard in his chest, he thought for a moment it was the pain of Cachamwri's nightmare birth.

But no. It had been a dream. With a groan of relief and pain, he fell back.

"Llyr?" Diana lay next to him, her head lifted, her silver eyes questioning.

"Go back to sleep," he said hoarsely. "It was only a nightmare."

Hours passed before he could sleep again.

"Now this is the werewolf breakfast of champions," Diana said, sliding the broiler pan into the oven. "Forget wimpy breakfast cereal—just give me half a cow on a plate."

She straightened and turned to grin at Llyr, her gamine face so alight with mischief, he felt his mood lighten.

He'd woken this morning to find her draped over his chest in her customary position, warm and drowsy as she'd lifted her head to meet his gaze with eyes of shimmering silver. Her pretty breasts had pressed softly against his ribs, the little nipples stiff with her habitual Burning Moon arousal. Her long legs shifted over his, the skin like silk.

He'd found himself making love to her before he'd even known what he was about, sliding into her tight little body with the reverence of a man taking a magical sacrament.

They'd showered together, and she'd combed her hair, and he'd kept thinking about watching that bottle fly out of the crowd and slam into her head. As she'd gone down, his heart had simply stopped with the memory of Isolde's death at the hands of Ansgar's assassins.

The next thing Llyr knew, he'd slammed into the fool who had hurt Diana. He'd beaten the mortal with a savagery he rarely allowed himself to express. He suspected he'd have killed the man if he hadn't seen Diana rise to her feet a moment later.

She'd promptly waded back into the battle, fiercely ready to defend her policeman friend against the drunken mortals who threatened him.

Unlike Isolde, any assassin who came after Diana London would be fortunate to escape with his life. And if anyone dared lay a hand on one of her children, there wouldn't even be enough of the man left to question.

The thought made Llyr smile until he remembered last night's dream. He was so wretchedly tired of losing those he loved.

Brooding, he watched her bustle around the kitchen, cutting up fruit with deft skill, the blade flashing in her delicate hands. She returned to the oven, grabbed an oven mitt and opened the door, then looked up at him with an expression of chagrin. "I guess you like your food cooked rather than kind of warm on both sides, huh?"

Llyr's lips twitched reluctantly. "I do prefer it that way, yes."

Diana sighed hugely and closed the oven. "I was afraid of that."

"You can take your own out now, you know."

"Yeah, but I've noticed guys tend to find something unsexy about a girl with blood running down her chin."

"You couldn't be unsexy if you tried. If there's even such a word."

"It's a word." She chopped an orange into slices, wielding the knife so skillfully, he found himself wondering what she could do with a sword.

An image popped into his mind: Diana teaching a towheaded little Sidhe boy how to use a wooden practice blade. Except she wouldn't be fertile with him anyway.

It made no difference. He couldn't put a werewolf on the throne of the Cachamwri Sidhe. His people would never accept it, assuming his father's ghost didn't rise in rage.

But what if Kevir had been a werewolf—resistant to magic and a shape-shifter? Would the boy be alive today?

The thought made Llyr's heart ache. He might be a grandfather now, a great-grandfather.

Instead of alone.

Unaware of his anguish, Diana had plucked the steaks from the oven and was busily transferring them onto plates. Suddenly she stopped and looked up at him, biting her lip. "Uh, I didn't fix any veggies."

"That's fine."

"Are you sure? Because I could open a can of corn or something." She frowned. "If you even want veggies for breakfast."

"The fruit's fine."

"I just don't like vegetables, I'm afraid." Carrying their plates, she started toward the table. "I mean, I'm willing to eat 'em deep fried, but otherwise they seem a little bit too much like rabbit food."

Llyr smiled reluctantly. "And you eat rabbits."

Diana shot him a guilty look. "Well, there's an awful lot of them around here. They're hell on gardens. I just thin the population down a little."

"Of course," he said, his mood lightening as he followed her to the table. "I'm sure the local farmers are grateful."

"And it's not like they're people's pets. Like cats. I never chase cats. Well, hardly ever. And when I do, I let them get away."

As they sat down, Llyr found the temptation to tease irresistible. "Are you sure? You never take just one little bite?"

"Of course not! That's disgusting." She glared at him, honestly insulted.

"Ah. I apologize."

"Okay, yeah, sometimes I'm tempted, but I always think that maybe there's some lonely little old lady waiting for Fifi to come home. I just couldn't do that to her."

"So you let Fifi go."

"Every time," she said firmly.

"Of course."

"You're twitting me, aren't you?"

"I'm afraid I can't resist you either."

"Eat your steak, you rotten fairy."

He dug in and found it delicious. They ate in companionable silence until she said, "You know, I'm considering asking my brother to give me a hand with this mess. I'd feel better if he was here to help make sure Ansgar doesn't get at you. Thing is, he's very alpha. I'm afraid you two would not get along."

"Alpha?" Another obscure mortal term.

"Alpha male," she explained. "A leader type. He's the kind of guy who walks into a room, and everybody else instantly wants to either follow him or start a fight. That's the guys—the girls just want to bang him. So there's usually a general kicking of the ass until he establishes to everybody's satisfaction that he's dominant."

Llyr glowered over his steak. "He would not be dominant over *me*."

She swallowed a bite and nodded. "There you go. You two just would not get along. And I'd spend all my time trying to mediate. So on the one hand, he'd be a great bodyguard, but on the other hand, he'd also be a huge pain in the ass. And I'm not sure which he'd end up being more, so I'm torn."

Llyr wasn't. The idea of turning to some strange male shifter for protection struck him as galling. "A better solution would be if I regain my powers and defeat the vampire, forcing her to confess she's working for my brother. Preferably before someone else is murdered or your FBI decides to arrest you and your police chief." He drummed his fingers on the table. "But in lieu of that, I'd take my people realizing there's something wrong and coming for me."

"Yeah, either would work. Wonder what's taking them so long?"

"I have no idea," Llyr said grimly.

* * *

The Dowager Queen Oriana swept into the High Council chamber with her Demisidhe servant fluttering at her shoulder, tiny rainbow wings a blur. A dozen Sidhe elders looked up at her entry. She watched varying expressions of dismay, irritation, and impatience cross their faces before every one of them took on a look of polite attention.

Dragon's Teeth, what whey-livered idiots.

"Have you heard from my grandson?" she demanded, advancing on the council table.

"Aye, Your Highness," Cradawag said from head seat, his face set in lines of elaborate patience. The officious old boor. "Just this afternoon."

"Did you tell him I wished to speak to him?"

"Yes, Your Highness, but he is most busy," Lady Oppida began. "He asked—"

Oriana stiffened. "Did he say he was too busy to speak to his grandmother?"

Oppida and Cradawag exchanged a quick look. "He is working on a very delicate spell, and . . ."

"I was crafting 'very delicate spells' two thousand years before that boy was born, and well he knows it," Oriana snapped. "If he's having difficulty with a spell, most likely I can help him with it."

"But he asked specifically not to be disturbed, Your Highness!" Cradawag protested. "I really don't think it wise . . ."

But Oriana had already turned on her heel and swept out the council door. As the guardsman stepped forward to close it behind her, she muttered, "And I really don't care what you think, you great fool. Dragon's Teeth, Becan, why does Llyr not fire the lot of those mincing idiots?"

"They did serve his father," the Demisidhe pointed out, darting along at her shoulder. Cynyr had made Becan her aide centuries ago, back when he first conquered the Morven Sidhe and married her. At the time, she'd wondered if he'd intended the Demisidhe as a spy, but Becan had proven a staunch ally. And, over the centuries since Cynyr's death, far more.

Not that she'd ever stopped missing the old rogue.

Llyr was a great deal like his grandfather, which was probably why she was so fond of the boy. A warrior at heart, a little arrogant perhaps, but courageous and true along with it, unlike that sneaking brother of his.

All of which were qualities his grandfather had had in abundance. That was why she'd fallen so hard for Cynyr to begin with, never mind that he'd conquered her people. The day that Morven rebel had slain Cynyr had been the blackest in her long life. Save, of course, for Dearg's death in battle against the Dark Ones.

Dearg. Foolish boy. If only he had not insisted on making Ansgar king of the Morven kingdom. She'd warned him there would be trouble, and she'd been right.

"I don't like this, Becan," she said, striding down the jeweled corridor toward her own chamber. "Why has Llyr not contacted me as I requested?"

"Perhaps he is simply busy with his vampire hunt."

"Or romancing that comely little werewolf. I like that even less. She's too personable by half. What if he falls in love with her? My grandchildren would be puppies!"

Becan's rich, masculine laugh rolled in her ears as they entered her chamber. She gestured the door closed. In a blink, he grew to full size—a thin, handsome man with clever dark eyes. It was really too bad she could never wed him, Demisidhe that he was.

"At least they would be able to take care of themselves,

Oriana," he said. "In any battle between a magical assassin and a Direkind shifter, I'd place my bet on the Direkind."

"Well, that's true enough." She sighed. "But still—puppies!"

As she flounced onto a divan, Becan moved to prepare the heated wine she preferred. "In all seriousness," he told her as he brought her a goblet, "I like not the fact Llyr has not contacted you. 'Tis not in character."

She took the heavy gold cup, lifting a brow. "I thought you said he was probably busy with his vampire hunt."

"And indeed, he may well be."

"Or Ansgar could be working some evil. That boy always was a sneaking creature. Did I tell you once I caught him tormenting a unicorn foal when he was but a lad? What sort of Sidhe would stoop to that? I told Dearg, but did he listen?"

"Well, he didn't will Ansgar both kingdoms," Becan pointed out.

"He couldn't. Llyr bore Cachamwri's mark." She squared her narrow shoulders and put the cup aside with a clink. "Get me my scrying bowl. I'll feel better once I've spoken to my grandson."

Oriana concentrated on centering herself while Becan filled the ornate bowl with water for her spell. It was normally a simple enough bit of work, but contacting Mortal Earth was always a chancy business, as magic did not work well there.

Becan placed the bowl before her. She looked down into its depths, waiting for its shimmering surface to still. When at last it had gone smooth and flat, she sent her mind reaching out.

And slammed right into a barrier of some kind. She frowned and probed again.

The barrier disappeared so quickly she wondered for a

moment if she'd imagined it. Llyr looked up from the bowl, an expression of annoyance on his handsome face. "What now?"

Oriana stiffened, hurt. He'd never addressed her in such a cold tone before. "I beg your pardon! I but wished to see that you were well!"

"Grandmother!" His expression flickered into alarm, then shifted into a warm smile. "I didn't realize it was you. Excuse me."

She studied his face in the water for a long moment. "Are you well, grandson?"

"Oh, aye." He waved a hand. "Just busy with a rather involved enchantment."

"If you need help, I have some expertise."

"No! No, that's fine. I almost have it."

Oriana gave him a warm smile. "I would be more than happy to assist you, dear boy. I haven't seen Mortal Earth in centuries. It might be a rather entertaining to see what the humans have got up to. I think I heard something about a moon landing, or some such absurdity . . ."

"It isn't a good time, Grandmother." Llyr's tone was so chill, she stiffened. As if sensing her hurt, he smiled a trifle tightly. "This vampire I hunt is a dangerous creature. I wouldn't want to risk you."

She relaxed, mollified. "As you will, then. But if you change your mind, let me know. I can be there in a blink. Good luck, grandson." Oriana gestured, shattering the image.

She sat for long minutes afterward, staring down at her own reflection in the bowl.

"Well?" Becan demanded.

"It felt like him. And yet . . ." She sighed. "Perhaps he is simply romancing his werewolf and doesn't want an old woman's interference."

"That's certainly possible," her lover agreed after a pause. Oriana shook her head. "Puppies!"

Ansgar fell back against his throne and wiped the sweat from his face. Fooling the old bitch had been a remarkably difficult piece of magic. She was much stronger than she looked. He'd thought several times during the conversation that she was going to see right through the spell.

He was running out of time. Sooner or later, they would trip to what he was doing.

Long before then, Llyr had better be dead.

Llyr was naked.

For once, however, he seemed to be completely un-aware of Diana.

Bemused, she watched from the door of her living room as the Sidhe slowly circled the room in a catlike crouch, an expression of intense concentration on his face. He'd pushed the furniture against the wall, clearing out a space.

Now he pivoted, bringing both arms up and around in a series of exquisitely controlled punches and blocks. His dragon tattoo seem to writhe as he leaped upward in a scything kick. One long leg kicked out as the Sidhe spun completely around to land lightly in the exact same spot.

A cold snarl of rage on his face, Llyr advanced on his invisible opponent, throwing kicks and punches in blurring sequence before he stopped, pivoted, and started back the other way.

The way he moved reminded her of the martial arts katas she'd seen demonstrated, though the actual fighting style was obviously different. The Sidhe were stronger than humans, and the techniques he used were so intensely controlled and demanding, she doubted a mortal could have used them at all

Llyr threw himself into another hard, low, spinning kick. Sweat flew off his body as he whirled, and ran in gleaming paths down his torso when he landed. Muscle flowed and worked under his pale skin as his unbound hair whipped around his body.

Diana had never seen anything so intensely male. Or as intensely erotic.

Then, as she watched in hypnotized fascination, she saw movement under the skin of his back. At first she thought it was a shadow, but as it slid around his torso, she realized it was something else altogether. Catching her breath in mingled fear and fascination, Diana stared hard as he pivoted into another blurring sequence of punches and kicks.

There it was again, a flash of blue along one long thigh. The outline of a tail snaked around his calf. Wings flexed across his back, blue shading into green. He whirled again, punching, and the image disappeared.

Llyr stopped pivoting to throw punch after punch into the air, muscles rippling under his pale Sidhe skin.

A shape began coalescing on his arm. She couldn't quite make it out at first, but as she stared, she could see the colors growing brighter, its outline sharpening. It looked like the dragon tattoo come alive.

Suddenly he froze in place, his bunched arm trembling with effort.

Cachamwri's mark flexed across his biceps. Then the dragon turned its head and *looked* at her. Its tail flicked out, wrapping down the length of his arm.

"Llyr!" she gasped.

He swore. The tattoo went flat again. "Dragon's Teeth, Diana!"

Shit. He'd almost done it, and she'd interrupted. "God,

I'm sorry! It's just—I think I saw Cachamwri. The mark—
it looked alive!"

Llyr tilted his head back and dropped onto the couch.
His body shone with sweat as if he'd run a marathon in the
past ten minutes. He lay there panting. "Yes, it was
Cachamwri. He answered. For the first time, I felt him."

Diana winced. "And I screwed it up. I should have kept
my mouth shut." She hesitated before daring to ask, "Is
your magic back, then?"

"No, there's still some kind of barrier blocking me from
reaching into the Mageverse to draw power." He shook his
head. "But I'm linked to Cachamwri through the Dragon's
Mark, and the block doesn't affect that. If I can only reach
him . . ."

"You should have told me what you were going to try to
do," Diana said. "What if it went bad? I mean, maybe you
should have a spotter or something."

Llyr's eyes flashed up at her and narrowed. Rising, he
started toward her. Offended male menace shimmered off
him. "I'm not in the habit of consulting others before I do
my duty."

Her heart started pounding in a kind of erotic dread she
didn't understand. "Well, maybe you'd better get in the
habit, particularly given the situation."

"And what situation is that?"

She considered attempting a diplomatic answer, but
she'd never liked attempts to intimidate her. And he was
definitely trying to intimidate her. "Your powers being
gone."

Llyr's eyes narrowed. "You think me powerless?"

She licked her lips and stiffened her spine. "When it
comes to your magic, yes."

A hand snapped out and wrapped around her wrist.
With a single hard tug, he jerked her up against his big,

sweaty body. His smile was downright feral. "I think you'll find I'm far from powerless."

And then his mouth crashed down over hers.

The kiss was hard, hungry, with none of the tender seduction he'd shown her earlier. Wrapping an arm around her waist, Llyr dragged her hard against him as he ate at her lips with teeth and tongue. She gasped and tried to pull back, but he grabbed the back of her head and held her in place. The other hand cupped her backside, canting her hips forward against his suddenly rigid cock.

Diana managed to drag her head back from his rapacious mouth. "What do you think you're doing?"

He gave her a dark grin. "Actually, I'm getting ready to fuck you."

FOURTEEN

Something about the way Llyr held her, about the hot gleam in his eyes, about the touch of his hands made eager little flames gather between Diana's thighs. She was appalled at herself. She should be kicking his fairy butt, not getting turned on. "Stop it," she growled against his lips.

"I don't think you want me to," he whispered back, and started pressing tiny, biting kisses along the line of her jaw. Long fingers caught and cupped her breast, stroking and squeezing. Her nipples peaked.

Diana braced her hands against his chest and pushed, but he refused to release her. "What the hell has gotten into you?"

"The Dragon's Breath," he rumbled, voice hot with anticipation.

Alarmed, she lifted her head to meet the burn of his gaze. "What?"

"There's a price for summoning Cachamwri." He raked his hands up under the hem of her shirt. Before she could stop him, he whipped it off over her head. "I'm afraid the Dragon God isn't particularly civilized."

Llyr reached for her sports bra, wrapped both hands in the tough material, and pulled. It ripped, loud in the quiet of the room.

Mouth dry, heart pounding, Diana stared up at him as he surveyed her breasts with satisfaction. "Very nice." He lowered his head and took her nipple with hungry lust.

Diana gasped as his tongue danced around the little peak just before his teeth closed in a delicate bite. She was swaying by the time he grabbed the waistband of her shorts and started pushing them down her thighs. Smoothly, Llyr knelt before her, still licking and biting at her breasts as he swept her pants down her legs. "Step out of them," he ordered, his voice harsh.

God help her, she could feel herself going wet between her legs. Responding. Politically correct or no, his dominant pose turned her on. Licking her lips, she stepped out of her shorts and stood naked.

He might be possessed by some magical dragon spirit, but she didn't care. It was as if somehow the animal in him called to the animal in her.

And her wolf was more than ready for whatever his dragon wanted to do.

When he pushed her back onto the carpet, she went willingly. Her gaze flicked from the wild heat in his eyes to the hungry jut of his cock.

Licking her lips, she reached for him.

Llyr knew now how Diana must feel in her Burning

Moon. Though Cachamwri had escaped him, the Dragon God left fire in its wake, shredding the careful control Llyr usually put on his own emotions. Now he kept remembering the moment when Diana went down under that bottle—and, what it felt like to thrust into her wet silk heat.

He had to have her.

When her small, cool hand closed over his cock, he tossed his head back and groaned. Her grip was pure, raw pleasure. "I won't be able to hold on if you do that," he gasped.

Diana's smile was slow and wicked. "Then don't."

For a moment he was tempted, but something in him growled an objection. This time he wanted to be in control, and he wanted her to know it. He grabbed her hand and pulled it gently from his cock, then caught the other wrist for good measure.

"Hey, what do you think you're doing?" she demanded. Judging by her grin, she had a pretty good idea.

"What does it look like?" He pulled her wrists over her head and pinned them to the floor as he settled himself more firmly between her thighs. The pose thrust her small, soft breasts upward until their tight little peaks pressed into his chest. Unbearably tempted, he transferred both captive wrists to one hand and twisted down to have his way with the tempting little berries.

She gasped as he sampled one, sucking greedily. "You do know there's no way you can really hold me?"

Llyr looked up and gave her his best dark grin. "Oh, I can hold you. Besides, you really don't want to get free." Tilting his head, he flicked the tip of his tongue over her nipple. "Do you?"

"No," she gasped. "Guess I don't, at that."

He cupped one breast so that her nipple jutted even more for his mouth, then gave it a slow rake with his teeth.

She shivered under him, bending her legs so her silken calves caressed his legs.

Dragon's Breath, he loved this. Loved the way she felt under him, so deceptively slim and feminine. He might be stronger than she was at this moment, but in a breath she could transform. If she submitted to him, it was because she wanted to.

The thought made him want to reward her—and slow the pace just a bit. He levered off her, still keeping one hand on her wrists just as a reminder that he was definitely in control. When he sought out her mouth, she opened to him in welcome, her lips sweet and damp against his. She tasted of the orange she'd just eaten.

Llyr entered with a mating thrust of his tongue, and she swirled her own around it. Deliciously seduced, he drew his tongue back, intending to nibble her lower lip. She slicked her own into his mouth instead. They dueled with thrusting tongues as he sought her breast to tease its hard nipple. She caught her breath in a maddening little moan.

Llyr lifted his head and looked down at her, panting. He couldn't remember the last time he'd been so aroused, and knew it was only in part because of Cachamwri.

The rest was all Diana. His sweet, hot little werewolf.

Some sane part of him knew there were good reasons he couldn't keep her, but the rest didn't give a unicorn's egg. She was his. He could feel it on some deep level beyond reason or kingship or anything else. And he intended to make sure she knew it.

Llyr pressed a tiny, biting kiss to her stubborn chin, then started working his way downward, pausing to nibble at the satin skin of her throat before continuing on his way. She writhed under him, gasping, but he tightened his grip on her wrists and threw her a molten glance. "You aren't going anywhere."

God, who wanted to? Diana groaned and rolled her face against her lifted arm. Instinctively, she tugged at her wrists, wanting to touch him, but she couldn't pull free of his hands. He was a hell of a lot stronger than a human male; she'd probably have to transform into the Dire Wolf to break his grip. And she had no intention whatsoever of doing that. She liked it just where she was.

Apparently the wolf part of her loved being pinned under him, though she'd always hated it anytime anybody else had tried it.

But too much thinking about why that was would probably spoil the delicious mood, so instead she simply lay back and enjoyed it. And there was a great deal to enjoy, because Llyr knew his way around a woman's body better than any man she'd ever met.

He was going after her nipples again, his tongue swirling a hot dance over each before he settled in for a deep, drawing suckle. Just when he was seriously in danger of driving her out of her mind, he'd bite down, ever so delicately.

Oh, yeah. He was definitely good at that.

Meanwhile his free hand was busy, stroking its way down the length of her body, pausing here to caress the delicate flesh of her ribs, there to circle his fingertips over her hip. When she felt him start exploring his way across her belly, she tensed in erotic expectation. When he levered his hips off hers, she caught her breath.

The sword calluses on his fingers felt just slightly rough as he slid his hand between their bodies. He lifted his head to look down into her face, and she drowned for a while in dancing opalescent flecks while he teased his fingertips through the soft hair between her thighs. He traced one finger over the seam between her nether lips, and she caught her breath in anticipation.

Then, with a dark smile, he sent his hand questing down to her thigh

"Tease!" she gasped in outrage.

He grinned. "Oh, yes."

"I'm going to get you back for that."

"Not at the moment." He stroked the thin flesh high on her leg until she squirmed in frustrated lust and gave serious thought to raping him.

Then, without warning, he cupped her sex and sent his middle finger spearing right up into her slick core. Diana gasped, throwing her head back at the delicious sensation.

"Like that?" he breathed against her mouth.

"Ever been raped by a werewolf?" she wheezed.

"Now, that's no way to talk to the man on top." He stroked out, added a second finger, and thrust both of them back inside. She arched, catching her breath as pleasure coiled up her spine in long, hot streamers.

"I like the way you do that," Llyr purred in her ear. "Do it again." He added a third finger and slowly pumped.

Sensing he was distracted, she twisted her wrists free of his light hold, grabbed him by the shoulders, and rolled over with him, landing astride his narrow hips. She smirked down into his surprised face. "That's much better."

Pale Sidhe eyes narrowed. "I think not."

Strong hands shot for her ribs, long fingers digging in a ruthless tickle. She shrieked out a laugh and fell backward. He pounced, shifted his grip to her hips, and angled her sex upward. Before she could even catch a breath, he speared his thick cock inside.

Diana gasped at the mind-blowing sensation of being filled so ruthlessly. Kneeling, her legs draped over his muscled forearms, he dragged her up his shaft, forcing his way in up to the balls. He gave her a feral grin. "Now *that* is better."

"You are not a nice man," she whimpered.

He considered the question, pulling out slowly. "No." He shoved in hard. "I don't think I am."

Diana grinned. "I never liked nice men anyway." Bucking her hips, she rolled her head at the sensation of his thick shaft grinding inside her.

Llyr straightened his knees and tightened his grip on her legs, pulling her backside off the bed and angling her body upward until only her head and shoulders were on the mattress. When he began thrusting, the angle made him feel like a baseball bat. She slapped her hands down to steady herself. "God, Llyr! That's deep!"

He grinned. "I know." Absolutely merciless, he began grinding hard between her helplessly spread legs. Diana sucked in a breath, fingers curling into claws in the sheets as the massive cock probed her slick flesh.

Each time he thrust, his pelvis rolled against her clit, sending shockwaves of hot delight over her body. Diana could feel the climax gathering like a firestorm ready to break. She bucked against him, maddened at the tantalizing delight just beyond her fingertips. "Llyr!"

Llyr gave her a feral smile. "Want something, love?"

"Yeah! Oh, God!"

"Beg." *Thrust.*

"Ah! *Please!*"

"Not good enough." He stopped, his cock only halfway inside.

She tried to buck deeper onto his shaft, but he held her effortlessly still. "Dammit, Llyr!"

"No."

"Let me come! Please!"

"Aahhh," he purred. "Very pretty. And here you are." He jerked her right up his cock, seating himself deep. Circling his hips, he corkscrewed the big shaft up inside her, grinding skillfully over her clit.

Her orgasm broke free like a blazing balloon. Diana screamed, writhing hard into him.

"Yes," he shouted, and threw back his head, the cords standing in hard relief on the side of his neck as he spilled himself deep inside her.

Until finally he fell forward, dropping her on the mattress an instant before he collapsed over her, panting and spent. Diana, gasping, could only curl her arms and legs around him and hold on as they fought to breathe, dizzy from the force of their mutual detonation.

An hour later, Diana sat on her bed with the television turned down to the lowest volume even she could hear. Even so, she could clearly make out the grunts and thumps from the living room as Llyr doggedly continued his efforts to call Cachamwri.

She hoped to heck he had better luck this time. Whenever she remembered how close he'd come when shc'd interrupted and ruined it, she wanted to bite herself.

Even in her irritation, though, she had to grin. What came afterward had almost been worth the guilt. Though whether she'd think so whcn Llyr went back to his people was another question.

Frowning, Diana thumbed the remote and clicked restlessly past two game shows, several reruns, and an endless round of cable news programs, all covering the same story from different political slants. She hit on a History Channel program on one of the more bloodthirsty medieval kings and settled down to watch.

Llyr was getting to her. Which should not have come as

a surprise, she supposed. The man was gorgeous, brilliant, dedicated to his people, and fantastic in the sack. Anybody would be smitten, particularly somebody without enough sense to come in out of the rain. Which apparently described her, because it was for damn sure that a romance between a werewolf and the King of the Fairies was doomed from the start.

She ought to be ashamed of herself. She'd grown up about as far as it was possible to get from magical royalty. Aside from the werewolf thing, the London family was solidly middle-class with occasional flashes of redneck. Her dad, Andrew London, was a Vietnam vet turned mailman, as well as a descendent of a long line of werewolves. Her mother was a high school art teacher with a ruthless willingness to bully those she loved into doing what was best for them. Diana often thought she'd inherited her taste for running cities from Marly London. Both her father and her brother, Jim, swore that was definitely where she'd gotten her bossy streak.

But even Marly, at her most ambitious, never dreamed higher for her daughter than becoming a lawyer. What the hell was Diana doing, setting her cap for the King of the Fairies?

This was *not* going to end well.

The preacher was working toward the fiery crescendo of his evening sermon, but Mayor Don Thompson scarcely noticed. He had weighty matters on his mind, and besides, this was his second Sunday service of the day.

However, Don also knew his constituents expected to see him occupying a pew every time the First Baptist Church of Verdaville opened its doors, and he always made sure he was.

Unfortunately, all the churchgoing in the world wouldn't save him from the political firestorm he currently faced. Not with a serial killer stalking the streets of Verdaville.

If, that is, it was a serial killer. Don wasn't convinced. It wasn't like there had been a letter from the killer claiming responsibility for those murders.

Anyway, he dearly wished Diana had kept her mouth shut instead of running to the media with a press release warning men to avoid picking up women in Verdaville, for God's sake. Which was a thoroughly ridiculous idea to begin with. First, it made it sound like the town was infested with prostitutes, which sent all the churchgoing ladies into a tizzy. And second, everybody knew no woman could have done the kind of damage the victims suffered. Women just weren't wired that way.

Don had to admit, he was surprised and disappointed by this turn of events. Diana had done a good job running Verdaville up 'til now, including digging them out of that little financial hole they'd run into three years ago after they'd bought the new City Hall property. They hadn't had to raise taxes in a couple of years, which was always good news. But this killer business . . .

People around him suddenly stood up, and Don jolted out of his preoccupation to labor to his feet and belt out a couple of stanzas of "That Old Rugged Cross" in his best baritone.

He went back to worrying over the killer issue while his wife gathered up her purse and they started working their way out into the aisle.

"Mayor! Mayor, do you know what that city manager of yours did?" Clara Davies demanded from behind him. "She arrested my Roger! Arrested him! And that boyfriend of hers broke Roger's nose! Why didn't the police arrest *him,* I'd like to know?"

He'd known this was coming. Don winced, then plastered a patiently attentive expression on his face as he turned. "Well now, Clara, they arrested Roger because he hit Miss London in the head with a beer bottle. The other man was just defending her." The chief had already briefed him on last night's debacle, knowing Clara went to First Baptist.

Her hazel eyes narrowed. "That's lies! Just pure lies! My Roger would never do such a thing. He and his friends were just talking in the parking lot when the police started harassing them. And that Diana London shouldn't have been pretending to be a cop to begin with. If she'd been at home, like a decent woman, she wouldn't have been hurt!"

"Now, Clara, you know how shorthanded the department is." Don carefully lengthened his drawl and broadened his smile. Nobody did good ol' boy better than Donnie Thompson. "Miss London was just helping out. As a volunteer, I might add. I think it's right public-minded of her."

"Public-minded? Who are you trying to fool, Don? What's she doin' running around in a city police car with a man? That ruffian blacked both Roger's eyes and broke his nose!"

"Was he blond?" a woman asked suddenly from Don's elbow. "I wonder if it's the same blond fella Terry was tellin' me about." Her eyes brightened with the pleasure of a woman sharing juicy gossip. Her voice dropped to a confidential whisper. "Terry's in my Sunday School class, and she lives next door to the city manager. She told me the last couple of days, she's seen saw Diana going in and out of her house with this man with a long blond ponytail. Thought at first it was a girl until she got a better look. He's obviously staying over there."

"Aw, now, I'm sure it's not what it looks like . . ." Don began, silently cursing the city manager.

"See! What's she doin' arrestin' my Roger when she's living in sin with some hippie?"

"Clara, I don't think they actually have hippies any more," Don's wife, Jenny, pointed out. Don shot her a hard look, and she quickly shut up.

"The council ought to fire that girl!" Clara raged. "What kind of example is she settin' for the young people of Verdaville? Shacking up with some man and running around pretending to be a cop, harassing innocent boys? I always said, women have no business being in positions of authority! They can't handle it."

To Don's disgust, a number of people had turned to listen to her rant. Now they were nodding in agreement. By tomorrow, the whole town would know Diana was screwing some long-haired civilian she let ride around in her patrol car.

Perfect. As if he didn't have enough to deal with.

"Well, rest assured I'll investigate this situation," Don said, narrowing his eyes to project stern determination. "If there's a problem, I'll deal with it."

Clara nodded, satisfied. "Good. You should fire her. She deserves it, the little tramp."

He gave her a tight-lipped smile and nodded. "As I said, I'll look into it."

It was beginning to sound like Diana London was becoming a political liability.

Diana scanned the shops and businesses that lined Main Street, looking for any movement beyond the darkened plate glass windows that would indicate a burglary in progress.

Llyr was conspicuously quiet on his side of the car. Probably still brooding about his failed attempt to summon his dragon. He'd taken two more shots at it after they'd made love, but he'd had no luck. She wished his mental logjam would break. They could use a little magic right about now.

Reaching down, Diana adjusted the volume on the patrol car's radio. She'd called the chief before they'd left for their patrol. Gist had told her there'd been no attacks last night.

Which made it all the more likely the vampire would strike tonight. Assuming they simply hadn't found the body yet.

Diana drummed her fingers on the wheel, wondering again if she was doing the right thing by dragging Llyr all over town on this vampire hunt. Ideally, she should be home with him, making sure he didn't get himself killed before his powers came back.

And if she'd been able to get in touch with Jim, she'd probably be doing just that. But she'd been unable to reach her brother on either his home phone or his cell. Diana had an ugly feeling he'd taken off for one of his weekend jaunts in the deep woods before his show. Dammit, she should have fessed up to him earlier.

Now, without backup, she had to balance the chance to keep somebody from getting killed against the risk to Llyr. Fact was, she just couldn't cool her heels while another man got slaughtered.

Llyr, for his part, had made it very clear he had no desire to sit on the sidelines. *"I have never believed in letting the enemy set the terms of engagement,"* he told her when she suggested staying home.

So here they were, riding around Verdaville waiting for

the other shoe to drop. Diana would rather be dodging magical fireballs. "Maybe Fangface has decided to pull up stakes and kill people somewhere else," she said finally, after the long silence had begun to get to her.

Llyr shot her a glance. "Not if she's working for Ansgar."

"Yeah." She sighed. "Maybe we should call it off and go back home to wait. If you're right . . ."

"She'd strike at a time of her choosing. I think not. I'd rather catch her in the act and possibly save a man's life in the process."

"Yeah, well . . ."

"Verdaville Charlie One-Nine," Dispatch interrupted. "Reported stabbing. Caller said she just got home from work to find her son nonresponsive and cold. 132 Huff Drive. Proceed with caution—the description of the scene sounds like the earlier incidents."

"That's her." Grimly, she scooped up the handset and clicked the talk button. "Ten-four, dispatch, Verdaville Charlie One-Nine en route. Does the mother think the subject is still on the scene?" Diana hit the gas and flicked on the car's lights and sirens with her mike hand as they accelerated with a roar.

"Negative."

"Ten-four."

"Is it our vampire?" Llyr asked.

"Probably." Grimly, Diana concentrated on driving the aging patrol car as they whipped along Verdaville's narrow streets, listening with half an ear while Dispatch started sending other units to the scene.

Huff Drive lay on the very outskirts of town—one street over, and the murder would have been in the county's jurisdiction. Diana wondered if that was pure chance, or if Fangface had a map and was deliberately doing her killing in the city limits. The road was lined with mobile homes, some elaborate brand-new double-wides, others rusting violations of half a dozen city codes.

She slowed the car, checking mailbox numbers until she found one marked 132. It sat in the curve as the road dog-legged, in front of spanking-new double-wide that probably cost as much as her house.

Diana popped the car door before the Crown Vic had even rolled to a stop. "Stay put and let me check this out," she told Llyr without looking at him.

"I don't think so." His tone was grim.

"Llyr, of the two of us, I'm the only one invulnerable to magic." She didn't wait to hear his reply as she swung out of the car.

She paused, crouching behind the door's cover as she drew her gun. A bullet might not stop Fangface, but it would keep her busy.

Glancing over to see Llyr reaching for his car door handle, Diana held up her free hand. "Wait." Carefully, she scented the wind blowing into her face. Her nose wasn't as good in this form, but it was still better than a mortal's. A cat lurked in the neighbor's bushes across the street, and a dog chained one house over barked like a lunatic. She wrinkled her nose absently; the dog really needed a bath.

Nothing else. Which might only mean that the vampire was standing downwind. She gestured at Llyr to stay where he was and scuttled around the car at a crouch, knowing its metal bulk would provide at least some cover.

When Diana reached his door, she straightened and motioned for him to get out. A quick glance at his face in the moonlight showed how little he liked her playing Secret Service to his President.

Unfortunately, she was damned either way. If she had him stay in the car—assuming he would obey, which she

didn't—he'd be a sitting duck the minute she went into the
house to check on the body. Better to keep him right at her
elbow.

Diana stepped back to allow him to get out of the car.
His frozen expression announced the situation went
against his every instinct—knowing him, he probably
thought he should be protecting her. Fortunately, he also
had the wit to know he wasn't magicproof.

They started across the yard for the mobile home, Diana's attention focused on the tree line across the road. Her
heart suddenly started pounding. She stopped, staring into
the woods, barely conscious that Llyr had moved past her.

The wind shifted, blowing out of the trees.

"Get down!" she yelled, and flung herself at Llyr.

FIFTEEN

The nimbus from the magic blast took Diana in the side as she barreled into Llyr, and she hissed in pain as they went down together. He spat a ripe Sidhe curse and grabbed her, instinctively trying to roll her beneath him.

But Diana was already changing, transforming into the Dire Wolf. She felt him freeze in astonishment as she went furry against him, but she had no time to worry about his reaction. She lifted her head.

The vampire strode toward her, bold as hell, dressed in some kind of magical glowing armor she'd probably generated from the life force of the poor bastard she'd just murdered. "Save us all some trouble and get out of the way," Fangface growled behind her visor.

"Not likely." Diana could hear sirens in the distance, but the humans were the least of her problems. She tensed, gauging the distance between them. "I've had more than enough of you."

"Whatever." The vampire lifted her hands, readying another blast. She obviously thought she was out of reach.

She was wrong.

Diana leaped in a long, flat dive, slamming into the vampire so hard, both of them went flying. She heard Llyr's shout behind her and ignored him.

She was damned well going to finish this. She'd deal with the fallout later. Plunging for the vampire's throat, she was dimly conscious of her prey's startled scream.

Fangface grabbed her jaw and managed to deflect her lunge; the bitch was strong, Diana had to give her that. Light exploded around her head as the vampire unleashed another spell. She smelled singeing fur and ignored it as she grabbed the vamp's hand and jerked it from her face.

"Why won't you die?" Fangface shrieked.

"I'm Direkind, you stupid bitch," Diana growled, and slammed her other fist into the vampire's perfect nose. "I was born to kick magic-using ass."

"Okay, so let's see how you do with steel." Metal glinted in her hand. Before she could twist away, the vampire plunged the blade at her eye.

Diana twisted her head aside, but the knife scored her cheek. She roared in rage.

Llyr, standing over them with Diana's gun in his hand, swore in frustration as the two twisted together like fighting cats. He didn't trust the weapon enough to chance a shot. He was damned good with a bow, but he'd never fired a modern pistol in his life.

Which hadn't stopped him from scooping Diana's weapon up when she'd dropped it to transform. It would probably do no good at all against the vampire, but at least it was something.

His gut demanded he wade in and start punching, but even Llyr knew that was a bad idea. His lithe lover had just transformed into seven feet of fur and fangs that was obviously more than capable of dealing with the vampire. And as much as it galled him to admit it, without his magic he could do more good with the gun, assuming he could get a shot he could trust.

Dragon's Breath, he hated this.

And those sirens were getting closer. Light flashed in the corner of his eye, and he turned to see a patrol car round the corner, speeding toward them.

The vampire's yelp of agony brought his head back around just as she jerked herself out of Diana's hold to spring onto her feet. An axe materialized in her hands, and she lifted it over Diana's head.

Llyr fired.

The vampire dropped the axe and staggered with a shout of pain. She shot him a look of glittering hatred and threw up both hands. A gate shimmered in behind her, and she whirled to jump through it. Diana, bleeding, rolled off the ground and dove, but the gate vanished. She hit the ground beyond it with a thud that made Llyr wince.

Brakes screeched behind them. Diana's long lupine muzzle turned in the direction of the sound and instantly began to shrink.

One moment she was an uneasy blend of woman and wolf, towering, muscles rippling under sleek black fur matted with blood. The next, she was herself again, a slim figure in a blue uniform with a gamine cap of dark hair.

She calmly walked over to take the gun Llyr held and slide it back into its holster. "Thanks," she murmured.

"What the hell was that?" a tall, heavyset Verdaville cop demanded as he raced up. "I thought I saw . . ." He broke off.

Diana turned to look at him, lifting a brow. "Yeah?"

"Nothing. What's going on? Where's the subject?"

"We wrestled with her, but she got away." She shrugged. "Ran off into the woods."

Two more patrol cars—these with different markings from Diana's—roared around the corner. Diana turned to look at them. "Why don't you take some backup and go see if you can find her? Llyr and I will check the house."

The cop shot him a look but obviously decided he didn't want to question Diana too closely. "Will do."

"And tell Dispatch to call the chief." Her expression was grim. "Our killer's struck again."

"Think it's the same guy?"

"Oh, it's definitely the same. But it's not a guy."

Llyr stared at the closed bathroom door and listened to the hiss of falling water.

Diana had told him she was going to take a shower. Then, before he could undress, she'd walked in and shut the door behind her.

Had she barred him from her body for failing to enter the battle against the vampire? He frowned, feeling a sense of inadequacy he hadn't known since he was a boy laboring in his brother's cruel shadow.

No. Llyr straightened his shoulders. He'd shot the vampire when she was about to use the axe on Diana. He had not done as much as he would have liked, but he'd certainly done all that was practical without making matters worse. If Diana believed otherwise, he'd simply have to convince her.

Without bothering to knock, he opened the door and strode in.

She stood with her back to him behind the slick mortal curtain, her head bowed and her shoulders hunched. She didn't look angry.

She looked defeated.

Well, he would address that, too. Squaring his jaw, he stripped off his shirt and the tough pantaloons she'd called jeans, then sat down to rid himself of his socks and shoes. It all took entirely too long. He wished he could simply magic them all away.

Diana looked around as he swept the curtain back and stepped inside with her. There was vulnerability in her wide eyes, a faint wince, a tightness to the mouth.

As though she was expecting a blow.

"I didn't think you wanted to join me." Diana reached up to sweep the wet curls off her forehead as she stepped back to make room for him.

He frowned. "You're the one who closed the door. I thought you were angry because I didn't join you in the fight against the vampire."

Her eyes widened as she recoiled at the thought. "God, no. Fangface would have blasted you or taken you hostage or something. Besides, you shot her before she could bury an axe in my head." Diana smiled slightly. It still looked a little wan. "Thank you for that, by the way."

Llyr snorted. "That blow would never have landed. You'd have blocked the strike or rolled clear—and probably fed her the axe in the bargain." He paused, studying her face. She looked away. "But if you are not angry, why did you close the door?"

Diana lifted one shoulder in a half shrug. "Oh, you know—I figured you wouldn't be up to wild jungle sex with Lon Chaney, Jr."

Junior? He frowned. "You were correct."

She flinched.

Llyr caught her shoulder and gently turned her to face him. "I do not have sex with men, so I am definitely not interested in making love to anyone named Lon Chanly." He tried out a small smile. "I assume this is another obscure mortal reference."

Diana laughed, the sound strangled. Some of the tension ran out of her body as she looked up at him. "Chaney, not Chanly. He was an actor, Llyr. He played a werewolf in an old movie."

"Interesting," Llyr said patiently. "I still don't understand why I should consider him a potential sex partner."

"Since he's dead, that would be out of the question anyway. I was speaking metaphorically. I meant I didn't think you'd want to make love to me after seeing me become a monster."

Llyr frowned, remembering her impressive beauty in Dire Wolf form. "Monster? Diana, Geirolf was a monster. A fire-breathing chimera is a monster. You, however, are no monster."

She braced her fists on her hips and examined his face, as if she didn't quite believe him. He was instantly distracted by the bounce of her lovely breasts. "Look, I don't have access to a Sidhese dictionary, but in English, anything that's seven feet tall, fanged, and furry is a monster. So quit pulling my chain." Diana frowned, seeing his eyes drop. "Are you listening to me?"

"No, actually I was admiring your nipples. They really are exquisite, you know."

"Argh!" She whirled, jerked the curtain aside, and stepped, dripping, out of the tub.

"Your ass is quite lovely, too," he observed, admiring it. "Very tight and . . ."

Diana spun with a growl and changed.

Magic shimmering around her, she grew to towering Dire Wolf height as silky black fur bloomed across her pale skin, her face stretching and elongating into a wolf muzzle, her ears stretching upward into long tufted points. He realized her basic build was the same as it was when she was in human form—long, lithe, and slender, though perhaps slightly more muscled than in human form. "You were saying?" she growled. Her voice was deeper than it was ordinarily, with a rough rumbling note underlying it. He found it intriguing.

"I was saying you're beautiful." Boldly, Llyr reached up and cupped one breast. The fur that lay over it was much softer than he'd expected, more like a cat's than a wolf's. Smiling at the silken sensation, he squeezed gently. "No matter what form you're in."

Looking up, Llyr realized that despite the shape of her body, her pale, lovely eyes were the same. They wore an expression of vulnerability now that tugged at his heart. She flinched back, bringing one clawed hand up as if to protect her breast. "You don't mean that."

He tilted his chin and gave her his most lofty stare—no easy task when she was ten inches taller. "Don't presume to tell me what I do not mean. Magic or no magic, I am still a king."

Diana laughed, a burble of relieved sound that spiraled higher as she changed. In a blink, she was herself again, naked and damp as she fell into his arms. "Oh, I love you, you arrogant fairy!" As if realizing what she'd just said, she stiffened and looked up at him, eyes anxious. "I didn't mean . . ."

"I know what you meant." Something hot lodged under his heart, but he ignored it to haul her into his arms and kiss her with a famished intensity. She kissed him back, sliding her arms around him.

As her smooth body pressed against his, hunger leaped, taking him by surprise with its heat. He growled against her mouth, and she purred back as he caught her firm backside in both hands and lifted her off her feet. Llyr turned to brace her against the wall as he deepened the kiss, ravenously drinking in her sweet response. She wrapped her long, strong legs around his waist as he pressed closer, grinding his aching, rock-hard cock against her smooth belly.

I can't just take her against the wall! some fragment of chivalry protested, but the wildness running through his blood didn't care. And she didn't seem to care either, biting and licking at his lips, pumping her hips against the thickness of his urgent cock.

He lifted her higher and bent until he could take one of her hard pink nipples into his mouth. She tasted deliciously of sex and wild things and magic. Llyr growled in lust.

Long, slim fingers wrapped in his hair and clenched. Suckling ferociously, he relished the slight pain as an indication of her need. He reached down between their bodies with one hand to find her sex. A thrusting finger found her slick and ready. He panted, his body shaking with need.

Diana rolled her head back against the cool tile, blowtorch lust burning every nerve. The idea that he found her beautiful even in Dire Wolf form was wildly exciting. She'd never expected to find that in anyone but another werewolf—not that she'd ever met one she wanted to love.

Yet Llyr's fierce desire couldn't be anything but genuine.

Now he was pumping two fingers deep in her sex, each stroke stretching her, readying her for the big cock jutting so hungrily against her belly. Any moment now, he'd stuff the whole massive thing inside her. He always felt as if he was almost too big. She loved that.

And then there was his mouth, skillful tongue swirling and laving her hard nipples. Her cunt clenched around his fingers with the first pulse of the orgasm she could feel building like a storm.

"Now." She gasped. Begged. "Now. Take me now. Here. Like this."

"Dragon's Breath, yes!" he gritted, and lifted her until he could poise his cock at her opening. With a hard roll of his hips, he entered her.

The sensation made her throw back her head and howl in pleasure. He felt so damn good, filling every nook and fold of her sheath with that massive shaft. "God, Llyr! More!"

His breath gusting hot against her ear, he braced her back against the wall and began to pump, riding hard and strong, those delicious muscles working with every exquisite thrust. She ground back at him, eager, panting, wanting, hungering.

The pulses started, long and rippling with ferocity. "Ah, I'm coming!"

"Yes!" Llyr shifted his grip until he held her more securely and started pounding her without any mercy at all.

Not that she wanted any.

His roar of pleasure was even wilder than hers as they shot together for the flaming peak. They froze like that, straining hard against each other, fighting for more.

And more. And more.

Until at last they slid to the floor in a helpless, sweaty tangle.

Diana knew good and damned well taking Llyr to work with her was going to cause talk, but she didn't have a hell of a lot of choice. He might be safe from the vampire, it being daylight, but there was no guarantee Ansgar didn't have another assassin waiting in the wings. She damn well didn't want to come home to find him dead.

So she told the clerks in the front office he was her cousin from out of town. They seemed to buy it, probably because the long hair made him look nothing like the glamor he'd worn in his FBI guise. While all three clerks eyed him in lusty admiration, Diana handed him a copy of the *Verdaville Voice* and pointed him to an empty desk. Then she retreated into her own office to call Gist.

The vampire had indeed murdered a thirty-year-old trucker she'd picked up in a bar, according to the dozen witnesses that had seen her do it. The chief had also learned Andy Evans didn't live with his mother; evidently the call to dispatch alerting them about the killing had been from the vampire.

"Though I don't know why the hell she did that," Gist finished. He sounded exhausted and depressed, probably from spending all night with either Andy's corpse or Andy's family. If past experience was any guide, neither could have been much fun.

"She was setting a trap for Llyr, Bill," Diana said grimly. "And she damn near got him that time."

For a long moment the chief didn't speak as he digested the ugly implications. "Jesus. You want me to assign a couple of the guys to guard duty?"

"Hell, no. They'd just end up targets or hostages or both. I'll keep an eye on him."

"You sure about that, kid? There's going to be trouble about him. And I ain't just talking about the vampire. Good-looking guy like that, staying in your house. People are going to talk."

She ground her teeth. "I know, but what the heck do you

want me to do about it? I'm stuck, Bill. If I tried to have him stay with somebody else, they'd both end up dead."

The chief sighed. "Yeah, I know. It's just not good."

"Look, I'm going to give my brother another call. Think he'd be a good enough chaperone?"

Gist snorted. "Probably not. People'd think y'all were having a threesome."

"With my *brother*? Eeeewww! God, Bill, that's sick!"

"Gossips have dirty minds, Di. Oh, and watch out for the coroner. Miller's got a real bug up his ass about this case. He was stomping around, grilling me and everybody else last night. He's insisting we call the FBI. I don't know how much longer I can stall him."

"Perfect. Just perfect. Any more good news?"

"No, that's it."

"Look, let's just try to keep it up in the air another day or so. I think Llyr's mojo is coming back—"

"Gee," Gist interrupted, "I'm sorry to hear it left."

"Ha. Funny. Point is, when his magic returns, he should be able to make all this crap just go away."

"That I want to see. Does he do ex-wives, too?"

"No."

"Figures."

Llyr sauntered in a half an hour later, bored with the newspaper. Diana handed him a magazine and tried to ignore him by working on the coming year's budget.

There was a knock on the door. "Diana, you in there?"

"Sure, Mayor," she said, frowning at a column of figures. "Come on in."

The door opened. She heard Thompson say in a frosty voice, "I don't believe we've met."

Diana looked up and cursed silently. Coroner George

Miller was with Thompson, his beady eyes focused on Llyr with obvious speculation. Balding and heavyset, George looked like a redneck cliché right out of *The Dukes of Hazzard*. Unfortunately, he was much smarter than that.

She stood hastily. "Hi, there, Mayor, George. This is my cousin, Llyr Galatyn. He's a writer, so I'm letting him follow me around. Llyr, this is Mayor Don Thompson and George Miller, our county coroner."

Llyr stood and shook hands with the two men with the innate grace that came so easily to him. Miller studied him like a bug under a microscope.

Oh, hell, she realized. *He's noticed some resemblance between Llyr and his guards.*

Thompson seemed oblivious. He gave Llyr an easy smile. "Mind if we have a moment in private with your . . . cousin here?"

"Of course not." Llyr inclined his head in a royal little half bow and strode out, closing the door behind him.

Diana could feel her stomach knotting, but she forced a pleasant smile anyway as she gestured the two men toward the chairs in front of her desk. "What can I do for you?"

"Well, there's been some rather serious questions raised, and I wanted to give you the chance to answer them," Thompson began.

"I'll be happy to answer any questions I can," she said easily. *Here it comes.* How the hell was she going to get out of this one?

"You said in your report that you had a run-in with the killer last night," Miller said. "Could you tell us about that?"

Oh, she definitely did not like this. "It was all in the report."

"I know, but we'd like you to tell us about it again," Thompson said, that good ol'-boy smile easy and broad.

Diana wasn't fooled. He was trying to catch her in a lie.

This was sounding worse and worse every minute. She settled back in her chair and plastered a polite expression on her face. "Well, I was taking my cousin out on a ride along—"

"You know, I don't think I've ever heard you mention a cousin," Thompson interrupted. "Where's he from again?"

"New York. I have a big family. Don, do we have a problem?"

"Why don't you just tell us about your encounter with the killer, Miss London," Miller said.

She gave them a long, cool look. "Dispatch radioed us about a reported stabbing. A woman claiming to be the mother of the victim said she'd returned home to find her son stabbed. In actuality, the victim's mother does not live with him. We believe it was the killer who called."

"Or an accomplice. Go on."

"I was the first one on the scene. I exited my patrol car and drew my weapon."

"Where was your cousin?"

She contained a wince. "He followed me."

Thompson frowned. "Diana, you know that's not procedure. As a civilian, he should have stayed in the car. You left us open to serious liability by leading him into a potentially dangerous situation."

"I was hardly going to leave him in the car with a possible serial killer roaming around."

"Which begs the question about why you let him on a ride-along when we're in the middle of the current crisis. That was stupid, Diana."

It was an excellent point, one she had absolutely no defense against. Under normal circumstances, she never would have taken a ride-along into a situation like that. But she could hardly explain why Llyr was an exception. "We were shorthanded, sir. Llyr has military experience."

"But he's still a civilian. Go on, Diana."

"We got out of the car and started toward the house. That was when the woman attacked us."

"You and your cousin," the coroner said.

"Yes."

"He's a big guy, your cousin. Between the two of you, I'm surprised you weren't able to capture this woman."

"She was armed, George." Sweat was rolling down the small of her back.

"With what?" the coroner asked.

"A knife." Keep it short and simple, she told herself. Less to remember.

"Were either of you hurt?"

"Luckily, no."

"The report said this Llyr Galatyn fired your weapon at the woman, and she ran off. How did he get his hands on your gun?" Miller asked.

"As I said, I drew it when I got out of the car. When the woman attacked me, I dropped it. Llyr fired, and she fled."

Miller leaned back in his chair. "Well, see, I'm having some trouble with this. Because Dr. Garrison did the autopsy this morning, and he said there's no way in hell a woman did what was done to the victim. Some of those bones were pulled right out of their sockets. It would have taken a hell of a lot of upper body strength to do that, and a woman just wouldn't have it."

Diana's Burning Moon temper began to steam. "I fought a woman. A woman picked that man up in that bar, and a woman called Dispatch and claimed to be his mother. And a woman ambushed us when we arrived."

"Could be a he-she," Thompson suggested. But his gaze was focused on her face. "It's funny you fought somebody that strong and don't even have a bruise to show for it, though. I mean, whenever the chief gets into a fracas like that, he's always got half a dozen cuts and bruises to show for it."

"I got lucky."

"Where's the cut on your head?"

Diana clenched her fists. Feeling her nails growing into claws, she struggled to contain her temper. "What cut on my head?"

"Where Roger Davies hit you with a bottle night before last. Your report said he bashed you a good one. Charged him with it, too."

"Are you accusing me of lying, Mayor?"

"There's no cut on your head."

"Fifty people saw him break that Bud over my skull, Don."

"He says he didn't do it."

"More important, his mama says her precious baby didn't do it, and his mama goes to church with you!" She clamped her teeth shut.

"Watch your tone, London!"

"I don't like being called a liar, Mayor!"

"Dammit, Diana, what do you expect? You shack up with some long-haired surfer and cause all kinds of talk. Then you run around claiming to fight serial killers you don't manage to arrest . . ."

"I've been busting my butt trying to catch that woman, Mayor."

"And yet all you've managed to do is cause a boatload of bad publicity and violate half a dozen city regulations! Even giving you the benefit of the doubt, your judgment has been abysmal in this thing. Now, I've got no choice but to call an emergency meeting of the city council for tonight to discuss your continued employment."

She stared at him numbly. "You going to fire me, Mayor?"

He looked away. "That's not my decision. That's up to

the council. But you may want to give serious thought to tendering your resignation."

As Diana stared at him, he rose to his feet and stalked out the door.

Then, softly, the coroner purred, "By the way, Diana, I understand the victims in that hotel explosion the other day checked in using your credit card. Want to explain that?"

She gave him a cold look. "Get out of my office, George."

SIXTEEN

When Llyr walked back into Diana's office after the men had left, he found her sitting very still. He stiffened in alarm at her pale face and wide, desolate eyes.

"What's happened?" he demanded, circling the desk to swing her chair around to face him. "What did they do to you?" Anger steamed through him as she looked up at him helplessly. His Diana was never helpless. "Dragon fry those bastards, I'll—"

"They're going to fire me," she interrupted in a small voice.

Llyr dropped to his knees to frown up into her face. "What?" It made no sense. "But why? You've risked your life to stop this killer and it's not even your job."

"I seem to have become a political liability." She turned the chair and stood. As he watched, bewildered, she bent and began to rummage into a set of cabinets against one wall.

"But why?"

"For one thing, you and I are setting a bad example for the youth of Verdaville." Her voice sounded choked, as if she was fighting tears. Pulling a brown box from the cabinet, she dumped its contents in the trash can and returned to her desk.

"I wish you'd explain." He frowned as she opened a drawer and started transferring items into the box. "What are you doing?"

Diana glanced up, her eyes red. "Cleaning out my desk. It's the traditional activity when us mortals get the boot." She swiped her tears away with an impatient hand. "Technically speaking, of course, the council will make that decision, but since I can't explain why I did a single thing I've done over the past couple of days, I'm screwed."

"Then explain."

She laughed, the sound strangled and bitter. "What, that I'm a werewolf and you're King of the Fairies, and we're hunting a psychotic vampire who's been hired to kill you by your brother? Oh, sure, that'll go over real well. Besides, the mayor's right about one thing—I am banging you." Snatching a small ceramic statue off her desk, she tossed it violently into the box.

He frowned ferociously. "That's irrelevant."

"Llyr, this is the South, and I'm a public official, and there's a mayoral race next year. All of which makes our sex life the unspoken nail in my coffin." She cupped a hand over the back of her neck and rolled her head to try to relieve the knot of tension gathering there. "And as if that's not enough, the fucking coroner knows I paid for the hotel rooms of FBI agents who weren't FBI agents. I'll be lucky if the Feds can't think of something to charge me with."

He stood. "No. This is not acceptable. I will not allow this! Everything you've done has been to save lives."

"Unless your magic comes back before tonight, there's absolutely nothing you can do, and no way we can explain." She rubbed a thumb between her eyebrows. "Maybe I should tender my resignation, but damn, I hate going down without a fight."

"Then don't. There must be some way . . ."

"I doubt it." Diana looked around at the room, then grabbed her purse and stepped around him as she headed for the door. "Oh, hell, I'm taking the rest of the day off. I didn't get enough sleep last night anyway, and I need some rest if I'm going to face that pack of jackals tonight."

Feeling helpless, he strode after her.

"You should eat something," Llyr said as they walked into the house.

"I'm not hungry," Diana told him without looking around as she headed toward the stairs.

Llyr stopped and stared at her, frowning. "You must be hungry. You transformed into your Dire Wolf form twice last night. Your body needs fuel."

"I just . . ." She broke step, shoulders slumping. "I don't feel like cooking, okay? I'll live."

He watched as she climbed the stairs, each step heavy with defeat. Silently, he cursed Ansgar. If he'd still had his powers, he would produce a feast for her.

Then again, if he still had his powers, he'd make every human in Verdaville mind his or her own business.

Llyr turned and eyed the refrigerator. His magic might be gone, but he still had hands. He'd cook something. Once she ate, she'd regain that fierce spirit he adored. At the very least, she'd lose the dull, beaten look that made his chest ache.

But what could he feed her?

He went to the refrigerator and opened the top compartment, as he'd seen Diana do the day before. It was filled with slabs of frozen meat, all covered with that transparent substance in which mortals seemed to habitually wrap their food. He chose one at random and examined it.

What had she called it? Ah. "The werewolf breakfast of champions," he muttered.

The thing to do was get the wrapping off. That, however, proved complicated. The transparent film clung to the meat and itself in stubborn folds that eventually reduced him to tearing the package open. Victorious at last, he pulled out the steak and tossed the frosty wrapping on the counter, then tried to decide what to do next. The meat was frozen into an inedible chunk. Automatically, he tried to spell it thawed, only to curse as nothing happened.

He hated being powerless.

Well, Diana had put yesterday's steak in the oven, so that was obviously what he should do.

Llyr crouched in front of the metal box and examined it dubiously, the frozen steak in one hand. The device had a great many knobs. Really, what were they all for? He leaned closer to read them. They were all inscribed with numbers. Temperatures?

Ah. That one read BROIL. One broiled meat. That would be the setting he wanted.

Llyr pulled the door open to pop the steak inside, then hesitated. It seemed Diana had put the meat on a pan of some kind.

Oh, well. This was good enough. He put the steak on the

metal rack, closed the oven door and twisted the knob to
BROIL. That should do it.

Satisfied with himself, Llyr rose to his feet. He wasn't
sure how long the cooking process would take, so it was
probably best to keep an eye on it.

A moment passed. He opened the oven. The steak lay
there, still frozen. Frowning, he twisted his head and contemplated the metal coils of the oven. Nothing seemed to
be happening. Perhaps he'd turned the wrong knob. He
straightened, located a second control, and turned it to
BROIL, too. A red light came on and began to glow.

Well, that was something, anyway. He wasn't entirely
sure how this metal box was supposed to cook a steak, but
mortals had been feeding themselves for thousands of
years. Presumably they knew how to construct the tools for
the job.

Besides, he was king of the Cachamwri Sidhe. He was
certainly up to mastering any technology humans cared to
create.

Diana lay stretched out on the bed staring sightlessly at
the ceiling fan as it spun lazily over her head. She knew she
should probably be working on some kind of defense, but
she was damned if she could think of one. There was just
no way to explain anything she'd done without mentioning
magic, vampires, or fairies. Which would be an even bigger career killer than no explanation at all.

Suddenly a shrill beep began to ring through the house.

Diana sat up, jolted from her preoccupation. It sounded
like the smoke alarm. "Good God, the house is on fire!"
She swung her legs off the bed and headed for the stairs.

As she ran down them barefoot, she heard Llyr growling something that sounded like Sidhe curses. Smoke

boiled from the kitchen door in a thick blue cloud that smelled of burning meat.

"Llyr! What are you doing?" Diana strode into the kitchen, stopping in the doorway long enough to reach up and key off the smoke alarm.

"I was trying to fix you lunch," he growled, shaking one hand and glaring at a chunk of partially carbonized meat. "I keep forgetting I don't have powers. I reached in to grab it and burned my hand."

"Oh, for the love of Pete!" She went to him and grabbed the hand he was shaking. The tips of two fingers were red. "Boy, you did toast yourself, didn't you? Come here." She towed him by the forearm over to the kitchen sink, turned on the cold water, and thrust his burned fingers under the flow.

"Ow!" He tried to pull back. "That hurts!"

"Quit being a baby, you big fairy. It'll help, I promise."

Llyr subsided and let her hold his hand under the water, still muttering musical Sidhe curses. Finally he wound down enough to ask, "There are not supposed to be flames in that oven of yours, are there?"

She looked up, alarmed. "Something caught on fire?"

"I blew it out." Blond wisps of hair had escaped his ponytail, leaving him looking adorably handsome and sullen. "Stupid device. One would think mortals would build things that worked the way they were supposed to."

Diana bit her lip to keep from laughing. "Go figure," she agreed.

He looked into her eyes and grinned. "That's better."

"What?"

"That smile. If I cannot feed you, at least I can entertain." He leaned forward and took her mouth in a kiss.

It started out mixed with laughter and self-depreciation, but Llyr was too dedicated a lover to leave it at that. A moment later, the kiss began to heat, became a lazy mating of lips and tongues. Pulling his hand from hers, he wrapped wet fingers around her shoulders and drew her close.

He felt so tall and strong and good against her. And whether he'd screwed it up or not, he'd been trying to feed her. He'd wanted her to feel better.

He cared about her.

And God, she cared about him. Not just because he was gorgeous and exotic and King of the Sidhe, not because he was brave and powerful, but because he was Llyr Galatyn, talented lover and lousy cook, funny and bright and an arrogant pain in the butt.

She was in love with him.

Diana moaned against his mouth and tried to pull back, shaken by the realization, but Llyr's arms tightened around her.

Before she could muster her defenses, he swept her up off her feet and strode out of the kitchen, carrying her like a doll. She yelped. "Where are we going?"

"Bed," he growled. "I'm cursed if I'll make love to you with the smell of burned cow in my nose."

She should tell him no, Diana knew, as he carried her up the stairs. Every time he touched her, she just fell deeper.

And yet . . . her life was going to hell. The only thing she had left was the pleasure of Llyr Galatyn's big body. And it would take a bigger fool than Diana London to turn away.

So when he swung her on the bed and followed her down, she wrapped her arms and legs around him as if she'd never let go.

His mouth sealed over hers in a sweet, deep kiss. She opened to him with a despairing moan and let him take her as he chose.

Yet he was tender with her rather than possessive, offering comfort with each stroke of tongue or lip over hers. She felt herself relaxing against him, melting into the warm strength of his body. He made a soft, encouraging sound against her mouth, one hand cradling her head, a thumb stroking her temple. His free hand slid down her body, pausing to dole out gentle caresses to breast and hip and thigh, soothing her. Deep inside her spirit, something wounded responded, releasing its bitter grasp on pain.

Then Llyr started taking off her clothes.

With each button, he paused to kiss, to murmur words of encouragement and praise.

It felt as though he loved her.

Diana caught her breath, entranced with the idea that Llyr Galatyn might feel the same tender adoration for her that she felt for him.

It was a stupid love, yes. She knew that quite well, but she didn't care. It was all she had.

But if he felt something, too, perhaps it wasn't as stupid as all that . . .

Then warm lips closed over one hard nipple, and he began to suck, tongue tip swirling and flicking, teeth nibbling. She let her head fall back and moaned.

He licked and tasted each breast in turn, slowly, lazily, before beginning a nibbling trek down her belly. Knowing what he intended, she threaded her hands through his long, silken hair. Reaching his objective, he pulled her thighs apart and bent to nuzzle.

His tongue flicked down between the soft petals of her sex, found her clitoris. Laved it until she had to undulate her hips against his face.

She murmured soft encouragement that grew more demanding as he kept licking, each tender tongue thrust driving her another increment toward orgasm.

The pleasure rolled up, sudden and surprising, a sweet

little pop of warmth. Diana groaned and shuddered, mindless.

But even as the first ripples faded, Llyr settled between her legs, caught his cock in one hand, and presented it to her sex. He slid inside, smooth and tight and filling. Diana moaned in need as he began to thrust.

"Oh, God, that's . . . Yes!" she whispered.

"Mmm," he purred in agreement, and bent low over her to murmur something rasping in Sidhe, the words both guttural and oddly lilting. Diana wrapped both legs around his butt and held on as he worked his cock in and out in strokes that quickly lengthened into driving jolts. Each one pushed her a little closer to another sweet explosion.

Until, at last, she could take no more. The second climax rolled free, hot and sweet, shaking her deliciously until she collapsed under him, panting.

He drove to the balls and froze with a soft, triumphant shout, coming, groaning something in Sidhe that sounded oddly reverent.

Almost like "I love you."

Diana lay still, listening to his panting breaths slow and calm. She wanted desperately to stay just as she was, warm and unthinking, but unfortunately, her rebellious mind refused to cooperate.

In a few hours, she'd have to meet with the council, who would likely fire her.

Ugly word.

When it was over, what then? The vampire was still at large, still killing. And Llyr was still in danger. Yet without the authority of being city manager, how was Diana supposed to fight her? The council wouldn't let her remain a reserve officer.

There had to be something Diana could do, some way she could defend herself against the accusations. Some way to save her job.

The maddening thing was that everything she'd done all along the line had been justified. She'd had good reasons for it all, up to and including sleeping with Llyr—she just couldn't explain any of them.

Under normal circumstances the council might find a way to turn a blind eye. Diana was well liked, after all, and she had pulled the town out of its financial tailspin.

The problem was that Clara Davies had an axe to grind about that abusive son of hers. Given that, Clara's influence among her wide circle of friends, and the mayor's general lack of balls at election time, and Diana was in deep trouble with little hope of recovery.

She sighed and closed her burning eyes. If only she could get a couple hours' sleep. She might be able to come up with something with a clearer head.

As if sensing her disquiet, Llyr rubbed comforting circles on her back with one hand. He felt big and warm against her, and she breathed in, inhaling his clean, masculine scent.

She wasn't going to be able to keep him either. He was going to regain his powers and go back to the Mageverse, assuming that damn vampire didn't manage to get the drop on them.

"That fuckin' vamp," Diana growled against his chest. "I swear to God, if it's the last thing I ever do, I'm going to kill that bitch. This entire debacle is because of her coming into my town and killing my people."

"We'll get her," he said softly. "Sleep now, love."

The tear took her by surprise. She wiped it away with her fingers, but another one took its place, rolling hot down her cheek. "I've worked so hard," she whispered.

His arms tightened. "I know, my love."

At the tenderness in his voice, the last of her barriers broke. She began to sob into the warmth of his chest.

Aching as she cried, Llyr stroked her hair and whispered Sidhe endearments he knew she didn't understand. But this time, she wouldn't allow herself to be comforted.

Finally she rolled away from him and curled into a ball of helpless misery. He followed anyway, spooning her with his body, trying to offer what comfort he could.

After a long, miserable hour went by, she went lax in sleep and he eased away from her.

Naked, Llyr rolled from the bed and padded soundlessly downstairs into the living room, where the furniture still stood pushed against the wall from his last attempt at calling the dragon.

Taking a deep breath, he slid into the first sequence of the Dragon's Dance, seeking to call Cachamwri once again.

He had failed so many of his women. Janieda. His wives. Even his children. What good was he when he couldn't protect those who loved him?

If he could call Cachamwri and break the spell, he was perfectly willing to make every mortal on Diana's council forget any grievance with her. Then he'd tend to the vampire.

And his brother would be next.

If he had to attack Ansgar directly and lose both his throne and his life, so be it. Llyr had always hesitated before because he'd known he'd not only die; he'd plunge both kingdoms into a civil war as the various factions in each struggled for power. The Cachamwri Sidhe, at least, lived in some semblance of peace; his advisors had vehemently argued that his people could not afford to lose him.

But enough was enough.

Ten Sidhe bodyguards lay in the mortals' morgue, their families unaware of their murders. Dead defending him from Ansgar's assassin. His wives and his children, too, were dead, murdered by his brother's pet killers. And Diana's life was in ruins.

All because of Ansgar.

No more. Llyr was done with playing the game his father had dictated all those centuries before. Cold determination filled him.

He pivoted, snapped a punch into the air with all his strength, followed it up with a kick, and spun. Sweat rolled down his naked body as he chanted, calling Cachamwri, reaching out to the Dragon God through the very cells of his body.

Llyr could feel the great beast coiled deep in the heart of the Mageverse, linked to him by its own vows to Galatyn the First. The vampire's spell might have robbed Llyr of his powers, but nothing could break that link.

"Heed me," he whispered in Sidhe, pivoting, stepping, punching into the air with all his strength. "You took a vow, Great One, to come to the aid of those of my line in our hour of greatest need. Come to me now. Breathe your fire over me. When I slid from my mother's womb, I bore your mark on my flesh. Come to me now. Come to me, for she whom I love suffers and my people are at risk."

Heat pulsed across his skin. From the corner of his eye, he saw color streak across his biceps and coil the length of his arm.

She whom I love . . .

Suddenly he heard his own words, and his steps faltered. Did he love Diana? Had he spoke the truth of his heart without realizing it?

His concentration scattered. The heat died, and he swore viciously. "No! Cachamwri!"

But the dragon was gone.

Llyr stopped and threw his head back, cursing himself. He'd almost had it! "Fool! Stupid fool!"

He squared his shoulders and pushed his frustrated rage away. He would just start over.

Doggedly, he turned and began again.

Diana and Llyr walked into the Verdaville City Council chambers to discover every off-duty city cop in the audience, all in uniform. Even Jerry Morgan was there, his face still bruised black and blue from the bar fight. Gist's expression was downright stormy, his eyes hot with outrage.

Unfortunately, the packed audience also included Clara Davies; her son, Roger, also bruised; the coroner; and two television cameras. Evidently somebody had alerted the media that the council was planning to fire her, because they did not normally cover Verdaville City Council meetings; the town was just too small.

Great. Just great. Not only was she going to be humiliated and fired, they were going to broadcast it on the six o'clock news.

Keeping her face expressionless with an effort, Diana walked over to the table she shared with the city clerk and the treasurer, while Llyr found a seat in the front where he could aim his regal glare at the council.

As she sat, she was aware of the cold, disapproving stares of all seven city council members flicking from Llyr to her. She stared back steadily. Dammit, she'd done nothing wrong—except possibly sleep with Llyr, and that was none of their business anyway.

City Clerk Tammy Jones leaned over to whisper in her ear, "I can't believe they're doing this. You're the best ad-

ministrator we've ever had!" Tammy, who was nearing re-
tirement after thirty years with the city, had worked with
seven managers. Professional administrators tended to use
Verdaville as a stepping-stone to something bigger and better. Or, depending on how things went, smaller and worse.

The latter evidently being Diana's destiny.

Jerry and the chief moved to join Diana at her table.
Both men looked equally indignant. "We're not going to let
them do this to you," Gist said in a low, intense whisper.

Diana sighed. "Chief, you're going to end up getting
fired, too, if you're not careful. It's not worth it."

He set his jaw. "Yes, it is."

"You're a good cop," Jerry told her, a mulish expression
on his face. "Whether you're a volunteer or not. I'd be in
the hospital right now if it hadn't been for you and the
blond guy." He lowered his voice. "But it might have been
better if you'd left him at home. They think—"

"I know what they think. I just don't care." She stiffened, seeing Bobby Greene get out of his chair with his
notebook, followed by two broadcast reporters. "Oh, God,
here comes the media."

The cops shot simultaneous glances of pure distaste
over their shoulders and went back to their seats as the
three reporters walked up.

Bobby grinned. "So, Diana—I understand you're living
in sin with a fairy."

Diana stared at the *Verdaville Voice* reporter, feeling her
face go cold with shock. Good God, how had he found out?
"What fairy?"

Instantly, all three reporters took on predatory expressions at her reaction. "The big guy," Bobby said, making a
gesture as if indicating the length of an invisible ponytail.
"With the hair."

Oh, that kind of fairy. She relaxed. "That's my cousin."
She hadn't lived thirty years as a werewolf without learn-
ing how to lie like a rug.

"Cousin." Bobby lifted his thick black eyebrows and
scrawled something down in his notebook. "Right."

"Ms. London," one of the television reporters began.
She was tall, slim, blond, and perfectly groomed in a suit
that probably cost as much as Diana made in a month. "I
understand some of the men who were killed in the motel
explosion had identified themselves as FBI." Gist had told
the local reporters some kind of bomb had gone off at the
Sleep Saver. So far they were buying it.

"Oh, the ones George thinks are aliens?" There. Now
Miller could fend off uncomfortable questions.

The other TV reporter's eyes lit up, and he scrawled
something on his legal pad. "Aliens?"

"That's what I heard," Diana said, shrugging. "But
you'll have to talk to him about that." Miller was a notorious media hound. With any luck, he'd get carried away and
shoot his own credibility in the foot. If Diana hit it really
lucky, talk of long-haired E.T.s would ensure even the FBI
would refuse to have anything to do with him.

Before they could ask any more questions, the Mayor
banged his gavel. "I hereby call this special meeting of the
Verdaville City Council to order."

The reporters turned and hurried back to their seats, as
eager for blood as any pack of wolves she'd ever seen.

"I requested this meeting to discuss the city manager's
contract," Thompson began. "Since this is an issue of employment, under the South Carolina Freedom of Informa-
tion Act, the council needs to go into executive session. I'll
entertain a motion."

"I make a motion we go into executive session to discuss matters of employment," Carly Jefferies said, her eyes

cold as she looked at Diana. She and Thompson were normally political enemies, but it seemed they were on the same page on this one. That wasn't good.

"Seconded," Roland Andrews said.

Thompson banged his gavel. "We'll adjourn to council chambers, but we'll return to open session before we vote, as required under the FOIA."

Diana relaxed slightly. She'd been afraid they'd start the process in open session, but evidently Thompson was wary of any potential lawsuit she might bring.

That was something anyway.

SEVENTEEN

Llyr turned to watch as Diana and the council paraded out. She'd explained the process to him earlier, and he knew he wouldn't be allowed to go with her, even to lend moral support.

His sense of failure nagged at him. He'd fought all day to call the dragon, but Cachamwri had refused to answer. He wasn't really surprised. He'd tried to summon the dragon before, but though the god had vowed to serve his line in its hour of greatest peril, Cachamwri's definition of "greatest peril" was evidently different from his. He'd actually gotten more reaction from it in the past couple of days than he ever had before.

But not enough.

Brooding, he folded his arms and stretched his legs out in front of him. He was aware of the stares of those around him—some curious, some outright hostile, some contemptuous. King that Llyr was, it irritated him, but he wasn't about to make matters worse for Diana by objecting.

Then to his astonishment, a short, heavyset dark-haired man dropped into the seat next to him, a notebook in hand. "Hi!" the fellow said, with the stubborn smile of a man used to rejection. "Bobby Greene, *Verdaville Voice*. I understand you're a friend of the city manager. What do you think of . . . ?"

Llyr remembered the front page he'd seen in Merlin's Grimorie. "*Verdaville Voice*. This is a newspaper?"

"Yeah, we're a weekly. Now, what—?"

"You're a reporter?" Diana, he recalled, did not seem to like reporters.

"Yeah. What do you think of the City Council's evident plans to discipline Di . . . ?" the reporter trailed off.

Llyr went on giving the man the look he usually reserved for those who had earned his coldest royal displeasure.

"Ummm." Greene swallowed.

Llyr lifted an eyebrow. *You're still sitting beside me?* his look said.

"Sorry to bother you." The reporter got up and fled.

Llyr grunted in satisfaction. He hadn't been a king for sixteen centuries for nothing. Perhaps he should try that trick on Diana's City Council. Or perhaps not. Lately everything he tried to do only made her situation worse.

Llyr aimed a brooding stare down at the toes of his mortal-manufactured shoes. He'd come to realize that his revelation this morning had been correct. He was in love with her.

Unfortunately, he had no more idea of what to do about it now than he had earlier. He was still powerless, out of touch with his people, and in constant danger of assassination.

And she was still a werewolf.

With luck, the first state of affairs would soon change, but Diana would still be a werewolf, and his people would still be reluctant to accept her.

The irony was, of course, that she'd make an incredible queen. He'd realized the full truth of that watching her stride from the room just now, head up and shoulders back, silently telling her enemies that they would never touch her dignity no matter what they did.

Oh, yes. He loved her.

The question was, what was he going to do about it?

As the council watched from their seats in the hearing room, Roger Davies glared at Diana. He was a big, floridly beefy man who could have used quality time on a Stair-Master. His piggy blue eyes revealed his sullen outrage that she didn't show him the fear he was used to getting from women.

"She police brutalized me!" Davies announced. "Her and that blond boyfriend of hers. You see what he did to me." Pointing at his battered face, Roger glowered down the length of the table at the council's members, who wore varying expressions of discomfort. "I'm gonna sue! Her and him and the whole city!"

"Mr. Davies, you blindsided me with a beer bottle," Diana said, holding on to her Burning Moon temper with extreme difficulty. "I'm lucky you didn't kill me."

"She is," Jerry Morgan put in. Cop and suspect had been called into the executive session to tell the council about the events of Saturday night. "He busted her head clean open. I saw him do it."

"They're lyin'," Davies spat. "There ain't a mark on her."

And there wasn't. The fact that both men looked like

they'd been through a meat grinder only added weight to Davies's accusation.

"I heal fast," Diana gritted. For once, her Dire Wolf powers were working against her. Though she'd taken a beating, both during the bar fight and in her battle with the vampire, both sets of injuries had healed when she'd shifted to Dire Wolf. But since she couldn't explain that, it made her look like a liar.

"Look, Roger's buddies were beating the living daylights out of me when Diana and her friend rolled up," Morgan said hotly. "If she hadn't waded in and helped, I'd be in the hospital."

"You started it!" Davies growled. "You swung at us with that nightstick of yours, just 'cause we said the cops was sitting on their asses instead of catching that serial killer." He looked at the council. "We weren't doin' nothing to nobody."

Morgan glared at him, his eyes hot with rage. "You know, I've known you since elementary school, and you've always been a lyin' bully."

As the two men began to shout at one another, Diana silently gritted her teeth. Despite the sideshow with Davies, she knew it was a lost cause. None of the council would look at her.

Carly Jefferies had made that clear as they all started to sit down half an hour ago. "Well, all I know is that everybody at the beauty shop today was talking about the man Diana's got staying at her house." She'd given Diana a long, cold look. "That's not the kind of image we want for our town. Not at all."

It was all over but the vote.

As the first hour of executive session slid by, Gist decided it was time for a bathroom break.

He was coming back from the men's room when he saw the coroner standing outside the open door on the steps of City Hall, smoking a cigarette.

Looked like a perfect opportunity to give the bastard a piece of his mind.

He sauntered outside. "Found out anything new on your aliens, yet, George?"

Miller turned, the cigarette halfway to his mouth. An expression of profound discomfort crossed his pudgy face. "Never said they were aliens."

Gist shrugged. "Well, you said they weren't human. That doesn't leave a hell of a lot of other options."

"You saw 'em. Did they look human to you?"

"You mean the ears? Ever heard of plastic surgery, George?"

A ruddy flush began to spread up Miller's face. "Hey, all I know is what the pathologist said." He gestured with his cigarette, smoke trailing his hand in snaking patterns. "Garrison swears their blood wasn't human."

"So what? You think you've found a fuckin' *X-Files*?"

The coroner threw his cigarette aside, his gaze cold with suspicion. "What I think is that you and your city manager know something, and you're covering it up. I don't know why, but I can just smell it."

"All you smell is your own bull—"

"Now is that any way for two public servants to talk?"

They turned in surprise. A woman climbed the steps of City Hall toward them, hips swaying. Despite his anger at Miller, Gist felt a distracting buzz of masculine admiration. The short skirt she wore showed a whole lot of long leg, and her red hair tumbled around her shoulders in artful disarray.

Then Gist frowned, taking in the fishnet stockings and handcuffs at her belt. She might be pretty, but she dressed like a hooker.

"Excuse us, ma'am," Miller said with the automatic chagrin of a Southern gentleman caught saying something he shouldn't in front of a lady. "We're just having a little professional disagreement."

The woman stopped on the step just below him. "See, the funny thing is, they are hiding something from you." To Gist's astonishment, her hand began to shoot light like a sparkler on the Fourth of July. In the fifteen seconds he spent staring, the sparks coalesced into a Bowie knife. The woman grinned viciously. "Me." She rammed the knife upward into Miller's ribs.

He gasped and doubled over. For a split second, his agonized gaze flew pleadingly to Gist. The woman pulled the knife away and let him fall.

"Jesus!" Gist grabbed for his gun, but she seized his wrist, stopping it before it got to his holster.

"Give us a bellow, baby," she purred. Those delicate fingers squeezed, and he felt bones break with a *crunch* and an explosion of white-hot agony. He screamed in shock and pain.

She grinned. She had fangs. "There you go."

Llyr reacted to Gist's bellow of pain on sheer instinct, springing out of his seat and running from the council chamber before even the police officers had time to react.

He met Diana charging for the exit, her eyes wild with Burning Moon rage. "That was the chief!" she snarled, flinging the exit door open.

They both stopped dead at the sight of the crumpled body lying on the stairs. "It's the coroner!" Diana's head came up sharply as she inhaled. "The vampire. She did this—and she's got the chief!"

"Diana!"

But it was too late. She leaped from the top of the stairs, transforming to wolf form in midair. Llyr cursed ripely as he cleared the steps in one jump.

Too late.

She was already off and running, a long dark shape streaking through the moonlight. He shot after her as, behind him, mortal voices lifted in shock and outrage.

Llyr ignored them, concentrating on keeping Diana in view, knowing even as he ran that they were probably headed into a trap. He also knew Diana was past caution. Or even reason. Between the Burning Moon, her fury at her lost job, and her fear for her friend, she'd completely lost control.

It didn't help that she was much faster on four feet than he was on two, even running full out. He'd never catch her in time.

As they fled through the night, male voices rang behind them. At least Diana's men were on the way. Unfortunately, they were human and even slower than Llyr was. He had the ugly feeling it would all be over by the time they caught up. He only hoped he could catch Diana himself before she ran headlong into whatever trap the bitch had set.

He saw the wolf streak into a stand of thick trees and plunged after her. Brambles and branches tore at his clothes and long hair, but Llyr kept going. He could scent her on the wind.

Along with the smell of blood.

He caught a flash of pale flesh and skidded to a stop barely in time to keep from tripping over her. Diana had turned human again to crouch beside a crumpled, blue-clad form.

"She stabbed him," she snapped, her silver gaze flashing up to his. She'd stripped off her jacket and wadded it up to press it against the chief's side. "He's still alive. Apply pressure to this—the vampire left a scent trail going east. I'm going to get that bitch!"

"No!" the chief groaned. "Di, don't!"

"He's right." Llyr dropped to one knee and reached to press the jacket against the wound. "Diana, stop and think. She's setting a trap."

His lover's pretty face twisted with frustration. Lowering her voice to a whisper, she hissed, "Llyr, I can smell her! She's right there waiting, maybe a hundred yards away. I've lost everything, but I am damn well going to stick a stake in that bitch before I'm done."

"Diana! Chief? Where are you?" It was Jerry Morgan's voice, rising over the sound of bodies crashing through the woods.

She lifted her head and shouted, "Man down! Somebody call an ambulance!" To Llyr, she added, "They'll be here in a second. Don't let up on the pressure!"

Before he could object again, she transformed and leaped off into the brush in a series of great bounds. "Dragon's Breath, Diana!" But he could feel her jacket going wet with blood even as he held it. He didn't dare let go, or the chief would be dead in minutes.

"She's nuts," Gist panted, his voice dangerously faint. He caught at Llyr's hand with icy fingers. "Go after her, boy. Don't let her . . . get herself killed."

"Not yet," Llyr told him grimly, refusing to let up the pressure. The crackle of brush and hoarse male voices grew closer, and he lifted his voice. "Over here!"

He just hoped he'd be able to catch up with Diana before she ran into the vampire's trap.

Deep in her blazing Burning Moon fury, Diana knew she was taking a huge risk, but she didn't care. The vampire

had destroyed her life, killed fourteen men, and stripped
Llyr of his powers. One way or another, she was going to
pay. Now.

Diana skidded to a halt to make sure she hadn't lost the
trail. The scent was so strong, every breath carried it. The
bitch had to be standing just around the . . .

Wait, what was that . . . ?

Something closed in the thick fur of her scruff and
jerked her off her feet as if she weighed no more than a
puppy. Diana yelped.

Suddenly she was crushed against a hard, armored
body, with a big hand clamped hard around her muzzle.
Terrified, she looked up into a handsome face that was both
familiar and horribly alien.

Her captor's grin stabbed ice into her heart. "So you're
Llyr's bitch," he said, in a deep, velvet voice that sent cold
fear shooting through her.

Ansgar!

Instinctively, Diana twisted in his arms and tried to
transform into the Dire Wolf, but before she could change,
he dragged her forward. Light exploded around her and she
felt the the magic of a dimensional gate rush over her skin.

Then they were through. Lifting her higher in his arms,
the Sidhe king kicked open a door. Diana felt her transformation begin with triumph and relief as he threw her to
the ground.

Pain blazed through her side as she hit hard. She came
up snarling as he turned, having just locked the door.

Wait. Either he'd grown, or she was much smaller than
she should be. Diana glanced down and saw white flesh
and her linen pantsuit. Somehow she'd assumed the wrong
form. Frustrated, she reached for her magic again.

Nothing happened.

Ansgar grinned at her, his mouth stretching into a parody of Llyr's wicked smile. "I use this room for execution," he told her, almost gently. "It's surrounded by a blanking spell that nullifies magic, which is what threw you into your human form." He moved toward her. She retreated, realizing he was even more solidly muscled than Llyr. His grin widened as he drew a knife. "In here, it's all about brute force."

Diana fought to hide her sick horror. If he'd been human, she'd still be more than a match for him in strength, despite his brawn and longer reach. Her Direkind muscle was that much denser and stronger than a human's. Unfortunately, though, he was Sidhe, and his size gave him easily twice her strength.

She gave him a sneer anyway as she fell into a combat crouch. "I'm afraid you've miscalculated, asshole. As we humans say, this only levels the playing field."

Ansgar laughed in a rolling boom that reminded her far too much of Llyr. "Oh, I don't think so." He moved toward her in an oiled slink, like a cat sneaking up on a pigeon. His smile of anticipation was as chilling as his gaze. "You know, you're very pretty. I see why Llyr is so infatuated."

Diana backed away, daring a quick scan of the room. Torches illuminated naked stone walls and a stained execution block with a huge headsman's axe buried in it. Other than that, the room was empty. "Where are your guards?"

"I don't need them." His gaze flicked over her body, deliberately insulting. "Besides, I'm afraid I'm not in the mood to share."

The chief's gun in his hand, Llyr moved through the night, every sense alert. A team of city firefighters, including a paramedic, had taken over administering medical care to Gist while he was being taken to a waiting ambulance.

As they'd carried him away, he begged Llyr to find Diana.

Now Llyr, Jerry Morgan, and two other Verdaville cops were searching the woods for Diana and the killer. But he hadn't caught so much as a whiff of wolf, and his tension grew with every step he took. Where in the name of the Dragon was she? Had she been ambushed?

A cold creeping on the back of Llyr's neck told him he was running a risk a king had no business taking. If he got himself killed out here, his people were going to end up wearing Ansgar's yoke. Yet it wasn't in him to simply cool his heels while the woman he loved charged into danger.

Llyr cursed silently as he ghosted through the brush with a hunter's skill. Diana's feral streak might be a delight in the bedroom, but it could be a pain in the butt in combat.

His instincts suddenly clamored, stopping him in his tracks. He listened hard.

Crack.

The snap of the branch was so faint he scarcely heard it. Leaves rustled.

"All alone, Majesty?" the woman's voice whispered out of the dark. He'd have said it was sexy if not for the evil undertone.

Llyr pivoted with a fluid skill designed to thwart any attack. Bringing the gun up, he aimed it toward the sound of the vampire's voice. His pounding heart slowed into the cool, steady rhythms of a veteran warrior. As he scanned the darkness, he saw no trace of the woman, yet his every sense thrummed.

Steel flashed toward his face and Llyr jerked aside. The blade sliced so close he felt the wind of its passage. He pulled the trigger. His borrowed gun roared in his hand, its flash lighting up a woman's wild eyes and snarling mouth.

The bullet struck a magical shield in a shower of sparks and whined off into the trees. Llyr fired again, but she had disappeared back into the darkness.

"You do know he's got her?" the witch purred from behind him. Llyr wheeled, fired, and dove aside.

She screeched in pain. "Bastard! That's it, I'm done playing with you!"

He saw the blazing ball of magic shoot toward him. Ducking, he fired. She hissed in frustration. Sparks danced as lead struck the shimmering energy field. "Aren't you worried about your pretty little friend, Your Majesty?" the witch taunted. "I mean, given your handsome brother's ugly habits?"

"What's Ansgar got to do with this?" Fear clamped around his heart, but he fought it. The chances were good she was lying.

"He just gated off to his palace with her. And you know, somehow he doesn't strike me as a very pleasant host."

Which meant Llyr better wrap this up before Ansgar killed the woman he loved, if she was indeed telling the truth. He fired toward the sound of the vampire's voice.

Whomp!

Something hot and viscous slammed into his face like a wave of burning glue, tearing the gun from his hand. The force of the magical bolt drove him backward until he slammed hard into a tree. Cursing, Llyr bucked, trying to tear free of whatever held him, but the spell wrapped him tight. He went on fighting anyway, struggling against the magic, but he couldn't break its hold.

Light blazed up, blinding him. Instinctively, he jerked his head away. Rough bark scraped his face.

When at last the dazzle faded, he found himself looking at the vampire. She smirked at him, one hand propped on her hip, the other holding an illumination spell that cast a cool blue glow over the clearing they stood within. She'd pinned him against a tree. He couldn't move.

Her carmine mouth exposed shining fangs as she spoke. "Here's the deal, baby. Ansgar takes care of your furry girlfriend for me, and I take care of you for him." Light flared in her right hand, coalescing into a butcher knife. "'Course, you and White Fang won't enjoy it much—but we sure will."

Ansgar's big fist flashed toward her face, but Diana twisted aside, blocking the blow with an upthrust forearm. Pain blazed in her wrist, but she ignored it, shooting a rabbit punch into his ribs.

He lifted a brow. "Very nice." Then he backhanded her with a slap that made her see stars. She danced back, trying to work her way over to the executioner's block and the axe it held. If she could just get her hands on that weapon . . .

Casually, Ansgar grabbed the neck of his velvet tunic and ripped it like paper. The ragged sound of tearing fabric was loud in the heavy stillness of the room. Diana sneered at his massive chest. "Is that supposed to impress me?"

He smirked, lips stretching across white teeth, his pale eyes burning through the black tangle of his hair. "Yes."

And as much as she hated to admit it, he was impressive—even taller and broader than Llyr, so massive as to look just shy of muscle bound. But even more frightening than his sheer size was the terrible anticipation in his gaze.

Diana backed up and started circling him, trying to get to the axe. Ansgar followed, thick brawn moving like boulders under the pale flesh of his torso. If he got those big hands on her, she was finished. He had too much reach with those long, powerful arms, and he was too damn strong. The axe was the only chance she had.

If she could get to it.

Luckily, Diana had grown up sparring with her brother, who was every bit as big as Ansgar. Unfortunately, she also knew Jim London had never gone after her full force, even when they were kids. She'd get no such mercy from the Sidhe king.

Seeing her chance, she leaped for the block. With a blood-chilling roar, Ansgar charged. Her heart catapulting into her throat, Diana spun aside, lashing out at the side of his knee in a vicious kick.

But before the blow could land, Ansgar grabbed the back of her jacket and jerked her off her feet. The kick went wide as he hauled her into the air. Instinctively, she threw her arms up and slid right out of the coat, hitting the ground on her ass. She rolled up onto her shoulders to power a kick up at his balls, but he leaped back, ugly malice in his laugh.

"Nice jacket," he taunted, holding the coat in the air as she bounced to her feet. Grabbing it between both big hands, he ripped it in two and dropped the pieces on the floor. "I'm looking forward to the shirt."

She sneered at him, hoping the ice in her belly didn't show in her eyes. "Fuck off." He meant to rape her before he killed her. She couldn't say she was surprised.

He laughed and charged again. "Oh, eventually."

This time she spun aside and shot a kick into the back of his knee. He went down cursing, only to roll to his feet again in one smooth motion. Dammit, she'd missed. If the blow had landed squarely, it would have shattered the joint.

Ansgar looked her over, his gaze chill with calculation. "You do know some technique, don't you?"

Diana didn't waste time answering. She had to kill him, that much was obvious. She was probably dead one way or another—she had no delusions that she could get out of the palace without being caught—but at least Llyr and his people would be free.

Her mind ticked through the lethal strikes she'd learned in the various martial arts classes she'd taken over the years. Unfortunately, she had to get in close to use any of them, and that gave him a chance to use those big hands. Not that she had a choice. She wasn't going to let him have the perverted pleasure of raping her.

Diana's thoughts flicked to Llyr. She just hoped to God he hadn't tried to go after the vampire, powerless as he was. If she had to die, at least he should survive.

The knife sliced into his skin in a shallow cut that burned ice cold. Llyr clenched his teeth as the vampire leaned into him, her skin damp with lecherous sweat. She'd stripped him and set up a field to keep them invisible to the mortals who still searched the woods around them. Llyr could hear them calling in the distance.

Unfortunately, there was nothing they could do to help him. He was alone with his killer.

"Oh, you're a stubborn one, aren't you?" the vampire purred. "That's good. I like a challenge."

Had Ansgar already killed Diana? Probably not. He'd want to play with her a while, like this perverted bitch. Which meant there was still time. Time to call the Dragon God—if only Cachamwri would answer.

Llyr closed his eyes to block out the vampire's smirk and sought to still himself. He had to concentrate, block out his fear for Diana and himself, block the pain, block everything but his need for Cachamwri.

Pain blazed up in his right shoulder, slicing diagonally across his chest. Just deep enough to hurt. Llyr fought to ignore it as he focused all his attention on calling the Dragon

God. *Cachamwri*, he thought in the Old Tongue, *you vowed to help the King of the Cachamwri Sidhe in his hour of greatest peril. This witch means to butcher me to feed her lust; my brother will enslave my people and rape my woman.*

Then save them, the Dragon breathed in his thoughts. Deep within himself, Llyr started. Cachamwri had never spoken to him before.

Evidently, this really was his greatest hour of need.

Hope rose in his mind, but he tamped it down. Carefully, he answered, *Ansgar has stripped me of my magic through treachery. I must call on your strength, Bright One.*

Another red-hot stab of pain almost jerked him from his trance, but he managed to hold on to Cachamwri's glowing presence.

"You try my patience, fairy," the vampire snarled in his ear. "If you're not going to play, I'll kill you now and be done with it."

She hurts you, the Dragon said. *I can feel your pain.*

"Yes!" The word emerged as a shout as a knifepoint scored his nipple.

The vampire laughed. "That's better. Oh, much. Now let's try this again."

EIGHTEEN

Help me! Llyr demanded.

The dragon's silence was nerve-wracking played against the backdrop of white-hot pain. *You are the scion of a line of heroes*, Cachamwri said at last. *In the past, I could count on the kings of Cachamwri to act for me in the realm of flesh. But I ask myself if your father's blood has run thin, given such a son as Ansgar.*

Llyr licked his dry lips. *Lend me but a fragment of your power, and I'll rid my line of him. As to your will, you need only make it known.* This time his ferocious concentration was such that the pain of the vampire's knife didn't even touch him.

He could sense the Dragon God's disapproval. *So willing to spill a brother's blood.*

The judgement stung. *Ansgar is no brother of mine.*

He's killed my wives and all my children, and he would make slaves of my people.

The Dragon was silent so long Llyr almost lost hope. *Still, I am not sure you are worthy of my Breath, and I do not care to give such power to one who cannot be trusted with it. But as I made a vow to your forefathers. I shall give thee a choice. I shall kill this mad witch and free you, or I shall kill your brother. I will not do both.*

It was all Llyr could do not to cry out in disbelief and despair. *If you restore my magic, I can save myself.*

That is not the offer. The Dragon's mental voice was unyielding. *Make your choice, Sidhe king. Live or die.*

Sick horror welled to choke him as he imagined what the next hours would be like. But there was no choice. *Then let me die. Save Diana and my people.*

Are you sure, Sidhe king? The witch means to scoop out your heart while you scream.

He wanted to curse, but he didn't dare. Cachamwri was the only hope Diana had. *My heart is already bespoke, Bright One. My woman and my people have it safe.*

A noble epitaph, Sidhe king. I hope you endure your fate with the same bravado. And the Dragon God was gone, leaving only cold, bitter darkness in his mind.

Llyr opened his eyes and sneered at the vampire. "What are you waiting for, whore?"

Rage blazed in the witch's eyes. "Oh, you're going to pay for that. I'm going to make you scream."

Diana leaped into the air in a scything kick aimed right for the side of Ansgar's jaw. It was riskier than hell; the kick might break his neck if it landed, but if she missed, she'd be vulnerable.

He jerked his head back. His hand blurred up. She twisted, but his fingers closed brutally hard over her ankle.

Ansgar jerked her out of the air so hard her neck whiplashed painfully. Diana yelped.

"Impressive move," the Sidhe said. "Stupid, but impressive."

Then, with an offhand jerk, he smashed her face first into the granite wall. Pain detonated in her head, and she went limp, stunned.

Distantly, Diana felt herself slam into the cold stone floor as he dropped her. Cloth ripped away from her legs. Her bra dug into her back as he grabbed it between her breasts and jerked. Weakly, she swung a fist at his nose, but he backhanded her. She saw stars and tasted blood. "Fucker."

His looming face grinned down at her. "Yes, thank you, I intend to."

Grimly, Diana fought to focus her swimming wits. She damn well wouldn't just go down like this. She lay still, trying to project stunned submission as she waited for her chance. Not moving felt much too good to her aching, battered body, but she fought the animal instinct to submit and hope he'd be satisfied with raping her. She knew he wouldn't.

Ansgar rocked back on his heels to look down at her, his cold gaze appraising her naked body. "Oh, you are lovely," he said. "Not as busty as I prefer, but rather lithe and charming. Perhaps I won't kill you after all."

A chance. Diana mustered a seductive smile, hoping the calculation didn't show in her eyes. "Please. You don't have to hurt me. I can make it good for you." Blood trickled from her swelling lip.

Ansgar snorted. "What kind of fool do you think I am?" He reached for her.

"Are you fool enough to waste the opportunity to have a willing werewolf in her Burning Moon?"

He hesitated, interest stirring in his eyes. "Burning Moon?"

Diana licked the blood from her lips with a slow pass of her tongue. She watched excitement flare in his eyes. "Take a deep breath, Ansgar. I know you feel it. No male is immune to the scent of a werewolf female in heat— not even Sidhe. How do you think I had Llyr so enthralled?"

His pale gaze flicked down her body. "I can think of any number of ways."

She forced a smile. "Flattering."

Suspicion darkened the heat in his stare. "You fought hard, for a willing woman—or whatever it is you are."

Diana shrugged. "No she-wolf yields easily. How else can one be sure a male is worthy?"

Ansgar sneered. "Oh, I'm more than worthy of you."

Not even on your best day. "Prove it."

She had him. She could see it in the leap of speculation on his face. The fact she might be trying to play him only made the temptation greater; it wouldn't even occur to Ansgar she could be a serious threat to him.

His lips curling into a taunting smile, he reached for her breast. She fought to keep the revulsion from her eyes as he touched her.

The knife plunged viciously into his side, forcing Llyr to clench his teeth against a scream.

"Ahhhh," the vampire purred, her green eyes bright with sick excitement. "That was good. Let's do that again."

He spat in her face.

Her head snapped back in fury. "Oh, you are a fool!" Slowly, she wiped the spittle away.

"It was worth it." Llyr laughed, knowing the mockery

would drive her into a frenzy. His only chance now was to goad her into killing him quickly.

"Bold words. Let's see if you—"

Fire! A searing explosion of heat and light detonated in his chest, so white-hot he thought for a moment she'd induced a heart attack.

Until he felt the vast, shining intelligence invading his mind. *What?*

It does burn, I fear. Cachamwri said in his mind. *But then, it is the Dragon's Breath.* That was when Llyr recognized the power that poured in behind the pain.

Magic. He had magic again. Cachamwri had answered his prayer after all.

I thought you'd decided I wasn't worthy, he thought, dazed by the sudden onslaught of hope.

I needed to make sure of you, Cachamwri said. *But you were willing to sacrifice yourself for your woman and your people. That is no coward's act, nor is the love in you a sham. It burns as bright as my power.*

Llyr felt the Dragon fill him, flooding him with strength and magic such as he'd never known in his long life. When the dazzle faded from his eyes, he saw the vampire staring at him, her mouth gaping. "What the hell was that?" she demanded, backing up a pace. "You lit up like a firefly."

"No." Llyr bared his teeth at her. "Like the Dragon's Breath."

The spell blazed out of him in a boiling wave of power, rupturing the enchantment that bound him on its way to her. She screamed and threw up a shield. The blast poured against it, sending sparks bouncing into the night. The vampire yelped as some of them tunneled through to scorch her skin. Llyr jerked away from the tree, grinning in furious pleasure.

Yet even in his euphoria, he could feel lead weighing his

legs. Blood ran hot from the dozen knife wounds scoring his flesh. He gathered the power and sent it swirling through his body. The gouges burned and tingled as they healed.

The vampire backed away, her eyes wide. "Where did you get all that power?"

Llyr bared his teeth at her. "From a god." Quick as thought, he sent his magic to summon a sword from the palace armory. Wary that his powers might disappear again, he drew the first nonmagical blade he found; it wouldn't vanish no matter what happened. He grinned in sheer ironic pleasure as it appeared in his hand. It was Galatyn the First's own blade that filled his palm with its massive, welcome weight. But there wasn't time to find nonmagical armor, so he generated some with a spell.

The vampire's gaze flickered as she saw the enchanted plate form around him, but she managed a sneer. "A god. Yeah, right. Big deal, baby—gods die. And so will you." A red glow surrounded her, leaving her armor behind when it retreated. The knife in her hand became a sword.

Baring his teeth, Llyr leaped for her, bringing the sword down in a savage two-handed swipe, using his magic to boost his stroke's power. She brought her blade up to parry, but the force of his blow drove her to one knee. The pleasure of it spread a grin across his face, broad and feral.

Until her sword burst into a blaze of power that lifted him off his feet and threw him.

He landed rolling, shaking off the blast as he surged to his feet. She threw up a hand and shot a lightning bolt at the tree next to him.

A massive rolling *crack!* split the air. Llyr ducked aside as the tree fell with a thunderous boom. "Missed," he taunted.

"I won't next time."

They began to circle, stalking one another, blades lifted.

Llyr watched her, calculating the power she was burning. How much had she bought by killing Miller?

Not enough, he'd wager.

Llyr dropped his guard to lob a power blast at her with lethal force. She shielded. Sparks showered as the attack hit, but he didn't even pause, following the strike up with another and still another, hammering at her shield, driving her to retreat. He followed, refusing to let up the pressure, forcing her to use more and still more of her magic.

"Bastard!" she screamed, realizing what he was doing.

"No." His lip curled. "That would be my brother."

Her shield barely held against his next blast. He summoned another, knowing it would be the last. She didn't have the magic left to block it.

And the vampire knew it.

She sank to her knees, her armor vanishing to be replaced by a shimmering gown of virginal white. Green eyes widened in an expression of pleading, the effect heightened by the tears that welled in her eyes. She lifted trembling hands. The sword she held shrank back into a knife, as though she no longer had the power to spend on the bigger blade. "Mercy!" she pleaded.

Llyr gave her a cynical sneer, the power blast hot in his fingers. "The same mercy you gave me?"

"It's not my fault!" she cried. "Ansgar told me he'd kill me if I didn't take care of you!"

"The way he made you kill all those men?" Furious, he stalked toward her, adding power to the spell he was readying. "Do I look like a fool?"

"He . . . I . . ." She lost her pleading expression in a snarl. Power exploded from her hands. Apparently she had enough for one more blast after all.

Llyr blocked it with a summoned shield, then stepped in and swung his sword. She fell, dead without a sound.

He blew out a breath, relieved, but he knew he didn't have time for triumph. Ansgar had Diana. Lifting his head, Llyr drew on the power of the god to find Diana's trail.

Blood. Magic. And the scent of wolf on the wind. She'd passed this way. With a flick of his wrist, Llyr sent the witch's body up in magical flames to avoid any questions Diana might not care to answer later.

Then he started to run, following the sweet, tempting wisp of his lover's scent. And prayed she still lived.

Llyr found the spot not a hundred yards farther. The magical traces of Ansgar's gate still lingered in the air, glowing gently to his Dragon-enhanced eyes. With a flex of his will, he opened a gate of his own, following exactly the path of his brother.

Then he stepped through.

Diana lay still as Ansgar fondled her nipples, fighting to keep the revulsion from her face. Judging by the lechery growing in his gaze, he was beginning to fall under the influence of her pheromones.

Not that he needed another reason to rape her.

Just a little longer, she told herself. Let his guard drop as his lust rose. Carefully, she lifted one leg, stroking it up his thigh. His gaze shot to hers, hot with lethal warning, but she kept the contact light and seductive.

She had to lull him.

There were three or four good attacks she could use, depending on where he let her touch him. If she could get a hand on his face, she could stab a thumb through his eye and into his brain. Even if she didn't manage to punch deeply enough to kill him, the pain would immobilize him long enough for her to get her hands on the headsman's axe waiting in the execution block.

There was also a palm strike up under the nose that would drive his septum into his brain. She liked that one; it was faster, not to mention less messy than delving into his skull with her thumbs. A trickier possibility was to drive her fingers into the big blood vessels on either side of his neck. Even without her powers, Diana had enough strength to rip his throat out.

The key was making him think she really was a bitch in heat. Luckily, Ansgar did not have a high opinion of women. She just had to be patient.

And lucky.

When Llyr stepped through the gate, he found half a dozen Morven Sidhe bodyguards on the other side in front of a single massive door. He could not feel what lay beyond it.

They gaped at him, startled that he'd been able to punch through the palace wards designed to block a gating enemy. He only wished he had time to eliminate the shields completely and bring in an army of Cachamwri, but that would take minutes of concentrated spell-casting he simply didn't have time for. "Back away and live," he growled, the god giving his voice a rumble of power. "I have called the Dragon." He let the God's Mark surface swirl across his armored torso in a shimmer of scales, far larger now that it was fully active.

"Cachamwri!" whispered one of the guards. "I saw it when the old king led us against the Dark Ones!"

Llyr met the awed fear in the man's eyes. "Then you know what I can do."

Calculation replaced fear. "I know if you turn that power on our king, your father's curse will destroy you."

"Then I'll die." He lifted his sword. "But you'll lead me into the afterlife if you don't step away from that door."

The guards glanced at one another, then back at the door. One shrugged. "At least you'd kill us quickly."

Llyr nodded grimly and braced himself. He hadn't really expected any other answer. Ansgar was too good at inspiring fear.

The first magical attack splashed against his armor. He sent one of his own shooting in return and leaped for the nearest guard. They closed on him in a frenzy born more of terror than loyalty.

With Cachamwri's magic pouring through him, he rammed his sword through the chest of the first guard, cutting enchanted plate and Sidhe flesh with equal ease. The man fell dead as Llyr whirled to block another's attack and fling a magical blast into the face of a third. He was all too aware that Diana waited on the other side of that door. He only prayed he'd finish the guards in time to save her.

Diana froze as a scream rang from the hallway, rising over a familiar battle cry.

"Llyr!" Ansgar jerked his head around to stare at the door. His left hand clamped down on her breast as he lifted the knife and turned back toward her. "Sorry, sweet. It seems there's no time to—"

Diana drove her palm up into his face with every ounce of her strength. He fell back with a roar of pain. She cursed, knowing that if he was capable of speech, she'd missed the septum. While he lifted the knife to stab, she tightened the thigh she'd slipped over his ass and flipped him off her. His knife scraped over the stone floor as it missed.

She surged to her feet as Ansgar leaped up, blood pouring from his nose. At least she'd broken it. "You're going to die for that," he snarled, lifting the blade. "And when Llyr steps in this room, he'll be powerless. I'll cut his throat."

Diana bounced on the balls of her feet and sneered. "What about Daddy's curse?"

"It's magic, bitch. It won't work in here either. Why do you think I really built this room? I was hoping I'd get the chance to kill him here."

He came after her in a low, hard rush. Diana tasted the sour tang of fear in her mouth as she twisted aside. Pain shot up her arm as the point of his blade scored it. Ansgar wasn't playing games now. He meant to murder her, then finish Llyr in the moment of shock when her lover saw her corpse. She had to keep out of his reach. If she could stall, Llyr would come through that door and the two of them could take Ansgar out.

But every muscle in Diana's battered body ached with pain, and exhaustion sat on her shoulders like a suit of solid lead. She just hoped to hell Llyr finished the guards before Ansgar finished her.

Doggedly, she fought, punching, kicking, trying to stay out of the Sidhe's reach as he sought just as hard to get his hands on her. Sweat ran burning into her eyes, and her breath rasped in desperate pants.

Until, ducking aside from one of his vicious swipes, she almost tripped right over the executioner's axe. She pounced on it, wrenched it out of the block, and reeled to face him. "Now," she panted. "Let's try that again."

She dove at him, swinging the axe in a stroke that almost took his head from his shoulders. Ansgar yelped and ducked.

"Oh, yeah," Diana growled. "That's better." Adrenaline surging through her in the last of her reserves, she stepped in close and swung like Barry Bonds going for a homer.

But exhaustion made her slow. He jerked back. The stroke missed. And then he stepped in with the knife.

It was Diana's turn to dodge, but this time she wasn't fast enough. Cold pain ripped a scream from her lips. Looking down, she saw the hilt protruding high in her chest. Suddenly there was no more strength in her legs. She went down, hard.

Panting, dazed, she watched numbly as Ansgar walked over and picked up the axe.

Snarling with frustrated rage, Llyr whirled to blast magic at the next group of reinforcements pouring down the corridor at him. He had to get through that cursed door, but they kept coming.

The Dragon roared and lashed within him, the power so hot it burned. He knew he'd have fallen a dozen times over without it. As it was, most of the blood that splattered the walls and floor belonged to the guards, and the smell of singed flesh rode the air, blending with the stench of loosened bowels and spilled guts. Sweat rolled down his chest, itching and inaccessible within his armor, stinging his eyes, but he barely noticed.

All his attention was focused on getting through that door. Diana could be dying even now. A Sidhe warrior leaped the pile of bodies around him, sword lifted. With a bellow of sheer fury, Llyr stabbed his blade right through the man's enchanted armor, then heaved the corpse headfirst into the wall.

At last the way to the door was clear. He threw himself against it with all the frenzy of his magical strength. The wood gave, bursting inward. As he landed inside, wild-eyed and sweating, he heard Cachamwri roar. *It's a trap!*

Within him, the Dragon's light winked out.

Astonished and furious at Cachamwri's sudden betrayal, he stopped dead. He still held his sword thanks to his own foresight in summoning a non-magical weapon, but his enchanted armor had vanished completely.

Diana lay naked and bloody on the floor, a knife protruding from her chest. Ansgar stood over her, an executioner's axe in his hands. "It took you long enough," his brother said, a taunting smirk on his face.

Numbly, Llyr heard the surviving guards fill the doorway behind him.

"Leave us," Ansgar ordered.

"Your Majesty!" a guard gasped in protest.

"Leave!" Ansgar roared. "I have long dreamed of this moment, and it's not for your eyes. Close the door and bar it!"

"Let me send her home," Llyr said as the door closed, his gaze on Diana, who had wrapped one hand around the hilt of the knife and was visibly steeling herself to pull it free. From its position—high on her chest, just under her collarbone—there was a good chance it wouldn't kill her, especially if she could transform to wolf form.

"I don't think so." Ansgar's grin was twisted and savage. "I plan to celebrate with her afterward."

"There won't be an afterward," Llyr said coldly. "Our father's curse will see to that."

"Not in here." His brother hefted the axe and started toward him. "Magic will not work in this room. Not yours, not mine, and not our fool of a sire's."

Llyr gaped as sudden, savage joy rose in him. This was it—the chance for revenge he'd long dreamed of. It might cost him his crown, but if it freed the Cachamwri and Morven from Ansgar's threat, he would count it well lost.

And if Diana survived, he would claim her for his own without his people or his crown in the way. Fifty years with her would be sweeter than a millennia with any other woman he'd ever known.

* * *

Panting through the searing pain as she worked the knife from her chest, Diana watched as the two Sidhe kings circled. Sweat and blood streaked them both, and she could tell from the way they moved that they were beginning to tire.

Not that it mattered. Each was determined to kill the other. Blade, bare hands, or teeth, they didn't give a damn how.

With a muffled shriek, she jerked the knife from her body and fell back, panting, the other hand clamped over the wound. Blood poured, hot against her chilled skin. She wished bitterly she could transform into a wolf and heal the injury. But that was out, at least until Llyr won.

Or Ansgar killed them both.

With a hoarse bellow, the bastard charged, swinging the axe. Llyr stepped aside and counterattacked. Sword met axe, clashing, scraping, ringing. The two men spun apart, their breathing loud in the tense stillness of the room. Growling Sidhe curses, they circled, long hair slicked to sweating bodies.

"Hero of the Cachamwri," Ansgar sneered. "The Dragon God chose the wrong brother!"

"He doesn't think so." As shock widened his opponent's eyes, Llyr grinned tauntingly. "How do you think I got here, brother? The Dragon helped me kill your assassin, along with two-thirds of your palace guard!"

"Well, he's not here now, is he?"

Llyr curled his lip. "I don't need him."

He swung his sword. Ansgar parried with a thrust of the axe, and the two men surged together, nose to nose, hate and fury blazing from them in waves Diana could almost see. With a grunt, Ansgar threw Llyr back. He caught himself and went after his brother again, his expression twisted with hate.

Diana winced and curled tighter on the cold stone floor,

shivering with pain and nausea. She suspected she was sliding into shock.

It didn't help that every time Ansgar swung at him with that axe, her stomach knotted with terror. Every time Llyr attacked him, she caught her breath with the hope that her lover would finish it.

And every time, it was damn close.

Yet it seemed to Diana that there was a special ferocity to Llyr's attacks, the relentlessness of a man finally unleashing his frustrated rage. Ansgar was intent on killing him with a passion born of years of hate and jealousy, but it just wasn't the same. He was the bigger of the two men, more heavily muscled, but watching them, she sensed it was Llyr who would never give up.

Which was no surprise, really. He was fighting to avenge his murdered children and assassinated wives. He wouldn't stop until Ansgar was dead. Period. He pounded at his brother relentlessly, meeting every blow of Ansgar's axe with a parry and a counterattack, his opal eyes blazing with a burning hunger for revenge.

And if anybody had ever deserved it, Llyr did.

A cold exultation burned in Llyr, singing in joy every time he launched an attack at his brother's twisted face. Oddly, he felt no fear, not even when one or the other of their blades bit into his skin when a parry wasn't quite hard enough. He was bleeding from a dozen cuts and gashes, yet he ignored the sting of those wounds. All that mattered was burying his sword in Ansgar's skull without getting the axe buried in his own.

That, and the fear in his brother's eyes.

Both of them were moving more slowly now, parries and attacks broader, clumsier with exhaustion. Yet Llyr had no intention of letting his body fail its job of killing Ansgar, and his brother knew it.

Then suddenly his foot hit a puddle of blood. He slipped, going down on one knee. Ansgar's black eyes widened, narrowed as he swung his axe. Llyr ducked. As the axe hissed over his head, Llyr thrust blindly.

The sword jolted as it bit into Ansgar's flesh, right through the gut. It was a mortal wound. For a moment, triumph sang through him.

"No!" Ansgar roared, jerking back off the blade. He clamped one hand over the injury. Even so, blood poured from it.

Llyr's lips peeled back from his teeth in a savage smile. Slowly, he began to stalk his brother.

"No!" Ansgar spat, his face going white. "Curse you, you'll not win!"

"Oh yes I will," he growled, hefting the sword. "I just have to let you bleed long enough. The way you let Isolde bleed. The way you bled my children and my wives, you unnatural bastard!"

Ansgar's eyes widened with malicious inspiration. His gaze flicked to Diana. "Now, there's a thought!"

Horrified, Llyr dove after his brother even as the man reeled around and started to lift the axe over Diana's helpless head. He glimpsed her white face as he drew back his own sword, knowing he wouldn't stop the axe's descent in time.

"Ansgar," Diana snarled, *"kiss my furry ass!"* She surged upward, driving the knife squarely between the Sidhe's thighs.

Ansgar bellowed in anguish and dropped the axe.

"Cachamwri!" Llyr bellowed in joy, and took Ansgar's head in one stroke of his sword.

The corpse toppled. The hilt of Diana's bloody knife protruded from his crotch.

NINETEEN

For a long moment, they froze, staring at Ansgar's twitching body. "Now that," Diana said finally, "has needed doing for a really long time."

Llyr huffed out a breath and bent to help her to her feet. "You have a gift for understatement."

"So I'm told." She sucked in a breath in a hiss of pain. "Let's get the hell out of this room. My life will be a whole lot more pleasant once I turn into a wolf and get rid of this frigging knife wound."

He gathered her against him as carefully as he could, pressing a quick kiss to her lips. "You did that well," he murmured.

"You weren't so bad yourself."

Together, they went to the door and wrestled it open.

To find dozens of Morven Sidhe warriors waiting on the other side.

Despite the hostile eyes on them, Llyr and Diana stepped from the execution chamber. She felt her magic return in a hot and welcome rush and promptly used it to transform, feeling her body heal as it changed. She'd never been so happy to shift into her Dire Wolf form in her entire life. And none too soon. She had the feeling they'd need all seven feet of werewolf muscle to get out of this one.

"They've killed the king!" one of the Sidhe guards said, craning his neck to look beyond them at Ansgar's decapitated body. His tone was more awed than outraged.

"And it was about time," Diana growled.

A man in the elaborate court costume of a Morven noble pushed to the front of the shocked crowd. He was as inhumanly beautiful as the rest of them, with hair that burned a deep ruby red against his pale skin. There was a touch of avidity in his golden eyes, the gleam of a man who saw an opportunity and had no intention of letting it pass him by. His voice rang with regal condemnation. "You have committed fratricide, Llyr Galatyn. Under the terms of your father's will, you are no longer fit to rule."

Diana saw Llyr stiffen as if from a body blow.

That's when her temper snapped. "Oh, spare me the hypocrisy!" In this form, her voice rumbled like a pissed-off lion's. "As if you would have said a single solitary world if Ansgar had killed Llyr, you gutless bastard. No, you only grow a pair when the good brother wins, because you figure he won't fucking *execute* you."

The man recoiled, his eyes widening in shock and outrage. "How dare you!" His hand fell to the dress sword hanging by his side. "I should run you through for that."

"Yeah, I'm shaking." She curled a lupine lip. "For sixteen hundred years, Ansgar has been violating the terms of Daddy's will, attempting to assassinate Llyr and killing every one of his wives and kids. I wonder where all this fine, holy outrage was then. Hell, I wonder where it was when Ansgar dragged me in there to rape and kill me."

"We didn't know!" the noble snapped. But his eyes flickered.

"Bullshit. You knew. You just didn't have the balls to do anything about it."

The man spun toward the surviving guard and extended a finger in her direction. "Arrest them! They have slain our king!"

"Lay one hand on His Majesty," Diana hissed, "and I'll rip the offending body part off and shove it up your ass. Assuming there's room, considering your head already occupies most of the space."

Llyr grinned, showing as much tooth as any werewolf. "Would you like help with that?" His dragon tattoo had come alive again, lashing its tail and coiling around his bare chest. Power rolled off him in waves. He'd healed his injuries while she'd been arguing with the Sidhe, but he hadn't donned armor. Probably so everybody could get the full effect of the Dragon's Mark.

"Yeah, actually. Hey, here's a thought. Let's kill 'em all." She bared her teeth at the guards. "I'll eat the evidence."

As one man, they stepped back a pace.

The opportunistic noble wisely stepped behind the nearest trooper before sneering, "Threaten all you like, but Dearg's Law is Dearg's Law. Llyr has forfeited his right to the crown. I say . . ."

Suddenly a quiet voice rose from the back of the crowd. "She's right."

The noble turned, indignant. "Trivag, you can't mean that. Dearg's Will—"

"Was violated countless times by our king, Jetad, and we all knew it." The man who had pushed his way to the front of the crowd was tall, and distinguished, still handsome as an archangel despite his obvious years. He looked sixty, which for a Sidhe must have made him old indeed. To Llyr he added, "It shames me I did nothing while you lost so much, Your Majesty."

Llyr sighed. "Ansgar would have killed you and your entire clan, Lord Trivag. You could not have done differently."

"Perhaps not, but I can now." He sank to one knee. "You have my loyalty, King Llyr Galatyn, belated though it is. If you'll have it."

Llyr smiled and bent his head in a slight bow. "And you have mine. I will not forget your support."

Jetad sighed. "Trivag, curse you, must you always be so bloody noble? I was hoping to be king."

"Indeed?" Llyr drawled. "Are you prepared to fight a civil war for the throne? For with me gone, many of your fellow nobles would likely have the same thought."

Jetad hesitated, clearly thinking that one over. Finally the calculation faded from his eyes, and he lifted his narrow shoulders in a sigh of surrender. "I suppose so. And I didn't like the last war at all." As Diana and Llyr watched, he, too, sank to his knee, followed by the rest of the Sidhe, including the palace guard. That they caved so easily probably said more about Ansgar than anything else.

"That's one kingdom down," Llyr murmured, soft enough for her Direkind ears alone. "Unfortunately, I'll wager my bunch are not going to be this easy."

"Are you nuts?" she murmured back. "They'll kiss your boots."

*   *   *

Llyr moved quickly to solidify his hold on the Morven throne. There was some grumbling, but Trivag and Jetad— the latter no doubt to score points—put a quick end to it. It helped that Llyr had the Dragon's Mark flexing on his chest, silent reminder of both his power and status as Heir to Heroes.

Personally, Diana thought he'd established he *was* one of those heroes.

He then closeted himself with his new nobles, after first showing Diana to one of the palace's chambers, then conjuring both clothing and a feast for her out of respect for her werewolf appetite. Transforming to human form, she attacked the food with joyous greed.

Diana had just finished off the crumbs and was considering a well-deserved nap when he returned. He was garbed once more in full court regalia, right down to velvet doublet, hose, and a truly impressive crown she'd never seen him wear before. "Nice hat," she said dryly, eyeing it, as he closed the door behind him.

"It's the crown of both kingdoms. Belonged to my father," he said, dropping into a slipper chair and rubbing his eyes. He looked tired.

"Have you talked to the bunch back home?"

Llyr nodded. "They're all here now."

"How'd they take it?"

"Surprisingly well. They've decided I acted in self-defense."

Diana grinned. "Told you. Your people genuinely love you, Llyr. There was no way they were going to kick up a fuss about your getting rid of that weasel."

He snorted. "Speaking of whom, I've put my grandmother over the task of planning Ansgar's funeral."

"I'll bet she's enjoying that."

"She is, actually. I don't think she liked him very much." Llyr's tired smile faded. "I've also recovered the bodies of my men from your county morgue. Along, I might add, with all medical records. Your Doctor Garrison no longer recalls anything unusual."

Diana sat back in her chair with a sigh. "Well, that's one less giant aching pain in my ass. Have you checked on Gist?"

"Not yet, but I can arrange it." His gaze met hers, searching and intense. "Along with seeing to it that your council and your people lose any interest in firing you. Though I would prefer to offer you an alternative post."

Her heart began to pound. Did he want her to become his mistress? And if he did, what should she say? "What exactly did you have in mind?"

Then, to her astonishment, he went to one knee before her and took her hand in his. As she stared, he gave her a small smile. "Be my queen."

"What?"

His beautiful opal eyes were earnest as he gazed up at her. "Diana, I love you. I want to marry you. I want you to have my children."

"Llyr, I'm a *werewolf*. I can't have children with a Sidhe."

His lush mouth tightened with cool determination. "I know, but I think I can come up with a spell to fix that. Marry me."

"What, fix my infertility or fix me being a werewolf?" Her head was spinning.

He gestured impatiently with one elegant had. "The infertility. Being Direkind is part of what you are, and I love everything about you." His gaze searched her face. "The question is, how do you feel about me?"

Diana huffed in bewildered frustration. "Well, I love you, of course. But that's not the issue."

"It's the only one that counts. Marry me, Diana. Be my queen."

She gazed at him, feeling helpless. "You're nuts. You can't make a werewolf Queen of the Sidhe."

A fine muscle worked in his jaw as his eyes narrowed. "Watch me. And marry me, Diana."

She sighed. "I love you, Llyr. Of course I'll marry you. But you and I both know it's not going to work."

"I'll make it work. I want you. I love you. And you'll make the greatest queen the Sidhe have ever known."

"You're insane!" Oriana exploded as the nobles of both kingdoms gaped at Llyr in astonishment. "You can't make a werewolf Queen of the Sidhe!"

"I can." Llyr sat in regal splendor on his massive throne, a magnificent ermine cape riding his broad shoulders. His black jeweled doublet and boots were so thickly encrusted with gems and gold embroidery, they weighed as much as his armor. "She fought for me. She saved my life time and again. But more than that, I love her, and I'll have her for my queen or no one."

Oriana wrung her hands. "Then make her your consort. None of us will object. But Llyr, she's mortal. She's a werewolf. Her children will be werewolves, assuming you can create a spell to make her fertile with you."

"Yours is a line of heroes," Lord Trivag agreed, his quiet voice as steady as his eyes. He'd supported Llyr before, but it was obvious he felt the king had stepped over the line. "You can't taint it with non-Sidhe blood."

A murmur of outraged agreement rose. Another man stepped forward. "I have advised you for sixteen centuries, Your Majesty. Listen to me now. Make her your consort if you must, but you can't marry her."

Diana stood frozen by his throne, her cheeks hot with humiliation. *That's what I get, she thought,* feeling sick. *I knew this was going to happen, but no, I had to ignore my common sense.*

Llyr's gaze met hers, anguished. She fought the rise of tears. "They're right," she choked out. "I'll be your consort. But not . . . I'll get old, Llyr. I'll die."

He squared his shoulders with the the same iron determination she'd seen there when he'd come into the execution chamber to save her from Ansgar. Rising to his feet, he shrugged off his ermine cape as if to do battle. "I said it once, and I'll say it again. I watched Diana London fight for me with a courage I have never seen in anyone, male or female, mortal or Sidhe. She protected me when I lost my powers, even though it meant endangering both her life and the job she loved. She protected the people of Verdaville with the same ferocity. And she would have been a queen such as the Sidhe have never known." Slowly, deliberately, he took off his crown, turned, and placed it on the seat of the throne. "And I will have her for my wife, even if it means the Sidhe must find a new king."

Oriana's gasp of horror was echoed by every Sidhe in the room. "You'd give up your crown for a handful of years with a rapidly aging mortal? Have you run mad?"

Llyr took Diana's shaking hands as she gaped at him. "No." He lifted his voice until it rang. "I watched four wives and ten children murdered without lifting a hand to claim the revenge my heart screamed for. I made that sacrifice because doing anything else would plunge both kingdoms into war when my father's curse struck me down. I endured my grief and rage, though there were times my life was one black, aching void." He turned a hard gaze over the assembled Sidhe. "I have suffered enough for you.

Fifty years, ten years—each *day* she is my wife will be precious."

"You can't!" Diana breathed. She tugged her hands free from his. "No! I won't allow this. You can't do this to your people, Llyr. There'll be a war!"

Llyr had never looked more remorseless, not even when he'd killed Ansgar. "Yes. And I think they deserve it. They did nothing while my children died, even though they knew Ansgar violated my father's will."

She stared up into those beautiful, coldly determined eyes. He was giving up everything for her. "What kind of life can we have, knowing we caused a war to get it?"

"Listen to her, Llyr!" Oriana pleaded.

Llyr turned and lifted a brow. "But she's only a were-wolf. Isn't that what you keep telling me?"

"All right, enough." The male voice was powerful, rich, and not one she recognized. There was a rustle as everyone turned to look toward the entrance of the throne room.

A man strode through the double doors, his strides long, yet with a smooth grace that was more animal than man. He wore full court garb, but there was something odd about the shape of his face, the tone of his skin, the long fall of his hair. His eyes glowed as brightly as blue candle flames with the power of his magic.

Llyr realized before any of them. "Cachamwri!" He sank to one knee in reverence.

The stranger was the Dragon God? Shaken, Diana went to her knees, too. He was no god of hers, but there was no point in pissing him off.

"On your knees!" Llyr ordered his people hoarsely, lowering his eyes. "Cachamwri walks among us."

There was a rising, startled murmur, but with a mass rustle and collective thump, the Sidhe obeyed en masse.

Holding her breath, not daring to lift her eyes, Diana listened to the click of approaching boots. The sense of power grew the closer Cachamwri came, until by the time he stood before them, it felt as if magic was crawling all over her body like thousands of invisible ants. Every hair on her body rose to quivering attention, and her heart thudded in a combination of excitement and panic.

As he stood looking down at them, Diana's senses insisted that he was much bigger than the six-foot male he appeared. His voice rumbled when he spoke. "I have not taken this form in six thousand years, and I am not pleased to take it now."

"My apologies, Bright One." Despite Cachamwri's overwhelming presence, Llyr's voice was so steady, Diana couldn't help but be impressed. "If you had something you wished of me, you had only to ask. You need not have made such an effort."

"Actually, this time it was necessary. I'm not pleased."

Llyr stiffened. Diana winced, silently praying he resisted the impulse to do something that would get himself killed. She dared a quick peek upward as the Dragon God braced big fists on his hips. "I have taken a great deal of trouble to put the Galatyn line on the Sidhe double throne. Do you mean to discard my gift, boy?"

From the corner of her eye, she saw Llyr lift his head and meet the Dragon's gaze. "It is not my preference, but I will not give up Diana to keep it. She's my love, and I want her for the mother of my children."

"Of course you do. You're not a fool."

Startled, Diana glanced up to find Cachamwri's gaze on her, a quirk of amusement in the corner of his mouth. "I knew you were the mother I wanted for the next Galatyn hero when you buried your knife in Ansgar's balls," he told

her in that awe-inspiring voice. "When you offered to eat
any Morven traitor who raised a hand to Llyr, I was sure of
it." The Dragon God turned toward the bowing Sidhe, his
cloak belling behind him with the movement. "If you don't
want her for a queen, you're all fools."

"But she's mortal!" Oriana whispered, her voice
strained and anguished.

The Dragon made a dismissive gesture that was thoroughly human. "Pah, that's nothing. Who do you think
gave the Sidhe immortality to begin with?" He turned and
looked down at her. "Would you become immortal to stay
with your handsome king, then? Would you bear his children, and give birth to the next of my heroes?"

Diana swallowed. The implications were terrifying. Not
only was the responsibility overwhelming, but she'd out-
live her family and friends. But she'd also have Llyr. "Yes.
To stay with Llyr. Yes."

Cachamwri nodded. "I knew you were a sensible child.
Stand up, then."

Diana obeyed. Her knees were shaking, and she fought
to steady them. Wide-eyed, she watched Cachamwri step
closer. His skin was tinged with blue. Looking closer, she
saw a faint, ghostly pattern of scales lay over his high
cheekbones. His glowing blue eyes had tight-slit pupils,
and on closer examination, his long hair was actually a fall
of rich iridescent feathers.

As she stared at him, hypnotized, he leaned forward and
pressed his mouth to hers in an avuncular kiss. Frozen with
a kind of dizzy terror, she didn't move. Then his lips began
to heat. Power blasted into her, pouring from his mouth in
a hot torrent that flooded her mouth, her nose, foamed its
way into every cell of her body until she felt stuffed and
glowing.

When he stepped back, her knees gave out. Llyr caught her as she fell.

"There," the Dragon said. "She's both immortal and cross-fertile with Sidhe. Her children will be Direkind, but they'll be magic users, too." He looked out across the kneeling Sidhe. "You were getting inbred anyway. A little genetic diversity will do you good."

Then, as the Sidhe watched, hardly daring to breathe, he swept out.

Diana scarcely noticed. She was staring, entranced, into Llyr's handsome, joyous face. As the door closed behind the Dragon, his mouth descended on hers in a kiss that was scarcely less powerful than Cachamwri's.

TWENTY

Diana was still floating the next day when they gated to Verdaville County General to play a visit on Gist. He was in intensive care, having spent several hours in surgery the night before. Doctors had told his wife it would likely be a long, painful recovery.

That prognosis changed, however, when Llyr rested one big hand on the sleeping police chief's injured belly. Magic poured from his palm in a wave of dancing light.

Gist's eyes opened wide as strength flooded his debilitated body. "Jesus!" he gasped, his gaze meeting the Sidhe's. "What'd you do?"

Diana gave him a happy grin. "Just making sure you can attend the wedding."

"Wedding?" The chief looked dazed. "What wedding? Would somebody tell me what the hell is going on?"

"Ours. Llyr has asked me to marry him in two weeks." She extended a hand, where she wore the impressive diamond Llyr had conjured in a nod to mortal custom.

"Some rock." Gist's eyes lifted to hers, going sharp as his mind began to catch up, thanks to the new strength of his body. "But I thought you said it wasn't going to work, since Legolas here is supposed to be some kind of king."

"I changed her mind," Llyr drawled with a smile, looking almost as lovesick as she did.

"I'm happy for both of you. But what about Vampire Bitch?" Gist glowered. "I'm nursing a grudge."

The amusement drained from the Sidhe king's eyes. "She's dead," he said shortly.

"Good." The chief eyed him shrewdly. "I don't suppose there's a body so I can give the families some closure."

Llyr hesitated, considering it. "I can probably arrange something convincing."

"That'll help." He turned his attention to Diana. "What are you going to do about the council? They think you're still missing, by the way. My wife said they'd be meeting around noon or so."

Diana smiled coolly. "Sounds like a good time to hand in my notice." And she planned to thoroughly enjoy it.

When Diana and Llyr walked into the council chamber, all seven council members turned toward them with varying expressions of amazement.

"Diana!" City Clerk Tammy Jones said, jumping up out of her seat, an expression of joy on her face. She sank back down when Thompson shot her a narrow look.

"Where have you been?" the mayor demanded. "We've had every cop in the county out looking for you. All anybody found was a circle of singed ground and splattered blood out in the woods."

"Did you catch the killer?" Councilwoman Carly Jefferies's eyes shone with avid excitement.

"Yes," Diana said. "And no, you don't need to know what happened."

The council was still gaping in offended astonishment when Llyr cast his spell.

"So," she announced, as they stared at her, bewildered, "I just dropped by to give my notice. I suggest you promote Tammy here to interim manager while you find someone else for the job. In fact, offer it to her. She knows the job better than anybody you can afford to hire ever would."

There was a shocked pause before Thompson drawled, "Well, I surely do hate to hear you're leaving us. You've done an excellent job as city manager. You'll be missed." He frowned. "I hope this isn't about that business last night."

"You know," Jefferies said, "I don't know why we all got so upset. In hindsight, it's obvious Diana was perfectly justified in what she did." She sighed. "We were just under so much stress. It's been a bad time for us all, with all these killings."

"I don't suppose you'd consider staying on with us?" the mayor asked.

Diana shot Llyr a veiled look. "I'm afraid not. I've had another offer."

"I'm not surprised," Thompson said, giving her the good ol' boy grin she'd come to loathe. "The good ones always use Verdaville as a stepping-stone to something bigger."

Diana concealed her smile with an effort. Yeah, she supposed Queen of the Sidhe definitely qualified as something bigger.

* * *

Simmering with a deep, gnawing rage, Jim London shoved open the door of his Atlanta apartment and strode inside. The muscles at the base of his neck were knotted with the tension that had only coiled tighter since he'd learned Tony Shay had been murdered.

Tony had been his best friend since their shared boyhood running wild in the Georgia woods. They'd gotten together for a little impromptu hunting just last month. The hysterical call from Tony's mother with the news had knocked Jim for a loop.

It was hard to believe. His laughing, red-haired buddy, murdered. What was worse, the local police department was stonewalling Mary Shay's inquiries into her son's death, which was why she'd called on Jim for backup. Tony's father was dead, and his mother had nobody else to turn to.

So Jim had gone to get Mrs. Shay and driven her to Clarkston to find out what the hell was going on. The Clarkston police chief had been, if anything, even more rude and obstructionist in person than he'd been on the phone. He'd told Mary her son had been involved in drug running and his Colombian associates had butchered him.

But that was bullshit. No way was Tony involved in drugs. He was Direkind, for God's sake. The very idea he'd traffic in poison was an insult.

There was something dirty going on, and Jim was going to find out what.

His mind working feverishly, Jim stalked to the refrigerator for a beer, then headed into the living room while he pulled the tab.

He rounded the corner just in time to see a whirling pool of light appear in the middle of the room.

Holy hell! Jim thought, recognizing the spill of glowing

magic from his grandfather's old tales, *It's a dimensional gate!* Instinctively, he jumped back, dropping the beer as he fell into a combat crouch.

But before he could shift to Dire Wolf form, Diana stepped out of the light, wearing a sunny grin of welcome. "Jim! Finally!"

He froze, stunned, as his sister flung herself into his arms. "Diana! What the hell?" Jim demanded as a tall, long-haired blond stepped out of the gate behind her, his expression indulgent.

She drew back. There was a trace of nerves in the silver eyes so like his own. "I hope you don't mind us dropping by, but I tried to call and you didn't answer. I've already told the rest of the family, and I just couldn't wait another minute. Finally I told Llyr to just cast a location spell to take us to you."

"Llyr?" Jim's jaw fell. He looked up at the tall blond, who wore a perfectly ordinary gray suit. "*King* Llyr Galatyn?"

The Sidhe smiled with a regal dip of the head. "The same."

Jim's eyes widened as he looked at his sister, remembering their conversation a few days ago. At the time, she'd admitted she'd broken her Burning Moon celibacy with the Sidhe king. And judging by the way Llyr was looking at her now . . . "You're kidding me."

Diana grinned, but the nerves didn't fade from her eyes. "Nope. We're getting married."

"But . . ." His jaw worked as he struggled to process the situation. "But you're a werewolf! You can't have children with a Sidhe, Diana!"

"She can now," Llyr said, stepping forward to rest a possessive hand on her shoulders. "Cachamwri cast a spell on her to make it possible." His smile at her was fond and proud. "He was very impressed with her."

Jim staggered to the couch and sat down, staring at her

helplessly. "You impressed the Dragon God? How the hell did you do that?"

"It's kind of a long story." Pausing, Diana took a deep breath. "And there's something else. He made me immortal."

"Immortal. And queen of the fairies." As he stared at her in dumbfounded astonishment, Jim saw a flash of something vulnerable in Diana's eyes, a shadow of mingled grief and regret. He realized suddenly what she was thinking: she'd never grow old, but her family would.

Jim had no intention of allowing that concern to darken her happiness. With a whoop, he sprang from the couch and snatched her off her feet, spinning with her until she dissolved into giggles. "I told you! I told you he wouldn't be able to resist you."

"And you were right," Llyr said softly.

Between the gold, the gems, and the fifteen-foot train, Diana's wedding dress had to weigh seventy pounds at least. It was a good thing she was Direkind, or she would never have been able to survive the long hike across the throne room in it. The lightest thing about the entire costume was the wreath of roses she wore perched on her dark curls.

Her father strode by her side, one warm hand covering the cold one she'd tucked into his arm. Giving away the bride wasn't a Sidhe custom, but Diana had insisted. A tall, bearlike man with a craggy face, Andrew London looked handsome in his royal-blue court garb. Still, like her brother and grandfather, he'd flatly refused to wear hose. He hadn't been any more thrilled about the snug trousers that were the only alternative, but at least he was athletic enough to carry them off.

But the most dazzling man in the room was Llyr, who waited before the two thrones, dressed in a blinding white velvet doublet heavily encrusted with jewels. His white hose and thigh boots made the most of his incredible ass. The double crown of the two kingdoms rode his golden head. It probably weighed as much as her dress.

A Sidhe Dragon Priest stood beside him, magnificent and alien in his scale armor in shimmering dark blue.

The vaulting throne room around them was packed with Sidhe in full court finery. Magic snapped and shimmered everywhere she looked, particularly around the arrangements of candles and flowers that decorated the Sidhes' seats. The smell of Sidhe roses was as rich and intoxicating as any drug.

A dizzying number of breathtaking faces turned toward Diana as she marched down the aisle, three Sidhe ladies following behind to help her manage The Dress. Her heart was pounding so hard, she was surprised it wasn't visible right through her jeweled bodice.

As she neared the front of the throne room by her father's side, she spotted the rest of her family: her mother, grandfather, and brother, all looking a little uncomfortable in their court garb.

Marly London beamed in the scarlet gown Llyr had conjured for her, while Diana's grandfather grinned like a Halloween pumpkin, surrounded by the Sidhe he'd been fascinated by since he was a boy. Brother Jim, tall and striking in navy blue, looked slightly grim and distracted. She resolved to hunt him down and find out what was bugging him as soon as she had a spare minute.

Then at last they reached the throne, and her father presented her hand to Llyr. There was a suspicious gleam of moisture in the big werewolf's eyes—along with a great deal of pride. Diana floated the rest of the way to Llyr's side, dazzled by his golden Sidhe beauty.

The ceremony itself passed in a blur as the Dragon

Priest requested Cachamwri's blessing on their union in rolling Sidhe phrases. Luckily, Diana now spoke the language thanks to a timely spell Llyr had cast on her and her family. She managed the expected responses without tripping over her own tongue, vowing to love and honor her royal husband. He returned the oath in a proud voice, the joy in his eyes making her heart draw tight in her chest.

Finally Llyr honored the customs of both Sidhe and Western humans by sliding a wedding band on her finger and clasping a Sidhe bond bracelet around her wrist. Then it was her turn to work the gold band over his strong finger. The clasp of the bracelet gave her a little more trouble, but with some excruciating fumbling, she managed it.

United at last, they shared a giddy grin before the priest leaned forward to prompt, "The crown!"

Reminded, Diana sank hastily to her knees as a Sidhe page approached with a more delicate version of Llyr's crown nestled on a velvet cushion.

Llyr turned toward the audience. No one stirred or coughed as he spoke in that beautiful voice of his. "I have asked Diana London to marry me because she has captured my heart. But I asked her to be my queen because I know she will serve you, my people, with courage, intelligence, and wisdom. You will come to love her as I have."

Her heart thundered like a bass drum as he turned and placed the crown over her head. It was much heavier than it looked.

Then Llyr snatched her off her knees and into his arms. The entire crowd rose to their feet with a roar as he took her mouth in a kiss that seared her to her toes. Thousands of watching Sidhe or no, she kissed him back with all the joy and heat in her heart.

* * *

Jim London hovered next to the Sidhe equivalent of the buffet table, holding a delicate plate piled high with tiny munchies, exchanging small talk with excruciatingly beautiful people, and counting the minutes until he could flee.

Swear to God, he'd never been so damned uncomfortable in his life.

And his baby sister was going to *live* like this?

Oh, well. At least she and her king were madly in love. Jim had cornered the big Sidhe the day before the wedding and given him a thorough grilling. It was obvious Llyr was just as nuts about Diana as she was about him.

Still, just in case, Jim had changed to Dire Wolf form for the king, ostensibly to demonstrate he'd be more than happy to serve as bodyguard if the need ever arose again. In fact, however, he was making sure Llyr knew it wasn't a good idea to hurt Jim's beloved baby sister. To his satisfaction, the king had looked thoroughly impressed. Apparently he'd seen Diana in Dire Wolf form, but Jim was a whole hell of a lot bigger.

Point made.

"Jim!" Diana's happy shriek brought his head up the moment before she threw herself against him. He pulled her into a hug, aware that Llyr was standing just behind her.

Sometime during the night, her dress had transformed into something a little lighter and less gem-encrusted, which was a good thing. Otherwise even Diana wouldn't have been able to dance in it. That intimidating crown was gone, too, replaced by a delicate little coronet that circled her dark curls.

Jim hugged her happily. "Hi there, Your Majesty. Are you tipsy?" There was more than a hint of alcohol on her breath.

She gave him a glowing grin. Damn, it was good to see her so happy. "Heck, yeah. That Sidhe wine is really, really good."

"I noticed." He'd had a few glasses of it himself. Good thing his werewolf constitution was up to processing just about anything.

Suddenly her brilliant smile faded. "I heard about Tony. I'm really sorry."

Jim's mouth tightened as he lifted his own glass and swallowed a mouthful of the wine. "Yeah. His mother . . ." He shook his head.

Diana's tipsy gaze suddenly sharpened. "I know that look. You're planning something."

He forced a grin. "Who me? Wouldn't dream of it."

She exchanged a look with Llyr. "Yeah, right."

Jim protested his innocent intentions, more for form than anything else, but his sister wasn't fooled.

She knew him far too well.

Diana made her way into the throne room with the exaggerated care of a woman who'd had one too many. Well, maybe more than one—she'd lost count. Now her nervous system was buzzing so loudly, she craved a moment of relative silence to herself.

Well, she'd rather find Llyr and a nice, quiet bed, but when she'd toured the ballroom looking for him, he'd disappeared. Didn't it figure? He'd been all over her all night, but the minute she wanted to disappear with him—poof!

With a sigh, Diana she stopped in the doorway and stared down the long, lushly elegant room at the two imposing thrones at the end of it. *One of those is mine.* It was a mind-blowing thought.

Unable to resist, she walked down the aisle to the thrones and stopped before them. Hers was slightly less massive that Llyr's, but it was no less ornate. The back was worked with gleaming jeweled dragon shapes: flying, hunting, roaring with spread wings. It would have been damned uncomfortable to sit on, but luckily the parts that would actually make contact with her butt and back were thickly upholstered in red velvet.

Deciding to try it out, Diana turned and sat down, settling back carefully.

The throne was surprisingly comfortable, though to be honest, just getting off her aching feet was heavenly all by itself. She settled back with a sigh and closed her eyes.

Just before she could sink into an exhausted doze, the double doors opened and shut. "Hello, Your Majesty."

Diana opened one eye and watched Llyr saunter down the aisle toward her, tall and male and thoroughly gorgeous. It was hard to believe she was married to such an incredible man. "Hello yourself, Your Majesty."

When he reached her, he went smoothly to one knee and lowered his head in a graceful bow. "How may your humble courtier serve you, Oh Queen?"

She grinned. "I'd suggest something obscene, if three thousand people and my daddy weren't next door."

Llyr lifted his head, opal eyes gleaming wickedly beneath his gold brows. "I would like to mention that this most excellent throne room has many intriguing features. Including a door that locks."

On cue, the double doors produced a muffled thunk, like a massive bolt sliding home.

"You see?" Llyr's lush mouth canted into a wicked grin as he slipped a hand under the hem of her skirt to close gently around her ankle.

Diana let her head fall back with a sigh. "In that case, your queen does have a request."

"And what would that be?"

"Rub my feet."

He laughed, the sound rich and rolling, and flipped her

skirts over her knee. She groaned in delicious anticipation as he pulled one foot into his lap, slipped off her shoe, and went to work massaging the ball with strong strokes of his fingers. Extravagant delight rose as he rubbed gentle circles over her instep and heel, then progressed to each toe. By the time he finished the other foot, she lay boneless with pleasure.

Which was when he swept up her skirts, draped each knee over his shoulders, and bent to nibble her thighs.

"Llyr!" She convulsed with a shout of laughter. "We can't do that in here!"

He looked up at her with a lift of a roguish brow. "You'll find one of the more pleasant aspects of royalty is that we can indeed do 'that' in here."

With that, he buried his face right against her crotch.

Diana arched her back as a wet, hot tongue traced between her folds. "Oh, God! I could have sworn—Llyr!—I had panties on a minute ago."

"You did." His voice was muffled. Teeth nibbled outrageously. "I made them go away. In fact . . ."

Cool air blew across her tightening nipples. She looked down and realized she was stark naked. Llyr, on the other hand, was still fully dressed—and fully occupied, as he slid a finger into her creaming sex.

Diana threw back her head to gasp and realized there was something heavy on her head. Putting up a hand, she discovered he'd transported the double crown of the two kingdoms onto her head again. She had no idea how it was staying up there. Magic, apparently.

Just then, a long, skillful tongue did something carnal and delightful to her cunt. Clinging to the arms of her throne, she admired her husband's talent for a while, panting.

He reached up a hand and captured one of her breasts

for a soft, loving stroke, then pinched and rolled its tight nipple. The pleasure piled on top of what he was already doing like whipped cream on a sundae.

Diana's climax bubbled up in sweet, hot pulses. Hooking her heels against his back, she arched her spine and stuffed her fist in her mouth to keep from yowling. The palace walls didn't look particularly thin, but then, Llyr was really, really good.

Several endless minutes of agonizing pleasure went by before she finally collapsed, her legs limp as noodles. Diana was still trying to recover when Llyr straightened, and she realized he was now deliciously naked. She didn't even bother asking where his clothes had gone.

The silken head of his cock pressed between her lips and entered in a slick, hard glide. Diana groaned in helpless delight. He felt so damn good.

Llyr buried himself to the hilt and stopped, wanting to savor the stark, hot pleasure of being inside her again. Her silver eyes blinked up at her, deliciously dazed. Her nipples were taut little points. He grinned in satisfaction, then sobered a little as he stared down into her face.

She was just so damned lovely, her mouth panting and flushed, her bright gaze so hot with need. He remembered how she'd looked walking down the aisle, so beautiful he'd felt a lump in his throat.

Finally, after so many centuries and so many wives, he'd found a woman who more than matched him in wit, courage, and strength. And even after so short a time, he loved her as he'd never loved anyone in all his long life.

Slowly, carefully, Llyr began to thrust. Her sex clamped around him like a wet velvet fist, massaging his ready cock with every slow plunge. She wrapped her thighs tighter over his shoulders and caught his forearms in her slim, pretty hands, bracing herself as he took her.

A wildness rose in his blood, sudden and fierce as a storm. Goaded, Llyr began to drive, lunging hard against her. She gasped and threw back her head, arching her back and thrusting her pretty breasts in the air. His brain was flooded with her scent—sex, woman, and wild things, potent pheromones goading him on.

Every breath he took shredded his control until he found himself mindless, grinding hard, working his thick cock in her sex, wringing every ounce of pleasure from every stroke he took.

"Llyr!" Diana gasped, and convulsed, her face twisting with the savage pleasure of her climax. "Oh, God, I'm coming!"

"Yes!" he panted. "Dragon's Breath, yes!"

Maddened, desperate, they lunged together, grinding their way through the last sweet pulsing explosion. He doubted he'd ever known anything so intense in his life.

The throne room was silent except for panting gasps. Diana had wrapped arms and legs around Llyr, holding him as close as he could get to her. He tightened his own grip. He had no desire to be anywhere else.

He felt . . . strange. Oddly weightless in a way he'd never known before. It reminded him of the times he'd visited a healer after suffering some grievous wound. The pain and exhaustion were gone.

Ansgar was dead, and those he'd loved and lost were avenged. His people were safe. More important, Diana was safe. And she was his.

This must be happiness. He closed his eyes and sent up a mental whisper of gratitude.

"Have I mentioned in the last few minutes that I love you?" Diana said, her voice still a little rough with exertion.

Llyr grinned against her dove-soft breast. "What a coincidence. I love you, Diana London Galatyn, Queen of the Cachamwri and Morven Sidhe, my delicious Amazon werewolf."

She gave him a sunny smile. There was so much love in it, he wanted to weep. "And I love you, Llyr Galatyn, King of the Sidhe and Heir to Heroes."

With a shout of delight, Llyr rose to his feet and scooped her into his arms, then plopped down on his own throne. Gazing at her face, so deliciously close, he couldn't resist a kiss.

When they finally came up for air, she hooked an arm around his neck. "Speaking of heirs, that reminds me. We really need to work on giving your grandmother some puppies."

Llyr laughed and rested a teasing hand on her belly. His eyes widened at what his magic told him lay within. "Actually, I think we already have."

"What?" Diana stared at him, shock and joy warring in her eyes. "You're kidding me! Just now?"

"Just now."

Stunned, they stared at each other.

Suddenly a pair of huge, glowing eyes opened up right before the throne. Diana yelped and grabbed for Llyr as teeth appeared in a mystical Dragon grin.

"Finally," Cachamwri said. "It took you long enough to get it right, boy."

Continue reading for a special preview of
Angela Knight's next novel

MASTER OF WOLVES

Coming soon from Berkley Sensation!

"*Are you sure* about this, Jim?" Ray Johnson asked. "I mean, think about it. Do you have any idea what it takes to kill a werewolf?"

Jim London stopped in midstep as pain knifed his chest. Ahead of them, the dogs in Ray's big kennel whined in sympathy. "Yeah, actually, I do. I saw the body."

"But how the hell did they *do* all that to him? Look, in Dire Wolf form Tony was—what?—eight feet tall?"

Frowning, Jim looked over at his friend. Ray was a slender man, graying and middle-aged, with a slight paunch and the most intense blue eyes he'd ever seen. He was also no dummy. "I don't know," Jim admitted, remembering all the times he'd gone hunting with Tony Shay in the Georgia woods. "You don't hunt rabbits as a Dire Wolf. He did become a fair-sized gray wolf, though. And he was about five-eleven as a human."

"Yeah? I thought he was more your height. What are you, six-four? Anyway, figure he was seven-three or seven-five as a Dire. The county coroner's report said he was alive when most of that damage was done. You know he'd have shifted if he was in that kind of trouble. So what the hell could have done all that to a seven-foot five-inch Dire Wolf who could probably bench press a Humvee?"

Jim shrugged. "Most likely it was one of those rogue vampires Arthur's crowd is hunting. My sister and Llyr fought one last month who'd butchered three men." Raking a hand through his dark hair, he stared absently across the backyard of his friend's sprawling farmhouse. It was June, which in South Carolina meant hellishly hot. Ray's dogs were panting even in the shade of their kennel, and honeybees were buzzing around the tomato plants. "Diana said that bitch had some serious power."

Ray frowned as they walked toward the kennel. "And you think the Clarkston cops are involved with a vampire like *that*?"

"The chief definitely is. He stonewalled all attempts by Tony's mother to find out what had happened to him. When she insisted on coming to town and asking questions anyway, he told her Tony was a drug dealer who'd been murdered by his own Colombian connection."

Ray stopped to stare at him in outrage. "Bullshit. No way in hell would a werewolf be involved in drugs. We protect humans. We don't prey on them."

"Oh, he was definitely lying. You could smell it on him. Mary knew it, too, and she was furious." Jim shook his head. "So she asked me to investigate. But when I went back last month to start nosing around, nobody would talk to me. Clarkston is a small town—no more than ten thousand really cliquish people. On top of that, a lot of the folks I talked to were seriously afraid of something."

"So you think you can find out more from the inside of the police department?"

Jim nodded grimly. "I'm sure of it."

Ray sighed. "And you probably can. But Jim, you and I both know there has to be more than one vampire and one cop involved in this." His friend spread his long-fingered hands. Claws slid from his fingertips, each an inch long and razor sharp. "Merlin created us to fight witches and vampires. Magical attacks just bounce off us. So to do that kind of damage . . ."

"You think I haven't considered all that?" Jim demanded. Ray was a great guy, but he did like to belabor the obvious. "You're right—odds are it wasn't just one vampire. It was probably a whole nest of them. That's why I'm going down there in a form they don't expect, and I'm going to damn well find out who killed Tony Shay." He clenched his fists, feeling his own claws grow against his palms with his rage. "And then

I'm going to make them pay, no matter many of them there are."

"Jim, anybody with that much power is going to know you're a werewolf. They'll sense it."

"Yeah, and I'll sense them, too."

Ray grabbed his shoulder, halting his determined stride toward the kennel. "Dammit, getting yourself killed is not going to bring Tony back."

Jim pulled free with a twist of his shoulder. "I can take care of myself."

"Against any normal threat, yeah. But these guys . . ."

"Look, you're not going to talk me out of this, Ray. So let it go."

"You could teach stubborn to a Georgia mule, you know that?" The older man shot him a frustrated glare as they stepped up to the kennel gate. The dogs surged forward, barking in excitement.

Jim ignored them as he closed his eyes and reached within himself for the core of his power. An instant later, magic rolled over him in a tingling, foaming wave. The bottom dropped out of his stomach.

When he opened his eyes again, Ray towered over him. "I wish you'd reconsider," the older man said as he pulled a chain choke collar out of his pocket. Jim sat back on his haunches as his friend crouched beside him and clipped the collar around his furry neck.

He woofed softly.

"Yeah, I know. You can take care of yourself. Asshole." Ray stood and opened the kennel gate so Jim could pad inside.

"This dog is going to be great for Clarkston," the police chief said. "Particularly if you can deliver the kind of drug revenues you did for your last department."

"That pretty much depends on the dog," Faith Weston told him. She smiled slightly. "Sherlock and I got the sheriff's office a house once. Detectives were able to prove it was bought with drug proceeds." Federal narcotics laws allowed police departments to seize drug money, cars, and even homes belonging to those involved in trafficking. For small departments eternally strapped for cash, the revenue was invaluable. Dogs, by alerting on hidden drug stashes, gave police the probable cause they needed for searches.

"I know. It's why I hired you." He gave her a long, suggestive look. "One of the reasons, anyway."

Faith stiffened. She'd been afraid he'd start something when he'd asked her to drive to Greenville with him to look at the dog. "I'm a very good handler," she said, giving him a cool, warning stare. *Back off, buddy.* "The dog may pinpoint the drugs, but I tell him where and when to look."

"Oh, I'm well aware of how good you are. I can sense these things." He smiled at her, all teeth and charm.

George Ayers was a handsome man—tall and broad-shouldered, with thick dark hair that was rapidly going a distinguished gray. He definitely knew how to use his looks to his advantage, yet there was also something faintly oily about his charm. At times Faith thought she caught a flash of cold menace in his sloe-eyed gaze, like Richard Gere playing a crooked cop. "Plus, the fact that you don't have to be trained to work with a dog will save the city a lot of money. You're already K-9 certified."

Faith gave him a cold nod, still simmering over that suggestive grin. Ayers had been coolly professional when he'd first hired her a year ago, but in the past two months, his attitude had undergone a nasty alteration. His gaze had grown speculative, and innuendo had started creeping into their conversations.

Worse, his boldness was growing. It was almost as though he thought he was somehow immune to sexual harassment suits. Evidently he figured he had her over a barrel.

Under the Clarkston employee policy code, Faith could go to the city manager and file a complaint, but she knew that would finish her in the department. It wouldn't take Ayers long to either invent a reason to fire her or make working conditions so miserable she'd be forced to quit.

And what if the media got wind of the situation? All it would take was one good story to give her a reputation for filing sexual harassment complaints. She'd be finished in law enforcement. No supervisor would want to take a chance on her.

It was infuriating. All she'd ever wanted was to be a cop,

and she'd worked hard over the past eight years to make herself a damned good one. Yet Ayers and his libido could destroy everything she'd fought for.

But no matter how much damage he did, she was damned if she'd give in to his harassment. Even aside from the questions of morality, taste, and the fact she couldn't stomach the smarmy bastard, a female police officer walked a very fine line.

There were only about thirty cops in the Clarkston PD; if any of them even suspected she was banging Ayers, the fragile respect she'd built would be instantly shattered. They'd assume she was doing it to advance her career, not to save it.

Faith's only hope was the dog.

If the animal worked out, she'd be expected to move to the second shift because that's when most drug-related traffic stops occurred. That meant less contact with the chief than she had to endure working first shift.

Besides, if he saw she was bringing in serious revenue, he might be more hesitant to piss her off. It was the best solution she was likely to find, short of looking for another job.

The latter was problematic, since Faith had only been with the Clarkston PD a year. Switching jobs so soon wouldn't look good; she'd do better to put off the job hunt for a few more months.

Though if the chief got too pushy, she might have to bite the bullet anyway.

"Ahhh," Ayers said suddenly, looking off to the right, where a white farmhouse stood across a sweeping expanse of lawn. A sign stood beside the blacktop driveway: JOHNSON K-9 TRAINING. "Looks like this is the place."

Thank God. The sooner they wrapped this up and got back to Clarkston, the sooner she could get the hell out of Ayers's big, black SUV.

The chief turned onto the circular drive and parked in front of the house. As they got out of the truck, a man sauntered up, his smile wide and easy. "Ray Johnson," he said, holding out a hand. "You must be Chief Ayers."

"That's me." Faith watched as Ayers went into his hail-fellow-well-met act, pumping the man's hand and introducing her as the department's K-9 officer.

Faith found Johnson's handshake warm and pleasantly firm, but there was something oddly wary in his eyes. Evidently, Ayers set off his instincts, too.

Smart man.

He offered them a glass of iced tea, which they refused, then led the way around the back of the house to the kennels. Faith was pleased to see they had to pass through a high chain-link fence to reach them. "The neighbors have little kids," Johnson explained, unlocking the padlock with a jangle of keys. "The dogs are basically gentle, but if a small child got in with them, you could end up with a tragedy anyway."

She smiled at him. "Not the kind of thing you want to take a chance with."

"So exactly who donated this dog to the Clarkston PD?" Ayers asked as they walked through the gate. He had to raise his voice to be heard over the boisterous barking from the kennels. Evidently the dogs were glad to see their trainer.

Johnson shrugged. "Like I told you over the phone, the donor wants to remain anonymous. He just decided to give a K-9 to a small town that didn't have one, and Clarkston won the draw."

"Generous of him," Faith observed. "A good drug dog can run as much as ten thousand dollars."

"Mine are a little more reasonable than that," Johnson told her.

"Oh?"

"It doesn't take me quite as long to train them." He smiled slightly. "I seem to have a certain . . . rapport with dogs. Besides, I want to make them more affordable for small departments. I usually charge five thousand or so."

The animals were in full voice now, tails wagging furiously as they greeted their trainer with deep barks. Nine of them were German shepherds, though there was one chocolate Lab. They were good-looking animals, well-fed and bright-eyed.

Faith's attention was caught by a towering coal-black beast that was the only one not barking his head off. "Man, now *that's* a dog," she called over the chorus as Johnson opened the kennel. "What the heck is he, part Great Dane? He's huge."

The trainer grinned at her over his shoulder. "That's Rambo. He's yours."

"Ours?" She grinned in delight as Johnson closed the gate behind him and pushed his way past his pack to reach the enormous shepherd.

Though some drug dealers wouldn't hesitate to challenge a cop, almost everybody respected a police dog's teeth. A beast the size of Rambo could intimidate a mob out of a riot.

Then Faith frowned as practical considerations reared their heads. "He's going to be expensive to feed," she told Ayers. "You think the council's going to give you any trouble over that?" They'd agreed the dog would live with her, but Clarkston would pay for his food and vet bills.

Ayers gave her a slight, smug smile. "Don't worry, Faith. The council's not going to be any trouble at all."

That was news to her. When the idea of a drug dog had first come up after he'd hired her, the chief had been doubtful he could convince the Clarkston City Council to foot the bill. Now he was acting as if he had them all under his thumb.

Ordinarily, Faith would find Ayers's confidence encouraging, but something about the look in his eyes made the hair rise on the back of her neck. You'd think he had pictures of the mayor dressed like a Victoria's Secret runway model, complete with fishnet stockings on his hairy legs.

Short of that, Ayers was pushing it. The council could fire him on a whim if they thought he was mismanaging his department.

Restless, Faith rolled her shoulders as her instincts set up a howl loud enough to compete with Johnson's dogs. Something was seriously off here.

"You don't have to worry about Rambo," Johnson said, as he led the big animal out of the kennel. His gaze was not entirely friendly; he'd evidently overheard their conversation. "He'll earn his keep."

Ayers smiled, all white teeth. "Of course he will." His gaze flicked to Faith and lingered. "He and Officer Weston will make a fantastic team."

Uh-huh.

"Give him a month," the trainer said. "If he doesn't work out, I'll take him back."

"Sounds fair to me, Chief." Faith walked to the fence as Johnson stepped out with the dog. She shut the gate for him before the other animals could push through, then sank into a crouch. The shepherd was so big, his head was actually above hers when she knelt. He had to be part Dane, though his body type said otherwise. She presented her palm to his long nose for a sampling sniff. "Aren't you a beautiful boy?"

Instead of smelling her, though, he stared deeply into her eyes. Just for a moment, she could have sworn there was human intelligence in the dog's chocolate gaze.

Then he swiped his long pink tongue over her palm, and the impression was gone.

Jim hadn't expected the handler to be a woman. That was going to complicate the situation.

For one thing, she was gorgeous. Tall and slim in her navy blue uniform, she had a surprisingly delicate face with a tilted nose and a lush bow of a mouth. Her smoky gray eyes seemed to take up most of her face, an effect enhanced by the way she wore her long red hair scraped ruthlessly back in a pony tail. He'd bet money her looks were the bane of her existence. She was way too cute to be a cop.

And she smelled just as delicious as she looked, a blend of shampoo and her own natural female scent. He was unable to resist an admiring sniff.

"Beautiful boy," she purred, raking her nails across the underside of his jaw in a caress that made him want to groan. She grinned, delighted with his reaction. "Like that, huh?"

Jim woofed softly, playing his part to the hilt. She cooed more nonsense at him, and he obligingly panted, tongue lolling as he wagged his tail. *Oh, man,* he thought, *This is going to get old fast.*

The last thing he wanted to do with a beautiful woman was pretend to be an overgrown puppy.

Unfortunately, he didn't have a choice. If he wanted to find out what the hell was going on with the Clarkston PD, he had to remain in dog form.

Besides, despite the cheerleader looks, she was as much a suspect as Ayers.